yolk

YO

SIMON & SCHUSTER BFYR

An imprint of Simon & Schuster Children's Publishing Division
1230 Avenue of the Americas, New York, New York 10020

SIMON & SCHUSTER BFYR is a trademark of Simon & Schuster, Inc.
For information about special discounts for bulk purchases,
please contact Simon & Schuster Special Sales at
1-866-506-1949 or business@simonandschuster.com.
The Simon & Schuster Speakers Bureau can bring authors
to your live event. For more information or to book an event,
contact the Simon & Schuster Speakers Bureau at
1-866-248-3049 or visit our website at www.simonspeakers.com.
Book design by Lizzy Bromley
The text for this book was set in Adobe Caslon.
Manufactured in the United States of America
First Edition
10 9 8 7 6 5 4 3 2 1
Library of Congress Cataloging-in-Publication Data
Names: Choi, Mary H. K., author.
Title: Yolk / Mary H.K. Choi.
Description: First edition. | New York : Simon & Schuster
Books for Young Readers, [2021] | Audience: Ages 14 up. |
Audience: Grades 10-12. | Summary: Struggling with emotional
problems and an eating disorder, Jayne, a Korean American
college student living in New York City, is estranged from her
accomplished older sister June, until June gets cancer.
Identifiers: LCCN 2020025065 (print) | LCCN
2020025066 (ebook) | ISBN 9781534446007 (hardcover) |
ISBN 9781534446021 (ebook)
Subjects: CYAC: Sisters—Fiction. | Emotional problems—
Fiction. | Cancer—Fiction. | Eating disorders—Fiction. |
Korean Americans—Fiction. | New York (N.Y.)—Fiction.
Classification: LCC PZ7.1.C5316 Yo 2021 (print) | LCC
PZ7.1.C5316 (ebook) | DDC [Fic]—dc23
LC record available at https://lccn.loc.gov/2020025065
LC ebook record available at https://lccn.loc.gov/2020025066

To Mike.

For going first.

This is a work of fiction that mirrors aspects of my own history with disordered eating, dysmorphia, and bulimia. For those struggling with body image and food, this story might be emotionally expensive for you. Please be gentle with yourselves—sensitivity is a superpower. And please know that there is no such thing as a bad body. Truly. Take up space, it is your birthright.

Love,

Mary

I could lie,

say I like it

like that.

—Billie Eilish

chapter 1

Depending on where I focus and how much pressure I apply to the back of my throat, I can just about blot him out. Him being Jeremy. Him who never shuts up. Him being my ex. He whose arm is clamped around the back of the café chair that belongs to another girl. She's startlingly pretty, this one. Translucent and thin. Achingly so. She has shimmering lavender hair and wide-set, vacant eyes. Her name is Rae and when she offers her cold, large hand, I instinctively search her face for any hint of cosmetic surgery. Her lids, her lips, the tip of her nose. Her boots are Ann Demeulemeester, the ones with hundreds of yards of lace, and her ragged men's jacket, Comme.

"I like your boots," I tell her, needing her to know that I know, and immediately hating myself for it. I'm so intimidated I could choke. She smiles with such indulgent kindness I feel worse. She's not at all threatened by me.

"I got them here," she tells me in faultless English. I don't ask her where *there* might be.

Jeremy says I'm obsessed with other women. He might be right. Then again, someone once described Jeremy's energy to me as human cocaine, and they were definitely right.

"Mortifying." He shudders, blotting his slick mouth with a black cloth napkin. Jeremy's the only one eating a full-on meal here at Léon. A lunch of coq au vin. I draw in a deep breath of caramelized onion. All earthy, singed sugar.

"Can you imagine failing at New York so publicly that you have to 'move home'?" He does twitchy little scare quotes around the last bit. He does this without acknowledging that for him, moving home would be a few stops upstate on Metro-North, to a town called Tuxedo. A fact he glosses over when he calls himself a native New Yorker.

I watch Rae, with a small scowl nestled above her nose, purposely apply a filter on her Instagram Story. It's her empty espresso cup at an angle. I lean back in my wicker café chair and resume lurking her profile, which I can do in plain sight because I have a privacy shield.

It's the typical, enigmatic hot-girl dross on her main feed, scones cut out onto a marble surface dusted with flour, her in a party dress in a field. A photo of her taking a photo in a mirror with a film camera.

In an image farther down, Rae is wearing a white blouse and a black cap and gown. Grinning. It's a whole different energy. When I arrive at the caption, I close my eyes. I need a moment. I somehow sense the words before they fully register. She graduated from Oxford. It's crushing that most of the caption is in Korean. She's like me but so much better.

My will to live leeches out of my skin and disappears into the atmosphere. I should be in class. I once calculated it, and a Monday, Wednesday, Friday course costs forty-seven dollars, not counting rent. Counting rent in this city, it's exactly one zillion.

"Yeah, hi." Jeremy flags down a passing server. A curvy woman with a tight Afro turns to us, arms laden with a full tray of food. "Yeah, can you get me a *clean* glass of water?" He holds his smeared glass to the light.

"I can," she says through her teeth, crinkling her eyes and nodding in a way that suggests she's garroting him in her mind.

"That's not our server," I whisper when she leaves. As a restaurant kid, albeit a pan-Asian strip-mall operation that charges a quarter for to-go boxes, I cringe with my whole body. Jeremy shrugs.

I check myself out in the strip of antique mirror behind Rae's and Jeremy's heads. I swear my face is wider now than it was this morning. And the waistband of my mom jeans digs into my gut flesh, stanching circulation in my lower belly and thighs. I can feel my heartbeat in my camel-toe. It's a dull pain. A solid distraction from this experience. I wonder if they were talking about me before I arrived.

I eye the communal french fries. Saliva pools in the back of my gums. Ketchup is my kryptonite. Especially swirled with ranch dressing, which I've trained myself to give up. The Raes of the world would never. Or they would and it would be quirky and wholesome.

Her leg is the circumference of my arm.

I smile at the room in a way I imagine would appear breezy yet bored in a film about heartbreak. I love this place. You'd never guess that a dumpy French restaurant from the seventies would be the new hotspot, but that's the other thing Jeremy's good for: knowing the migratory practices of various clout monsters. That and ignoring the tourists as he sweet-talks Oni the hostess into ushering us past the busy bar and into the seats in the way, way back.

Someday I'm going to eat a meal in a New York restaurant by myself without burning with shame.

"I have to get this dog, right?" interrupts Rae, lifting a fry to her mouth. When she chews, a pad of muscle pulses at her temples. She leans into me and shows me a Pomeranian puppy. "I want a rescue, but look at him." She strokes the photo with her thumb. "I don't know if I can wait."

I glance at Jeremy, who's paused with his fork raised to his mouth. "What time is our thing?" he asks her.

"What thing?" It's out before I can think.

Rae's eyes flit to Jeremy's and skitter back to me.

They let my question hang in the air like a smell.

"Oh, don't worry," I recover, smiling stiffly. "I have plans."

"No, come!" exclaims Rae, squeezing my forearm for emphasis. "God, I'm so awkward." She laughs at herself ruefully. "It's just an intimate gathering at a dear friend's home. It's a safe space, so I have to make sure it's okay." Her eyes narrow meaningfully, placing an open palm on my leg. "But if it's a no, I hope you can respect that it's nothing personal."

"Honestly," I tell her, convinced that all her friends are sylphlike and terrifying. "I have to leave right after this."

Jeremy pushes his plate away. I hand him my water before having to be asked. His eyes dart past me to beetle all around us. Party eyes. Shiny. Hard. Roving for people to say hello to. I get it. I love New York precisely for this reason. The culture. The vibration. The relevance. The crackly frisson of opportunity. When we first met, it was this gleaming, hungry aspect of him that I liked best. His magnetism was contagious, especially when he motormouthed at you about his grand plans. You felt like you were on his team.

He pulls his sunglasses out and cleans them with my napkin. Not so long ago he was beautiful to me. Partly because he's tall. Not even New York tall but objectively tall. Over six feet. But it was his ambition that drew me to him. I'd never met anyone who could talk at that pace. It was astonishing. But now, I can see him how others might. His straw-blond hair and skin tone blend his features together in a vague soup, blurring an already uncertain chin.

But then he'll say something so quintessentially, winsomely New York that I'm scared to let him go. And he knows everyone. From models to door guys. Once we ordered weed to the house and it turned out he played basketball with the delivery dude. When they gave each other a pound, I was so envy-struck I could barely speak. It doesn't help that on the rare occasion Jeremy introduces me to his friends—their eyes glaze over in disinterest.

Jeremy calls himself a poet. And a performance artist. But, for him, neither of these things particularly mean anything, and combined they mean even less. Mostly he focuses his efforts on a literary magazine that I've designed pages for but never seen in real life. In short, he's a bartender at Clandestino over on East Broadway. I try not to think about how much money he owes me. And how we shared a bed for months and then stopped.

The only time I don't hate him is when I think he's mad at me.

"I'd rather die than go home," I say to no one in particular.

chapter 2

"Be right back."

I get up, grab my wallet, and thread my body through the crowd by the bar. I swallow hard, guts curdling. I feel callow and gullible and unspeakably sad. I need to forget how, at an earlier point in the day, I'd dressed as though my loose plans with Jeremy were a date.

"Hey, Mike." I up-nod the bartender, weirdly a near dupe of Jeremy but with a pornstache and more tattoos.

"Hey, baby, what can I get you?" I'm heartened that he seems to remember me without Jeremy as a cue.

"Vodka soda. The cheap kind." I always get my drinks separately. I'm too poor to split bills at the table. "I'm going to need to see an ID, babe." I hand it over, and he gives me a heavy pour. "You want to keep the tab open?"

"You can close it out," I tell him, sliding him my credit card. "Thanks."

He hands me a sweating glass. Part of me already doesn't want it. I take a sip right where I stand, ignoring the glares and pointy elbows of couples waiting for their tables. The drink's strong. And thoroughly disgusting. I feel it work immediately.

I pocket the credit card and fake ID. It's funny how no one ever notices that the names don't match. And that the photo isn't my face. Partly it's that they don't expect criminals to look like me, an Asian art student dressed in black, but it also confirms a horrible suspicion: that no one's ever looking at me. Really looking.

I'm staring at the halo of her before recognition kicks in. There she is, in the mirror behind the bar. Like an apparition. A Japanese horror movie. I want to laugh, I'm in such disbelief. She pushes through the crowd, scanning the clustered bistro tables by the front window, openly searching their faces. When she falls out of frame, I almost turn my head toward her but hesitate—superstitious—thinking that she won't be there. I lift my hand to my lips, watching my reflected self do the same, confirming my own presence as she double backs toward me. Now we're both in the mirror, and still I don't face her. She has different hair—shorter—but it's ludicrous how enormous her gourd is. Even without our nursery-rhyme names—Jayne and June—you'd see how we belong to each other. Our heads are twinned in bigness.

The joke goes that I practically slid out of Mom after she'd pushed June out. Even after the two-and-change-years between us. Normal-size heads look as though they'd orbit mine, and my sister's is even huger. The other joke is that June, eleven days late, at eleven pounds and two ounces, hadn't wanted to come out at all. She's like one of those parasitic eggs that hatch on a caterpillar, casually eating it for sustenance, using it for shelter without any sense of imposition. If June had her way, she'd have kept growing and worn Mom like a hat.

The last time I saw her, I hid. She'd been transferring for the uptown 4 at Union Square. Her nose was buried in her phone and she was wearing a slate-gray businesswoman's dress to the knees, looking like someone I'd never be friends with.

It's only then that I realize: My sister is looking for me.

With my back pressed against the wall, I wait for her to reach me like a Venus flytrap. I steal a glance back to my table. Rae and Jeremy are both on their phones.

She startles when I grab her. "What are you doing here?" I whisper angrily, pulling her behind the hostess section and pinning her, hiding us both. She knows better than to lie. This isn't her part of town. I quickly assess her appearance. She's dressed all wrong. The baseball cap on her head reads DARPANA MUTUAL. The putty-colored trench I recognize, but under it is a strange orange shirt, swishy silver workout pants, and ultramarine rubber clogs.

"Why aren't you in class?" she demands, shaking me off her arm and pulling away. I scoff. It's so classic. Of course this is the first thing she says to me in almost a year.

"Why aren't you at work?" I counter. "And what are you wearing?" I haven't seen her out of a suit in years. Honestly—and this is fucked up—she's dressed like a rural Chinese person on holiday. I take a step away from her. I want to make clear to anyone observing that we are not together. That this is an intrusion.

"I've been calling," she says. I feel her eyes land judgily on the glass in my hand. I take a long sip, holding her gaze.

"I left, like, three voicemails," she continues.

"I didn't see them," I lie. All of the messages were "Call me."

"You're so unreliable."

"So, you stalked me?"

"I wouldn't call it stalking," she says. I need to stop geotagging everything. I forget that my sister's even on IG. The last thing I saw on her grid was from Halloween, where she's dressed as a

Yu-Gi-Oh! character. It stressed me out so much, I muted her.

She crosses her arms archly. "You know, you could have just gone to San Antonio Community College if you're hell-bent on being some lush," she finishes.

I'm tempted to smack her, but we're mushed against the wall by a party of four inching past us.

"Seriously, what the fuck?" I whisper angrily. "What are you doing here?" For a second we're back in high school. My adrenaline's spiked. I slide my left foot back for stability.

But instead of pushing or shoving, she takes a deep breath and refuses my eye.

My heart judders.

"Fuck, is it Mom?" I ask. She's dead. I'm totally convinced of it. It's the only thing that would make my sister come see me like this.

"No," she says. "But we have to talk."

"So, talk, fuck." My indignation sounds performative even to me. I realize I'm drunk. The glass in my hand is suddenly empty.

"How are you?" she asks conversationally, doing this little brow-knitting concerned thing.

"You can't be serious." Truth is, she's really beginning to frighten me. This isn't who we are to each other.

"Fine," she says quickly. "But I don't want to tell you here." She reaches for me. I recoil so fast, her nails scrape my bare forearm. I raise it between us, glaring accusingly even though it doesn't hurt. We stand there, the radiant resentment between us throbbing.

"My friends are waiting for me," I counter, practically in singsong. It's old hat that I goad my sister this way. Flaunting my comparative popularity. I dislike myself as I do it.

"Look," she says. "It's not Mom, but it's important. Text me when you're done. I'll send a car."

"Fine," I tell her.

Jeremy barely glances at me as I sit down. "How is it privilege if it's a lottery? Nobody asks to be white. Especially nowadays." It genuinely pains me to rejoin this conversation. "It's a class issue, not a race issue. *That's* the scam. Why is it practically illegal for cis, het, white men to have any cultural relevance anymore?"

"You know," Rae says, gaze trained on her phone. "I think we can take the J train over."

I grab my coat and bag. "I just have to . . ." As I head toward the front, the bathroom door swings open. The dappled glass pane that reads TOILETTE almost hits me in the face. I let myself in and twist the lock shut. It's tiny. A single commode and a gemlike sink in the corner. The coffin-sized room features floral wallpaper and the kind of European flusher where you pull down the knob on a chain.

I collect bathrooms in the city. I like knowing where they are. The LGBT center in Chelsea with the Keith Haring mural on the second floor. Whole Foods on Bowery in the back of the food court with a passcode on any receipt. The tiled floral beauty of the New Museum stairwell, where you can catch video installations for free. Dank Irish dive bars all over the East Village also make for safe refuge, and they're always open. The real winners are in hotels and certain clubs. The ones that feature stall doors that go from the floor all the way up to the ceilings, those are best for secrets.

I pee and check my phone for a while. Just enough to make June wait.

When I glance back at the table, it's empty.

chapter 3

The city isn't how I'd left it. The light's dipped and it's getting loud. There's an urgent thrum that crackles. It's that disorienting feeling as you leave a movie theater in Midtown and the skyscrapers with their LED lights come at you.

New York is an ambush.

Outside feels IMAX.

Plus, drunk New York is the shit. I love drunk New York. It glitters with potential. It feels like gambling.

"June?" asks the driver when he rolls down the window.

"Sure." I don't bother correcting him and get in. It's a black SUV with its own atmosphere. I wonder if I've been given an upgrade or if June only commissions Uber Blacks. I hailed one once, on accident, all the way home during a surge, drunk and cross-eyed, treating myself to not-Pool. I felt rich. When the eighty-dollar charge showed up the next morning, I cried.

It's not fair, I think, as we crawl up First. New York nights are for anyone other than family. Still, my saltiness eases as I lean and stare out the tinted window. It's a miracle that I get to stay here. This place commands total dedication or it will eject you. I really would rather die than go home.

New York's never been for lightweights. It takes a tax. Eloise was chill if you related to a six-year-old asshole living at the Plaza, but that was never the romance for me. Give me the Hotel Chelsea any day. Growing up, I'd moon over Tumblr pictures of Debbie Harry, Patti Smith, Basquiat, Daang Goodman, Anna Sui, Madonna hanging out like it was no big deal. Diane Arbus's haunted children. Tavi, a literal child, front row at New York Fashion Week on her own merit. Max Fish. Lafayette Street. That the cofounder of Opening Ceremony was a Korean girl, Carol Lim.

There were promises here. A young, loose-limbed Chloë Sevigny plucked from SoHo retail to star in that movie *Kids*. Lady Gaga, Nicki Minaj, and Timothée Chalamet all going to the same fucking high school. That's the energy.

I love it all so hard, but just as much, I love that the guys at my deli know my coffee order. That I know to avoid an empty subway car as confidently as the closed mussel shell in a bowl.

The car stops.

I even love how it takes sixteen minutes to get to June's house in a taxi and thirteen if I'd just taken the F at Second Avenue. Nothing makes sense and it's perfect.

I have a vague idea of where June lives, but I'm unprepared for the glass turret. And that her apartment and my school are separated by 1.5 long blocks.

The lobby is as silent as a museum, with recessed lighting, dark walls, and enormous artwork bigger than a life-size floor plan of my entire apartment. There are tasteful sitting areas and hardcover art books on the coffee table that are ripe for stealing by anyone other than the people who can afford to live here.

As I wade out onto the gleaming marble, approaching the front desk, I hold my right heel high to keep the tinny clack of the exposed nail in my worn-down boot sole from ratting me out as poor.

"You sisters?" asks the younger doorman in a pale-gray uniform when I speak her name. Feels racist even if it's true.

He's dressed as if manning the bridge of a spaceship. All high collars and embroidered insignias.

There are two door dudes. Both white with brown hair. One young, one old. I wonder if younger door dudes grow up to be older door dudes. Or if you need one of each at all times.

"Can you just tell her I'm here?" I'm annoyed that I've been summoned. Annoyed that I'm related to someone so basic they'd live in a testament to architectural phallic inadequacy. Even one with a Chipotle a block over and a grocery store literally inside the building.

They let me by. I pass the mailroom and a mixed-race couple wearing matching puffer vests with a shih tzu. I barely have to glance at their faces to know he's white and she's Asian.

My ears pop in the elevator.

June works in hedge funds. Which means she devises high-stakes gambling schemes for despots and oligarchs, and this is what she gets for her soul.

The overheads in the hallway light up when you approach. It's cool. Also creepy. Like the type of building that tries to kill you when the security system becomes sentient.

Thirty-four F. Two floors shy of the penthouse. It's petty, but I'm happy that there's at least something for her to work toward. I stand outside her door for a moment. If she didn't know I was already here, I'd leave.

I ring the doorbell. Wait. Hear nothing. Wait for another moment. Ring again—nothing. I knock.

"I'm coming," says June tersely as she unlocks the door.

"Sorry," I say just as she opens it. We stand there.

"Hey." Absurdly, she seems surprised to see me. She's changed. Now she's wearing a pale-gray silk bathrobe, the diamond of her neck and chest exposed. It's strangely sexy. A TV booty-call outfit.

"Hey." I clear my throat to not giggle from the awful awkwardness. "I'm here."

"Come in," she says, leading me into the kitchen behind her.

There's a formalness neither of us can shake. I take forever removing my shoes. I don't recognize any of hers except the sad clogs I saw her in earlier. There's a pair of shearling boots similar to ones I've been eyeing, but they were over a hundred bucks and I'm willing to bet these are fancier.

"Do you want anything?" she asks, padding over to the brushed-silver fridge. It's the kind with an ice machine and water right in the door. The cabinets are skinny and white, and there's a matching kitchen island with two barstools that separates the kitchen from the rest of the living room.

"Water?" She looks over at me. "I have sparkling. Wine?"

It takes everything for me not to roll my eyes. I feel as though my sister's masquerading as a dynamic careerlady from a Hallmark movie. I want her to cut the shit immediately and tell me what's going on.

"Yeah, I'll take a glass of wine." Mostly I want to see what happens when I ask for one. We've never had a drink together.

That's when I remember her ID in my wallet. Fuck. This is a trap.

I walk farther into her apartment, into a morass of tasteful beige and oatmeal furniture. The entire back of her apartment is glass, and her view is spectacular.

"Red or white?" she asks.

"June," I deadpan. "It could be fucking blue. I don't care." Across the way, in an office building, I watch two women separated by a cubicle type into black monitors. I wonder if they're friends. Or if they're locked in an endurance contest to see who leaves first. I wish I had binoculars.

I never get to be this high up, and it's wild how June's New York has nothing to do with mine. Sort of how some people's news is the opposite of yours or how their phone configurations are alien even if the icons are the same. Part of me is proud that she gets to have all this—knowing that we come from the same place and that she's earned it. Another part of me wonders if she's secretly Republican.

I take a seat on her tufted beige couch, staring at the matching love seat. I've never met anyone in New York whose living room can accommodate two sofas.

She hands me a glass of white wine. "The red's nicer," she says.

We both look at it. I can never tell if she's fucking with me.

"I couldn't find the bottle opener," she explains, and sits down across from me. I feel like I'm in therapy.

I turn the wineglass in my hand. I'm tempted to snap the delicate stem in my fingers. If she brings out a cheese board and throws on smooth jazz as the lights dim, I'll bolt.

"Thanks," I tell her, taking a sip. It tastes like grass. "Your place is nice. That's how I guess you know you've made it, right? When nothing's IKEA."

"Yeah," she says, with an anemic little chuckle. "Thanks. And you're still in . . . ?"

"Windsor Terrace."

"Is that Queens?" I watch her for any hint of a joke.

"Brooklyn."

June tilts her head. "Right, you live out by that cemetery."

"It's closer to the park." She's definitely spying on me. I've never told her where I moved to. I couldn't risk her telling Mom I slept near corpses. I take another sip of wine. "We have a park in Brooklyn, you know. It's older than Central Park. Plus, they didn't raze a Black-owned neighborhood to build ours."

June knows everything there is to know about a handful of subjects. On everything else, she's wildly indifferent. For the longest time June said "intensive purposes" and not intents and purposes, claiming I was the asshole for correcting her because everybody knew what she meant.

"So, you're good?" she asks. I'll give her two more questions before I break.

"Yeah," I tell her. "Good. Work's good. School's good."

"Mom was saying how last semester—"

"Last semester was *last* semester," I interrupt. So that's what this is. Mom's guilted her into checking up on me. Fucking narc. First-borns are the goddamned worst. "This year's better. There was this one teacher, Hastings, total pervert—he really had it in for me. And everyone who was on my group project was an absolute nutcase. Flakes and drug addicts basically. This semester's . . ." I wave her off.

"I hated group projects," says June sportingly. "Always ended up doing everything on my own." She takes a sip from her water glass. I briefly wonder if she's pregnant.

Fuck. That would be so weird.

"Yeah." I sit up straighter and set my wine down on the broad, mirrored coffee table. "And my job's going well," I continue. "Honestly, it's much better this year. It's fine." I hate how defensive I sound. Having a genius for an older sister, who scored a full ride to Columbia, has not been optimal for my professional self-esteem.

"Look"—I cross my arms—"it's fine. Tell Mom to calm down."

June winces and shoots me the stink eye. See, there. That's the June I know. "Who said anything about Mom? I'm the one asking. You're smart when you focus. I'm tired of people giving you a pass because you're *emotional*."

I stare at her long and hard. She's like Mom when it comes to mental health stuff. June thinks anxiety is for pussies. That you can banish it with intestinal fortitude. According to her, depression is laziness that can be fixed by high-intensity interval training and caffeine.

"What do you want, June?"

She sits up and leans in. I lean in too. Monkeying her.

"I'm sick," she says.

"Yeah, well, what kind of sick?"

"I have cancer."

chapter 4

My mouth snaps shut. I vaguely sense that I'm smiling. It's a horrible tic. A placid little placeholder while my brain catches up. "What?"

My scalp prickles. Everything else is numb.

Cancer.

My sister is going to die.

I wonder if in a few years this will have been the worst thing that's ever happened to me. Or if things get worse. If this moment defines me as an adult, I need to know right now by how much. *My sister died,* I imagine myself saying. *My sister died. Well, my sister died.* I wonder if a sister dying is worse than a mother dying. I'm deciding it is.

I imagine the viewing. I'm dressed in a vintage Dior suit I don't own. My sister's gleaming casket on the pulpit above us, me turning to Mom, her unseeing face wild with grief as Korean hymns swell around us, the flower-perfumed air coating my throat.

Fuck.

My therapist, Gina Lombardi, says I need to name five things I can see, feel, and hear when I catch myself losing it.

My lungs expand with as much air as I can hold.

I tap the cool glass in my hand with a nail.

Black socks against cream carpet.

Fuck.

I make it as far as my sister's lap. Her hands are gathered there. My gaze retreats, skittering to the window behind her.

Christ, this is unbearable.

I yank my attention and force it to land on her face. I'm trying not to blink. I'm momentarily terrified that I might yawn.

"I might have cancer," she says crisply. "I'm pretty sure I have cancer." My sister nods several times with grim finality. As if it's settled. As if she decides what's cancer. "I have cancer," she tries again. "I just don't know how much."

"What?" I rise to my feet. She stands too.

I pound the rest of the wine, tilting my head way back. "So, do you have cancer or not?" I can't feel my arms.

"Well," she says. "We're still hoping it's something else. Like endo or PCOS."

I don't know what any of these words mean or who "we" refers to.

"So, your doctors think it might not be cancer."

"They've been telling me it's not cancer since I was eighteen. We thought it was polyps or fibroids or—"

"But they think it's cancer now?"

"They're looking into whether it's cancer."

I sit back down. She does the same. "Um. Is it, like, I had a weird pap smear, or are there clusters of shadows all over the X-ray or whatever—the scans?" I'm running through every episode of *Grey's Anatomy* I've ever seen.

"There are masses," she says.

"The fuck does that mean?"

"They won't tell me," she finishes. "They want me to see an oncologist first. But it's cancer. I can tell."

The thing to remember is that my sister is a known psycho. Her convictions are stigmata level. Her palms would bleed at will to win a fight. For a week in third grade, she decided that daylight savings was bullshit and showed up an hour late to everything. She took it all the way to the principal, saying the administration was infringing on her First Amendment rights and her freedom to exercise her beliefs. She served a full week of detention before they threatened her grades, which is when she finally gave up.

My sister stares me straight in the eye. "I swear on Mom's dead baby I have cancer."

That shuts me up.

It's been a long time since June's sworn on Mom's dead baby. Since either of us have, as a matter of fact. When we were really little, we used to do it several times a day. Instead of *I'll bet you a billion dollars*, it was *I bet you Mom's dead baby*. We'd swear on it like the Bible. It was the biggest deal we could think of. We did it until the time we accidentally did it in front of Mom. She stiffened visibly even though we never think she's listening when we're talking in English.

The baby was a girl. Older than me, younger than June. I've often thought she was the missing link. The middle bit of the Venn diagram that made me and June make sense. That almond shape, the eye, is called a vesica piscis. I think about her all the time. I imagine her being everything that June isn't.

"Don't tell Mom," she says. "About any of this."

I flinch.

"Promise me."

"Jesus, I would never." I'm insulted. "Why would I start calling her now?" I haven't talked to Mom in over a month. And I know better than to drum up a whole boondoggle that'll send her straight to church, lighting candles and browbeating every Korean Catholic in the hundred-mile radius into a prayer circle.

"Okay."

"So, what do you know?"

"I had a pelvic exam, a transvaginal ultrasound, and a biopsy. They shove this insane bendy stick in you and scrape . . ."

The other thing about June is that there isn't a surgery reality TV show that she doesn't love. Me, not so much. I let out a shaky breath.

"So, it's in your uterus?"

"Or my ovaries," she says. "Or both, I guess."

I imagine the goat head that is the female reproductive system in all the diagrams I've ever seen. It's hugely embarrassing, but I couldn't tell you if the ovaries are inside the uterus or around it. Probably around like those behind-the-head earphones that asshole runners mostly wear. I'll google it later. That and what a *womb* even refers to.

"What happens now?"

"A bunch more doctor's appointments." She seems eerily calm. I try to imagine what my sister would look like with cancer. I wonder whether she'll lose her hair. She's always had a better face than me. With an aquiline nose that came out of nowhere. She'd look good with a pixie, which means she'd probably look good bald. You have to have very specific bone structure for that. I feel an old twinge of jealousy followed by a large transfusion of self-loathing. I'm not allowed to be jealous of my sister's cancer.

She's staring about middle distance into her own living room. Her eyes are like a shark's, her hands clasped together between her knees.

A searing sensation rises into my chest as I stand. My heart is liable to burst out of my sternum. I grab my phone.

"So, you'll let me know when you know more?"

She nods. "I'll walk you out."

We don't say anything in the elevator.

I almost pat her arm but don't. I breathe through the rolling panic, watching the elevator display change as we hurtle toward the ground, trying to exhale without making a noise.

chapter 5

"*I'll just take the subway;* it's faster," I tell June in a stage whisper. I'm keen to let the people in the lobby know I'm with a resident. In the same way I always make sure I have my purse if I'm carrying a plastic bag so that no one mistakes me for a delivery person.

"Okay," she says. June's thrown her trench over her robe. If she had curlers in her hair, she'd look every part the suburban mom in a sitcom waiting for the school bus, and the visual churns my guts. I wonder what womb surgery means for having kids. June's an asshole sister, but she'd be a good mom. At least she wouldn't be worse than ours.

"Okay." I give her a little wave.

"Okay," she says.

I don't move. I don't even know what I'm waiting for. It's not as if we're going to hug. "Thanks," I tell her, which is entirely the wrong thing. "Um, keep me posted."

"Thanks for coming by," she says, and just as I nod stiffly and turn around, I almost bodycheck a woman with an enormous clear trash bag filled with recycling slung on her back.

"Whoa," I yelp. She's tiny, a hundred years old, and bent over to boot. The dimensions are surreal. It's mostly plastic bottles and cans, but the load is twice her size. She's like old-lady Asian Santa. Or Atlas. With veins purpling the hand clutching the neck of the sack. She smiles and extends her other palm. She's holding a piece of paper. She's closer to me but dismisses me to talk to June.

"*Kalambosewko,*" she says, extending the note and nodding. Everyone asks June for directions. It's a thing. The woman's eyes disappear when she grins, and her mouth is so puckered she looks like she's missing all her teeth. Her hair's pulled back into a bun.

"I don't read Chinese," says June, enunciating as if volume is helpful. Mom made us take Mandarin because it was the "language of the future," according to Korean Christian radio. We took it for three years before she gave up. We retained astonishingly little.

"She's probably going to East Broadway, right?" June asks me.

"I'm sorry." I shrug, smile apologetically, and show her my palms in the universal sign for total uselessness. The woman bobs her head a few times, still smiling, and turns to leave.

"Wait!" June holds out her phone. "I have this app for real-time translation. Say again?"

The woman tries again. Also louder this time.

"Oh my God." I urge June out of the way. "She's going to Columbus Circle. She's speaking English. We're such morons."

I give her directions to the R and W, showing her the map on my phone.

"Yellow line." I pull out a pen and write on her paper *R/W to 57th Street. Columbus Circle* in tidy capital letters in case she needs to show someone else on her trek.

The woman smiles again as featureless as a fist and nods appreciatively before leaving. She merrily jaywalks at a diagonal, far from the crosswalk.

"Columbus Circle? What the hell is she going there for?"

I shrug.

"I would have put money on East Broadway or Flushing," June says, shaking her head. "When did I become so racist?"

I turn to my sister, ready to tell her she's always been racist, when I stop. June has dark smudges under her eyes, and her hair's stringy. It startles me. I recognize her so essentially that she may as well be an avatar. She's sick. I hadn't known that June can be sick. I'm overcome with the urge to touch her.

"You know, I've never seen a recycling lady on a train before," she muses, watching the woman go. I stand next to her, nudging her shoulder slightly with mine.

"Me neither."

The observation reminds me of all the times I've wanted to call her over the past two years. The list of things in my phone that I know June would love to weigh in on.

"You think the churros lady at Union Square takes the train?" I've never seen her haul the cart downstairs.

"No way. Her man drives her. He has to help with the stairs. She gets up at four in the morning to make them, and she sells them, too, because he bitches too much about all that standing. He has to make up for it by driving."

We keep watching as the recycling lady gets small. "I've never seen a recycling lady at night," I tell her.

"Really?" My sister turns to me. "I've never seen one during the day."

I imagine the woman on the train, clutching the subway pole

because no one will give up their seat for her. I want to fight them all.

"Don't you kinda want to go with her? Make sure she gets where she's going."

"Yeah."

The canner seems so small yet certain. She turns the corner. I'd hoped she'd look over and wave.

"How are you gonna keep all this from Mom?" I ask June finally. I haven't seen them in over two years, but June talks to her every day.

June smacks my chest with the back of her hand, laughing. I turn in surprise. "Mom would be so fucking pissed that you thought of her because of that old-ass woman."

I shove her back, smiling.

It's true.

chapter 6

I stare at the other passengers in our shared jaundiced lighting. There's no equalizer greater than the F train. There's a heavyset blond dude in a lime-green rugby shirt across from me.

Next to him, with her legs stretched way out, is a youngish girl in an enormous hoodie and platform sneakers. Her teen-spreading is so surly, I can't help but smile at her. I wonder what their deals are. It's absurd that there are so many people walking around who aren't sick.

And still so many others who are. I googled it. There are seventeen million new cancer cases every year. I don't know how to conceptualize that number. I don't even know what one million looks like. The teen rolls her eyes at me behind her stringy bangs. I shift focus to outside the window.

Several bluish skyscrapers dot the horizon. If I'm honest and if I had the money, I'd probably live in one too. I've always felt safer off the ground.

I unlock the metal gate at my apartment. My knees throb from the boots and my back aches from sucking in my stomach. I can't wait to get out of these fucking jeans. All I want to do is peel off this costume, step into the shower, eat the world, and go to bed.

Something tells me to listen for noise before I insert my keys.

Quiet.

Good.

When I open the door, all the lights are on.

Fuck.

I was so certain he'd stay out. He being Jeremy.

There are two glasses on the kitchen counter with inky remnants of red wine and an unfamiliar orange leather tote. It has a blue-and-white ribbon stripe running up the center of it.

I check for her shoes by the door but spy only his New Balances and my sandals. I can't believe he's letting this bitch wear shoes in my house. I'll bet they're expensive, too.

My keys dig into my palm as I tiptoe to the bedroom. The mattress is just about flush on all four walls. And it's only a twin. Before I can press my ear to the door, I hear it. Laughter. Rage clutches my throat tight. I taste bile.

For the record: I know that Jeremy has never been my real boyfriend. We were hooking up and then we weren't. But he still lives here. If you ask him, he'd tell you that we found each other on Craigslist. That he'd answered my ad for a roommate.

That's not exactly true.

I'd seen him before. The summer I moved to New York, I knew no one. June loaned me money for the mattress and I'd found an airless room in a three-bedroom apartment with two other girls, Megan and Hillary, who'd been best friends since high school. It felt as though they were locked in a contest to see who could be less interested in me. It was a dead heat. I'd seen Jeremy outside of a coffee

shop in Bushwick with his cream-colored bike. And when he intro-
duced himself, extending his hand, I was as stunned as if a painting
had spoken to me. I'd spent weeks longing for anyone to address me.
My roommates went everywhere and did everything together. At
first, they were civil. Until I made the mistake of buying the wrong
trash can liners and then it was a bonanza of crisp, passive-aggressive
Post-it notes remunerating my failings. They'd pointedly ignore me
when I dared enter the living room. So, I went everywhere people my
age—art students, design students, aspiring musicians, actors—gathered. I'd sit near them with a book and wait to be invited.

He asked me to watch his bike while he grabbed a coffee because
he'd forgotten his lock, and I did. When he thanked me and rode
away, I was bereft.

He wore this white shirt that billowed behind him like a cape,
and I was fascinated that he didn't seem to carry anything while I
lugged around chargers and granola bars and novels that might pro-
voke conversation. All Sally Rooney Everything. A little poetry.

When he rang my buzzer four months ago—almost two years
later—and I watched the top of his head ascending the stairs, it felt
like kismet.

I was stuck in a kind of constant, rambling bewilderment that life
wasn't perfect in New York. It wasn't solely my roommates' chilly dispo-
sitions. I'd search every face for any sign of rapport. A knowing eye roll,
a bemused smile, but in their absence, I convinced myself I was doing it
wrong. College was impenetrable. The dorm kids forged quick loyalties.
Design students flocked by major. And the hard-faced girls—real New
York natives—with their artfully applied makeup, the ones who knew
where the parties were, clung only to each other. I was a marketing
major at fashion school living an hour outside of campus. Fashion Avenue, which is what they call Seventh, wasn't glamorous at all.

I remember little of the first year beyond how the cold never left my bones. My second year, I started going out. I met Ivy at a dive bar famous for their free personal pizzas with any order of a drink. She sat by me, promptly complimented my Telfar tote since she had the same one in green, and proceeded to point out all the people in the dark, dank room that she'd slept with. Ivy's twenty-three. She has bleached blonde hair, brown eyes, and is the kind of pale where the blue tributaries of her veins are so close to the surface that her forehead reminds me of those glowing babies in fetal development pictures. Free pizza is the perfect metaphor for our friendship. It's an anemic facsimile for the real thing, but when I'm drunk, it's a miracle.

This is the kind of person Ivy is: under her bed she keeps a trash bag filled with duplicates of crap—bedside lamps, milk frothers, hair dryers—disposable flotsam she scams off Amazon by telling them they sent the wrong thing.

We partied every night. It was easy. I wasn't even sure she knew my last name. It's my fault that when my roommates kicked me out, I was surprised that Ivy didn't text me back for a full week. It's not my fault that those vicious harpies turned on me so fully. I was stunned by Meg and Hill. Or Mean and Hell as Ivy referred to them when she finally called.

I couldn't ask for June's help. By then we hadn't properly spoken in over a year. The roommates gave me a week and I didn't fight them, I was so cowed by the hostility that pulsed off them like heat. In a frenzy, I searched Craigslist, Street Easy, and dubious message boards for shared apartments but eventually landed on the cheapest one-bedroom I could find. And even then, I'd need a roommate to occupy the living room. The photos were a grainy Google Earth satellite photo of the entire block and an inset thumbnail of the Pepto-colored bathroom sink. I called the phone number, met a rangy Latino man named Frankie wearing a mesh vest in South Brooklyn with a deposit borrowed from what Mom and Dad had given me for fall tuition. I was told not to make any complaints and that if anyone asked, we were distant cousins.

In hindsight, it's a miracle that it wasn't a scam.

Jeremy wore the summery white shirt again that day, and a thin gold chain glinted at his throat. It held a delicate rose pendant, a keepsake I decided on the spot that his grandmother had given him because he was her favorite. He had three brothers, I surmised, and he was the youngest, as I was.

Turns out Jeremy is an only child. An only child who carries nothing because the kindness of strangers never fails him.

He'd found the necklace in the bathroom at the bar where he works and made no effort to return it.

Since late May, Jeremy's been staying with me in fits and starts. I don't know where he goes on the nights he's not here, and I pretend not to have noticed when he returns. Sometimes while he sleeps, I mouth *I love you* to his closed eyes to see how it feels. We haven't had sex in a month, but I find myself searching for signs of improvement.

More laughter. Then the smear of a moan. Followed by the insistent, unmistakable thumping of mattress against wall.

I don't know where the humiliation ends and the rage begins or if those two sentiments are ever unlinked.

I want to hurl myself against the door. Rip it off its hinges. Tear into him and her, kicking them both out of my home. But failing that, I'm too embarrassed to make a sound.

Perversely I keep listening. Who is she? Does she know me? What if she's someone important? It has to be Rae. The conviction that it's beautiful, willowy Rae who'd matriculated at Oxford fucking University, bucks at my chest. I'm startled that he'd bring her here.

To this dump, where for the past few weeks, we've been wearing our coats to bed when the heat fails and the summer brings roaches with wings.

I can't stand to be in my skin, be behind my eye holes. And I can't bear to signal my presence. If they catch me, I can't pretend to be someplace else. Like a bandit in my own home, I mince and scrape and quietly wash my hands and face. Take off my pants. Put on a dirty T-shirt and some shorts. I think of June's washer and dryer. What she'd think of me if she saw how I live.

I climb onto the couch, folding myself up on my side so I can fit onto the love seat. I don't know anything about Jeremy's finances. The first month he lived here I gave him a pass since we immediately fell into bed together. That second month too, since it was agonizing to discuss. Eight weeks ago when I was convinced we'd get evicted, he Venmo'd me seven hundred dollars. His half for August. I was sitting on the floor and he was standing above me with his sunglasses on, halfway out the door. He pushed a few buttons on his phone. No big deal. He may as well have thrown crumpled bills in my face. He sent the flamingo pool-float emoji as the note. Later that night, he brought someone home.

My stomach rumbles. I need to drink water. The orange purse throbs in my sight line. It's expensive. Probably Clare V. I try to recall if there'd been a bag slung on Rae's chair. I'm intimidated by this handbag. It's whimsically hued, which suggests one nice purse among many. A Wednesday tote for eight hundred bucks.

The purse goads me, and without thinking, as if guided by invisible wires, I get up, walk toward it, peer over the rim before grabbing both upright handles and jawing it open.

Predictably, there's a laptop, the teeny MacBook Air in a purple leather sleeve. Tempting but bad karma. AirPods, sunglasses case, keys with a neon-pink rubber charm that reads GIRL BOSS in white, and a patent-leather Tory Burch wallet. Heart pounding, guts clenched, I glance at the door and flip the billfold open. A freckled brunette with a heart-shaped face squint-smiles at me from her California ID. I'm both relieved that it's not Rae and affronted that it's someone else.

Someone basic.

Her eyes are dishwater gray, and on the day the photo was taken, she made sure to match her lipstick to her sweater exactly. Her last name is hyphenated, which to me means she's rich, that she's a horse girl with vacation homes. My heart sinks. She weighs twelve pounds less than I did this morning even after I went to the bathroom.

I return the purse and spy a slouchy velvet makeup pouch. I unzip it, its belly moving in my palm like a live animal as a feeling of calm bleeds into me. As if easing into a thermal bath. I pluck the half-full bottle of perfume with its steel cap, Flowerbomb by Viktor & Rolf, girly and pink, and return everything else. I drop it into the trash can, where it plummets past the soiled paper towels on the top, and then I return to the couch.

I want to set shit on fire.

I try to count the five things that I see around me. Acknowledging the articles that will ground me in this room, in this time and space.

One: fridge.

Then I fall asleep.

chapter 7

The alarm jolts me awake. My phone is on 15 percent and my mouth tastes furry. Acid clambers up my windpipe. I'm somehow more fatigued than when I went to sleep. I rub my eyes and blearily register that the orange tote is gone and the bedroom door is open.

I stumble over to the bathroom, turn on the hot water for the shower, and sit on the toilet to pee. As the steam builds, an acrid, rancid sourness barely masked by the air freshener hits my nose, jolting me into memory. Shit. Right. I have to take care of a few things before school. Things to replace. Acts to undo.

Somehow it's always my latest first class that I have the most trouble getting to on time.

I wash my hair. I can't detangle the knots fast enough and tug impatiently, breaking all the ends. I dry myself hurriedly, throw on a bra and sweatshirt, pull on jeans, jumping up and down to get them over my thighs, and grab the plastic bag I'd shoved under the couch in a haze early this morning, away from prying eyes. I open it, survey its contents to confirm that it's real, that I did it again, tie the handles up in a double knot, and shove it deep into the garbage.

A pinprick of pleasure weasels its way through my self-loathing as I recall what else is in the trash. The bitch's perfume.

I wonder what she looked like naked. If she had better boobs, a flatter stomach. I drink water from the tap, promising myself that next time—which there won't be a next time—I will stay up the requisite enamel-preserving half hour and remember to brush my teeth before passing out.

I smear on liquid liner in case the hot deli guy's working the register and dash to the far bodega. There's one on my corner, but they're dicks, so I leg it across the street and down the block. But of course it's not the hot guy but the old one. He adds a convenience fee when you charge your groceries to a credit card, which the hot guy doesn't. I wish I were the type of person to confront him about it, but I'm not.

I tear down the aisles, say hi to the black-and-white deli cat, grab the medium-size box of Cheerios, a jar of Nutella with a regular label—not the seasonal one—English muffins, which I don't even like, and a thing of turkey cold cuts. It's the wrong brand, but it'll have to do. Honestly, he's lucky that I'm even making the effort. I also grab a cup of coffee, black.

Back in the apartment, I replace everything in the fridge and cupboards, tipping half the bag of Cheerios into a ziplock baggie so that the level will match up, and shove the surplus cereal into my dirty clothes pile.

Before I leave, I grab the shower cleaner from the back of the cupboard. I keep two back there. Jeremy hates the smell of ylang-ylang. He says the floral citrusiness reminds him of getting carsick in his father's overly air-freshened Volvo. It's triggering, he tells me. *You're triggering,* I want to say back. *And your face is triggering.*

I spend precious moments dedicating myself to bombing the ever-living shit out of the bathroom far more diligently than I did last night. I pump ylang-ylang deep into the bathmat, grinding it in with my foot and drenching his towel before closing the door firmly behind me.

My hands still smell of flowers on the train. I wipe them on my jacket and stare out the windows. I like the aboveground part of the commute best. They demolished a building just before I moved here, smashing it into a mountain of rubble that they've been removing bit by bit. I try not to think about how quickly things change. Whenever people complain about neighborhood businesses shuttering or how their favorite bakery's now a Citibank, I feel a tremor of panic. As if the ground beneath my feet isn't reliable. How can I ever get to know a place that changes so quickly? I'm late enough as it is.

I thumb through Instagram. I almost exclusively follow people who make me feel bad about myself.

Models, photographers, influencers, aspirational fitness entrepreneurs, actors.

My heart stops when I see someone I know. Someone I actually know in life. Not even New York life—my real life.

It's Patrick.

His tattooed arm is flung around a fashion designer who makes animal-print fleeces that cost six hundred bucks. I'm astonished by the happenstance, but it's him. He looks almost the same as he did when he was fourteen. Slightly less skinny but not by much. He's pointing at the sky with his mouth wide. He appears to be singing.

His hair is unimpeachably excellent. Not too coiffed. Not fussy and stiff with product or the calculated androgyny of boy band members. Patrick unfailingly wore hats, until he got this transformative haircut that made him hot overnight. He was utterly forgettable until he absolutely wasn't. Patrick was partial to bucket hats. I've never understood the appeal of looking like a giant toddler.

Back then, I wasn't ever sure my infatuation with Patrick made sense. School was rife with cues as to who to desire. The jocks were kings. You could see it in how adults behaved. The way teachers nodded along to their jokes, lips drawn back, readied for the laugh. Holland Hint was objectively attractive. The bathroom walls told me so. There was no controversy in gold hair and green eyes at six foot one.

At church, Patrick was a feeling. A giddy, swirly bubbling that flushed my face, but I couldn't talk to June—or anyone from school—about some boy from church.

I zoom in. Patrick's cheekbones seem swiped with highlighter. Especially with his mouth hung open. He's wearing a somewhat clingy Rick Owens shirt. It's either Rick Owens or very, very old.

I click on his name.

@40_7264N_73_9818W.

We get it—you do art.

The tagged pictures set a different tone from his feed. There's even a photo of him at Léon. We could have been at the restaurant at the same time, except that the caption reads that he was at an impromptu album release for a reclusive singer-songwriter. A party I would never have gotten into. Jeremy wouldn't have either for that matter. I take some satisfaction in that.

I feel foolish now that I'd been right all along. About Patrick's hotness. Less that I'd squandered the chance to stake my claim but more how clear it is that he'd been out of my league then, too.

Patrick's account has more than fifty-three thousand followers. Way more than anyone I personally know. In fact, Jonah Hill follows him, which seems significant to me. There are only two selfies. One in glorious morning light, where his face is slightly puffy. Another with a black eye.

Most of the images are mood boards. Typefaces. Buildings. Album artwork. Some very thin Asian girls with explosively big lips and freckles dressed in designer goth layers. I wonder if he's dated any of the women. Probably. He's either an art director or a photographer. I had no idea he moved to New York. Not that he'd have told me. His family left Texas forever ago, so the church network wouldn't have dispatched the all-points bulletin either.

I go to his saved stories. The one called shoots.

I open on a beautiful white loft with a curved wall on one side, which gives a Stanley Kubrick spaceship effect. There are windows all along the back, with fifteen people standing around.

They watch a screen instead of the model in front of them. A model with dark hair in a blue-and-white dress who lifts her arms and waves them, the sleeves billowing dramatically.

She does this over and over and I'm transfixed. The delicate, translucent fabric refracts the light. The dress is familiar to me. The woman laughs, throwing her head back, her wavy hair coiling around her pale cheeks.

I recognize her too. She's not a model but an actor. Korean, but Korean American. She'd won an award from an indie film about CEOs who moonlit as contract killers. And as she gathers the full skirt around her, lifting its hem, I realize she's wearing a variation on a hanbok. Almost exactly the gown my mother was married in, the one in her wedding photo. The one that still hangs in her closet. It's startling to see someone who resembles me, us, in such a setting. Commanding attention without being ninety pounds, without backing from a girl group.

I go to my own grid. See if there's a photo of me at Léon. There isn't and I'm disappointed. I start deleting. It's mostly pictures of magazine covers from the nineties, dressing-room selfies of clothes I can't afford, and close-ups of my hands and mouth.

I tidy it up. So it's more aesthetic.

I find that the more I hide, the more presentable I am to the world.

Then I follow him. He probably won't even notice.

I'm filled with the urge to tell June. But the version of June I want is the one I sat with at church. The one I grew up with. The one from long ago, before all the screaming fights in high school, and not this one at all.

June.

I imagine her from last night. I dislike that every unkind thought will now be tempered by this other feeling. Pity. I hate it.

I glance up just as I'm about to miss my stop. It's by some kind of magic that I always manage to step out at Twenty-Third. My stomach gurgles from the coffee, but I need the caffeine. I promise myself not to eat today.

I hustle into my entrepreneurship lecture. Total adjunct professor struggle. The teacher's a youngish, sandy-haired dude in glasses and a blue shirt. He seems the type of guy who'd rather host a podcast than have anything to do with us.

Last year, there's no way I would have made it to class. If I stopped partying even for a moment, I couldn't get out of bed. It was fascinating that if the feeling of impending doom and dread made my limbs leaden and my head cottony, no one ever found out. You could get away with anything if no one cared enough to check. Far away from my family for the first time, I learned that everything was profoundly optional. So I opted out. I couldn't not.

Podcast Guy drones on about Recent Business History—youngest self-made billionaires, Harvard grads that go onto entrepreneurial greatness, upwardly mobile white women who seed their businesses from well-connected families, and the industry disruptors and influencers whose parents happen to be celebrities or early employees at tech monoliths. As if any of these lessons apply to me. As if any of these relics aren't ancient. As if any of it is ever to be repeated in my lifetime.

He insists the lesson is that we're supposed to be able to isolate unmet needs in the marketplace, but I can tell he doesn't believe his own bloodless recitation. He may as well be crossing his fingers behind his back. Or have a massive hashtag above his head that reads: ad.

I stare out the window. What's the point? The planet is on fire and everything is random. June is one of the smartest people I know and she got a job at a prestigious hedge fund without a master's because her first roommate was a finance scion who also happened to be obsessed with *Animal Crossing* and shojo manga.

I start clicking through the spring collection slideshows for next year. During last fashion week some rando Ivy was dating got us onto the list for an after party at Le Bain, that club with a hot tub in the middle of it. But of course she didn't show up and I was her plus-one so I didn't get to go.

I know that attending college is like praying to God. It's not that you believe in it; you do it just in case. Because other people are. Design school in Manhattan is *Hunger Games* for East Asian kids with severe haircuts. I can't tell if I'm the racist one for feeling like we're interchangeable, but all the incentives seem scammy to me.

I've never met a single person whose job I can remotely admire.

I google "who is the richest Asian in the world" for sport. Jack Ma's up there. He's the founder of Alibaba, the Chinese e-commerce site. I had no idea he looked like that. His features look like they should be on a much smaller face. He needs longer bangs. It's eerie how much he resembles a fetus.

Then I google image uteruses, thinking of June; turns out ovaries *are* outside the uterus. The uterus is weirdly small, too. Picture the goat head: it's the nose.

I check the time. I've only been here for twenty-three minutes.

Jeremy texts. I wonder if he's going to say something about last night, apologize or at least acknowledge in any way what an asshole he is.

He wants to know where I am. Class. He wants to know if I can do him a favor. My mouth drops open. What? He wants a high-res TIFF of a portrait I took of him. Jeremy's shockingly bad at technology. I once accused him of being homeschooled by Mennonites and he didn't speak to me for days. He says he needs it for a magazine that's doing an article on him.

I don't respond, seething. Instead I check Tinder. I swipe and swipe and swipe and swipe. It's dazzling how disposable we all are.

chapter 8

"**It's why everyone** thinks the Monopoly man has a monocle, but he doesn't."

"Does he not?"

"No, we're mixing him up with the Planters peanut guy. And it's called the Mandela effect because everyone believes Mandela died in prison, but he didn't."

On Tuesdays at 1:00 p.m., I have therapy. I love therapy so much. Mostly because I'm an excellent patient. Gina Lombardi's a social worker, not, like, a psychiatrist or psychologist, which made me dubious at first, but she's soothing to spend time with. She's super tanned with a deep side part, and sometimes I just pretend that I'm talking to Miuccia Prada.

"Does that make you question your own long-held beliefs? What you thought you knew?" she asks.

I shrug. "Sure." I mostly want her to know that I've read entire Wikipedia pages about South-African political revolutionaries.

"Don't you find it *fascinating* that we don't know what we don't know?"

Gina gets my best material if I'm honest. For the past two months I've been saving up clever bon mots for her benefit. For our initial appointment, I'd spent the whole ride reading up on the news and world events because her office is on the Upper West Side. She's in the garden apartment of a town house, and you can see everyone's calves and purebred dogs on the street level out her windows. She has built-in bookcases and a white-noise machine, and though I've only ever seen the little waiting area by the downstairs entryway and her office, I like to imagine this is her actual home. I feel giddy at the possibility that there could be an Egyptian cotton pillowcase with her silvery-blond hairs on it mere feet from where I'm sitting. I bet she wears a pajama set. And that it's monogrammed.

It's moments like these when I wish we could be real friends. I've only made her laugh out loud once, but I felt high all day. When we first met, she said she didn't know who Rihanna was, which made me almost walk out until I thought about what that signifies. She has no loyalties. To not know about Rihanna means she's a total nihilist.

Gina's constantly telling me that it's my negative self-talk that's derailing my productivity, not a debilitating laziness. The first time we met, I tried to ice her out because I was so pissed that student services made me wait five weeks for the appointment, but then I forgot I wasn't talking to her and complained about a stupid documentary. It was about violin prodigies. Gina mentioned that I was responding with undue hostility that someone would dedicate themselves to a single pursuit and then she said something that blew my mind.

She said that there was more than one type of perfectionist. And that I qualified because the kind of perfectionist I was, was the kind that abandoned everything if I wasn't good enough at it. And *that's* why I couldn't finish tasks. Meanwhile, I thought you had to be

Natalie Portman from *Black Swan* to be a perfectionist, all shivering from malnourishment and eighteen-hour practices, but she's right. I'd rather fail outright than be imperfect. It's why last year, when I was on academic probation, I couldn't bring myself to cram for finals and end up with a C average. I just kinda gave up. There's nothing more humiliating than trying so hard for everyone to see and still ending up a loser. Right now I have As and Bs, and I like to think that's due to Gina.

"It *is* fascinating," she says. I beam back at her proudly. "Knowing that we don't know everything leaves room for mindfulness. It opens up the possibility that thoughts and feelings can change. Perception is a lot more subjective than anyone feels in the moment."

"Totally." I nod enthusiastically, before serving up a thoughtful pause. "But don't you think that sometimes it's better not to know anything at all? My sister, June, is the least self-aware person in the world and she's really fuck—she's extremely accomplished." I try not to curse in front of Gina. She has Diptyque candles on her desk and wears pantyhose.

She glances up. My therapist removes her hand from her chin and uncrosses her legs.

Unclasping the enormous silver cuff bracelet from her wrist, she sets it down on the tasteful coffee table between us and studies me. I wonder if she's about to tell me something unbelievably profound.

"How old is your sister?" she asks.

"Tw-twenty-three," I stammer, holding my breath.

"And she's extremely accomplished?"

I nod, watchful. I know it's not how psychology works, but a part of me really believes Gina's like an oracle.

"You know you've never mentioned your sister before?" she says, and then writes something down in her notebook before I can answer.

"Where does she live?"

"Twenty-sixth and Sixth."

She writes even more down. I feel like I'm failing a test.

"Are you close?"

"Yes?"

"But you've never mentioned her before and you both live here."

"Okay."

"Do you find this significant?"

I hate when she does this.

"I guess so . . ."

"How so?"

"Well, we have nothing in common. She doesn't like me and I don't even know why."

"What would she say if I asked her?"

That she resents me for being popular. That she blames me for her own unhappiness and wishes I was never born. That I'm a burden on Mom and Dad because I'm a baby who can't get over herself. That I'm vapid and vain and that I'm selfish. That I'm a slut and an attention whore. And that I don't call my mother or hang out with my sister because I'm ashamed of where I came from and that's why I'll never be happy.

"That she doesn't approve of my decision-making."

"Why?"

"Did you ever see that documentary where the brother murders the sister's boyfriend because the sister groomed him into believing that her boyfriend stabbed their mother to death?"

It's a true story. The sister was on *America's Most Wanted.*

"No."

"Well, it's streaming on Netflix or Amazon right now." I wonder if Gina even watches television. "They're Korean."

"I haven't seen it."

This session isn't going the way I'd planned.

"Well, sometimes siblings don't get along. For whatever reason, it's the path they're on," I tell her.

"How do you feel about your sister?"

My sister died, I imagine myself saying to Gina in the future.

I feel the tears teasing at the tip of my nose.

There's this whole theory that younger siblings are spoiled. That we're enfeebled from all the mollycoddling. Soft. That by the time it was our turn to rebel, our parents had already given up. I disagree with this wholly. It's firstborns who can't take no for an answer. Youngest kids have iron constitutions. Hardy hides from lifetimes of rejection. A hundred million entreaties for their older siblings to hang out answered by shoves, eye rolls, slammed doors, and stone-cold ditches with peals of laughter.

It's always felt like pressing into a bruise to talk about June.

It's why I don't do it.

I shrug. "I just wish she liked me."

chapter 9

After therapy, in the hour before work, I meet up with Ivy at the Chinese bakery on West Fourth. She kisses the air near my ear and her hair's wet. "I'm sorry I'm late," she says as if she's ever on time. "I'm coming from SoulCycle." We went once, together, ages ago and I almost passed out in the dark, throbbing room. Everything about it felt like an exorcism.

When the class let out, all the hardbodies shiny and triumphant, I watched Ivy slip the borrowed cycling shoes into her bag instead of tossing them in the return chute. She just kept right on talking to me as if it wasn't happening.

For a second, I'm tempted to look into her gym bag, but it's not my business or my problem.

"I'm so glad you picked this place." She nods to the bakery display cases behind us. "I haven't eaten since yesterday." She grabs a pair of orange-handled metal tongs and begins to pile tarts and sweet buns on her plastic tray.

This was a mistake. Seeing Ivy after therapy is like slamming mezcal after a juice fast.

When I join the line behind her empty-handed, she cocks her head. "Really? Nothing?" The dark-haired woman behind the counter slides the pastries into individual wax paper sleeves. "Hold on," says Ivy to the cashier, turning to me. "Go get something right now. My treat."

I shake my head. "I'm okay." There are at least four people behind us in the line, but that's not the kind of thing that trips Ivy up. She rolls her eyes. "You know, you're kinda being a wack friend."

I order a milk tea, and when I ask for it without sugar, Ivy grimaces.

"Now you're just making me feel bad," she says, angrily stuffing her bakery bag into her tote when we walk outside. We cross the street to watch the basketball players. There isn't a game on, but there's a few dudes shooting around and there's a larger crowd gathered at the handball courts beyond it. I love the way the small, hard ball sounds when it hits the wall. I sip my tea.

"You want to go the diner instead?" Ivy rummages in her pocket and pulls out a vape and offers it to me.

"I have work," I remind her. Her shoulders slump dramatically as she takes a long drag. Her gel nails are painted like pineapples.

Smoke curls out of her nostrils. We both pretend to watch the game even though we can't see shit for all the backs turned toward us. "How's the apartment?"

"Fine."

"I still can't believe those cunts kicked you out."

"Yeah."

"How's the boyfriend?" I can tell she thinks Jeremy's the reason why we're not close.

"He's not my boyfriend." With my free hand I cling onto the

cold wire of the chain-link fence, watching through the diamonds as a taller guy dressed in all black shoots a three.

"Are we not friends anymore?" she asks in a small voice after a while.

It's the unexpected vulnerability that silences me. Makes me want to turn around and disappear into the subway station behind us. I pretend to be mesmerized by a guy strapping on a bright blue knee brace. His broad face is slick with sweat and his chest is heaving, but he's grinning and talking shit the entire time.

"Whatever," says Ivy coldly. I don't dare look at her. "You're no fun anymore."

I can't say what I'd expected. I'd entertained the thought of telling Ivy about June, forgetting for a moment who Ivy was. Who I was to her.

"Where's that vape?" I ask her instead.

She hands it to me. It's white with a gold ring around the middle. "It's a really nice Indica forward hybrid," she says. "You'll like it."

I take a deep drag and hand it back. "Thanks." When I hug her to leave, she smells like singed vanilla. "I'll text you."

I turn up Erik Satie on my headphones as I walk to work. When I approach Union Square, I notice how weird it is that I was just at a park by a movie theater and now I'm by another movie theater nearing an entirely different park. I realize I'm high, but I love the way the piano music turns the plaza into a movie. On the steps, there's a protest, making the foot traffic that much slower. Little kids are holding signs. It's about Medicare. I'm watchful for police presence and unmarked fed vans, keeping my head down.

My posture gets shittier the colder it gets. Growing up in Texas means that you only ever need denim jackets and hoodies and maybe a peacoat if you want to be pumpkin spice latte about it. But New York is no joke. I have a bone-deep fear of cold weather, but at least this time of year, there's a festive energy in the air. The Halloween decorations are up. Blink and it'll be New Year's Eve.

I duck into the store where I work, Fishs Eddy. I was enticed over the summer by the busyness of it. The resplendent displays, the strings of lights, the barrels of raffia-bundled coasters, and so many candles. They have a chandelier made out of antique eggbeaters. It's the land of milk and honey. The abundance is ridiculous.

I have twenty minutes before my shift, so I wander down the aisles with everyone else, playing house. Checking out the new merch. Someday, when I have the kind of furniture where the sales associate orders fabric swatches, I'll own all this shit and more. I scan the faces around me resentfully. All the customers feel rich. So many excellent jackets. Colorful scarves in complicated Parisian-seeming knots.

I finger a smooth porcelain butter dish with a lid. I love the romance of it. The decadence. Not only a dedicated place for butter but a roof over its head for protection. Who thinks of such things?

Even with a 30 percent employee discount, I'd never be able to buy everything I need. I want egg cups and cake stands and cookie jars and café au lait bowls. Antique milk jugs for succulents and the wooden, weather-beaten shelf to go with it.

When guests come over, to my home, the place that will one day exist and be mine, I want to convince them that I grew up being this person. That I've always had so much crap. Superfluent in the super-fluous. That I'd been allowed as a kid to pick a bedroom wall color other than white for self-expression.

I'd roast chickens and mix pitchers of drinks, smiling, always smiling, appearing as though I were the type whose parents knocked—knocked!—before entering her room. Because sleepovers were things that I was allowed to host and attend and privacy was honored. I want to appear as though I'd had a family who knew how to celebrate Christmas. Real Christmas. With a tree and presents that are gift wrapped and asked for. Not stacks of SAT workbooks and a twenty-dollar bill folded around gas station candy.

"Ay," says Mari, looping her arm into the crook of mine and steering me toward the glassware. "I have tea to spill." Mari started the same week I did but immediately started dog-sitting for people and going to Wednesday karaoke nights with everyone. She always has gum and tampons. I think she thinks we're friends.

Mari widens her eyes at Chinara and Trev at the registers. "He lost his virginity to her," she whispers gleefully. I look over and try to imagine them having sex. It's not altogether unpleasant. Trev's short but lean, Latino, and sometimes brings a skateboard with him, and she's Nigerian with a pixie cut and a nose piercing.

"Recently?" They've got to be in their late twenties at least.

"No." Mari shakes her head sharply and rolls her eyes. "When they were in high school."

"Oh." I smile, unsure about the appropriate reaction. "That's cool."

"But don't you think that's so New York?" She gestures hugely, platter-eyed and expectant. "They hadn't seen each other in ten years before they both got jobs here. Plus, she married someone else!"

"Random." I nod carefully. I know I'm disappointing her. I'm dying to know the right words to say, but I'm still a little stoned and failing. She probably thinks I'm a freak.

"See." She sticks her tongue out and grins. "See, that right there. That's why you're hard to be friends with."

As I go stow my stuff, I'm reminded of something I overheard a few weeks before I was kicked out of my old apartment. We all had shitty drywall bedroom walls, and mine had a six-inch gap where it didn't meet the ceiling. I heard my roommates talk about how I was selfish because I was an only child. I remember thinking how absurd that was. Everything about me is a little sister.

As I'm restocking displays in the four-thousand-square-foot store, I can't stop thinking about June. How we used to play restaurant with real cups and dishes from the kitchen because we didn't have toys. The way she brushed my hair. How she'd make me eat things like whole garlic cloves and once her toenail clipping, laughing when I would.

In a slatted wooden fruit crate beside a stack of trays that read YOU'RE A MESS, there's a burlap-lined tangle of bright-orange bottle openers. The chalkboard sign reads $12. I flip the corkscrew part out like a switchblade. It snaps out beautifully, and snaps back in. It's perfect.

As I walk it up to Mari at the register so I can buy it on break, my heart rate quickens with how easy it would be to put it in my pocket. The only reason I don't is because it's for June and that feels unlucky. If I wind up karma-killing my sister because of a stupid $12 wine opener, I'd feel like a real dumbass.

After work, when I get back to my block, I'm gripped by a cold wave of nausea. I take a deep breath, press my ear to the apartment door. I haven't responded to Jeremy about his stupid portrait. He hit me up a few times but thankfully he's not home. I kick off my shoes, shuck off my clothes, and toss myself onto the bed in my underwear. My face mashes against a pillow. I'm so exhausted I could sleep for days. I miss this bed. My bed. But now the sheets smell of him. Not unpleasant but just the way his skin smells. It's incredible how attraction works. I used to love the familiar scent of him. The plane of his chest. His hair. And now it's othered. Dank. Musky. Foreign.

I get up, pulling the elastic straps of my cotton Calvin Klein sports bra down and leaving it looped around my waist. I'm too lazy to take it all the way off. I throw on my Jonas Brothers sleeping sweatshirt. I'm happy that Nick came back. He's always seemed like the smart one. I can't help but wonder how the other two managed to bully him into returning. What exactly they had over him.

I investigate the fridge and the cupboards and then I ransack both.

I fill up a jar at the faucet. They call New York tap water the champagne of water. They say bagels and pizza taste different because of it. I've never told anyone, but sometimes when I'm drinking it, I wonder if it'll imbue me with an essential New York *something*.

Even if it's trace amounts of lead.

I chug it in great tidal gulps, spilling it down my chin, feeling like a snake eating an egg, the fluid sluicing through my throat with such force that I almost choke.

I raise one hand above my head and heroically burp into the living room as I lower it.

I put the kettle on for tea and make myself a mug of rooibos, immediately burning my tongue. Fuck. This always happens. For twenty years of life you'd think I'd have a cup of tea that was the exact right temperature at least once. I fling open the freezer door. Of course he's finished the vodka. Or maybe that was me.

Honestly, fuck Jeremy. I'm glad I never sent him the photo he needed. Fuck all these awful Jeremy feelings. My fuck-it switch is flipped as I shake off the shame and dread and heartache.

I pull out my phone, scrolling and chewing. I've been checking Patrick's feed obsessively without liking any of the photos. He doesn't post often, but he's tagged on random images. But this time, feeling nostalgic and lonely, I DM him. *Hey. Nice photos.* Like some kind of poet laureate.

I cringily jump up and down a few times to get the douchechills out of my spine.

When I go for my tea, it's ice cold.

I drink it, looking over the rim of the mug at the wreckage. The emptied tub of ice cream, the crinkly bag of Life cinnamon crumbs, scattered Cheerios, and the square crusts of Jeremy's oat bread where I've bitten out the pillowy centers.

There are seven of them. I arrange them into diamonds.

chapter 10

The coffee tastes burnt but sweet and my heart skips when I see her. Thank God. Hot-pink sweatpants with exactly matching coat and shoes. She's holding her slice of pizza, and the pockets of her fuchsia fur jacket are stuffed with napkins. I check the time—we're both running a little behind.

I'm heading east from Eighth Avenue. It's almost residential over there since the broad side of an apartment complex pretty much takes up the whole block. And as I hustle back under the shadow of where the art and design center bridges over Twenty-Seventh Street, there she is.

I don't know her name. In my head I call her Cruella. She has Vantablack hair. It's the kind of black where no light escapes. Its blackness is as eye-catching as neon. It's usually teased like cotton candy on top of her head, and today it's in a beehive.

We're walking toward each other on the same side of the street. She must live nearby because I see her all the time. Usually with a plastic bag around her wrist. Sometimes with a small white Chihuahua. She's alone today, but she's wearing my favorite outfit. She only ever wears three different sets of monochromatic clothes with renditions in miniature for her dog.

The first time I noticed her was because she walks like a newborn foal. It registered somewhere in my peripheral vision as someone falling, but that's just the way she moves. It's that clattering mayhem of a fifteen-year-old Eastern European couture model on a catwalk, where the hips and knees slice through the air several feet ahead of her chest and arms, which dangle way back. From the side she looks like she's limboing.

She's so thin it makes my teeth hurt.

Her skin is powdery white. With a slash of crimson lipstick. I try not to stare as she folds her slice in half, tacoing it in her paper plate. She lets the oil from the cheese drip onto the street for a moment, off the rumpled wax paper onto concrete.

Just as I pass, she chews off the tip of her pizza and works her jaw in a rhythmic rabbitty fashion. I lock eyes with her for a second as we pass, and it feels exquisite. I turn around as if to check the street sign. She pulls out a napkin. I know she's spitting into it.

I wish I could break the wall and talk to her. I wonder if she notices how often she sees me. God, what I wouldn't give for a four-hour documentary on her. I have so many questions. She searches for fucks to give, this woman. The first time I saw her do this with her food, I couldn't believe it. That it was happening in public. It was a Papaya dog, and it was as revealing as a man masturbating on a subway car. Another time I saw her unfold the paper towels and deposit the spit-sodden masses into a bush, calling to a squirrel. It was performance art. In New York there's at least one of each of us.

Seeing her always makes my day.

My phone comes alive in my hand as I take another sip of coffee. It's June. Calling.

This time I do something crazy and pick up. My sister asks me to come over later. I find myself wanting to go.

Class is itchy. It's disrespectful how slowly time goes by. Sometimes I think about the other me. The me I'd be if I'd gone into design instead of merchandising. I'd be insufferable and self-satisfied. "Je m'excuse?" I'd drone. "How is the Serger broken *again*?" I'd be wrapped up in all the high drama of calling forth a physical product. "Garments," never "clothes." "Pieces," if you're serious. "Wearable art," if you're a dilettante with an Etsy page.

I had no idea a plural for dilettante is dilettanti.

After several hours of monastic focus, I check Instagram. I like saving it, waiting until the messages pile up, especially after setting thirst traps in stories. I tap the paper airplane. My insides go liquid.

Patrick.

Hey, it reads. *I never check DMs.* And then *Holy shit Jayne from Texas.* And a phone number.

I check to see if he's viewed my stories. He hasn't. I'll wait at least a few days to text him back.

On my way to June's from school, I learn that endometrial cancer and uterine cancer are the same. Uterine cancer sounds meatier. As if it's farther inside of you. I picture blooming cells with rows of teeth. I also hadn't known that certain cancers are overfunded, like breast cancer and leukemia, whereas esophageal and uterine cancers are underfunded. Even the scariest diseases aren't immune to branding. I catch myself stopping at a deli to consider buying flowers and immediately feel like an asshole. June would ridicule me if I stopped for a bouquet of daisies.

I still have the wine opener in my bag. I vow to give it to her only if it naturally arises in conversation.

"Hey," she says when I come up. When she opens the door, there are clusters of jars and opened spice bags, with a large spill of peppercorns marching across her counter like an army of ants. I remember this about my sister, how you'd find stray ingredients for days after she cooked.

"What are you making?" I take off my jacket and Vans. She's leaning into a comically tiny mortar and pestle with unnecessary force and nods at the hall closet between us. There's only a black parka and a camel trench in there. I hang my coat, marveling at the superabundant closet space. A life beyond breaking shitty plastic hangers every time you shove excess clothing aside.

"Mapo tofu." She resumes her grinding. It's Dad's favorite. "Since I'm doing the spices, I thought I'd do a big batch. You should take some with you."

"Thanks." There's a package of tofu on the cutting board. It's deep-fried, not silken. And the cutting board is shitty and plastic, dinged up and discolored. Fobby. I fantasize about getting her a really nice checkerboard wood kind. The ultra-expensive Williams Sonoma one that lasts forever because it's made of the butt ends of wood blocks.

"Uh," says June, bumping her elbow into me. I'm hovering, which she hates.

"Do you cook a lot?" I perch on a barstool on the other side of the kitchen island. I imagine intimate get-togethers, dinner dates, charcuterie. She probably has a book club or something.

"Not really," she says, keeping her eyes on the pan. "Never had time."

She scoops up the escaped peppercorns. They look like tiny cannonballs. As she returns them to the bag, she wipes her brow with the back of her hand. "Careful with your eyes, Juju." My jaw stiffens. She goes about her business, acting as if she hasn't heard, crinkling the cellophane loudly.

I hadn't meant to call her that. It's been years since I've called her that.

"How was school?" she asks after a moment.

"Fine." I sound sharper than I'd intended. I hate when she polices my whereabouts.

She tosses the pre-fried bean curd from the cutting board into the sauce.

"That's not the right bean curd." The adult part of me wants to bop the little sister part right in the nose.

"So don't eat it," she says without skipping a beat and then sucks the ends of her cooking chopsticks.

This shuts me up. It smells good.

She stops midstir to study me.

"What?"

June looks pensive. Like a baby taking a shit. There's no telling what she's thinking.

"Nothing." She looks away. "I had something to tell you, but I forgot."

I wonder if she's mad at me.

"Seriously, what?"

"Nothing," she snaps.

It's probably about the tofu. Or calling her "Juju."

"Uh, um, so . . ." I hop off the stool and go to my bag, desperate to defuse the tension. "I got you something. It's dumb. And small. It's from my store—the store I work at. I just figured . . ."

I offer her the paper sleeve. One of her hands is manning the pan that's smoking; the other's tossing its contents with chopsticks.

"Sorry," I say hurriedly, removing the corkscrew, crumpling the bag and shoving it in my pocket. "Worst timing for a present." I lay it down on the counter. "It's not even really a present. It's more just . . . functional."

"No. It's perfect. Thank you," she says, a little too brightly, throwing her aromatics into the pan. They crackle, and the apartment air fills with a convincingly Szechuan bouquet. She coughs as the peppers smoke. "Oh shit," she says, turning back to me. "Is that what you wanted? Do you *want* wine?"

"No." I shake my head. "I mean, sure, but I can get it." I open her fridge. I'm shocked by its contents. It's crammed with random half-eaten, uncovered food. I shut the door, averting my attention, embarrassed to have spied. "I got you one because you couldn't find it last time. Remember you offered me red because that's the one you liked better, but . . ."

"Oh." She's smiling with so much effort. "That's so thoughtful."

"Oh." I wave the air. "It was only twelve bucks."

We are so cringey. I barely know what to do with my hands. She turns and busies herself with the rest of the cooking.

"So, did you want red?" I ask her.

"I'm okay," she says. "Did you?"

"I'll just have water." I watch as she slices scallions, and the rhythmic motion of it—the scratchy sound—soothes me.

"Remember when you wanted to take over Mom and Dad's restaurant?"

"Yeah," she says distractedly. "What a nightmare that would've been."

I open a cabinet. It's completely empty. "What do you need?" interjects June.

"Water glasses."

"It's this one." She points at the cabinet over the sink. I grab two from the four in there, fill them with tap water, and set them on the bar. "Thanks," she says.

"Want me to do the rice?"

"Sure." She turns, opens the drawer behind her, and hands me a flat white paddle. There's a tiny rice cooker on the counter by her fridge. It's small and cheap and doesn't match the other gleaming appliances, but I'm surprised she even has one. She hands me two blue bowls.

We both make shit rice, at least according to Mom. We never add enough water and never bother to soak it the way she does. The trick is to add enough water so that it just about meets the first line on your ring finger. Even still, we both eyeball it and get it wrong. I open the steaming lid, digging around the cooker to break it up.

I scoop her two lumps because it's bad luck to give someone a single scoop and then portion out a tiny clump for myself. I don't think the luck thing counts if it's yours.

She inspects my meager bowl. "I had a late lunch." She frowns briefly and hands me the ladle so I can serve myself. I spoon a little. I can probably get away with two pieces of tofu. The sauce is thickened with cornstarch and glistening with oil. She fixes her plate, grabs kimchi from the fridge, which we add to our bowls with chopsticks. I pause at the white barstools. "Those make my ass numb," she says. I follow her to the couch.

I warm my hands on the bowl and take a small taste. It's amazing to eat something hot for once. I haven't had home-cooked Asian food in forever. I take another bite. "This is really good."

"Right?" she says. "I had such a craving this morning. You sure you don't want more tofu?"

"No, I'm good."

We eat silently.

"Do you have roommates?" she asks after a while.

"Just one."

"How's that going? Is she cool?"

I think of Jeremy fucking that woman in my bedroom. I nod a few times. Something must have passed across my face because she stops chewing. She lifts her sock-covered foot off the floor and pokes my haunch, hard.

"It's a dude, isn't it?" she asks with her mouth full.

I pull my chopsticks out of my mouth.

"You're living with a boyfriend, aren't you?" I have never been able to lie to June. She also has this way of rolling her eyes without rolling her eyes.

"He's not my boyfriend."

She chortles.

"Who's on the lease—you or him?"

"It's fine," I tell her quietly. "He's leaving soon."

"You broke up?"

"No, we didn't break up. We can't break up because it's not like that."

She makes a rumbly noise in the back of her throat as I stare at my food. "Well," she says, shaking her head. "At least you're consistent."

I set my bowl down on the mirrored coffee table harder than I'd meant to.

"He's not on the lease."

Truth is, I'm not either. There is no lease and it's some guy called David Buxbaum's name on the apartment because I'm living in a rent-controlled illegal sublet, and I still get his jury summonses.

"Okay," she says.

Again I sense the math in her brain, the deepening of the wrinkle between her brows, but she lets it go. I'm staring down at my bowl when her blue cotton foot creeps back into my sight line and prods me again. This time on my arm.

I glare at her. She keeps nudging me, smiling as she pushes her bowl toward me. She wants me to get her seconds. "With more kimchi, too, please," she says sweetly.

"Ugh, fine." I roll my eyes, getting up. "I need sauce anyway."

"Am I ever going to meet this asshole?" she calls out from the living room. "I guess it's pointless to ask if he's white." I add more rice to both our bowls in silence, along with kimchi. I dump a fuckton angry scarlet chili shards into June's bowl. I'm annoyed at my sister, but I'm aware that something's loosening between us.

"Here you go." I hand her the bowl before sitting down, smiling just as sweetly.

"What's his name?" She picks up a whole pepper with her chopsticks and sets it on the chrome top of the coffee table.

I eat my food.

"Let me guess—it's Tyler. Ooh, no, it's Tanner. Oh, what's up with that guy Chase Rice? Isn't he on a TV show? How perfect is that name for a white dude who only fucks with Asian chicks?"

She sets another chili beside the first one. I get up and hand her a paper towel torn in half. Even in such a nice house, June's a slob.

"So, what's up? Like, cancer-wise?"

June raises her brows. "Cancer-wise?"

I just wanted a change of topic.

"Got my pathology report," she continues, extracting more peppers.

"And?"

"They referred me to a gynecologic oncology surgeon."

"And?"

"I'm gonna go see them."

Gynecologic oncology surgeon. I glance down at the gloopy red-brown sauce in my bowl. "When?"

"In the morning."

She's not smiling anymore, utterly focused on her napkin. It's why she called me. It's why she wanted home-cooked food.

"Wait? You have surgery tomorrow?"

She sets her bowl on the table and doesn't immediately respond.

"June?" Everyone in my family does this, gets really pissed off or shuts down when you ask them a question they deem too personal.

"June?" I ask my hands quietly. My nail polish has chipped off except on my thumbs. I try another tactic.

"Where's the appointment?" I ask conversationally, pretending to take another bite of food.

Past her head, on top of her pale wood credenza, on a shelf below the TV, I see the pastel-colored DVD case from the *Gilmore Girls* box set. The familiar sight makes the tightness in my chest catch at my throat.

"Everything's on the Upper East Side," she says finally. "Total fucking schlep. And I hate when they take the FDR."

"Take the Q."

"I have cancer. I'm not poor."

I choke a little.

My phone lights up on the coffee table. Jeremy again. Her eyes flit over to it, so I flip it over.

"We're just talking tomorrow. Going over the biopsy results."

I wonder if I'm supposed to go with her, but I feel stupid asking after all this time. She probably has friends she'd rather be with. People she's close to.

"Thanks," I tell her. She looks up at me as if I've said something stupid.

"Will you do something for me?"

I plonk my bowl down in my lap and nod solemnly.

"Can you just go the fuck to school? Please? I know that *boy problems*"—I wince at the wording—"are a lot for you, but don't get distracted." She sighs and closes her eyes for a beat. It's painful to see how annoying she finds me. "Focus in class, do well, and over the next few weeks, or even months, try not to give Mom and Dad anything to worry about."

I glance up at her. "Do you really think it'll be months?"

She sighs again. I'm insufferable. "I don't know, Jayne."

"Okay." I keep nodding.

"You're so smart when you make the effort," she says, and instantly my eyes well up. It's all I've ever wanted to hear her say. Just not in this context.

"I'll never be as smart as you," I tell her.

June picks her bowl back up and laughs. "I didn't say you were anywhere near as smart as me. Just . . ." Another loud exhale. "I'm smart in ways that make me stupid in others. I've made so many fuck-ing mistakes, Jayjay."

My throat tightens.

"You're going to be okay though, right?" I hear the warble in my voice.

"What do you want me to say?"

I want her to tell me the day, the hour, and the exact minute when she'll die. And I want her to go away so I can start preparing for it now with zero new memories because I have enough that I'll miss.

She gets up. The conversation is over. When I stand, I'm struck again by the heft of it. My sister has cancer.

I follow her into the kitchen. From behind she's so small. There's so little of her to invade.

She stoops to start loading her dishwasher. "Siri, play *The Graduate* soundtrack," she calls into the room.

I snicker, I can't help it. "Have you ever even seen *The Graduate?*" She turns to me. "You know I haven't."

"It's a classic."

"I'm good." She leans over to pop a Cascade pod into the machine. "Who has time for whole movies? I've seen clips. I love the soundtrack. I get the idea."

It takes every ounce of restraint not to fight her again on this. She switches on the dishwasher.

"I can't believe you have a dishwasher," I tell her, genuinely impressed. It's like having a backyard in New York. "And that you use it."

"I know," she says, smiling, leaning up against the counter with her arms crossed. "Every time I run it, I imagine Mom shitting a brick." Our parents have a dishwasher in Texas, but they only use it as a drying rack. June once modeled an elaborate graphic to prove how much *more* water was wasted doing dishes by hand, but they wouldn't hear of it. Mom would have an aneurism if she found out detergent pods were even a thing. She dilutes dish soap.

"Man, when's the last time I had your mapo tofu?" I rinse my bowl and hand it to her. "Probably high school."

"It *was* high school. Couple months before I left for college." She takes a long, pensive sip of water.

That's when I remember too. She'd made it for Dad. As a consolation. And how on that lonely night, the three of us barely ate any.

chapter 11

I'm clutching the still-warm Tupperware on my walk to the subway. Cancer must feel like such betrayal, knowing that somewhere deep in your body you're manufacturing tiny bombs that detonate and catch fire.

I barrel down the stairs to the train.

June doesn't *look* sick. She always looks that way. Piqued. She has resting antagonism face. If there was visual evidence of frailty, all of this would be more believable. It's not as if I don't know how mortality works, but for June it doesn't track. It's that absurd cognitive schism where when somebody dies, all the thunderstruck dummies go, but I *just* saw them. The totality of death is inconceivable. It's intolerable that you're completely, utterly, irrefutably alive, filled up with decades of inside jokes, goofy facial expressions, all the love of your family, and then not.

It's also so weird that any news of death makes you almost immediately think of yourself. I'm determined to know how I'll feel when

June dies. I want to be able to see it, touch it, taste it so I can make sure I'll survive.

The smoke of my breath on the subway platform seems like it should be warm, but it isn't.

Fuck. Juju is going to die.

One: black-haired girl in a red toggle coat.

Two: the kind of laughter that seeks an audience.

Three: trash can with a LITTER STOPS HERE sticker—torn.

Four: movie poster with a Sharpied mustache.

Five: another puff of my breath.

One, two, three, four, five. *Onetwothreefourfive.*

She'd better not die. She's nowhere near done.

One, two, three, four, five.

June's first word was "milk." Mom was convinced she'd read it off the formula canister as an infant. That's weird too. Like death. One or zero. Words have no meaning, and then boom—reading. My first word was "cow." I'd heard Mom telling someone on the phone that it was June's first word and I wanted ours to be the same. That makes my brain itch. How babies go from gurgling lumps to spies in one day. Illiterate and then illuminated.

June was always precocious and was conscripted into dirty-diaper duty the moment she could be mobilized. Ferrying the clean and scuttling the shitty, the sun rising and setting behind her bobbling head. Thinking about June as a baby makes my heart hurt. Every picture of her as a kid is of her laughing. And most of them are blurred—she could never sit still.

I couldn't either. In our small, high-rise apartment in Seoul, way up on the eighteenth floor, I'd open the window and climb out. Lowering myself into the fish-tank-sized concrete flower bed by the kitchen, the small, square tiles biting into my dimpled knees. Finally, free of that cramped flat, I'd blink into the breeze. The first time I escaped, my father had stalked out as far as the parking garage, confounded. The second, June found me, and we were both yelled at as Mom cried. Another time, when we visited a family friend's house, on the twenty-second floor, I wedged my head between the balcony railings as an experiment and was trapped there by my neck. My father had to negotiate my narrow shoulders, my warm, compact torso, and my pudgy, squirming feet through the balusters, where I soared in the abyss before being pulled back over the handrail to safety. It was by some feat of kid proportions that I could get my head out but not back in without getting stuck by my ears.

I couldn't be reasoned with.

Until June threw the doll.

I can recall exactly how it felt when she took my sticky palm in hers, tottered me along the stretch of cool concrete hallway, the crackled pattern of the ground so close beneath my chubby legs, and rode the elevator down with me to see.

It was a porcelain-faced doll, a dark-haired girl in a plush, silken onesie with pom-poms down the front, like buttons, a clown costume, and she was utterly shattered. Her hollow china hands lay broken too. We peered into the conch shell interior of her face for secrets, but there was nothing inside.

She forced me to look up at our apartment window and then back down at the doll.

"Don't ever hide from me," said my sister, eyes dark and serious. She pointed to the wreckage, then prodded my tiny chest. "Or you'll die."

We took the doll, shards and all, and threw her away in a plastic bag and into the trash chute. We heard her mangled body *whoosh* and then *thunk* somewhere deep in the dark.

I was three; she was six. I never left her side after that. Even in Texas, where we moved later that year. Enormous, ridiculous Texas. Where everything was so flat you could feel all hundred and eighty degrees of sky at your shoulders. Where if you lay on your back look-ing up at the sky, it felt so heavy you couldn't breathe. It was as if the horizon could crush you. There was nowhere to hide in wide, bound-less Texas. No escape at all.

We never had a plan to forestall June's death. Only mine.

Maybe she shouldn't hide from me, either. Just in case.

The subway jolts to a stop.

I hug the container of tofu closer to me.

I blot the tears from my eyes with my hoodie sleeve and pull out my phone for distraction. I open up Instagram and it lands me right at Jeremy's sunglassed face. God, June would loathe him.

I click through the slideshow he's posted. Link in bio. Link in stories. Link everywhere. It's an article about small-run zines. How New York, Seoul, London cool kids are flocking to printed materials and hand-selling them. Or else not retailing them at all and giving them away as limited-edition artifacts at parties. It's incredible to me how much press you can get about something that barely exists.

So, this is what he needed the photo for.

I click to the article. There he is. Mugging for the entire city. He's used a portrait I've never seen. I wonder who took it—it's not cred-ited. It's his best angle, the three-quarter turn of the head. Where the generosity of the onlooker's mind envisages both profile and direct aspects as more handsome than either truly are.

I scroll through the write-up quickly. There's a sidebar with bullet points about all the people who have helped him. His mentors, a pair of famous brother directors I know he barely knows. Another rich-kid friend who's larded with trillions of social media follows through twin careers of modeling and skateboarding. And Rae. Again. This time cited as his muse.

I'm sick. The next page is an entire story dedicated to her. Mostly photos. Of pale, ink-stained hands, eyes peeking behind pastel hair, chapbooks she's written alongside generous bowls of turmeric latte, a tree pose with her hands up, nipples teasing the gossamer of her shirt, laughing. Every picture is striking. All featuring her avian body only just skirting nudity. There's even a photo with her on the toilet. Another of a shower drain with pink water whirlpooling and a stanza as caption about moons and menarche.

A tidal loathing rolls through me. She's so girlish, so delicate and quintessentially lovely that biological truths on her are blushingly seductive. Titillating and carnal. It's a subversion that requires nothing from you. Arousal that makes you feel like a feminist. Sometimes the female gaze is just as systemically toxic the way it postures as provocation.

I'd so much rather they were fucking.

I'm shocked when I have no reason to be. I'm ashamed that I feel robbed. Contrary to everything he's shown me, I'd thought that Jeremy would mention me. Name me. Obviously not as his girlfriend but at least as the brains behind the visual aesthetic. Thank me for the sleepless nights he's hovered above me nitpicking as I made tweaks to his logo. Acknowledge me in any way for the lost time, the small hours when he brought me coffee with kisses and encouragement, when my rip of InDesign crashed, dropping fonts and losing layouts because he had a last-minute "ideation all-hands."

I don't exist in his story.

I never do.

chapter 12

The next moment, I'm at our door. A glitch of dissociation. He's home. I hear the muffled sounds of his laptop and his *huhuhuh* chuckling as I slide my key in the lock. I steel myself. When I open it, he's on the couch, ass to the pillow I put my face on, watching his computer, which is hooked up to my Bluetooth speaker.

"Jeremy." I toss the keys on the kitchen counter with too much force. They slide straight into the sink. I set my sister's Tupperware on the stove. He shoots up, his basketball shorts drapey on his chicken legs. He lays his laptop beside him, out of the way. I know he's using my Netflix account. I should have kicked him out when he asked for my password and canceled his subscription without talking to me first. If they show you who they are, believe them. What more fuckery did I need than his smiling green avatar on the landing page?

"Babe," he says. "I'm glad you're home." He comes over to me in the kitchen. "Not to be a dick, but I've been meaning to ask. Did you smoke all the weed? Because that's not chill . . ." He rubs his face.

"And yo, did you kill the rest of my ginger ice cream . . . ?"

"What?" I'm blindsided by his gall. "Are you serious?"

"It's a seasonal flavor," he explains gravely. "They only made, like, thirty pints. It's for tastemakers. I'm supposed to social it."

"I saw your article," I snap. He takes a half step. I wonder if he's always had such weak shoulders. If they've always sloped at this unbecoming, defeated angle from his neck.

"The reporter was a moron," he says, pulling out his phone. I know he's checking how the post is doing. "And thanks for sending the photo," he says sarcastically. "It would have taken you a second. I wouldn't even mind you eating all my special stuff, but the least you could—"

"You have to fucking leave my house," I tell him.

His tiny peanut head jerks back. "Now, hold on," he says, palming the air between us. His attention flicks down to his thumbed screen one final time as he pointedly puts it facedown on the coffee table.

His expression hardens when I roll my eyes. "You owe me twenty-one hundred dollars in rent," I continue. "And I don't know what the fuck happened to your precious limited-edition douchehole ice cream."

The lie comes out smooth. It was delicious. Especially when I was high on his weed.

"Wait a minute—" He stammers.

I cut him off again. "I'm kicking you out."

I shuck off my sneakers and head for the bedroom, but as I do, a single, hot tear crests over the ridge of my right eye and tumbles. I brush it away and sniff hard. He gives me a simpering look as I push past him, misreading my traitorous rage-tear.

"Is this about the other night?" He reaches for me, but I shake him off, pulling the suitcase from the closet. "When I had . . . company?" A belabored sigh. "You knew I've been seeing people. Polyamory is important to me. I've been abundantly clear on my truth."

I pull out two blazers, a tangle of cardigans, and some silky things for going out. Jeremy's dirty clothes are in *my* white plastic hamper, so I shake them out and slide his flannel shirts off *my* flat black velvet hangers and drop them in heaps.

"What are you doing?" he calls from the hall. "You don't have to be an asshole."

I drag the suitcase and the hamper filled with hangers, backing into him forcefully. I start packing in the living room.

"Can't we talk about this?"

I turn to glare just as he brightens, as if struck with a genius idea. "We can switch," he declares, nodding toward the couch that I've been sleeping on for the past few nights. "I'll take the sofa." Then he smiles indulgently. "Look, it's healthy for us to move through this. Honestly, living with you hasn't been good for me, either, what with the hostility and the silence. You know she was just some Raya chick."

That's when I tune out. I lose myself in the packing. I love packing. Always have. When I was little, I was constantly gathering hobo bags with Mom's tablecloths and scarves, tying them to the end of broomsticks, filling them with snacks and toys. Mom would always remark on how keen I was to leave.

Later, I'd laugh at her hypocrisy.

The packing isn't as tidy as I'd like. My school books take up half the suitcase. The Spacesaver bags are in the high closet, and I'd sooner eat my own eyes than ask Jeremy for help. I mash everything together and zip it up. I head to the kitchen with the hamper and press every Trader Joe's cooler bag I have into service.

"Jesus, what is with you and food?" I unzip the first bag. "You're lying about the fucking ice cream. I know it. The way you lie about my cereal. Bread, Beyond Burgers, everything. What is wrong with you? Why can't you talk like an adult? You don't get to shut down right now. Jayne. Jayne? God dammit. This is important. Look at me."

There's a lot to do in the pantry. I grab sesame seeds, sesame oil, rice wine vinegar, Chinkiang vinegar, red chili flakes, soy sauce, fish sauce, and seaweed. I seize both Maggi sauces, the giant Jeroboam one and the mini because I deserve them.

I pop open the fridge, removing every banchan and condiment. Prepared Korean food is extortionate, so I hoard it like a pepper flake coveting Gollum. Every kimchi jar, even the wack white cabbage garbage that hipsters eat for the probiotics, the preserved dried squid, the marinated soybeans, seasoned radish, the fermented bean paste, frozen dumplings, frozen rice cakes, and the stupid fucking frozen edamame that I buy from Trader Joe's to illustrate a point even when Jeremy keeps ordering edamame from Seamless for eight bucks, and splitting the bill down the middle when he's done.

"How many times have I told you, it's the same fucking soybeans." I wave the bag of pods in his face. "Japanese curry comes from a brick. Restaurant udon isn't from scratch, either. Jesus."

Why is he so dense? I take the almond milk and his oat coffee creamer.

On my tiptoes, I fling open the snack cupboard and hit pay dirt. I grab the economy-size five-pack brick of Shin Ramyun Black by the corner of the plastic bag and fling it onto the counter.

"You're not taking that," he says, stepping closer, trapping me between him and the counter behind me. He's wearing his Birkenstocks in the house, which he swears he doesn't wear outside when he totally does. "I bought it. You don't even eat ramyun anymore, remember? It makes you bloated."

That he calls it *ramyun*, the way Koreans pronounce it, sets me aflame. I shudder at Jeremy's entire schtick. The way he was so proud of how he knew how to use chopsticks before we met. Or how showy he was about loving spicy food until the time we got hot pot and he ordered stunt-spice levels and had fire shits for a week. Plus, he's constantly passing off my tastes as his own. I overheard him tell a girl that Kinokuniya was his favorite bookstore though he'd never even heard of it until I took him.

"Are you breaking up with me?" He runs his hand through his hair, riffling it out a little. This tic of preening almost makes me shudder. Watching him self-consciously finger his eroding hairline disgusts me. I let him see my revulsion.

"I can't break up with you," I tell him, shoving everything into bags. "We obviously aren't together. It's like how you can't fire me."

"Wow," he drawls. "Okay. But you're legally obligated to give me time. I paid rent."

"You paid rent once. Two months ago. It's October." I'm lightheaded that we're finally talking about money again.

"You have to give me at least thirty days," he says crisply. "It's New York law."

"I'll give you a week."

He nods at the neck of the bottle sticking out of my blue tote. "Maggi's European, you know. Knorr's Swiss."

I can practically hear the fissure in my brain. It's as if every splinter of frustration from every nonconfrontational moment in my entire life forms this dense thorny morning star of rage that I'm desperate to hurl at him.

"Fuck you, Jeremy!" I scream inches from his face, and push him with the hand still holding the instant noodles. "You don't get to have this! In fact, you don't get to have any of this anymore." I hate how I've upgraded this fuckstick's life in any way. Especially this way. That this asshole now knows how superior Shin Ramyun Black is to regular Shin Ramyun by the grace of an extra flavor packet and all that bonus garlic.

This fucker doesn't deserve bonus garlic.

"If I so much as see you at H Mart"—I get right in his face—"or even Sunrise Mart, I will fucking ruin you."

chapter 13

My head is hot, my ears flooded with blood. Something's biting into my palm, and I look down to find a tangle of iPhone charger cables clutched in my fevered fingers. Two are his. One of the dangling white cubes is even labeled J in blue Sharpie. Jesus Christ, Jeremy's a dipshit. It makes me laugh that both our names start with *J*. My mind hones in on the memory of when I told him Koreans don't get BO because we have dry earwax and not wet like most people. Later, when we went to get dumplings with his boys, he kept raising my arm up by the wrist and smelling my armpit in front of them, saying, "Seriously, get in there. She smells like air!" I socked him but felt secretly proud. It made me feel thin and virtuous to smell like nothing.

When the car pulls up, one of the IKEA bags lurches painfully into my shin.

I click the seat belt fastener a few times before realizing I never buckled myself in.

I stagger through the lobby, looking like a bag lady.

June buzzes me through, but when I get to her floor, she takes a look at my stuff. "What happened?"

"It was a boyfriend," I tell her. "He was a scumbag."

"You shouldn't have left," says June, blocking her door.

"You're the one who's always saying I shouldn't waste my time with these guys!" I panic momentarily that she won't let me in.

"Not like this." She's wearing pj's and her face is creased.

"Were you asleep?"

She ignores my concern. "Dummy, do you know how much harder it is to get him out now?"

"But . . ." I glance down at my hands helplessly. They're lashed red from the heavy bag handles.

"Christ, Jayne." She crosses her arms and gives me a hard look. "You know I have a doctor's appointment in the morning."

The tears come without warning. "I'm sorry," I whimper. "I know this is the worst possible timing, but if you just let me stay for tonight. I promise . . ."

"Is he on the lease?"

"He's going to leave," I insist. "I told him he had to by the end of the week. I completely lit into him."

Her eyes drop to my bags again. "Dude, did you only bring groceries?"

"Please, June."

She sighs, bumps her door open with her butt, and shuffles back inside. I hobble in after her, shoving all the frozen foods in the freezer, and leaving the fridge stuff in the cooler bags for the morning.

I take a long, hot shower, luxuriating in the water pressure, the steam, and how the tub isn't blackened with mildew. She's left her bedroom door ajar, so I get in beside her in the king-size bed. The sheets are cool and expansive, and I'm calmed by her steady breathing. I wake up six hours later.

"Have whatever," she grumbles when I find her in the kitchen. June has never been a morning person. I open the fridge to finish putting away my things. The smell is so intense, it feels invasive. It has the piercing quality of ammonia. In the back there's a jar of pickles that's carpeted with a thick layer of fur, which I didn't even know was a thing for brined foods. In the crisper drawer is a ballooned sack of mixed field greens that have matured into a sludge. There's also a container from Domino's Pizza. In New York. We live in the town with the best slices in the world and my sister is ordering Domino's Pizza. If there were ever an indication that your sibling was unwell, it's this.

Her uncovered bowl of mapo from last night sits front and center. Complete with stale rice and chopsticks still stuck in it. Behind it are stacks of takeout containers and a petrified slice of red velvet cake in a plastic clamshell that hasn't been shut. It looks like a wax sculpture.

I locate eggs and check the expiration date. I pair my Hidden Valley ranch dressing with her bigger one in the fridge door. I also slot my soy sauce and fish sauce in the pantry. I love that we have two of mostly everything.

"I'll sleep on the couch tonight," I tell her, cracking two eggs and depositing the whites into a ramekin with a damp paper towel on top.

"What did you do with the yolks?" she asks.

I glance at her guiltily. Her face is puffy from sleep.

"I chucked them."

June hits her trash can pedal with her foot to peer inside.

"Not the literal trash. I'm not a total monster. The sink."

"That's fucked up."

I don't tell her that what's really fucked up is the elaborate ecosystem that's going on in her refrigerator. Her hair's tied in a sloppy ponytail, and I can't believe she's wearing the woolly blue pajamas with yellow roses that Mom gave us two Christmases ago. The temperature's in the sixties today, but June's favorite thing has always been to crank up her central air and wear winter clothes inside. I bite my tongue about how she can be wasteful too.

"Next time get your own eggs," she says groggily. I don't tell June she has sleep in her eyes, out of spite. Even though I'm the only one who has to look at the goo.

"Fine." I put the eggs in the microwave silently. I can't wait until the week is out. "You did say help yourself to whatever, though."

Something softens in her expression.

In the hazy morning light, a corona of baby hairs dance around her face. "I got those eggs from the farmers' market," she says. "They're nonconflict, organic, grass-fed eggs that cost nine bucks for a thing."

"Jesus." I'm genuinely taken aback. "I had no idea."

I check the carton. They look like regular eggs. If a little hipster because the label is a tasteful line drawing of chickens. It looks like a wine label. Or a sixties animation where real shit pops off, like the farmer kills a character for food.

"Whatever," she says, waving her hand. "Take them. I thought I should start eating better and then forgot about them."

I look down at my shriveled breakfast. I could have kept the yolks. Pretended I was ever in my life going to make hollandaise. Or flan. "Damn, the farmers probably christened each one."

She smiles at my stupid joke. "Are you a farmer if you have chickens? Or is that only for, I don't know, crops? Can you be like 'I'm a chicken farmer'?"

"Hi. I'm a 'cow farmer.'" I try it out and grin. "Are we stupid? Why don't we know this? I think it's right though." I raise a hand.

"Hi. I'm a pig farmer. See there, I feel like I've definitely heard of pig farmers. That's a thing for sure."

She starts laughing. "I don't know why, but the 'hi' is the dumbest part."

I start laughing. "Is it the 'hi' part or the fact that I keep waving each time?"

We both crack up. Then it dawns on me. What the eggs signify. June once told me that organic food was a scam.

"Yeah, you can stay for a few days." She pulls out a Chinese food container from the fridge and sniffs it. "What'd the bastard do?" She pries off the metal handle of the cardboard Chinese food bucket, folds it shut, and sticks it in the microwave.

"He was just a fuckstick," I tell the back of her head.

I study her while she watches the box spin in the microwave.

June is scared. There's no way she'd go to the farmers' market and get ripped off on eggs if she wasn't.

chapter 14

"I'm going to my thing," she announces as I'm rinsing our breakfast plates. I watch her pull her hair out from the back of her coat.

"Okay," I tell her. "With the gynecologic oncology surgeon." I hear myself recite the words carefully, as if reading.

"Yeah." She checks her pockets for her keys and then holds on as if she's forgotten something.

I want to ask to go with her, but I'm watching myself not do it.

"Um, when are you done?" I ask instead.

"I don't actually know. Juju's first cancer, so."

I feel stupid for having asked. "But like—" My voice breaks.

She glances over with the door cracked.

"Do you want me to come? With you? To the place?"

"Why?" she says in a withering tone. "No." She shakes her head briskly. "Don't you have class?"

"Yeah, but . . ." I get on my feet and shrug. "I could come. And help you or whatever."

"Honestly," she says, raising her brows. "You'd just stress me out."

"Fine." I blink back tears.

She sighs and tries again. "I need to process. Give me a little space, okay?"

"Yeah, okay."

She's punishing me for being here. I know she is.

"Um," she says. I hold my breath, wondering if she's changed her mind. She pulls a set of keys out of a drawer, dangles them, then sets them on the counter. "The top key's squarish."

I nod.

"Don't lose them. It's, like, two hundred bucks for the outside one."

"Got it." My nose stings. The full weight of the indignity hits me as the door shuts.

I lie around staring at my phone dejectedly and then finally go to the bathroom to fix my face. I open June's medicine cabinet to an avalanche of tampons. Gathering all the plastic-wrapped bullets from the floor—since my sister uses OB like it's 1954—I quickly dismiss the niggling unease of how my period's been missing for the better part of a year. I open the under-sink cupboard to find a large plastic bag of hotel toiletries, including two pairs of terry-cloth slippers in cloth drawstring pouches. There are also countless individual packets of Advil and NyQuil. And a half-used ring of birth control pills.

I miss my sister, I realize. I feel cheated out of the past four years. In the span of time we were becoming adults and I had so many questions, we barely spoke. I return everything, put on eyeliner, and head back into her kitchen to open her fridge.

I know a pathology when I see one. June's always been a slob, but these are multiple cries for help. I drag her trashcan close and throw out everything I'd set my sights on last night. I continue snooping in the kitchen. Every cabinet is filled with random garbage. The shelf beside the stove, the one where I'd keep spices, features a packing-tape gun, a roll of toilet paper, and a tennis ball.

The ball reminds me of the first guy I hooked up with in New York. I knew it was damaged that I slept with three random guys in barely a week when I arrived, which is why I don't think about it. He wore Gucci moccasins, the ones with the fur, and had a single mattress on the floor of his room. The only other objects were a flat-screen TV and a candy-colored tangle of video game controllers. He had zero toilet paper, and as far as I could tell he washed his hair with bar soap, but he owned a brand-new tennis ball in the cabinet under the sink. I have no idea why.

I squeeze June's tennis ball.

I pad into her bedroom. It's sun-drenched and girlie. Tall, high, huge bed with white sheets and a pale-lilac reading chair in the corner. The closets cover the entire wall beside the bed. The mirrored panels remind me of my mom's closet, but June's are smudged with fingerprints. When I slide it open, there's a handful of suits in dry-cleaner bags, an overflowing laundry hamper, and a shelf with stacked T-shirts. One of them, a tie-dyed *Lord of the Rings* tee, I recognize. When June first left for college, I was constantly hiding her stuff under my mattress to rescue them from Mom's church donation pile. On her visits home, I'd wordlessly stow them in her suitcase before she left. I draw the heathered cotton tee to my nose and sniff deeply, expecting to invoke our old house, June's old Clinique perfume, anything, but it smells of laundry detergent.

In her living room there's a credenza below her TV. Inside is a row of encyclopedias. I look around to confirm—there are no other books in the house.

I stoop down to pull one out. Thankfully, they're not conjoined decoy book spines that are featured as an aesthetic choice in the homes of asshole people. The navy hardback's dusty as hell. I flip to a random page.

"Fernweh. Noun. Origin: German. Translated as wanderlust but more literally, far woe. Or, far pain. Longing for a distant place. Could be characterized as a homesickness for somewhere you've never been before."

I'm struck by how I feel this way about New York even though I'm here.

Back in the kitchen, I fling open another cabinet door at random. Inside is a single wineglass. Beside it the wine key I brought. I open every cupboard and the dishwasher to verify what I feel I already know. That the wineglass she offered me was the only one she owns. There's something so distinctly broken about this that it squelches a muscle deep in my body.

I check my phone. If I leave now, and run, I'll be on time to class. Instead of putting my shoes on, I sit on the floor and text Patrick.

Last 10 yrs
Quick synopsis
GO
Read 10:04 a.m.

chapter 15

Oh my God. What did I ever do to him? Honestly, what kind of psychopath sets read receipts on? I'm scandalized and confused. I'm running up to Twenty-Eighth, the wind flying in my hair, zigzagging through pedestrians, hands jammed in my pockets. It's cold. Freezing. I don't remember the weather turning at all. I feel sort of high. Is Patrick rude? Deranged? Did he do an OS update and something went weird? Jesus, forget it.

Cancel Patrick. What a weirdo.

I'm in a flopsweat when I take my seat in Sociology. The fog at the small of my back dampens the waistband of my sweats. I look around furtively. I'm convinced people are watching me, judging me for my breathlessness, thinking I'm out of shape. The room is hushed. I'm in a row toward the back, but with the stadium seating, I can see kids going over their notes. I check my gCal. There's a quiz.

I flip open my notebook. The reading was on scatterplots and distribution, basically how to interpret data sets and deduce correlations.

The lecture was depressing yet faintly reassuring. It was about how humans compulsively categorize information because we need the illusion of control. Sorting scary, unfathomable variables like infant mortality rates by relating them to economics makes us feel safer. That if we can predict it or draw a little line, we'll be protected from, at the very least, feeling stupid.

It's why randomness is unacceptable. Why organized religion is a salve. It's far more palatable to think of a divine order. Why conspiracies are easier to stomach over psychopaths making a rash decision that alters the course of history.

But then you have people who seem to know what they're doing at all times. My favorite thing about June is that she mows through life with purpose. To me, nothing she does seems random. And when I'm within her reality distortion field, I feel like I know what I'm supposed to do too.

I'm only in New York because of June.

Ever since I can remember fashion's the only way I can organize facts. I know when World War II ended, because Dior's New Look was two years after. And I have a photographic memory for Marc Jacobs's 1993 grunge collection for Perry Ellis, including how it got him canned. Ask me anything about why the Antwerp Six are so influential, and how I'm obsessed with its most elusive and iconoclastic member, Marina Yee, not solely because she's Asian.

Even still, it was June who kept sending college catalogs to the house, addressed to me with no note, since we weren't technically speaking.

June who filled out the paperwork for tuition assistance with her home address so I could qualify as in-state.

June also partially answered the application essay of how technology and media had affected my life.

But I couldn't let someone who only listens to movie soundtracks speak for me entirely.

I responded to the other essay prompt, the one she'd never be able to answer, the one about art and culture. I wrote about Wong Kar-wai's *In the Mood for Love*. It was the first movie I'd ever seen without any white people that was part of the Criterion Collection. It was that or the lesser-known movie *Hyo*, a word that non-Koreans can barely pronounce, a term that means "duty" or "filial piety," this super-slavish devotion to doing well by your forebears, to do your parents' bidding, often at the cost of your own dreams.

Everybody condemned the Danny Song casting. He'd just shot a superhero movie and critics presumed he'd be ill-suited for a micro-budget film about a Korean brother and sister in Oklahoma trying to keep their Chinese restaurant afloat after their parents are killed in a car accident. It had a 100 percent score on Rotten Tomatoes, which stunned everyone. It was produced, directed, and distributed by Korean-Americans and felt so distinctly Korean-American that it had never occurred to me that anyone else would relate to it. When I watched it, I knew I had to get out of Texas.

I'd considered applying to the design program. I'd gone as far as creating the mood boards, sketches, and sewn the garment projects but chickened out at the last minute. The jacket I'd made fell lumpily across my chest since I didn't have a dress form and the cheap, chintzy fabric I'd ordered was all wrong.

I got in without declaring a field of study and it felt like a miracle. When I found out, by myself, after school, screaming and jumping in that hot, sticky house, I picked up the phone to tell June. But I chickened out on that as well.

I overheard Mom telling her on the phone a few weeks later. I closed the door to my room, face burning. But the next time June was home, I left the bath towel for her on the bed, the one we always fought over because it was the biggest and softest. And I reminded Mom to make rice without red beans because June hates them.

When I get out of the quiz, I see Cruella sharing a string cheese with her Chihuahua on a park bench. It's as if they were waiting for me, vivid and sunny, both dressed in yellow.

Life is random, I think. Data sets are fine, but mortality is random. Cancer is random. But seeing Cruella and her dog today feels like good luck somehow.

Instead of dicking around at McDonald's for a coffee, I go home to my sister. I want to finish cleaning her fridge. Maybe do her laundry. I need to know how her doctor's appointment went.

I run the long block, darting through the people with their heads bowed over their phones, earbuds glinting. I want to make June a cup of tea. Gather the remotes and phone charger and place them in her lap. I want to look after her in some way. Let her know I'm aware of what she's done for me.

By the time I'm at her building, I feel stupid for sprinting back. Recalling that she wanted space. I press my ear to her door, nervous. I hear nothing. It's cold, inert, and mute. Six inches of titanium or something crazy. It strikes me how even rich-people keys feel different, the way they glide in without catching or requiring any tricks of wriggling to turn.

June's flipping through a Vermont Country Store catalog in the kitchen. Back in pajamas. I knock belatedly, feeling stupid.

"Hey." I pointedly return the keys to her drawer.

"Hey," she says, not looking up from the gift guide.

I study her for any news. I can't even tell if she's had blood drawn; her sleeves are pulled over her knuckles. It's maddening how withholding she is. And she's barely looking at the Corn Chowder set or the Summer Sausage basket as she's turning pages.

Hanging up my coat, I make sure that my suitcase and bags are stacked behind the couch at an angle you can't see from the front door.

"School was good," I offer. "I, like, went."

I shuffle into a spare pair of her house slippers. "So, how was your thing?"

"You know what's weird?" she asks me, shutting the catalog.

"What?"

I reach across the counter to grab her forearm, partly as a joke, and when she doesn't withdraw, I really begin to freak out.

"They talked to me for, like, an hour," she says. Her eyes are glassy, and that groove between her eyebrows bites in deep.

"Okay," I say. "Did they do more tests?"

She shakes her head. "No, it was just . . . I met my doctor. My special cancer gyno. She seems fine. Her engagement ring seemed a little excessive but whatever. I guess we're going to run more tests. They want an MRI. Or I guess I want an MRI. I think I'm not supposed to eat beforehand, but they scheduled it for two p.m., so I'm going to be fucking starving. . . ."

"What happens after the MRI?"

"I don't know," she says. "We'll schedule the surgery."

"Is that what they said?"

"Pretty much." I can tell she's barely listening. She grabs the catalog again and rolls it up tight.

"Okay, but what's weird?"

"What?"

"Is the two p.m. MRI the weird part?"

"Huh?"

"You said, 'You know what's weird?'"

"What's weird?" she asks me, scowling impatiently, as if I'm the one being distracted and annoying.

I slowly exhale the breath I've been holding. "That's how you started this conversation, June. You said, 'You know what's weird?'"

"Oh," she says, waving my attention away. "It's not even that weird. I just can't believe I was in there for an hour, because I don't remember anything she said. I feel like I just watched her mouth move for sixty minutes."

I tug on my lip. My nose fills in anticipation of tears. I don't know what to do. Or what to say. I feel like leaving immediately, calling Ivy and getting drunk. But I also know that people who "do the work" would stick around. I wish I wanted to.

She shuffles over to the couch. I make myself follow her.

"I feel so dumb that I didn't bring a notepad." She gives her head a slight shake. "Once the doctor left, the nurse told me everything over again, but I don't know if I retained much of that, either." Her eyes track back and forth as if she's scanning her memory. "I should have voice memo'd it."

This doesn't sound anything like my sister. My coding math-brain sister. I hate it.

"Jesus, June." My voice cracks on her name. "I told you I'd come."

She kisses her teeth. "Whatever, I'll record it next time."

"When's the MRI?"

"Next week."

"I'm coming."

She shakes her head. "It's an MRI. I just lie there."

"Well, I'll sit there."

"That's the other weird part," she says with a faraway expression. "There was this pregnant woman in the waiting area. She was huge. And she was Asian. But with bangs. It felt like some kind of fucked-up psychology experiment."

I glance down at her coffee table. The rug underneath needs vacuuming. I hear her sniff. We're not big criers in our house. Once, a long time ago, Dad burst into tears, and June and I just backed away from him as if he were plutonium. We couldn't even make eye contact with each other for the rest of the day.

The silence hangs horribly between us.

"Do you want to watch *Gilmore Girls*?" I ask.

"Yeah, okay," she says. June always wants to watch *Gilmore Girls*.

I make her start on season two, when Jess appears. June likes Dean, which is all you really need to know about her even though I'm a Logan apologist, which makes me emotionally unwell. It's weird—we've only ever watched from season two to six.

When we were kids, we'd watch *Gilmore Girls* and *Friends* on a loop. Dad bought a TV/DVD combo player on sale from Costco, and we'd made him buy the box sets because we didn't have cable. Everything we owned was from Costco. It's where June's movie soundtrack obsession started. Mom bought her the *Cruel Intentions* soundtrack, and we listened to that on a loop for a year.

"I can't believe she doesn't just go with him," I muse when Jess tries to get Rory to follow him out the window.

"I can't believe the little poser steals Lorelai's beer when Luke saved his homeless ass," says June pointedly.

We both love Paris. Total personality disorder.

I don't even check my phone until Dave leaves Lane because Adam Brody's turncoat ass went to *The O.C.*

Patrick's texted me back. It's a string of emoji.

Korean flag.

British flag.

Highway.

Cactus.

Palm tree.

Camera.

Laptop guy.

Money flying away.

The little dude bowing or doing push-ups.

Then he goes: I'm shit at brevity. And emoji. I can give you a long synopsis if you'd like.

I try to wait until morning to respond. That way he'll know that I read it too, that fucker. But I break.

Use your words, I tell him.

chapter 16

Fuuuuuuuuuuuuuuuuuck. I can't believe Patrick went to Yale.

Also, Patrick is not only the type of guy to leave read receipts on, he texts bricks. Huge walls of texts. Sermons.

I lived in Seoul, he's written, when I check my phone the next morning. Moved to London for a bit. Went to art school in Cali. Straight to Yale for my MFA. Moved here because I've always wanted to be here. It's everything I thought it would be and nothing like what I'd expected. Walking around with music on feels like I'm living inside a movie. What about you?

It's stupid how unprepared I am to have the question turned around on me.

All day in class, I think about what to write.

I painstakingly transcribe the text on notes, typing and deleting.

My roommates kicked me out, I imagine myself telling him. *Then I ran out on my other roommate who's also my fake boyfriend and an unrepentant skeez. I only graduated high school by hate-studying because I couldn't bear to see any of those people ever again. I'm living with my sister because she feels sorry for me, when she's the one who deserves compassion. Because: postscript, she's dying. My sister died of cancer, Patrick. My sister.*

The question sets me on edge. I can't show the work. I don't know what I've done. I barely know where I've been. The next day, during my shift at the store, I almost have a meltdown behind the register. A long-necked, older redheaded woman tried to use an online gift card for an in-store purchase. "I don't have a computer," she says in a high-pitched voice, bobbing her head for emphasis. Six people suddenly materialize in the line behind her. "My late-husband, Morty, gave it to me," she says. There's something cartoon ostrichy about her that I can't shake. "Why would you sell a real-life, physical card if it's not for the material world? Why are you making life so hard?"

"I'm sorry," I tell her over and over. "I don't know why life's so hard."

"Want to get dinner or a drink or something?" Mari asks me just before eight. "Either Mercury's in reggaeton or it's a full moon. Everyone's being a pill today."

I shoulder my backpack. Not going straight home to June's storminess is enormously appealing, but I can't leave her alone. Over the past few nights, there were moments that I got up to watch her sleep. To make sure nothing awful is happening on my watch. I need to stop googling the symptoms I'm observing—irritability, fatigue, forgetfulness—but I don't know what else to do when she can't retain what her oncologists are saying.

"I have homework," I tell Mari, swiveling around to show her my book bag. It's partly true. On top of everything else, I'm way overdue on sending Patrick thirty words about my existential purpose.

I love what he said about feeling like he's in a movie when he's in the city. This pierces me to the core. It's why I want my streets scored to music with no words, because the lyrics get in the way of the faces. It's part of why I can't write him back. I don't know how to speak honestly without sounding corny.

I want to say how the grizzly dude in the flak jacket selling political buttons is why I love Union Square.

Or that Cruella gives meaning to Seventh and Eighth Avenues.

When I recognize people, it lets me hope that maybe they recognize me, too.

Over the next few days June and I ease into a routine where she slinks off for appointments as I mince around, physically collapsing into myself, cringing about the imposition of leeching off her resources. I have no idea what she's told her office but she's suddenly around at all hours, watching me. Every morning I spring off her couch to shove the pillow into my suitcase, folding up the blanket as small as it will go. To earn my keep, I cook and clean. I break down cardboard from a confusing onslaught of disparate Amazon Prime, interspersed with daily assaults on my already porous self-esteem.

"Those mom jeans do nothing for you," says my sister, fishing a foam roller out of a box.

"Seriously? A *New Yorker* tote bag? No one believes you read that shit." A single bottle of supplements is set on the coffee table.

"Why bother going to design school and not taking design?" she asks, peering over the top of a cookbook entirely dedicated to meals for one.

"You look like an idiot spoon-faced Steve Madden ad. Eat some carbs—what's wrong with you?" She prods me with a second, demonstrably longer, foam-roller purchase.

"Why do you worship white-people things?" That one was close. I'd almost made it out the door.

"Who even asks someone that?"

"You're not someone," she says, twirling a pen over a brand-new, thousand-piece jigsaw puzzle of a chessboard. "You're my sister."

Meanwhile: *Hey, June. Did you get the results of the MRI?*

Nothing.

One night, I get home from work at a quarter to nine. Lately, June's taken to hate-watching *Seinfeld* and heckling. "How is it funny that Jerry gets a South Asian immigrant deported after he ruins his restaurant?" I have a distinct suspicion she's been muttering into an empty living room all day. I wash the subway grime off my hands.

I don't know how cancer people are supposed to act, but you only ever hear about them running remission 10Ks or traveling the world searching for answers. It's not as if I'm waiting for June to become inspirational, but so far she's acting like a forty-year-old dude going through a breakup who's moved back in with his mom.

"Is your office cool with you taking all this time off?" I ask gently. She needs to go the fuck back to work. She might be sick, but she's pelting me with eighty-hour work weeks' worth of determination and problem-solving. Well, me and sitcom legend Jerry Seinfeld.

"Fuck work," she snaps. My spine stiffens. Okay, this is bad. This is depression or some other kind of mental health issue, because June does not refer to work in this way.

"Did you tell them what's going on?" I take a seat on the couch, careful to keep the concern off my face.

"I haven't told them," she says. "I'm taking vacation days and you'd think I took a shit on the conference table."

I wait for her to say more, but she doesn't. She raises her thumb to her mouth and chews on the nail. In my peripheral vision, she's tilting her whole head slowly as she makes her way across like she always does instead of rotating the finger which is so much easier.

"Did you eat anything today?"

"Whatever," she says, still gnawing on her thumb. Eyes affixed to the screen. "You know, it's not just that the show's racist. It's this institutional expectation that everyone will understand *Seinfeld* jokes that's racist."

I get up and open the pantry. "Do you want ramen?" I hold out the block of Shin Ramyun Black.

"Sure," she says, and then, "The fuck is Shin Ramyun Black?"

"It's like regular Shin Ramyun, but it's way better." I fill the pot and set it on the stove to boil. I'm starving.

"But we don't have kimchi," she calls out.

I check the fridge, knowing full well that we ate the last of it yesterday.

"Ramyun's garbage without the fixins," says June. "Kimchi, egg, and scallions. That's how Mom would make it."

With my back to her, I close my eyes. I can't believe she invoked Mom.

I throw my coat back on. "I'll be back," I tell her, letting the door slam behind me.

I love a new deli. A fresh location. I've been eyeing this one for a while. I grab kimchi first. A squat plastic square the size of a wallet that's eight dollars. I get a grapefruit from a pile since June needs vitamins and then switch it for the tub of cut-up mango. I splurge since June gave me her card.

Next to the eggs is a selection of dubiously healthy snacks strung up on a vertical display. I finger the chocolate-covered dried banana chunks through the black foil packaging. There can't be more than six or seven in there. I check the price tag. Five bucks. Criminal.

I pluck them from the hook, taking them for a walk. I pick up a can of seltzer. Two since it's me and June. I wish I could get some Chex, but this isn't the kind of deli that has regular cereal. I check out the buffet offerings on the long steam tray. There's congealed chicken and broccoli behind the sneeze guard and fried noodles. A chicken drumstick's been dropped in the vanilla pudding. It makes me sad for whoever thought to add a maraschino cherry and a dollop of whipped cream to the dessert. While peering at egg rolls, I slip the packet of chocolate banana into my pocket. They make a satisfying swish against my nylon coat. It lies beautifully flat against me.

My phone buzzes in my pocket. It's futile to wish it was Patrick. It's been a week since I ghosted him.

Can we have Chipotle instead? It's June. Except that her name in my phone still says Juju. I scroll through our iMessage chain. It's been forever since she texted me. She usually calls because she's an emotional terrorist. Her last dispatch was from a year ago. It says **call Mom.**

I have the goofiest picture for her contact. It's from tenth grade, when she was growing a perm out. I snapped it while she was sleeping, and her mouth is hanging open. I click on info to change her name, and that's when I see it.

A little croak escapes my throat.

Of course. I smile up at the groceries around me.

I'm so stupid.

That's how June knows where I am.

On her info page, I can see her big-mouth avatar, smack-dab on Twenty-Sixth and Sixth Avenue. We've had our locations shared for years. We started even before Mom left. I stopped checking because I got too jealous when she went to college. Watching her pie hole gallivanting around Manhattan while I was stuck in Texas without a driver's license was too painful. I leave it on. I can't believe she never just told me she was trailing me when I asked. That sneaky bitch.

I scroll through my contacts. I've got my location activated with so many people. Girls from high school I don't even talk to. Jesus. What *have* I been doing for the last ten years?

I wonder if telling Patrick that I did the brand identity for Jeremy's literary magazine would make me pathetic or pathetic *and* delusional. Mostly I want to ask him what kind of ramen he eats. Whether he thinks *Seinfeld*'s racist. If he remembers what an asshole June was. I love that he's a year older than her.

My pocket crinkles as I reach for paper towels.

I can't believe he has his master's degree. I wonder if there's any way we would have started dating in high school. I'd have been a freshman and he'd have been a senior and ...

I slide my hand all the way into my pocket. I find myself pinching the packet, tearing it open between my thumb and two fingers, hand cramping with effort. They slide out into my pocket but when I pop one into my mouth, I'm thrilled that it's somehow even better than expected.

There's no way one packet is enough. And if they sell out, I won't be able to stop thinking about them. I head back to the fruit. This time, as if checking the nutritional information on the Tate's cookies, I smoothly grab another packet with my other hand and slip it into my other coat pocket.

Just as I turn around, I startle at a woman in workout clothes and AirPods in the aisle. I smile, and she even takes an earbud out to smile back as if to tip her hat. My sight line rises to notice the enormous shield of mirror rigged to the ceiling.

I casually look behind the register. My palms dampen. Behind the salad bar I'd studied so intently there are four flat-screen TVs of the security cameras' views. My heart races and my breathing along with it. June will murder me if I get caught. I watch my hand unsteadily place the rice on the shelf in front of me. The mango's returned to the cooler. I force myself to ditch my groceries quickly and calmly. I leave with my head ducked. I'm convinced I'll be found out. That it's a matter of seconds before someone dashes out from the back to block me from leaving. I hurl the door open, rushing into the cold night, and hurriedly walk back to June's, stuffing the stupid banana pieces into my mouth and tasting nothing.

chapter 17

The next day, June's sprawled out on the couch eating Pringles when I get out of class. It's Halloween, and Halloween at design school is its own exhausting spectacle.

"Hey," she says, when I hang my coat up. Rory's well into Yale on *Gilmore Girls*. No matter the season it always seems like Christmas in Stars Hollow.

"Hey."

She studies me. "Where were you?"

I stop myself from rolling my eyes.

"Class."

The kitchen counter's a mess again even though I wiped everything up this morning. A half-dozen condiments left out. Loose sesame seeds. A Diet Coke that's been there since yesterday. I open the fridge. A few days ago, I broke down and removed the shelves to air them out in sunlight. The bottoms of the produce drawers looked like the contents of a shark's stomach during an autopsy. I wouldn't have been surprised to find an old toilet seat cover in there.

I tip the soda into the sink.

"Don't clean," she says. "I'll call someone to come."

"It's okay," I tell her, noisily crushing the bottle. I can't believe that this time last year Ivy and I spent hours dressing up as prescription pill bottles with *Euphoria* makeup. We ate so much candy I googled whether you could give yourself diabetes. Sometimes my memories are so remote they may as well have happened to someone else.

I twist all the lids back onto the various seasonings and return them to their shelves.

The year before that, Megan and Hillary had a party at our house. It was nineties themed. They were actually kind of nice to me that day.

I sponge down June's counters. I may as well. I looked up this building on StreetEasy and rent is, like, thirty-five hundred for a one-bedroom.

"Seriously," she says, sitting up. "Don't clean. It's fucking annoying."

I know this mood. June's bored.

I check the time on the microwave. It's 4:00 p.m. "Did you go outside today?" I already know she hasn't. The air in the room is comprised of 100 percent mouth-breath.

She glares at me and bites into the stack of Pringles, which shatter across her sweatshirt. She brushes at them hard even though one of the crumbs is basically half an entire chip.

My sister is so jonesing for a fight.

"What?" she demands hotly. Every single baby hair on her head is sticking up in attack mode.

I can't keep a straight face. A lactic-acid burn sears in my cheeks from keeping myself from smiling. I shake my head. "Nothing," I say innocently. My chin wobbles.

I spray down the counters.

"I told you to fucking stop," she says, doubling down. "So fucking stop."

I can't even look at her. She sits up. Covered in chips. Jutting her chin out.

I raise my hands and set down the Formula 409.

June and I have had fistfights and even drawn blood, but this isn't that.

I'm trying to clear my throat. Reset. But chortles keep audibly escaping my nose. I bite my lips.

"What?" she counters again, but I hear her voice waver.

She gets up and marches toward me.

I back away from her with my blocking hand up. "I'm not fighting you, you psycho."

At that, she reaches over and smacks my shoulder with her open palm.

I look down at my shoulder, then back at her.

Eyes hardened, hand aloft in a swat, she's about as menacing as a Labradoodle in a tam-o'-shanter.

"What the fuck was that?"

June continues to glare.

"Look, I'm not hitting a bitch with vagina cancer," I protest as she smacks me again, harder and harder, this time laughing.

"Uuuuuuuugh, I hate you," she wails, dragging her ass back to the couch. "I'm so bored."

"Go walk around the block."

I slump on the couch next to her, undoing the top button of my pants. I'm just glad to be home.

"Let's go to your apartment," she says, kicking me for sport. "See if he's gone."

"What?"

She's animated now, eyes gleaming. "Yeah, let's see if that fucker's out."

"Now?"

"It's been over a week."

"Well, I can go check," I tell her, getting to my feet. I wonder if this is her way of getting rid of me. "You don't have to come."

"I need an activity," she whines. "It's Halloween."

She's such a child. "Yeah, dick, also known as the worst subway night ever."

"It's early."

I groan. "I don't know, June. What if I need space too?" I echo her earlier sentiments. "What if this is personal and I need to process it?"

She appears to consider this.

"Bring me a glass of water."

I fill a glass, remembering that I haven't had water in several days, and take a long thirsty sip before refilling it to hand it to her. I already know she's going to bitch about that.

"You should've served me first and then had your water. You act like I'm not older than you."

God, she's petty.

"I'm coming with you," she says, dragging her hair into a sloppy ponytail. "It's not the same thing."

"What if I don't want you there?"

She shrugs off her pajama top and pulls on a wadded-up hoodie over her T-shirt. "Really?" she demands. "That's where you want to take it right now? You've been here for a week, all up in my shit, and you won't invite me over? I just want to see. I know there isn't a medicine cabinet or a drawer in this bitch that you haven't snooped through, so suck it up. It's my turn."

"No!"

"Fuckface," she says. "Either you invite me to your apartment and introduce me to your asshole boyfriend or . . . I'll beat your ass."

"God," I rage, putting on my sweatshirt. "Fuck, you're so inconsiderate. You have zero fucking noonchi."

"I don't need fucking noonchi when it comes to you," she says, shoving her feet into mules. "You're my family."

"How is that even a thing?" I put lipstick on in the mirror by the door.

"Matter of fact," she says gruffly, pulling on her coat. "Not only are you my family, but you're my younger family. Fuck noonchi, asshole. You don't count. I'm the heir; you're the spare. You owe me your whole life. You wouldn't even be here if it weren't for me."

I can't tell if she's talking about New York or Planet Earth.

We take the F to Brooklyn in silence. June was right. It's early yet. Other than a small cluster of school kids in desultory costumes, it's manageable. The one nice thing about Halloween on a Monday is that the hardcore weirdos are partied out from the weekend.

The train rises aboveground at Smith and Ninth, and even though I'm still aggravated, the ride is calming. The atmosphere's electric, all the surfaces gilded at the edges. I love New York on crisp days like these. It's magic hour, and I can't help but feel grateful. I read on a new age blog somewhere, probably while perusing supplements, that there are places on earth that are a vibrational match for you. That certain energy vortexes thrum along yours. I want to say that the fine print claimed it was a thing with Native Americans. Or Australian aboriginals. Hawaiians maybe—something that makes white women hawking powders and elixirs seem like they have any kind of history. But I'm sold on there being a home for your soul. New York feels right to me in moments like these. When I take a second to look out and remember where I am.

"See the Statue of Liberty?" I point her out on the other side of the train. She's the size of a thumb on the horizon, a pale-green queen, arm raised high out in the water. To me, Lady Liberty's like the moon, the way she can look bigger even from the same spot.

"Jesus," says June. Marveling at the skyline. "You live in Butt-Fuck Egypt." There are six more stops to go.

"It's chill."

And cheap.

I check on my rubble piles when we coast by.

"How long does it take you to get to school?"

"Hour."

"Damn. That's a hike. Takes me ten minutes to get to work." She's sitting in the seats facing me and crosses her legs at the ankles, looking out the window. Then she cranes down and tugs at the edge of her sock. "Look at this shit." The bright-blue lip of fabric bites into her fleshy ankle. That's when I notice that her other sock is lighter, with a scalloped white edge. "I'm losing it." She looks at me stupefied. "I don't think I've ever done this before."

"You should get all the same socks." Mine are uniformly black, from Uniqlo. I stick my toes out at her. Shaking my feet so she sees, but when she doesn't say anything, I look up. That's when I realize, to my horror, that June is crying. Again. The expression on her face is unchanged, but there are fat droplets coursing down her cheeks and falling onto her hands, which are lying in her lap like upturned bugs.

"June . . ." They announce our stop. I get up and she follows.

We walk the three blocks to the apartment. I beep the fob on the door, and we march upstairs, her behind me, our footfalls matching.

"Is he gone?" June asks, even before I've opened the door. She's clearing her throat and blotting her eyes. I unlock the door and switch the light on. We remove our shoes.

At first glance I can't tell. There is, however, an enormous dead cockroach right in the center of the living room.

I rush into the bathroom, bundle up some toilet paper, and throw it out. My face burns. I can't stand to look at her.

The sunken West Elm love seat off Craigslist is still there. Same with the bookcase and the particle-board café table and chairs that I use when I'm doing homework. The house smells the same. Lightly floral from a candle that sits in the kitchen. Not a hint of ylang-ylang shower cleaner. My bedroom door is ajar, and as I approach it slowly, I feel a crawling dread, as if I'm the final girl in a horror movie. I peek in.

The curtains are drawn. I feel my way in the dark, turning on the bedside lamp on the floor inside the closet since the overhead bulb shorted out ages ago. The bed's been stripped. He could be out. Just as I say "He's not home," I'm shoved from behind onto the mattress.

"BWWWAAAGH!" screams June, standing over me.

I flip around, heart pounding. "You're such a dick!"

June laughs in my face, pinning me to the bed. "Why are you scared? It's your house," she says. Then she looks around the room. I see it through her eyes. This is precisely why I didn't want her coming. I watch as she registers the mattress that's flush to the walls. The bubble of condensation trapped under the white paint above the window. I brush the crumbled pieces of ceiling plaster off the bed and grab a fitted sheet from a shelf to put on. The bare mattress suddenly seems obscene. June reaches out to tame the bottom of the elasticated clump of fabric. She has to stand in the hallway to do it.

I eye a yellowing hexagon on the white terry surface of the mattress. I don't remember the last time I changed the sheets. It looks like the outline of France.

"Is this the mattress I bought?" She pulls the quilted corner away from the wall to hook it into the sheet pocket expertly. "Didn't I tell you to get a full?"

"I paid you back." I do the same from atop the bed. "And a full didn't fit." I'd love, just once, to live in an apartment where I had my own full bed.

June smooths out the sheet. "Jesus, haven't you heard of a mattress protector? This is a year old."

"Two and a half."

She glares at me. "I just hope these cum stains are yours."

I drag her onto the stain and when she falls, she laughs so hard it makes me laugh.

"I hate you," I tell her.

I check the bathroom. And the coat closet and the cabinets. From what I can see, he has every intention of coming back. Most of his stuff is still here. I immediately change my Netflix password and delete his profile. Fuck him.

June's in my fridge. "Jesus, he doesn't eat food either?" she says, flinging the door open, causing condiment bottles to clang. She pulls out a crusty jar of honeyed yuzu from the shelf, so I put the kettle on. She holds her palm above the radiator and looks at me with concern. Then she puts her coat back on. It's cold in here.

"I don't think he's gone," she says.

"I have no idea," I tell her, noncommittal.

"Mom would shit if she found out you were shacking up with some dude." She turns on the kitchen faucet and holds her hand under the water. Then she turns the hot water on full blast.

"Jayne," she says.

I watch her fingers wriggle in the stream.

"You can't be serious."

"What?" I glare at her.

"Look around, asshole," she says. "You can't live like this! You have black mold on your bedroom walls." She points accusingly. "It smells like cats have been peeing in here for centuries. Please tell me you withheld rent this month—you don't have hot water."

"You can't tell Mom I'm living with a dude," I tell her, nudging her out of the way to open the cupboard by her head. I might live in a hovel, but at least I want her to see how normal people store their mugs.

I make our tea.

"Jayne."

I give her the good mug, offering it to her with the handle facing out, burning the shit out of my fingertips.

She takes her sweet time reaching for it and walks over to the couch. For a split second I see her wrinkle her snobby nose before perching on her seat. I sit down next to her, squishing in.

I want to put my coat back on too, but I don't want to give her the satisfaction. I lean back and stretch my legs out as if June's being a priss.

I set my mug on the floor since we don't have a coffee table but pick it up again. It's gross down there. There are so many dust bunnies and hair clumps that I've never noticed before.

"Why did you move out of your old place?"

"Does Mom still call you every weekend to ask if you went to Mass?" I ask instead of answering.

"Yeah," says June, irritation flashing across her face. "It wouldn't kill you to pick up once in a while. It just doubles my load."

I never thought about that. "Is it true that parents go to hell if their kids don't go to church? Mom keeps wailing in her voicemails about how she's going to hell."

"Just lie. Also"—she chuckles—"why are you asking me if it's true? Hell's not a real place." June takes a swallow of tea, then sticks her tongue out. "Fuck, burnt my tongue."

She always burns her tongue. Even worse than I do. She also salts her meals before she tastes them.

"Lie?" Honestly, it's never occurred to me. It also never occurred to me that June wouldn't believe in hell.

"It's not lying if it's to protect her," June reasons. "She's happier not knowing. Most people are."

Just then my phone lights up on the floor in front of us. It's Mom.

"How the fuck does she do that?" We look at each other and then back at the phone.

She's worse than Alexa or Siri or Amazon ads. "Fuck," I breathe. I watch it go to voicemail. "That's creepy."

Mom's like June. She only leaves a voicemail after power-dialing at least six times in a row.

MOM appears on the screen again.

"Does she do this to you?"

"What do you think?"

June's phone buzzes in her coat. She shows it to me. Mom. Of course. And, of course, June picks up.

"Yoboseyo?" she says into her phone. And then, "I'll call you right back."

"What are you doing?" A trill of anxiety shoots through me. "Why'd you pick up?"

June then goes and FaceTimes her.

I fix my hair.

Mom picks up. "Yoboseyo?"

We're treated to a visual of Mom's ear. She mutters in Korean about the crappy sound quality.

"Umma," June calls out, laughing. "You're supposed to look at us. Look at the screen!"

"Hi," I pipe up from behind June.

Mom's scowl turns into a smile. "What are you guys doing together?" she asks in Korean. Her expression shifts again. "Why is it so dark where you are? Turn some lights on. You'll ruin your eyes. Is everything all right?" It's astounding how quickly she goes from happy to worried.

"We're fine," says June. "We just thought it would be nice for you to see us."

"Oh, okay." Mom's wearing a mint-green golf shirt with what appears to be a fake Ralph Lauren logo. The embroidered polo player's missing his horse. "Not that I can see you," she reiterates. "Do you need me to send a lamp?"

We ignore that.

"We're drinking yujacha," I tell her, lifting my mug. I always do this. Inform her when I'm doing Korean things as if to ingratiate myself. As if this will make her proud of me.

"Where'd you get it?" she says. "Is it the red label or the green and gold?"

I'm not going back to the fridge to check. "Green?"

"That one's all sugar. Get the red label next time. Red and yellow, I think."

"I will." I will do no such thing.

I haven't seen my mother's face in so long. I don't even recognize the silver wire-framed glasses she's wearing. A lump forms in my throat. It's like staring at the sun.

"I'm coming home," June announces.

"Really? For a business trip?" Mom's face brightens immediately. "When? Can you stay for a few days? You must be so busy."

"Yes, for work," says June. "Dallas for a meeting, but I'll come down."

There's a falling feeling in my stomach. I can't believe she hasn't told me about this. I can't believe how easy all of this is for her.

"How long?"

"A weekend."

"You're still coming for the holidays though, yes?"

"For Christmas," says June. Even with Mom's birthday at Thanksgiving, we don't usually celebrate. It's never felt like a real holiday to us, and Mom hates turkey. "What a tasteless bird to eat," she says. "And so huge." She thinks it's a perfect allegory for American food.

"Send me your flight information," she demands. "Is Jayne coming?" I duck out of the frame and glare at my sister.

"You're going to have to ask her."

I reach over and pinch her thigh.

"Jayne?"

June points the phone right at me and raises her eyebrows, smiling prettily.

"I want to," I tell her in English. "But I'm busy with school and work."

"Of course," she says, face tightening. "You have to focus on what you have to focus on. You poor girls, working like dogs in that gutter-filthy city. I heard the subways are always broken. You couldn't pay me to go inside a tunnel on the subway. Are you at least taking exercise and eating proper meals at proper times? What's good grades and money if you don't have your health? Are you okay for money, Ji-young?"

"I'm fine," I tell her, sick with guilt.

"So this weekend?" Mom asks my sister.

"Yeah."

I watch June intently. She's stopped blinking, which means

she's lying. I'm willing to bet there's no business trip to Dallas. She's just going because she wants to. Which she can because she's so stinking rich.

"Friday to Sunday," she says. "I miss you guys."

"Maybe you can bring something back to Jayne, some myulchi or something for soups," says Mom to June, while looking at me. With her glasses on she appears older.

"Thanks, Umma."

June has cancer! I want to scream into the phone.

"Maybe I'll see you before my fiftieth birthday," she says. Mom knows how to lay it on. She's not turning fifty for another three years. "Did I ever tell you girls the dream I had before my birthday last year?" Mom's partial to the notion that she's more than slightly clairvoyant. "It was beautiful. I was swimming in the most clear, placid water and the temperature was exactly the same as my skin. Like a bath. And in the sky was this white dragon. Coiled across the horizon and then whipping toward me. It had green, green eyes. I was filled with so much joy. You couldn't ask for a more auspicious dream."

She says this as if it's Korean tradition that the mother has an auspicious dream before her own birthday and not the *birth of a child*.

"Do they have Catholic churches where you two live?" she asks. I have a feeling Mom thinks me and June are neighbors.

"Of course," says June. "It's, like, all Irish and Italians."

"Well, not as good as our church," says Mom. "It'll be good to go together, June. You have so much to be thankful for. We all pray for you girls so much."

When we hang up, I slap June's arm. "What the hell?"

"What?" June slaps me back.

"Why are you going home all of a sudden? I know you don't have a business trip."

"Who the fuck cares?" she says. "I just . . ." She looks around my house. "I want to go home."

"Yeah, but you have a home."

"Look, I don't know what you've got against Texas," she says. "But I like it at Mom's. It's chill."

It's funny. Even though our parents are together, it'll always be Mom's house.

"I'm tired," she says, and swallows. "I want to see Mom and Dad before all this shit goes down. I want the feeling of being in San Antonio, where people search for fucks to give about emerging markets, how fat my bonus is going to be, or what my bowl order is at fucking Sweetgreen. I'm wrecked. I just want to eat those little anchovies fried in garlic and that potato thing she makes with a mandoline. I want soup with every meal, and I want my mom to buy me shit at Costco."

"*Our* Mom," I correct her saltily, thinking about her clear soup with the oxtail and the turnip.

"Whatever. I've known her longer," says June, scrolling through her phone for flights.

"I fucking knew you didn't have a business trip. Liar."

She shrugs, ignoring me. She's not even going to Orbitz or anything, but going straight to the commercial airline app like some kind of millionaire.

When she clears her throat repeatedly, basically right in my ear, I want to punch her in the face. If I were June, I'd be so nice to my little sister. June is such a shitty older sister. She's more of a shitty older sister than she is a good daughter. I know it's a bonus that she gets to be mean to me *and* suck up to Mom at the same time.

If Mom's dead baby were here, she and I would be best friends. We'd never put up with this shit. June would choke with jealousy.

My middle sister would be Mom's favorite because she was sick as an infant and then June would finally know how it felt to be left out.

"Well, what am I supposed to do?" I blurt once June's entering her credit card security code.

Finally, she puts her phone down and smiles triumphantly. "You know what? I don't fucking care," she says. "No offense, but I wouldn't mind not thinking about you for a few days either."

"Thanks a lot." I sniff. "I'm the only one who cooks or cleans. I washed all of your linens, had to practically run that shit twice with extra hot water and rinse. Maybe I'm tired too. I don't want to think about you, either."

"Well, then it's perfect," she says, putting her phone away. "Quality time apart."

I can't believe she'd leave me at a time like this.

"Serves me right for buying you that wine opener." I also bought her some kitchen towels. They were on sale, but they have really cute taxicabs on them. I know it's not unreasonable that she's sick and wants to go home, but I still feel like she's going home *at* me.

"You're the one who doesn't visit," she says. "Such a fucking drama queen. New York would still be here when you got back."

"Well, I can't afford it," I tell her. "It's like four hundred and fifty bucks around the holidays."

It's not as if I didn't look it up last year.

"Oh my God," says June, sticking her tongue out on "God" and rolling her eyes. "If you want to come, I'll buy you a ticket—just fucking tell me one way or another."

"I'll have to get off work." Not everyone has a trillion vacation days like my asshole sister.

"So get off work."

"Fine," I tell her, looking up flights of my own.

"I'll buy your ticket. I'll get it on miles."

"Fine."

"Fine what?" she says, knocking my knee with hers.

"Thank you."

"Thank you what?" she says, really joggling me this time.

"Thank you, Unnie."

"That's right, you little dickhead."

We drink our teas. "I'm pretty sure this is expired." I peer into my mug. The yuzu's bloomed at the bottom, but it doesn't taste like much.

"This shit always tastes kinda expired to me," says June. She points at the empty bedroom behind her. "So, what now? Are you staying here? It's so fucking depressing. Like, Christmas-morning-at-a-strip-club depressing. I feel like I've only seen places like this in night-vision goggles because the feds in the movie are about to do a raid."

I look around. I don't want to. In the last week, I'd forgotten how deeply unhappy I've been here. I'd only thought as far as checking if Jeremy had left. I can't imagine closing my eyes and trying to sleep in this place. "I guess I should," I tell her. "It's where I live."

I didn't know I'd be leaving June's for the night when we left. She'll probably abandon all the wet towels in the washing machine and let them get smelly again. Plus, she'll Seamless fried chicken instead of heating up the leftover lentils and turkey I made her. And we're only halfway through the episode of *Gilmore Girls* where Christopher comes back. For the third time.

June gets up. "Okay."

I get up too.

"Text me if you need anything," she says.

"Thanks for the ticket."

"It's just miles."

She holds her mug out. "Should I? Just put it in the sink or . . . ?"

My sister moves toward me just as I step in the same direction.

"Sorry."

"Let me . . ." I take the cup from her, relieved to have something to do with my hands. "I'll see you soon," I say, suddenly not knowing when I'll see her. "I guess at the airport."

"Oh," she says. "Sure."

"Okay." Friday sounds like ages away.

We face each other.

"Actually, you know what?" she says abruptly, rolling her eyes. "You're such a numbnut. Did you even bring any of your things? Do you have your toothbrush?"

"No." I shake my head theatrically. "I'm so stupid."

She kisses her teeth. "You know I haven't had a single cavity?" My sister smiles big with her lips pulled back, going slightly cross-eyed from the effort.

I nod approvingly. "You're really lucky," I offer.

"Look, just come to my house," she says. "It's so fucking cold and depressing here. And you have fucking roaches."

"I had *a* roach," I correct her. "One. And it's dead."

"Okay, asshole, do you want to stay here or . . . ?"

"No."

"Besides," she says, ordering an Uber. "You can't sleep on someone else's cum stains. That's just not right." I shove her as she laughs.

We take a black car back. With Halloween surge pricing it's a depraved amount of money *and* it has heated seats. I settle in, feeling warm inside and out. June leans over the middle seat to show me something on her phone that I barely register. When she gets back on her side, she feels far. On long car rides as kids, she'd twist, practically strangling herself with the seat belt as she hurled her legs over mine to stretch out and sleep. It never seemed particularly comfortable. It was more the principle of it, that she could because she was older.

I bite my lip to stop from smiling. June really is such an asshole.

chapter 18

"Okay, so Buc-ee's we gotta go to for jerky...."

June's counting off all the stores we need to hit while we're in Texas.

"Totally."

Buc-ee's also has the absolute hands-down best bathrooms in the entire solar system. Clean and enormous.

"Also, I want the Izzy roll." The sushi rolls at Mom and Dad's restaurant are the size of burritos. "And I want migas. And puffy tacos. And Taco Cabana chips."

I realize there are things I miss about Texas. Sweet tea, the velvety quiet nights, people in flip-flops and shorts who don't discuss prestige TV shows like it's a competitive sport, the eye contact and nodded acknowledgments in grocery store aisles. I might not miss the house we grew up in, but there are plenty of nice things to be said for San Antonio. Like how it's 82 degrees right now.

We stop by June's dedicated mail room. That might be my favorite feature of her building. At my place and the one before, if you ever actually received a package, it was a miracle. Plus, none of the bougie tenants at June's apartment ever want their catalogs. There's always a stack in the recycling area. I bend over to scoop the L.L. Bean and a Harry & David for the holidays.

June grabs someone's *New York Times*, still in its blue sleeve, which has been left on the marble shelf. "What?" she says when I shoot her a pointed look. She flashes the address label at me. "4C's an asshole. Have you seen the way he treats his dog?"

"June."

She rolls her eyes and puts it back. Then she reaches over and snatches the Harry & David from me. "Hey," I protest. She smiles gummily. "Maybe if you're good, I'll be inspired for Christmas." She waves the rest of her mail in my face until I carry it. We know the deal—while June's paying for everything, I have to be her rent mule. "So, I got those Delta tickets," she says. I'm presuming the ones she'd shown me in the car. "It's the only direct. But I sprang for Delta Comfort Plus. Even for you, you fucking freeloader." She pushes the elevator button a trillion times as if to make it hurry.

I look through the rest of the mail while she flips through the catalog and land on a bill in a familiar envelope. I didn't know June and I had the same health insurance. Mom once told me June's coverage was so baller, she could get chemical peels for free.

That's when I see. That the envelope is addressed to me.

"What the fuck is even up with these pears?" June asks, shoving the Harry & David catalog back at me. "I don't get why they're so expensive. Everyone knows Korean pears are superior. These ones don't even have that white mesh protective jacket thingy."

I'm barely listening. When we get inside, I open the envelope while June's back is turned.

Listed are blood tests for cancer antigens.

Transvaginal ultrasound.

In-office biopsy.

"What is it?" June asks when she realizes I'm silent. I confirm the name. It's repeated on every single page. *Jayne Ji-young Baek. Jayne Ji-young Baek. Jayne Ji-young Baek.* It's the diabolical headfuck of reading your own name on a tombstone.

"Wait, what is that?" she asks again. "Did you open my mail?"

"June?" I show her the paperwork, the page after page of deductibles and explanation of benefits. "How come . . . ?"

Her eyes widen as she snatches it from me. "Fuck," she says, and then swallows.

"Why does this . . . ?"

"Fuck," she says again, this time inspecting my face.

There's not enough air getting to my lungs. It's the way she looks. She hasn't blinked in a minute.

"Is everything okay?"

"I didn't want to worry you," she says finally.

"June." I'm smiling again. That stupid, idiot smile. "What's going on?" I hear the rising edge in my voice.

"Jayne, okay," she says. And then, "Do you want to sit down?"

I shake my head.

My sister exhales noisily. "Fuck, shit. So, for the whole past year I knew something was wrong," she says hurriedly, watching my eyes. "I could feel it. Even before they told me to get an ultrasound, I knew. They thought it was fucking polyps or cysts or endometriosis, but I knew."

I shake my head, confused. "But why does it say my name?" I snatch the paperwork back and show her. "June, why do I have cancer?"

"I got laid off nine week ago," she says.

"What?" I don't understand why we're having two separate conversations, but the fact that June could be jobless reorganizes everything I thought I knew. "Are you going to be o—"

"There was no other way," she says. Her mouth sets. "I had no health insurance so I used yours from school. I stole your ID and . . ."

"What?" I keep shaking my head like a dummy. I know I'm still smiling. I look to my sister helplessly.

June pulls out her wallet from her purse and shows me an ID. It's mine. My Texas one. "I know you have mine. . . ."

"I never—" I start to protest. She'd asked about it, but I'd stonewalled.

"Jayne," she cuts me off. "I know you've been using mine as your fake ID. I saw it in your wallet a year ago, so—I took yours. Just to fuck with you. I was going to give it back, but then I didn't."

She hands me the card, and I take it. I stare at my face smiling up at me. Mom hates this picture. I wore spaghetti straps that day. With my hair down, I look naked. It's the worst ID. The hideous vertical format for Texas minors. Everyone unfailingly wanting to know why it's not a driver's license and why I didn't learn.

"Nobody noticed." She looks up at me, wide-eyed. "I changed the address for the mail because I didn't want to scare you. I had to get the diagnostic stuff done as you so that if I needed surgery or treatment, I could do that as you as well. I had no other choice. I did my due diligence. Your deductible is huge, but I can pay that. You have to know that I did everything I could. I looked at every single angle. I gave it a lot of thought." She tucks her hair behind her ear and chews on her lower lip.

It finally dawns on me. This isn't a clerical hiccup. A typo that erased the two people that we were and made us one. June did this.

"I couldn't afford to pay out-of-pocket for cancer," she barrels on, rapping a fingernail on her kitchen counter. "It's like twenty thousand dollars for the surgery alone. The testing and hospital . . ."

I place the ID facedown on the kitchen counter next to us. My head swims.

"But I thought companies have to offer health insurance for a few months."

"Well, not this one. It's complicated."

"What about Obamacare?" I blink rapidly. I'm still smiling, still trying to be helpful, still angling to give my sister an out.

She snorts. "The first bill went to Mom and Dad's for some fucked-up reason, and they never open their mail so they dropped me for nonpayment."

Our parents aren't the type to be overly concerned with fat envelopes from New York State of Health. Mom and Dad's genius strategy is to wait to age into Medicare and fly to Korea for the big shit.

"It's so fucking typical. Other people fuck up and I'm left holding the bag."

"Wait a minute." I raise my hand. "That's your read on this? That you got fucked over? You stole my identity. You took my health insurance without asking me, you made a mistake with your permanent address, how are *you* left holding the bag?" I pick up the paperwork from the kitchen counter and shove it at her.

"You could have fucking asked me." Finally, my voice rises. She glances at me, warily. "You don't just take something like that from someone, June."

"I did it to protect you," she says. "Why would I implicate you?"

"Wow." My sister is incredible. "Well, thanks for looking out for me." I cover my hot eyes with my cool palms as another thought clicks into place. I pull my hands away. "That's why you didn't want me to come to the doctor with you, isn't it? You were hiding this from me."

I can't help it. This time, I really do laugh. "God, I can't believe I was worried about you." I shake my head. My sister's mercenary.

June's mirror neurons fire because she's smiling too but her eyes are watchful.

"You were being so weird. I thought you were depressed or . . ." I feel my fingers rake through my hair. "You just didn't want to get fucking busted."

"You didn't want to be there anyway," she shoots back, pointing at me. "I could see it on your face. You hate when people need anything from you. It terrifies you. I know it does. Don't pretend to be something you're not with your bullshit Florence Nightingale act. No one has any expectations of you, Jayne. Ever. You're always going to run away with your loser friends that treat you like shit and get fucked up. That's what you do. That's who you are."

All the air in my lungs escape. I have never doubted that my sister, as alienated as we were, had my best interests at heart. I knew I annoyed her. I knew she judged the way I dressed, who I hung out with, the way I studied, but even when we were at each other's throats in high school, I knew that somewhere deep down she loved me. She might not have liked me, but she loved me.

"You know what? You're right. You're so right. Everything you've ever thought or said about me is right. Thank you."

I grab my bag off the floor.

My sister watches.

"See?" she says, shaking her head with another bitter smile.

I open the door.

"God, you're predictable," she adds.

I glare at her. My sister is not a good person. And she is not my friend. And the pathetic truth is, I'm devastated. I was better prepared to hate her before she came back into my life. A kaleidoscope of images troop through my mind. Of us at different ages.

Making each other laugh at church.

Speed-washing glasses at the restaurant.

How she'd look up from her homework late at night waiting on Mom and Dad to get home.

"Are you still coming to Texas?" She says it quietly. In a tone I don't know how to parse. I let the door close behind me.

I can't deal. I can't feel my face. As I frantically hit the elevator button, heart speed-bagging the back of my throat, I realize that she never once said she was sorry.

And that, despite it all, I left my ID for her on purpose. Just in case she needs it.

chapter 19

"You could be twins," says everyone when they find out that June's name is Ji-hyun and that mine's Ji-young. "Both your names are Ji!" As if anyone would ever name twins the same thing. Nobody would do that. Not even sadists.

Mom and Dad thought June would be easy for an American name. It's basically a portmanteau and it's a breeze to pronounce in Korean and easy to say in English. For June, Ji means "meaning," or rather, "purpose." And the Hyun means "self-evident." It's a strong name. No wonder she's had Columbia banners on her wall from infancy. She's known what she wants since in utero.

My Ji means something else. That's a thing with certain Korean families, that siblings' names have the same first syllable. Homonyms. My Ji's not as good. It means "seed." It's diminutive. I'm a fleck, a crumb, a mote of something but not my own thing. It sort of reminds me of the way people are named in *The Handmaid's Tale*. I'm Ofmyparents. Ofjune.

I'm not wild about the "Young" in my name, either. It means "petal." Teeny and pretty and entirely inconsequential. I wish I'd been named after a war general or some kind of poison. When June and I got our green cards renewed, before we got our US passports, people couldn't get over how close our names and social security numbers were. Someone even remarked, "Oh, you're Ji-young and you're younger. That's how you remember." As if June and I need a mnemonic device.

I march downtown from my sister's, hugging myself, tears streaming down my face, mayhem in my heart. It's freezing. My breath puffs out in little Miyazaki clouds with each step. With so many crews of people in matching costumes, I've never felt lonelier. I hadn't known it was possible.

There's no need for a mnemonic device to distinguish you from your sister when the difference is so apparent. With sisters, like twins, there's always a better one. Around our house and certainly at church, June's and my assets were public knowledge to be debated right in front of us. June's grades. My hair. The paleness of my skin. June's coding camps. My lissome limbs. Her accelerated math courses. With us, there was a smart one and a pretty one.

Except then I got ugly.

Or "healthy," according to Mom's church group, who'd gamely pat my love handles and pinch my cheeks. "It's not the meals she eats at home that are the problem," Mom would say in a stage whisper. "Texas sized means Texas thighs." Once, one of the Theresas at church suggested that it could have to do with an unstable home and Mom looked as though she'd been slapped.

Sisters never stand a chance to be friends. We're pitted against each other from the moment we're born. A daughter is a treasure. Two is a tax. God, how they must have wanted a boy when they tried a do-over after a dead baby girl.

A thought teases and then expands, collapsing my rib cage and wrecking my heart. June wasn't worried when she came to the restaurant to find me. She saw me cutting class on her phone and needs me as a full-time student because of my health insurance.

I rummage at the bottom of my purse for my earbuds when I hit Broadway.

Flatiron building.

Bald man with the face of a baby, dressed like a baby.

Maleficent with a cigarette.

Sexy witch mom with a despondent preteen son.

Crosswalk.

I let myself cry. My face is instantly numb from the cold.

Whatever this feeling is, I never want to feel it again.

I hate that somewhere out there, somehow, June and I are melded into one. Even on paper. That me and June are together again in this way. I may as well be the twin that's absorbed in the womb. I'm too scared to talk about it, but sometimes I worry that I don't exist. That I don't count. It's not solely that June's superior to me in every aspect. Or that I lack conviction, which I do. It's that I have this awful, unshakable suspicion, an itchy, terrible belief that I'm some kind of reincarnation, the recycling of my middle sister's spirit. That I don't have my own personality or destiny and I'm just a do-over for someone else and that's why my life doesn't ever feel like it fits.

My family thinks it's a play for attention. My depression. The anxiety. Or as June put it, my "emotional" nature. Mom thinks anxiety is about as insufferably first world as it gets. Like lactose intolerance. She thinks it's an idle mind searching for things to bitch about at the lack of famine or war. If you've got a full belly, you've lost your right to bellyache.

I'm too terrified to ask if Mom's dead baby was called Ji-young, but I'm convinced of it. I know it's not unheard of that people name their younger children after dead ones. Everything about my existence feels like a costume. And losing my name to June makes this wobbly feeling stronger.

It is my greatest fear to have this horrible nonexistent, disembodied feeling I carry with me realized. I brush the tears off my face and sniff hard.

I don't know where I'm headed, but around Union Square, I weave through the road closures and find myself swayed by the current of people heading for the L train. I pull out my compact and salvage what's left of my makeup on the subway platform. I'm a shop-worn trope. So many girls have done exactly this before me and so many more will. It'll be fine, I tell my tear-stained self. I observe myself as though from afar. Asian girl. Hair. Decent boots. All that tristesse. It's easier to watch myself be sad than actually feel sad.

I reline my eyes, fix my lipstick, and put away my reflection. I allow a smile to tease at my lips, summoning someone beguiling. I imagine myself in a movie. It usually helps. I glance around for any attractive people. Male, female, old, it doesn't matter. Someone to see myself through.

I stare at the train tracks and imagine myself falling.

I want to text Jeremy but don't. Instead I buy a pack of gum at the newsstand, pop all the pieces into my mouth, and chew big. I really need someone to look at me.

"Vodka soda!"

I hand over June's ID and her credit card to a genuinely frightening Pennywise and drain my drink immediately. I also still have her house keys. Her stupid $200 "do not duplicate" house keys. I get another vodka soda. Pound it. I'm instantly drunk. I take a deep breath, praying that he'll show. I'd almost told him to come to Léon just to see what would happen, but instead I'm in a terrible bar that's a close second to how much trouble I can get myself into in the shortest amount of time. It doesn't matter if he flakes, I tell myself. I'll just pick a different one.

The bar's a dive, but when the side door's open it's almost like a house party or a cookout. Last time we were here, Ivy and I started drinking at noon, and I loved how that felt. Like we were hiding in plain sight. Something in the mutuality of saying "fuck it" to the rest of the day made everyone behave appallingly.

She called the bar Tinder Live for its hookup potential, and it's true. You can feel it. The vibe in a word? Ravenous. It reliably runs a special of Pabst Blue Ribbon with tequila shots from brands that have labels that look like Photoshop disasters. There's one called Luxxx, which I'm pretty sure isn't certifiably a thing unless that thing is personal lubricant.

I gaze vaguely into the space. Glazing over everyone's eyes. Trying not to betray how desperate I am to recognize anyone. The guy to my right bumps me, not even turning around to check if he cares. He's got this reedy voice, Hawaiian shirt opened to his midriff. "I don't know," he says through his retro pornstache. "Aren't cargo pants strictly for botched-surgery Chads?"

The boy with the bowl cut next to him nods. He's wearing cargo pants. I watch as he discreetly pulls down his shirt while listening. Tag yourself; he's me.

There's a spidery jitteriness in my heart. I can't believe what happened. Fuck June. How fucking dare she.

I take another swallow of my drink to blot out the intolerable discomfort of reality.

Truth is, part of me wishes I could un-know all of this. June hit that nail on the head. I don't want to deal. And if I hadn't opened the envelope, I would be eating pad Thai she paid for, watching TV with her. I would feel moderately but not sincerely bad about being a mooch. I'd do her dishes. Everything would be otherwise fine.

Maybe I did know, though. On some level. June has never been this accommodating to me. Or nice. I've been cooking and cleaning, but old June would've conscripted me into all sorts of other menial tasks. I haven't massaged her shoulders, lotioned her heels, or walked ten paces behind her holding her bag.

The Cure plays at a volume so loud, I have to squint in an attempt to dampen the noise.

I make a beeline for the smoke-filled patio, carrying my drink past the split vinyl booths, the old-school video games, and the line for the bathroom on the right, which has snaked in the narrow hallway. I try not to meet anyone's eyes. Everyone else's need to be seen is embarrassing to me because I so badly need the same.

Despite the chill, it smells human outside. Sour. My phone lights up in my hand. *I'm here. You?*

Instead of responding, I finish my drink, pulse racing. I check my reflection. I could still leave, I think. As long as he doesn't come to search for me, I could dip out the side entrance. Even if he calls my name, I could ignore it. It's loud enough. I slide an ice cube in my mouth and take a deep breath.

I exhale with my eyes closed, breath cool as I sigh.

I imagine myself as an entirely different person. Someone new. Someone strong. Someone whole.

chapter 20

I return to the main bar, flitting through the crowd, excitement unraveling down my spine. I shrug off my coat and then extract my arms from the lumpy sweatshirt, throw it over my head as my skin prickles to gooseflesh. Everything off except the black silk camisole.

I swing my eyes left, then right, enjoying the smearing in my vision. Now, I tell myself, I'm fascinated by everyone.

Next to a girl with glasses pulling on a vape, I see him. He smiles easily.

I make my way over, smiling stupidly at the ground, tilting my head up at the very last minute.

"Graduated, applied to design school, grew my hair long, moved to New York, met up with you," I tell him as a greeting. I'm giddy with relief that he's not in costume. "That's what I've been up to in the last ten years."

Patrick smiles wide and opens his arms for a hug. I sense an unlatching in my chest as I fall into them. It feels like fate that he picked up immediately when I called.

"It's good to see you." I sigh into his cashmere-clad sternum, my disguise of someone carefree and confident slipping ever so slightly.

"You too," he says from above. He holds me longer than I'd expected him to. I leech everything I can out of the hug. Bleed it.

I pull away and look up. His cheekbones are positively architectural. His teeth, impossibly white. His sweater is a heathered gray that brings out his creamy skin. "Hi," I say, attempting to be a normal, appropriate adult person. "So, we live in New York."

"We sure do," he says, taking me in. Then he laughs, looking around. "And of all the places in New York, we've chosen to be here. On literal Halloween."

"It's the worst." I smile back at him. "I love it."

His eyes alight from mine, and I wonder for a split second if he sees someone he knows. But instead of turning away, he touches my shoulder gently to let the person pass. "Do you want a drink?"

We're standing right in front of the bar. "Vodka soda," I whisper into his neck. His wallet is slender and expensive.

When he hands me a glass, I take a sip and notice it isn't the kerosene I've been drinking. We toast each other.

Then he grabs my hand with his free one and guides me to a quieter part of the bar. My palm throbs when he lets go.

He rummages in his pocket and pulls out a single-dose pack of antacid and offers it to me. "Pepcid gang," he says. A beat. "Don't you get redface when you drink?"

I shake my head.

"Outlier," he says, downing it.

"Is that a thing?"

"Yeah," he says. "A lot of East Asians can't break down the toxins in alcohol. It's us and Ashkenazi Jews that won that particular genetic lottery."

I'm embarrassed what I don't know about us.

"It's good to see you, Jayne," he says, and my cheeks flush for altogether different reasons. I love hearing Patrick say my name. And that he knows how it's spelled. And that every time he speaks, he leans in close to be heard. "I honestly wasn't sure you were going to text back. I'm fucking horrible at texting."

He shakes his head.

"How long have you lived here?"

"Almost a year," he says. "But I've been visiting since forever."

"Two and a half for me."

"Right, you're at school."

"And you went to Yale," I tell him, sidestepping the inevitable question of where I go. "I can't believe I didn't hear it from the church ladies."

"I don't think art school counts," he says, chuckling.

I smile into my drink. He's right.

"Where do you go?"

"Not Yale." I say it in a disgustingly goofy way. "June went to Columbia, though. Full ride."

"It's so nice that you're both here."

"Yeah, totally."

"We should all hang out sometime, get food."

"Yeah, totally." I feel instantly clumsy and inarticulate.

He watches me in a way I remember from when I was a kid. With intensity. Almost as if he's recording me with his eyes. It's the opposite of everyone in my life who is constantly looking past me. I don't have to vie for his attention. It's mine to lose.

"What about Kirsten?"

"Kiki's in London," he says of his sister. She had a blunt bob when we were younger. It made her seem sophisticated. "Or she was. She's in the Peace Corps now. Panama."

"Fuck."

"Yeah." He smiles the good-natured smile of a younger kid with an impressive older sibling.

"But you, creative director. That's awesome."

He runs his hand through his hair. "Yeah." He clears his throat, nodding a few times.

"Is it fucked up that I have no idea what that means?"

He laughs. "No." He shakes off the cocktail stirrer from his drink and, absent a place to put it, shoves it in his pocket. It's exactly what I would do. "Most creative directors are carpetbagging dilettantes who think they're brands. Generally, I'm overpaid to answer questions about a company's point of view. Or I guess I've been overpaid a couple of times. I only just got out of school."

"How does that work? Do you work at an agency or . . . ?"

I studied up from his website but couldn't tell. Flash sites make me crazy.

"I'm freelance," he says. "Which means I'm either panicking about starvation or I have a weird amount of money sitting in my checking account."

"So, you work for yourself?"

He nods. "For now."

I can't believe he's only twenty-four.

I search for clues as to whether this means he's homeless. Nails: clean. Clothes: freshly laundered. His hair: not only washed but fiddled with long enough that a light, a mirror, and some privacy were required. Then again, I've heard of a girl who used her SoHo house membership to scam dates and roomies for the night. See also: Jeremy.

"That's amazing."

"We'll see," he admits. "Mostly, I have a truly despicable advantage . . ." Patrick glances around and leans in. "I don't pay rent."

"You're squatting?"

"Yes," he deadpans.

When my eyes widen, he shakes his head, smiling. "My mom went to NYU in the nineties and kept her apartment downtown."

I take a half step back. "Where downtown?"

"East Village."

"Fuck you."

He laughs. "See."

"So, it's rent-controlled?"

"No." Then he cringes.

I love that I feel completely comfortable grilling him like this. "God, she owns it, doesn't she?" I steel myself against the tidal jealousy.

"She does."

"My dude . . ." I jerk my head back from him.

"I know." He looks a little like the gnashed-teeth emoji. "I've told no one. I feel like if fucking Bane came to my apartment in the middle of the night and killed me just to level the playing field it would be fair."

"So it's not that amazing that you work for yourself."

"Way less amazing."

"Fuck." I shake my head, cutting my eyes at him. "Wait, are y'all rich?"

He pauses. "I *was* going to say we're comfortable, but that's literally . . ."

I finish his sentence. "What every rich kid says. Wow. I'm torn between admiration and rage. You're so lucky."

"That's what I'm saying," he says. "It's not fair. It's not a testament to anything that I can afford to be freelance."

"Maybe you're talented."

"I'm okay," he says. "But I don't *not* know that a huge reason I even have a career is that my crew from art school blew up. I shot Danny Song for a *GQ* cover when I was twenty-one because he requested me."

I feel special. Like he's confiding in me because of our history.

We smile at each other.

Someone's put on Lil Peep, so all the white girls treat the bar to shouted karaoke.

"You picked the place," he reminds me.

I search the bar around me, hoping for a more acoustically amenable area just as a booth frees up. I grab his arm and lead. We slide in facing each other across the table.

A lanky Black dude up-nods as soon as we're seated. "Just the two of you?" he hollers. He and his friend have matching septum piercings, and they're both wearing bleach-spattered sweatshirts.

I nod helplessly, but just before they can squeeze in with us, Patrick slides next to me. "Executive decision," he whispers in my ear. "Is this okay?" he asks. "We could also stand if I'm crowding you."

I smile. "This is good."

The boys sit opposite us and start making out athletically. We grin into our glasses.

He slings his arm around the back of our seat. My ears heat up.

"So, you were saying," I remind him. "About work." I don't ask what Danny Song smells like, even though Danny Song was my celebrity husband before he became the Internet's boyfriend. I couldn't even tell if I wanted to be *with* him or *be* him. Just that when I fantasized about him bowing deep to my mom, greeting her in the honorific when they met, I'd feel warmth spread in my chest. All the horrible, shameful mistakes I'd made with other boys would be wiped clean. I know it's somehow defective that I've never dated anyone Korean before. Asian even. But marrying someone like Danny Song would fix all that. Marrying Patrick, too, for that matter. I'm flustered at the thought.

"Um, as I was saying"—he clears his throat; his thigh is pressed against mine—"I don't know. I have all these ideals that are probably going to bite me in the ass. Everything's so fucked. Billionaires don't pay taxes. Idiot racists rule the world. I'm trying not to work for evil people, even peripherally. I'll probably starve, but I'm okay for now." He glances down at his hands.

I clear my throat. Stare at the ring of wet on the black tabletop. Sincerity always throws me.

"What about you?" he asks finally.

"What about me?" I croak, shrinking a little under his gaze. "I didn't know there was going to be a speech portion."

I wish he'd turn his eyes down a little.

"But what are you studying? New York's incredible for creative people. What do you want to do once you're all good and learned up?"

"Well . . ."

The truth is, I know all the socialist talking points, but if anyone threatened to pay me enough for a cute apartment and a forever sofa, I might happily be stuck on marketing calls all day for a company specializing in murdering honeybees.

"Well, I wasn't done talking about you," I demur. "The job suits you."

"How'd you figure?"

"You've always been into details," I say, wondering if he agrees. "Keenly observant."

At least that's how it felt. Back then. When four years really did feel like such a long time. I was still in grade school when he started high school. I somehow felt invisible and conspicuously ungainly at the same time. I had awful hair and awful skin. Chipmunk cheeks with an explosion of pimples sprinkling my chin.

This was before I knew how to be seen. How to hide, too.

chapter 21

It's not that I had a crush on Patrick at the outset, just that I noticed and appreciated the way he moved through space. Unlike other boys at church who constantly horsed around with a basketball and lunged into you as part of the game, Patrick mostly read graphic novels. He had this smoldering intensity. Like, he had everything he needed right there, right then, all by himself with his book. He wasn't like the guys at school, either, where the popular ones seemed to glitter with erratic menace. I couldn't tell if Patrick was popular in his other life, his real life, his non-church life, during the week, but he seemed quietly confident. He would rarely look away when I caught his eye. If anything, he'd lean into it. I always looked away first. I wasn't ever sure whether he was mocking me.

"You see quiet things," I practically whisper.

"You do too," he says. "At least you did then."

"I've changed a lot though." I finish my vodka, hoping to make it true.

"Yeah," he says evenly. "I see that."

"All right." I show him my empty cup. "My round. What are you having?"

"No way, Baek Ji-young. Your money's no good here. I'm older. I'll always be older. It's on me."

"Ew." I laugh. "I am not calling you oppa."

"Ew," he says back. "Then don't."

When he leaves, I check my phone. June hasn't texted or called.

"I like your hair," I tell him when he returns.

He runs his hands through it. "I mostly still wear a hat, but I thought I'd make the effort."

I gather my hands so I don't reach out and touch it. It's killing me not to. It's something I've been aching to do since he arrived. Since before, if I'm honest. Patrick hat watch was personal church tradition.

"This is going to sound psychotic," he says, studying me again. "But you feel so familiar even though I barely know you."

I untuck my hair from my ears so that it hides the side of my face closest to him. I feel exposed that he finds me unchanged even though he makes it sound like a good thing.

"I know what you mean," I tell him, not knowing what he means at all.

At several points during the evening, I have to remind myself to listen and not just stare at his lips. In the booth across from us, there's a revolving cast of characters, but I barely notice their comings and goings.

It occurs to me, too many drinks later, that I should have eaten dinner. I'm not good at drinking. I know I'm talking way too much and I'm desperate to pee.

"Okay then," says Patrick. "Bathroom break. And you're not talking too much."

"Oh." I laugh, rising to my feet. I hadn't known I'd said it out loud.

We squeeze out of the booth. The floor underfoot feels spongy. And my left haunch tingles with pins and needles. I place my hand on his shoulder to steady myself. I know I'm closing my eyes longer than I should, but it feels exquisite. I'm exhausted.

"Whoa, okay," he says, assessing me. "How are you doing?"

I focus on the central Patrick of the three in front of me, which pulse along to my heartbeat. "Seems wasted." The sibilance of my words slide way longer than I'd intended them to.

He grins.

"Don't make fun of me," I plead.

"I would never," he says, offering me his arm. "So, we're going to deploy the buddy system on this, Baek Ji-young. We're going to pee, optimally not together, and then we're going to get you a coffee and possibly an entire loaf of bread and then pour you into a cab."

"I haven't eaten bread since eighth grade," I tell him.

He escorts me away from our booth toward the bathrooms. This is nowhere close to the dazzling seduction I'd had in my mind when I first texted.

"And I'm not shy anymore, you know," I blurt. "I'm . . . I'm gregarious and effervescent."

He has the decency to keep a straight face, but I can detect the mirth bubbling just underneath. "No one's accusing you of being shy . . . ," he says, regarding me seriously. "And you're extremely fun and . . . fizzy."

I swat his arm. I want to tell him that the greaseball fat kid he knew back then is dead. That I'm exciting now. Desirable. That admirable people have made all sorts of terrible decisions with me.

The line for the bathroom spills out of the red-lit hallway and wraps around the old-school jukebox. I lean on it, pushing the buttons that flip the CDs. I want piano music. Something keen and unsentimental. I want Ravel, but I'm also open to Jason Mraz.

I turn around and almost collide into him. Patrick's eyes widen. His lips are inches from mine. It occurs to me how preposterous it is that our mouths had to travel this far over this many years without ever once touching. I press my mouth on his. After a moment, he pulls away.

"All right, killer," he says affably. I can't tell how mortified to be about the brush-off. It doesn't matter. My light is on now. I'm sparkling above this moment, this room, this entire city. All I know is that whatever else happens tonight, Patrick will like me before it's through.

I flip the pages of the CDs in the jukebox. When I see the *Cruel Intentions* soundtrack, my palms sweat. I turn back to Patrick.

I feel like I'm in a dream. My fingers caress his cheek. Possibly with more force than is required.

His hair's curling in the back from the humidity. I reach out and touch it this time.

50 Cent comes on. There's a wall of screaming to "In Da Club" at our left.

Just then the bathroom door opens somewhere behind him, a bright slice of yellow light. I cut the line, grab him by the wrist, and pull him into it with me. I need him to pay attention. To see me as I am now. The bathroom's covered in a thousand stickers that are tagged over with a thousand different Sharpies and smells so overwhelmingly of pee that I feel like I can taste it.

"Hi," he says. "This is a variant on the original plan of peeing separately, but it can be remedied." Patrick grabs the door to leave.

"Stay for one second. I can't hear you out there."

"Oh," he says. "We're here to talk."

It occurs to me that my makeup's running down my face. There's no wall mirror. Only one of those plastic handheld ones. This one's black and chained to the faucet. The glass has been broken out of it.

"Wow. Metaphor much?" I ask.

He smiles indulgently. It really does smell so much like pee. I gag slightly.

Someone knocks at the door.

"Just a second!" I call out, laughing.

Right then the unmistakable trill of a Tinder match erupts from his pocket. His hand shoots to his phone.

"Oops!" I blurt jokily. "Guess the night's looking up." Even in my soused fog, I know this is not going smoothly. I'm trying to be a good sport, to be fun, carefree.

"Sorry," he says, and looks at me with such compassion I want to hit him. I wish he'd made a joke. Suddenly I'm weepy. I don't know what I'll do if he leaves for his date.

I reach for him and kiss him again. A Hail Mary pass. His mouth is warm and bittersweet from his cocktail and I know this is the weirdest thing to think about, but it's the perfect moisture level. God, he probably remembers to drink water throughout the day or something annoying. Again he pulls away.

I keep staring. Boldly. He leans into me then, grabbing the back of my neck and kissing me. His other hand is on my hip. I grab him by the waist of his pants and pull him toward me. I kiss his neck. It's briny and slick. I wonder if the Tinder girl he matched with is prettier than me.

"Okay," he says, breaking away again when I squirm the tips of my fingers down his pants. I've never had sex in a bar bathroom, but I'm game. Patrick is safe. I just don't want to leave. I can't face going back to that apartment. Either apartment.

More urgent knocking at the door.

"All right," he insists, pulling away and reaching for the lock. "I'm calling it. I'll put you in a car if you want." Then he kisses me lightly again before turning. "This is not the place," he says firmly, as if convincing himself. Before he leaves, he looks at me as if he can see all of me. As if he's privy to something I don't know about myself.

I close the door on him.

God. Maybe he's religious. Fuck that. Maybe he's one of those good Catholic boys. Or maybe he's just not into me.

I hover pee, thighs burning in my heels, and then wash my hands for a long time, grateful for the cold water on my wrists, grateful that I can't see my reflection. I'm sure my face is sticky. I don't want to touch my face, this bathroom is so filthy.

Now that I'm taking a breath, I'm glad we stopped. I like Patrick so much. Even if his ethics feel like poetry in that the meaning behind the words evade me.

When I open up there's a girl on her phone, dressed like a nun. She shoots me a look like, "Seriously?" and then slams the door in my face.

I'm surprised to find Patrick waiting in the hall. "Jayne," says a voice from behind. I look over. Patrick turns too. It's Ivy.

"There you are," she says. She's wearing blue lipstick and a matching boa.

"Hey," I say, throwing myself into her arms and hugging her. "What are you doing here?" I run my palms through her soft feathers. I'm so happy to see her. It feels like a miracle that we're reunited like this.

"Jayne," she scoffs, pulling away. "You literally told me to meet you."

I did. I had. I feel Patrick's eyes on us. I'd texted her when I was scared that he wasn't coming.

"Fuck." I smile and roll my eyes. "I'm so wasted."

"Okay, well, come with me to Pete's." Ivy pulls out her phone to show me. "His Halloween parties are mental." The IG stories are full of beautiful bodies in lowlight heaving to loud house music. Pete is Benzo Pete. Or Pedo Pete. This creepy forty-something A&R who last year tried to guess my age and was delighted that I was nineteen.

"You said you weren't going to hang out with him anymore."

"Jayne." She says in singsong, teeth flashing, "I have shrooms."

I sense Patrick's attention on us. The thought of him meeting Ivy is intolerable somehow. I don't want my worlds colliding.

"I can't." I take her hand in both of mine, but she snatches it back. The idea of partying with Ivy and returning to my body three days later turns my stomach.

"You're the worst." She turns on her heel for the bar.

I force myself to smile. "Let's get some air." I link my arm gamely in Patrick's and march out without meeting his eyes. My chin dimples from the effort of keeping my mouth shut. My nose clogs. I cannot let myself cry.

chapter 22

"So," he says once we're outside. "Can I make a confession?"

I nod, bracing myself for the news that he's leaving.

"I really still need to pee. You'll stay here?"

I nod. "Of course." I don't expect him back.

I watch him go. At least the air on the street is deliciously cold. Sweet. The best air I've felt in ages.

I check my logs. That I had no memory of texting Ivy until she showed up feels itchy in my brain. I wonder if that was it for us. The thought that she'd be angry with me makes me vaguely ill. Karl Lagerfeld, the late designer of Chanel, said it was best to be sort of afraid of friends, to have a sword of Damocles hanging over you. To have tension where all parties had something to lose. I don't know that I have that with Ivy beyond how she's my only friend.

I'm reminded of an evening with her on my bed in my old room. We were smoking cigarettes out of the window, which drove my roommates crazy, but they weren't home. We'd gotten all dressed up but changed our minds and dumbed out on TikTok and ate junk instead. We'd dipped into Ivy's good credit card, the one from her dad for emergencies, and tossed all the wrappers and crap onto my floor as we ate until we were numb. I wanted to ask if she did things the way I did. Whether she left her body on the fizzy, glittery, shit-faced nights we saw each other and collected it on the other side of the morning trying not to think about everything that happened in between. Instead Ivy told me she'd been super depressed in high school back in Jersey. She told me how much everyone hated her. I was picking all the breadsticks out of the Chex Mix since the rye chips were gone when she told me her boyfriend in junior year used to "throw her around a little." She'd slept with his friend as revenge and been so badly bullied for being a slut that she transferred.

As soon as she said the word, it appeared on the movie screen at the back of my mind.

Slut.

It's bizarre how the word loses its sting after high school. I hadn't even thought about it since I saw it scrawled next to my name on the third-floor bathroom. JAYNE IS A CHINK SLUT.

I felt Ivy's eyes on me. Impatient for a response. An acknowledgment of this gift of trust. I let the silence hang as I observed her naked need for my approval. It was so keening. She wanted it so badly I didn't want to give it to her. The smoke curled out of my mouth. I could have asked her what happened. If the incident had changed her. If ever she went a little dead inside any time a dude touched her since. But I just kept my head turned to the street outside until she cracked a joke to fill the silence.

All I could think was how I didn't want a friend who was anything like me. I have enough of me to go around.

"Bet you can still make that Tinder date if you leave now." The line sounds practiced, but my gratitude at Patrick returning makes my heart thunder in my ears.

"Don't do that," he says, putting on his coat and fixing his collar. As he does, I see a tendril of tattoo lower on his neck, by his clavicle. I try to steal another glance but snag his attention instead.

"You want to talk about what just happened?" he asks.

My head's swirling. "Nope."

"Fair enough." He nods.

"What does your mom think about your tattoos?"

"She's glad they're not in color because that would make me a yakuza poser, which is the only thing worse than actually being in a gang."

"Wow. That's cold."

"She also thinks it's my dad's problem since she doesn't have to deal with a criminal-looking son on her side of the bathhouse."

She seems chill. Even if in appearance she looked like any other Korean Catholic golf mom. I still can't believe she had an apartment in the East Village this whole time.

"Move to the left," the bouncer bellows at us.

We duck next to the entrance of a Chinese takeout.

The black metal cellar doors have been left open, a yawning maw in the sidewalk, and Patrick steers me way out so we don't fall in. A skinny Asian girl, about eight, pops up out of the stairs, as unexpected as a gopher, and is trailed by another a few inches shorter. Sisters. They both have wet hair. As a restaurant kid, I know this means that they went home at some point, showered, and then had to come back here. Probably for homework.

They file into the small restaurant, taking their seats at a corner table closest to the glass-front window, and set up an iPad. They share a single pair of earbuds. Watching them, I feel as though I got socked in the solar plexus.

I remember being a restaurant kid. How it sets you apart from others. I wonder if their mom and dad ever took time off work for a parent-teacher conference. Or if they're able to help with homework beyond checking to see if it's done.

"Do your parents speak English?" I ask Patrick.

"Yeah," he says, smiling and putting his phone in his back pocket. "Mom works in NGOs, so she speaks French, Mandarin, Spanish, and conversational German, and she thinks it's pathetic that we don't. I guess Kiki speaks a little Spanish now though."

I force myself to smile back. I only vaguely know what an NGO does.

"What about your dad?"

"He went to Berkeley, so . . ." Patrick clears his throat.

"Did you know we had a restaurant?" I ask him.

"Yeah," he says. "My parents went, I think. It's off I-10, right?"

"And 410."

Patrick watches me watch the girls and taps a cigarette loose from a soft pack out of his jacket pocket. He lights it with a black lighter that reads A24 in white.

"I should call Kiki," he says, nodding at them.

I snatch the cigarette from Patrick's mouth and take a deep drag. I haven't smoked in a while. It catches deep in my chest, scratching the length of my throat, making me spasm in great whooping, mortifying coughs, coughs so seismic I can't catch breath between them. I turn away from him just in time as a stream of scalding acid ejects from my guts.

I really should have eaten.

"Holy shit," I hear somewhere from behind me. I can't tell if it's him.

"Ew," another street voice chimes in.

I double over and wipe my lips with the back of my hand. "Whoa," I breathe.

I open my wet eyes. My vision's blurred. I'm in the street, staring at the dark hole of the storm drain. All the storm drains, since my eyes are crossing. They're pulsing together along with my heartbeat. I experience a sudden stunning moment of clarity.

A gentle pressure on my elbow pulls me back.

"Come out of the street," he says. I can't look at him.

Patrick hands me a bandanna from his back pocket.

"I'm sorry," I mumble, covering my mouth, desperate to catch my breath.

It's gauzy from many washings and smells like fabric softener. It's such a tender personal gesture. "It's clean," he assures me.

"I'm so sorry."

I feel a hundred times better for having voided my stomach. I always do.

"Don't sweat it," he says.

To his credit, he seems more concerned than horrified. I pull away, to save him from my sour breath. Now that I've got a clearer head, now that the spell of hooking up with him, of trying to be attractive, is broken, I shoot my shot.

"Okay," I begin carefully. "I have to ask you something." This is humiliating, but if I'm going to be banished to the friend zone for all eternity, I may as well go for it. "Can I come over?" I smile weakly. "Don't worry, I won't try anything. I'm just not entirely ready to go home yet. And for what it's worth . . ." I touch the tip of my nose with both hands. "Instantly sober. Ish."

He seems amused. I try not to read it as pity.

"Look," I tell him. June or Jeremy aren't options right now. "I'm between homes."

"So, you're asking if you can move in?" he deadpans.

I laugh gratefully. "I'm experiencing some roommate turbulence. Me and June live together. We had a real barn-burner earlier tonight."

"Ah," he says, nodding, and a strange look passes across his face.

"That's not why I called you," I assure him. I'm rummaging around in my purse for a piece of gum I know isn't there. "I wanted to call. Honest. I've wanted to text for a week."

I take a beat, lean into his whole sincerity thing. "I got scared of how accomplished you were. The whole art school, Yale . . ." I gesture widely. "I was embarrassed because I have no idea what I've been doing for ten years. But I wanted to see you."

He nods evenly. "I feel like maybe it's an ESL thing, but I never know if a barn-burner is a fight or a party."

I locate a cough drop and pop it in my mouth, training myself to look at him when he looks at me. "I think it's a political thing," I tell him, rolling the lozenge with my tongue so it extinguishes my breath. "Or sports? Every trending topic I don't recognize is a politics person or a sportsperson."

"That's me with most famous people at this point. It's a running joke with my friends."

"Well, that's 'cause you're old."

The corners of his mouth tug upward. "Yeah, we can hang out at mine," he relents.

In the car, he's silent. Seemingly lost in thought as he looks out the window.

"Do you want to split the ride?" I pray he won't take me up on it—I can't remember what card I have synched to Lyft.

"Don't sweat it," he says. I wonder if he regrets inviting me already.

chapter 23

The car stops on Ninth and A. Right across from Tompkins Square Park and around the corner from a gelato bar. It's a part of New York that I wish I knew better. The part that you read about in books and see in documentaries about kids and drugs from the eighties. I know it's changed a lot, but I'm impatient to recognize it from my own memories.

"Wow, so it's you who gets to live around here," I tell him, looking up out of the car. "Sick."

"Yeah," he says, getting out and holding the car door for me. "The first time we stayed here, back when me and Kiki were in grade school, it was so different. In the last few years, it's gotten unrecognizable." He points over my shoulder as he handles his keys. "All those highrises are new. My mom said that when she bought the place, Tompkins was choked with drug addicts. Syringes everywhere. Called it Tetanus Park. But now . . ." He up-nods at the pristine artisanal café on his block with an Instagram-bait mural about love.

He leads me into the narrow foyer of his building, and we trudge up to the second floor. "I'm right here." He gestures to the left. It's an older building, with patterned tilework on the ceilings, and the hallways are cool stone and smell a bit like basmati rice. My buzz from the drinks is wearing away at the edges. I feel as tense as I ever do walking into a guy's house for the first time, but I remind myself that this is Patrick. He's my church pal. Also known as a man with whom I have successfully extinguished any possibility of romantic entanglement. Patrick's seen me puke. We're good.

He holds the door for me.

His apartment is tidy. A little stuffy if anything. I peek into the cramped galley kitchen on the way in. The walls are lined with bookcases, with additional stacks of books on the floor under the windows. On the windowsills there are rows of the smallest flowerpots I've ever seen, with miniature cacti standing sentry. The furniture is old. And stylish in an aggressively retro way. Probably his mom's. His sofa is enormous, cushioned in mustard leather, an overstuffed, oversized freestanding futon mattress that stays bent by some trick of interior design magic. It's concertinaed at its hinge and almost resembles a giant catcher's mitt. It's ugly in a way that speaks to its expensiveness. It's jolie laide. The Marni of sofas. We take off our shoes.

The coffee table is see-through plastic, an upturned U, and he doesn't have a TV. Instead he has a projector mounted to the ceiling above his couch. The far wall, the one with the windows, is exposed red brick.

"Do you want anything?" he calls out from the kitchen.

"What, other than this apartment?" I clear my throat, standing in the middle of the living room, wishing I could brush my teeth. On the walls hang old movie posters, huge ones, seemingly from actual movie theaters, framed. The hardwood floors are dark, and out the windows behind the couch, I see the guard railing of a fire escape. It's so gloriously, enviably, unmistakably New York.

I look down at his feet when he reappears.

He's wearing what is tantamount to Uggs.

"Um."

He opens a shoe cabinet crammed with sneakers and pulls out another pair of fur-lined boot moccasins. They're conspicuously smaller. Either his mom's or dedicated for overnight guests from dating apps. "I highly recommend them."

"Thanks." I slide my feet in. I wish I could take off my socks, but I don't know whose feet have been in these. Still, they're toasty. "Nice place."

He takes my coat, hangs it up, then walks across the living room. "Thanks," he says, and cracks the window.

Even the honking of the cars outside sounds New Yorkier than usual. I take a closer look at the movie posters. Truffaut, Kurosawa, Maya Deren.

He has a Wong Kar-wai *In the Mood for Love* poster. Of course he does. "I love that you have the French edition." I've stalked the poster on eBay since freshman year. It's the one that features Maggie Cheung on one side of a brick alley and Tony Leung on the other. Both with their eyes downcast, and Tony's shadow doing what his body can't and touching her. It's devastating.

"I can't take credit," he says. "If you're feeling a commotion in your loins, it's my mom you're attracted to."

"Commotion?" *Loins?*

He smiles and shrugs. "This is mostly her stuff," he explains. "Except the books.

"Okay," he says, washing his hands in the kitchen sink and drying them on a red-and-white-striped towel. "Not to be all, I'm going to slip into something more comfortable, but I'm going to slip into something more comfortable."

He pads into his bedroom and closes the door partway.

"Hungry? Thirsty?" he asks when he returns in gray sweatpants and a hoodie.

I eye his cozy ensemble longingly.

He smiles knowingly and shakes his head. "You want sweats?"

"No, I'm okay."

"Lies."

"Okay, fine, I want sweats so bad I'm willing to, like, purchase them from you."

He goes back to his room and emerges with an exactly matching duo. "I hate mismatched sets," he says, and I smile, thinking about my socks. "These are on loan." He places the pile in my hands meaningfully. "I'm tired of getting robbed for my staples."

Again, I can't help but be curious about all the other women he's had over. Whether the slippers and sweats are a part of some move or M.O.

"Thank you." I raise them, as if toasting him. "Is that the bathroom?" I point down the hall past the kitchen.

The bathroom is small and perfect, with even more plants and an old claw-foot tub.

I barely recognize myself in the mirror. My face is oily. My eye makeup smeared. I open the medicine cabinet, locate some mouthwash, swish, gargle, and spit it out, and feel marginally better.

When I close the mirrored door, I realize I deliberately avoided reading his prescription bottles.

Shit. I like him.

There's a pump dispenser of face wash on the sink, and as much as I want to scrub my face, I still have some sense of decorum. No one's seen me without eyeliner since I was twelve. My face disappears without it. I don't have a double eyelid, and Mom and Dad refused to let me get the surgery even though in Korea it's basically as much a rite of passage as a bat mitzvah. I wash my hands, running warm water over them for a while. And then wash *around* my eyes and brows with my soapy fingertips like a lunatic.

Peeling off my jeans that are so tight I can never get them off without rolling them inside out, I realize how filthy and sticky I feel.

"Um . . ." I crack open the door, cringing. "Can I take a shower?" I grit my teeth. Maybe I should remind him again that I'm not homeless so that he'll extra, really be convinced that I'm homeless.

God, he thinks I'm a grifter.

I shiver, remembering the puke. How that must have appeared.

"Knock yourself out," he says. I turn on the hot water and hear a tap on the door.

I crack it, hiding behind it. He hands me a towel. "You've got to run the water while you press inside the little spigot guy to make it come out of the showerhead," he says.

"Thanks."

"It's old and cranky."

"Thanks," I squeak.

I pull back the shower curtain. Not only is the tub spotless, but there's a powder-blue rubber mesh over the drain to catch hairs. I've seen these exact ones in the household appliance section of H Mart. I smile picturing him tossing it into his shopping basket or else his Mom sending it to him in a care package with the same lime-green square exfoliating washcloth that I keep meaning to use but don't.

Even with his fancy parents who speak fluent English and a sister in the Peace Corps, Patrick isn't above the stupid blue hair catcher. I feel like squeezing his face into mush.

The spray of hot water is a miracle. I'm so grateful for this moment no matter how the rest of the night goes.

When I put on the sweats, I feel like weeping.

I find Patrick in the kitchen. He's wearing black reading glasses, with a tea towel on his shoulder and his sleeves pushed up. I study the thick lines of ink on his forearms without staring directly at them. I feel another commotion. Definitely in the loin region. "I'm making spaghetti aglio e olio," he says. "Or aglio e olio e pepperoncino. I guess."

"Beg your pardon?"

He laughs. "Pasta."

The kitchen's tiny, with high white cabinets and insultingly abbreviated counter space, but it's the kind of room that's perfect for entertaining, the way it opens into this little nook where he's set up a café table. It's the sort of cubby that never puts on airs, where if the host is gracious and organized, cooking becomes a collaborative activity. Everyone chopping on whatever available surface, drinking and eating without a sense of imposition or resentment or slavish, burdensome labor.

Basically, the opposite of the way my mom cooks.

I try not to move into his apartment in my mind. It's while attempting not to picture us in matching aprons making pancakes that my eye lands on an old egg timer shaped like an avocado sitting on top of his counter.

I pick it up. It hums lightly in my hand. I didn't know I had a hole in my heart in the shape of an avocado egg timer.

I glance at him again, utterly charmed. Between this and the handkerchief, why is he so adorable? Why the fuck can't he use his phone timer like everyone else in the world?

"Guess an egg was too on the nose?"

"It would be depraved to have an egg complicit in another

egg's demise," he says distractedly, checking his pan.

"God forbid a chicken," I observe.

Finally, he turns to me and appraises my outfit. I smile goofily.

I feel ridiculous. He holds his hand up for a high five. I reach over and slap it. "We look like Japanese game-show contestants."

"We *look* like a million bucks," he says. Suddenly everything is easy. Comfortable. It's as if we shucked off some film of self-consciousness when we both put on house clothes.

When the timer goes off, I watch closely. He spoons a little pasta water into his pan of garlic, adds olive oil and bits of red pepper. In deft, economical movements, with a tea towel in hand, he drains the spaghetti, gives it a good shake in the colander, and dumps the pasta into the pan, making it sizzle. It smells dementedly good. When he looks back at me, his glasses are fogged. If I were braver, if this were a movie, I would step forward and polish his glasses with my sleeve. He removes them and smiles.

He piles two blue-rimmed bowls with nests of noodle. "Whatever you don't want, I'll eat," he says, and hands one to me. He wipes his glasses, puts them back on, and opens the drawer by the stove.

"Fork or chopsticks. I could do either."

I marvel at his lack of self-consciousness or formality. Nothing he does is showy. It's a quiet kind of confidence that's unfamiliar to me. I grab forks for both of us.

"There's Parmesan in the fridge," he says. "And parsley in the blue thing." I'm standing between him and the door.

I find that I'm holding my breath when I open the fridge. There are cans of LaCroix and beer. Oat milk in the door. A rotisserie chicken from the supermarket. There's also a squat jar of kimchi, a tub of red pepper paste, and a stack of plastic containers with various prepared banchan.

I'm torn between the relief and this stirring, sparkly almost triumphant other feeling. It's a revelation to open the fridge door of a Korean person who isn't related to me.

See, I don't fucking worship white-people things, I want to tell June.

"Right there," says Patrick, pointing at a dedicated drawer in which there's a Saran-wrapped wedge of cheese. And, as promised, in a blue-topped container, there are green sprigs. I open it. There's parsley with a white paper towel lining the bottom. I can imagine him so vividly, carefully blotting the fronds after washing them and it makes my insides evanesce. I want to give his parents a plaque.

"Grab a drink?" he asks.

"Sure. What are you having?"

"Seltzer?"

I grab the cans. Suddenly I'm starving.

We sit on the couch to dine at the coffee table, but when I scooch down onto the floor, he joins me. "That's how I usually do it, but I didn't want you to think I was an animal."

I love this feeling. Like we're kids having a midnight snack.

The pasta is delicious. Perfectly cooked. Expertly salted. He offers the cheese grater and then stops me.

"Um," he says, eyeing my hands intently. "Is it okay if I grate it for you?"

"Excuse me?" My hands pause above my bowl.

"That fucker is weirdly slippery and a total health hazard. It's a design flaw that I always forget about until someone else uses it."

"Sure," I tell him. "Grate my cheese . . . *Oppa*."

He rolls his eyes. "Just say when."

"That's good," I tell him, watching the flecks fall.

He winds noodles into his spoon and shoves them into his

mouth. "Where'd you learn how to cook?" I notice that his wedge of Parmesan is the real deal. That his olive oil is bright green. That even his salt and pepper seem considered, special, extracted from a small wooden bowl and crushed out from a large, well-worn peppermill.

He keeps chewing. "My pops cooks," he says finally. "This isn't a recipe though. Good pasta's only ever four things."

"Your *pops*?"

"Yeah."

"Pops? That's what you call your dad?" I take a sip of soda.

He nods.

"So American." Again I wonder what his childhood was like that he has gochujang *and* the good kind of Parmesan in his fridge.

He laughs.

"Wait, what do you call your grandmother?"

"Uh, halmoni?"

"Okay." I take another bite of food, reassured.

"Why do you seem relieved by that?"

"I don't know." I cover my mouth, smiling. "I am though."

I look down at my bowl. I'm mowing through it faster than I'd like. "So, Pops went to Berkeley, Mom's a genius, but what are they like?"

"It's weird," he says. "For the longest time, I was totally incurious about them. They were just my parents. But going back to Korea was a game changer. Moving there for two years and seeing what they were like with their friends and family was wild. My mom is a different person in Korea. It's fucked up, but I had no idea that she was funny until then. They weren't people to me before. You're going to think this is so dumb, but I could see that my parents were, like, popular."

At the mention of popular, I don't even know what to envision for my parents. I picture my mom smoking a cigarette like a little street urchin. I try to imagine her at a poetry reading, but now, in my head, she's just wearing a beret. My archetypes for cool are astoundingly limited. There're emoji with more depth than I'm willing to assign to my parents.

"I know nothing about my mom and dad," I tell him. "Black boxes, both of them. And I want to know everything. I used to have this fantasy that I'd invent an app where we could talk to each other through a filter with translation and microexpressions and tone and all this stuff so we could properly communicate. But then I realized it wouldn't make them want to talk to me. My dad's family was wrecked by the banking crisis, so everything's about money and success, and my mom's from some tiny village, but I don't even know what that means."

I've never talked about my parents this frankly with anyone. Not even June.

He sets his fork down. "How'd they end up in Texas?"

"I don't know. I'm beginning to think they didn't even have a plan. It's not as if we knew anyone out there."

"You miss it?"

I shake my head. "You?"

"All the time," he says. "Nobody in New York can make iced tea for shit."

It's true. It's been an ongoing secret source of pain. "I keep ordering it at restaurants for, like, six bucks and getting so sad. Plus, they charge for refills."

"Iced tea in New York is such a scam."

"And it's not like C-Town has Mrs Baird's Texas Toast for French toast."

"Brioche is pretty good for that."

"Fuck outta here." I shake my head. "You know, I'm going back this weekend."

I hand him my half-eaten pasta and sit on the sofa.

"Oh yeah? How do you feel about that?"

I shrug. My leg's fallen asleep. "I haven't been since I got here. Where are your parents right now?"

"Korea," he says. He eats like a boy. Wolfing.

"Do you ever look at your parents and wonder why they make their lives so hard?" I ask him.

"Okay," he says, getting up on the sofa with me. "I guess we're going in."

"Sorry." I bite my lip.

"No," he says, and reaches over to touch my forearm. "I didn't mean that. I just . . ." He shakes his head. "It's like you said the exact thing I've been thinking for the past few years. It's just a bit uncanny, I guess."

He leans back. "As the kids of immigrants, we always have to think about that whole 'I am my ancestors' wildest dreams' thing. I know my parents made sacrifices, but I also don't understand their choices. Like, uprooting their lives three times for me and my sister's schooling. And my dad gives so much money to his abusive brother, who we have to pretend isn't a narcissist and psychopath because he's the firstborn or some shit. There's so much that goes into the collectivist mind-set, considering the good of the whole before prioritizing yourself, but sometimes it's like, give it a rest already. Just set a boundary and break some patterns once in a while."

I lean back with him. His shoulder's warm against mine.

"Does your family have secrets that you don't even know why you're keeping?" I ask him.

"Yeah," he says. "My uncle has a second family that we don't talk about. What about you?"

I think about June. How we're keeping her cancer from Mom.

How she kept her job loss from me. "My mom left for three months when we were in high school and we don't talk about it. We have no idea where she went, why she left, and when she came back, we all pretended it never happened."

"I'm sorry," he says. "Do you and June talk about it?"

I shake my head. "Not really. It's crazy how lonely it is to be in a family. Even if the stuff with my mom didn't happen, even if everyone was super evolved and therapized, I think just being in a family is what screws you up. I'm never going to fully understand them. And it's fucked up because that means they're never going to understand me. But who knows." I shrug. "Maybe it's designed that way for a reason. Families are such fucked-up tiny cults."

"Makes sense," he says. "Marriages are the original tiny cult."

"Siblings too."

"God," he says. "That is the truth. I feel like Korean families are extra fucked up though. Because of Han. Because we've been invaded and occupied and split up without retribution."

"We're so repressed."

"So repressed." Patrick crosses him arms, lost in thought. "Did you ever have that thing where, like, staying out late, drinking forties, breaking shit, or making out with people in public was, like, white-kid shit."

"Totally!" I think about my friends with ripped-up jeans, face piercings, and dyed hair. "Bad-kid shit was always white-kid shit."

"I'm sure being an Asian woman is its own thing, but being an Asian dude in America is such a head trip. College was weird; Texas was weird. Especially with those Asia years in between. Even at international school in Seoul, Asian guys were the jocks, the bullies, the stoners, the hot guys, all of it. We didn't think about it. There wasn't the ambient trauma of not being taken seriously as a man that I've seen Asian-American dudes carry around, where they have to be ripped and mad alpha or else they're a nerd. But then again, my dad's a professor. My mom lived in Europe. I lived in Korea, but kids in Southern California act like I'm not Asian *enough* because me and my sister didn't have the whole signing up for Kumon and living with our grandmother deal. I'm not a restaurant kid or a store kid. My parents actually encouraged me to go into the arts. . . ."

"You call your dad frickin' pops," I offer, grinning.

"I call my dad frickin' pops."

"Wait a minute," I ask him. "Were you allowed to go to sleepovers?"

"Not you, too," he says, reeling in mock injury.

"Well?"

"Not, like, every weekend, but . . ."

Patrick might be salty to have his Asianness tested, but to me he's a unicorn. "Wow." I reach over and touch his cheek. "We look the same and yet . . ." I touch my own cheek with my other hand. "So different."

He shrugs me off. "I don't know what to tell you, fam. I went to sleepovers. Had sleepovers. I had PB&Js in my lunch *and* brought kimbap and didn't fucking think nothing of it."

Patrick leans over to drink his water, which reminds me to do the same, and then he stacks our bowls.

I follow him into the kitchen.

"Oh, wait," he says, turning to face me. "I know something that's real Korean. Deeply Korean."

"What?"

"My dad had bypass surgery when I was in college," he says, running the water for the dishes. "*And* they didn't tell me because I had finals."

Again my sister flashes into my head.

"That," I tell him, nodding, "is deep Korean. And also deeply messed up that you're so vindicated by his coronary issues."

I feel better that Patrick doesn't have a dishwasher. He's only out of my league by a factor of thirty-nine, not seventy-three.

I grab the first bowl from him and dry with the kitchen towel on the oven door. "Did they wait until the holidays to tell you while they were gossiping about someone else's health?"

"No," he says, eyeing me. "They FaceTimed and bought me a plane ticket to see him the day finals wrapped."

"Yeah." I frown a little. "I don't know. Feels like you might need an asterisk on that achievement. Feels emotionally stable and transparent now." His parents sound positively Scandinavian.

"Great," he says, walking over to the bathroom. "I'm going to spend all night tallying traumas."

"Do your worst," I tell him. Even with his head start, I'm pretty sure I've got him beat. Being an Asian woman really is its own thing.

Patrick returns with a brand-new toothbrush with the name of his dentist printed on the handle. Plus a tiny wheel of floss.

"Whoa." I take both from him. "Thank you. I'm beyond grateful to you, for your hospitality, your company, and your sofa." I lay my palm against the leather and slide onto my side. It feels so good against my cheek.

He laughs and yawns.

"No, you get the bed." He yawns again. "It's super comfy. You can't sleep here. My mother would murder me."

"How would she know?"

He scoffs. "She'd know."

Guess he really is Korean.

chapter 24

I brush my teeth, body listing forward I'm so tired. Patrick's bedroom is spare with heavy blue curtains blotting out the streetlights and a big, broad bed with enough room on either side to walk completely around it. I struggle to keep my eyes open but when I slip into his striped sheets, burying my face in his cold pillow, smelling dryer sheets and a scent I imagine the back of his neck to carry, I'm haunted by the image of the two, wet-haired girls in the window of the restaurant.

The picturesque sweetness of a matching set is never experienced by either of the people in it. I'd get so sick of being tethered to June. How we were always displayed as a pair. The way customers would address us as if we were one person. Or even more disembodying, the way they'd talk to us as if we weren't there. As if we canceled each other out. Sometimes June would pipe up, once snapping at a baby-talking white lady, "Take a picture, it lasts longer," and laughing straight in her face. I was thrilled. It was exactly what I would have said if I were brave enough.

June never held her tongue. I seethed. My thoughts festered and it was a tailor-made hell that I couldn't hide anything from her. I'd sit there at family meal, eyes downcast, cheeks ablaze, next to our parents, the cooks, the busboys, and the dishwashers, pretending I wasn't there. Pretending I didn't know them. June would crack on me in front of everyone the way I'd jolt when the door opened, scared that someone from school might see. "You think you're so cool," she'd remark, shaking her head, munching on all the broken fortune cookies, piling up the paper ribbons of fate without bothering to read them. "It's so embarrassing."

Her taunts stung, staying with me for days the way Mom's did, cutting over and over. The funny thing about having an older sibling play babysitter is that you're only vaguely aware that they're also a child. I remember once when June had turned eleven. I was still eight and we were in the rare months where she became especially intolerable since she was three years older instead of two. Eleven was properly in the double digits. "I'm basically an adult," she'd announce. Back then we'd walk home after dinner at the restaurant to put ourselves to bed. The worst, scariest part of the trip was the stretch of road under a patch of the Loop 410 highway, past the middle school and an enormous H-E-B grocery store. That's where you felt most exposed to the whoosh of cars at your back. I always walked as fast as I could. Taking shallow, vigilant breaths.

June knew how much I hated that walk. The solemnity with which Mom instructed her to hold my hand. It all went straight to June's giant melon head. She acted as if I owed her my life. At the critical expanse, she'd purposely slacken her grip on my sweaty palm. "Uh-oh," she'd say, eyes widening dramatically.

That night she held out her backpack for me to carry.

"Take it."

I shook my head.

"I said, 'Take it.'"

Again, I refused.

June dropped the bag where we stood and boldly skipped ahead. "I'm telling Mom," she declared, sprinting into the light of the H-E-B supermarket parking lot.

I ran after her.

"Mom's going to kill you," she sang, grinning back at me wickedly. I knew it didn't make sense, but June was wily with words when Mom interrogated us in Korean.

"You'd better go get it," she yelled once she crossed the street that led to our house.

I turned around. Anyone could've run away with it if they wanted to.

Heart jackhammering in my chest, I ran all the way back. I could feel my bookbag banging against me. When I reached the nylon straps of hers, I heaved it up with both arms and hurtled back. My lungs burned and my feet slapped against the hard concrete as I bolted.

With each footfall June got closer and closer. Bigger and bigger.

Her head turned as her eyes widened.

Twin headlights flooded my vision as screams fill my ears. I wondered if I'd feel the pain of my body being crushed by the oncoming car. Whether I'd fly into the sky at a strange angle from the impact. But then my face and neck were hot from the engine. My eyes were shut tight. I heard a loud sustained honk and a slammed door from somewhere above me.

"What are you doing?" screamed a tall woman with huge hair as she got out of her enormous SUV. She made the sign of the cross. "I could have killed you." She had moles all over her face, and as she leaned toward me, I could see down her flowered shirt to her cheetah-print bra.

June ran up and grabbed her bag.

"You idiot," she said, pinching my belly and pulling hard. "We're sorry," June called out, waving to the lady.

I was instantly in tears. Bawling and rubbing my side where I'd been pinched. I was shocked by the near miss and outraged that my sister could be angry at me.

"I can't believe you didn't look," said June, storming off. "You're such a stupid baby."

She left me to cry on the street. I wept and wept, hiccupping and furious. I wept about what kind of sister would be that hateful. I wept as if I were at my own funeral.

Moments later she returned, tears streaking her face, red as a busted tomato. She shouldered her bag and mine. "I'm sorry," she moaned, hugging me hard. My face was mashed against her bony shoulder as I continued to sob. "Shhhhh," she said again, stroking my hair so hard it hurt. "I'm sorry." That made me cry harder. Somehow it was even sadder that I'd made June cry.

Whenever I think of my sister in that moment, it hurts my heart. How lonely she must have felt marching into the house, breath held, closing the door, leaning up against it, and bursting into tears before coming back for me.

No matter how much she resented me and however much I disliked her, it was June's bed I climbed into every night. I was convinced that if I fell asleep before our parents came back they would die. I never had to tell her that. She knew. Back then she knew everything. And as long as I was big spoon, creeping in quietly and wrapping my small body around hers without touching, she'd pretend not to notice. I'd have to be careful to breathe softly because if I breathed out too hard or too much, according to her she'd be poisoned in her sleep from my carbon dioxide. As far as I knew, it was the only thing June was scared of.

chapter 25

Patrick's standing at the window when I get up. It's pouring outside.

"Morning," I croak, opening his bedroom door and yawning, pretending like I've been asleep this whole time. Pretending like I didn't set my alarm for 7:00 a.m. to remove my crusty makeup and reapply it by early windowlight and phone. I even thought about trying to poop without detection while Patrick snored softly, hugging the couch, dead asleep, but I'd rather hold it, poison my microbiome, and die slow.

He shuffles into the kitchen and returns with a cup of coffee. "Sleep well?"

I nod, taking the hot drink.

We stand side by side at the large window. It's miserable. The kind of umbrella-flipping torrent where everyone's huddled under awnings, waiting it out.

In his glasses, hair sticking up in the back, with his coffee mug, grinning down at the sad sacks on the street, he looks totally different from the version of him on social media, even the kid from church. This is nice, I tell myself. Other than Jeremy, I've never spent a morning with a guy in this way.

"What about you?"

"Great," he replies, toasting me with his mug.

I search for any hint of resentment at my staying over.

"I guess I should be heading out," I tell him, before he can beat me to the punch.

He frowns and nods toward the street. "In this? What time do you have to be at class?"

"Eleven."

"Breakfast?" he asks hopefully. It's just after eight.

I look to the sky for any indication it'll let up. It's a woolen moody mess up there. Patrick smiles. Honestly, I don't need any further encouragement to ditch.

"I just have to text someone."

Gina Lombardi's office texts me back that I'm canceling within the twenty-four-hour cancellation period and that it'll count as a session.

Whatever. Besides, I'm a little mad at her. Frankly, it's irresponsible to rile me up with all those questions about June without teaching me how to deal.

"Where do you want to go?" I ask Patrick. I find myself wondering how this memory will feel in the future. If wherever he picks will become our special place and we'll return for special anniversaries.

"Well," he says. "Scale of one to ten, how gremlin monster are you feeling?"

"Is ten the gremliniest or . . ."

He nods. "Ten is comatose, don't even shower, and roll over to the diner and eat eggs in our matching sweats."

The idea of staying in his sweats is the closest I've come to true joy in a minute.

"That one."

I borrow two pairs of socks and a pair of Timbs to add to my tab.

"Man," he says, eyeing me. "Fucking adorable."

I look down at my feet, cheeks heating, and throw on my coat.

He wasn't kidding about how close the diner was. It's a half block, and we bolt, leapfrogging under awnings and storefronts. When we get there, he holds my hand briefly. His palm is warm where mine is wet, and he leads me into the open door and to the counter. I keep reminding myself that it's not a date. That you don't go on morning-after, rainy-day dates with someone you almost barf on. The worst part is, I don't even care that we're dressed like dorks; I'm so happy. I feel like half of that couple who dresses in onesies and takes selfies and I like it.

The short, beefy Latino guy behind the counter turns Patrick's cup upright on his saucer and pours steaming coffee as soon as we sit down. He looks to me, and when I nod, he wordlessly pours me a cup as well. "I'm here a lot," explains Patrick, just as the dude asks him if he's having the usual.

I've always wanted to have a usual.

"I'm going to need a minute," he says, picking up his menu. "I could hit you with a total curveball today, Angel."

Angel gives an unimpressed shrug and returns the coffeepot.

"What's your usual?"

"Two eggs, over medium, sausage, home fries, rye toast, dry, side of hot sauce. But everything here's good."

I scan the menu. "Have you had the Streamline Special?" It's described as a mound of cottage cheese with canned tuna and a side of peaches.

"Yep, and it slaps," he says. "I don't know why; it just does. It's like peanut butter and bacon."

I realize that I'm starving. "I'll have what you're having."

He nods approvingly. "Donut for the table?"

"Sure."

"Power." He shuts his menu. "I'll have the usual," he says to Angel.

"I'll have his usual." I nod to Patrick.

"And a glazed donut."

I'm proud of the order somehow.

"You think we would have been friends if our parents hung out?" I ask him. "When we were younger?"

"Totally," he says, and then cocks his head. "I guess, all four of us would have. You would've been obsessed with Kiki, I wouldn't have gotten off my phone, and June would've probably kicked all our asses. We look a little different now, but we're still basically the same." He reads something in my face and qualifies. "But I don't know. You *seem* the same."

I narrow my eyes. He said a similar thing last night. I try to decide if I feel insulted by this.

"But maybe not as intimidating. Actually, fuck it. I don't know. You're still intimidating."

I laugh at this. A sharp bark. I glance around, stunned by the assessment. "Me?"

"Yes, you. You were so intense. Big goth energy. Always reading some humongous book with a level of focus I'd never seen in a kid. You were *way* too busy to talk to me."

"Oh, because you ever tried talking to me." I remember the books. Mostly horror and romance paperbacks. I also remember Patrick with his comics, his video games, his earring, and once his dyed-purple hair, which had scandalized the church ladies. He also brought a few non-Korean friends to mass who ate the fishy-smelling soups and everything after church. It was fascinating that he'd reveal this part of his life to his friends, who seemed cool judging by their sneakers. Everyone was always talking to Patrick. I wish he'd stuck around to see me a few years later. When I pulled myself together.

"I tried talking to you," he says, sipping his coffee.

"You talked to June, not me." This I remember too, with a flutter of jealousy. June could talk to anyone.

"I talked to June because she yelled at me all the time. Acting like we already knew each other from the second we met. She high-key bullied me into lending her all my Civil War comics right as I was starting them. She said I had to make the concession because I was older and that was my duty."

I laugh. It sounds exactly like June.

"But I talked to you," he says, tapping his chin. "Or at least I tried. It was right around Easter because that mass was fucking brutal. You were wearing a Forest of Endor Summer Camp sweatshirt."

I remember the sweatshirt. It was purple and it was June's. My heart sinks. "Nope," I tell him. "Wasn't me. That was June's."

To be mistaken for June by strangers is one thing, but I'm upset. I feel duped by the premise of this nostalgic conversation. I flip through the plastic specials menu on the counter. "I've never seen a single *Star Wars* movie ever in my life," I say coldly.

I'm relieved that this diner serves alcohol. I could order an Irish coffee without it seeming too big a deal. I can feel my face tightening, but Patrick's oblivious. He nudges my knee with his.

"That's exactly what you told me," he says, barely keeping a straight face. "I swear to God. You said it just like that too. So snotty." He leans in. "I spoke in *Ewokese*. I thought it was so cool." He laughs, searching my face.

I grin. He's right. I don't remember.

"Wait, what did you say?"

"No fucking way."

"Tell me," I plead. "I might remember it."

He shakes his head. "Nope. You gave me the most withering look and said, 'Excuse me?' So, I explained, which won me zero points, and then you said, *I have never seen a Star Wars movie ever in my life.* End quote."

It certainly sounds like me. "God." I shake my head. "What a dick."

"And!" he says, remembering another detail. "June wasn't even there. She was at some genius NASA thing that weekend. Me and Kiki wouldn't hear the end of it from Pops. To this day he's gutted that none of his kids inherited his math brain."

That's when it comes to me. He's right. June was in Houston. LBJ Space Center. She'd won some big-deal data contest, and she and Dad had gone. I'd thrown a fit because Mom hadn't washed any of my clothes, so I'd had to wear June's top. I don't remember Patrick talking to me, but I do vividly recall how the entry fee and hotel for that event was three hundred bucks. Meanwhile, they'd refused to pay for my gym membership, saying that I could just do jumping jacks in the driveway.

Our food arrives, so I proceed to cut it all into pieces and move it around. Breakfasts are easy because there are so many stations—your egg area, the potato pile no one finishes. Bacon's easier to fake than sausages, but that's fine. Fried eggs are a cinch because once you pop the yolks, no one checks how much you've eaten.

He cuts the donut with a knife. I take a huge, enthusiastic bite of my half and widen my eyes. I can practically hear my pupils contract into pinpricks. Sugar always does this to me. "Mmm," I moan, and deposit the rest of it back onto the plate. I'm glad we're sitting next to each other and not across. It makes the optics easier. Patrick tucks in with zeal, going nuts with the hot sauce and the ketchup and talking about his father.

I only vaguely remember his dad, but another memory of Patrick coils up to the surface. It was later that same year. He'd been gone all summer, and when he returned, he'd changed. Enough so that June noticed it first. "Did Patrick get hot?" she asked, jabbing me in the ribs when he and his family walked in.

All of a sudden, he was a head taller than his sister, who'd always been modelly. That wasn't it though. There was an ease to the way he moved. I'd wondered all summer where he'd been. But I couldn't admit that to June.

Right after mass, before the communal meal, Mom asked me to put the hymnals back in the car, and when I did, I saw him. He was at the other end of the lot and suddenly an adult. I kept my eyes on the ground, wishing I'd had earphones, debating whether or not to say hi. But just as I glanced up, he'd gotten a call, and the way his face broke into a smile, I could tell he was talking to a girlfriend or a crush or something. I kept my eyes straight ahead, ignoring him, even as I purposefully marched at an angle where he'd see me.

"How was it?" he asks, nibbling on his last triangle of toast. I swallow at the memory. God, I was such a dork.

"Great." He glances down at my plate, so I drape my napkin over the leftovers and order another coffee. I hit the bathroom, and then we head back to his apartment and watch TV. He checks his phone for some work things, and while I try not to look down at his screen, I wonder what his real life is like. How I'd fit into it. If there's any room. I wonder if he's dating anyone. Who the Tinder match was. Whether or not he's dated any of the models he's previously photographed.

He smiles, apologizes, and puts his phone down on the coffee table, and while I'm overjoyed that this man's idea of a good time is to watch *Bake Off* on Netflix sprawled on the couch, and even though I'm nestled beside him, I can't help but wonder if I'm getting too comfortable.

I let my eyes wander over to him. It's Patrick from church, but it's also profoundly not. Me and Patrick need a reset, I decide. I have to keep this from going off the rails.

"Do you mind if I shower?" I ask him suddenly, springing to my feet. He tilts his head up sleepily and smiles. "Go for it."

I don't wash my hair, but I scrub my face, removing all my makeup, and wipe the foggy mirror down to start over. I fluff out my hair. It's wavy and full, and I give myself a little pep talk. Part of me is intrigued. Flattered even. No dude has ever set out to be my friend, but what does this mean philosophically? The thought of him not being attracted to me is unbearable. I can so easily imagine him keeping me apart from his work life, his personal life, the way Jeremy did. I need to convince him of my value.

"What do you have to drink?" I ask him when I emerge, still in his sweats but so much cleaner. So much more focused.

He looks up. The laptop on his coffee table drones on about the temperament of hot-water crust pastries in a hand-raised pie.

"Bourbon and . . ."

"I'll have that." I nod. "Don't make me drink alone," I admonish. He pads to the kitchen, then hands me a drink in a squat glass and clinks his to mine. He toasts me, watchful.

"Maybe I should shower too," he says. "I need to wake up."

"Do it," I tell him. He drains his drink, Adam's apple bobbing, ice cubes clinking as his head tilts back. He disappears into the bathroom. Sometime in the last half hour, I've made the decision that we should sleep together. I want the data. I need to know how I'll feel after. If Patrick will be different.

I'm reminded of Malcolm Ito. Malcolm Ito was a forty-year-old Japanese furniture designer with a big beard and tinted glasses who had recently divorced a French socialite filmmaker fifteen years his senior. We'd met at a party at the New Museum. It was a springtime launch event for an art magazine that Ivy's ex-girlfriend was involved in, and I was wasted on champagne. We kissed on the roof deck. It was terribly poetic. His beard rubbed up against my chin. I touched his face, and when we broke away, I heard him gasp. He was the first Asian man I'd ever kissed. I decided to fall instantly in love with him.

It was as though I could feel my heart fasten to his like the interlocking of precision machinery. It was everything I'd imagined it would be if I'd kissed someone tailor-made for me. Someone worthy and good who would accept me for me. Who I'd see with such a deep and profound recognition that they'd never be able to leave me. He excused himself for a phone call and never returned. I'd waited, shivering in my drunk haze, handkerchief-thin dress fluttering against me. I stared at a far-off water tower, convinced he'd come back. When I googled him a few months ago, he was engaged to a Norwegian model with a dynamic ceramics practice. That's how they described it. Dynamic. Ceramics. Practice.

Suddenly Patrick feels like the answer to a question. He belongs with me. I belong with him. I'll finally know how things went wrong all those times before.

I'm not great at drinking and I'm not great at sex. So far, I don't particularly excel at adult things. I've tried it. Sex. And it's never how I'd want it to be. For all the talk of first base, second base, third, it's more like a light switch. You go from not having it—barely kissing really—to all of a sudden having it. Full-on sex. When it's over, I feel like I've failed to make it better for myself. That it's somehow my fault that I'm startled each time.

It's the way they aggressively and incessantly initiate sex. The way I always feel cornered, by the text, in the bar, in the car, in their apartments. Sometimes I wonder if I'm confused by how purposeful they are. They're so sure they want sex that I try to convince myself I must be wrong about my ambivalence.

I go to pour myself another drink. It's noon, but it may as well be the weekend. The booze bottles are on a silver tray on top of his fridge. They shiver, clinking slightly when the refrigerator runs, but the bourbon's been left out on the counter. I quietly ease out another inch, so he doesn't think I'm a lush.

I look at myself in the circular wall mirror hanging just outside the kitchen. I watch myself take another sip. I marvel at how convincing I am as an adult. I rub my lips between my fingers, hard. Pulling them so they color and hopefully swell a little. They'll stay bruised and puffy for at least thirty seconds after he comes out of the shower.

Men don't enjoy the taste of lipstick though they like the look of it.

It's as if the transmission was fed into an earpiece, it's so fully formed and not mine.

I smile silkily. I look crazy. I suck in my cheeks and make fish lips. Clear my throat. Suck in my gut, let it out. Take another sip. Put the glass down on the counter and slap the apples of my cheeks with the pads of my flattened fingers. I drink even more, warming my insides. I want a third glass and listen for the running water, but I shouldn't risk it.

I settle on the couch, wishing there was music on. Arrange my arms and legs so they don't flatten against the leather and appear wide. Even with the boozy buzz, another layered distraction would be good. I can't deal with bodies. The smells, the tastes, all that rubbing, the occasional mortifying flatulence if my chest suction cups his in a way that I wish we could laugh about but never do. It's the worst. Usually he'll grunt in a porny way, masking it, so I'll do the same in a whinier, pleading tone, and we'll both keep ignoring it because breaking character would reveal how fucking embarrassing it all is.

Consent?

Yes.

Yes?

It's like a spell we're taught the words to, but how do you cast it? Where am I supposed to stand? What do I do with my arms? There should be a laminated poster in all bedrooms. The way restaurants have Heimlich maneuver guides. Why is the invocation so awkward? All the sex I've ever had seemed inevitable. It wasn't wrought but ordained. It was like watching someone fall from a height. We all know where it's going.

I hold an ice cube in my mouth to quiet my brain. I know this will be different. It has to be. When Patrick returns to the couch, back in sweats, I climb onto his lap, on my knees, facing him, and touch my lips to his. He tastes like toothpaste. His mouth is cold, then warm. The alcohol begins to blur the lines, soothe the spikiness of my thoughts, the impatience. I feel and hear the tremble, a low rumble in his throat. His hands find their way to my waistband and pull me into him. I pull away a fraction. His face is blurry up close, and for a brief moment, as if a single foreign frame has been spliced into the reel, reality warps and my mouth is full of some random I hooked up with the first time Jeremy left. I never learned his name.

I pull away completely.

Wordlessly, I get up, take his hand, and lead him toward his bedroom. He follows.

Everything is as I've left it. Queen bed. Striped linens. But in the blued afternoon light, each article throbs with a new significance. The bedside table with a stack of books. His half-drunk water. Reading glasses.

I insert myself into his future. Slot my copy of *The Secret History* onto his table. A scrunchie by his water glass. If I leave something—an earring, my compact, an eyelash—it would secure my safe passage back.

I wonder if we'll know each other after this.

I sit on the edge of his bed while he stands. Watching. The rest is muscle memory. Old choreography. I touch the soft hem of my sweatshirt, holding his gaze while I pull it off, judging from his expression how much he's into this. Into me. How much of him I'll get to keep afterward.

He drinks me in. I'm not wearing a bra. I tug on his pant leg, and he joins me on the bed. We're kissing, scooching higher up on the mattress as he lies on top of me. From this angle he could be anyone. I close my eyes, waiting. But then the warmth of him leaves. He pulls away, propping himself up. I peek just as he hooks his finger against my cheek—pulling—and a hair slides out from the back of my throat, tickling the wet of my mouth, and is freed. It's such a small movement. Tender. Patient. There's a pleasant buzzing in my ears as my senses go all syrupy, and then the room snaps into focus. That Patrick would consider my comfort above his even for a moment grounds me back into my body. I freeze.

"Let's pump the brakes a little," he says, studying me. I nod. He pushes away and lies on his back, holding my hand as we stare up at the ceiling.

I raise his hand to my mouth and kiss it. "Do guys hate the taste of lipstick?"

I feel the tremor of him laughing beside me. "What?"

"I don't know . . . Is it a thing where you like the way it looks but hate the way it tastes?" I shift to my side and kiss his cheek.

"I have never noticed that it has a taste, and I have no real opinion on its appearance. I guess it's nice."

He goes quiet. "Is this a quiz?" he asks after a while. "I'm trying to remember if you were wearing lipstick last night."

This time I laugh. "No. I just had this dumb thought that men have these strong feelings, but I don't know where it came from."

"I like mouths," he says, facing me and kissing mine. "Humans like mouths. I'm indifferent to the ornamentation, I think."

We lie there for a while. Listening to the street. Not talking. I want to ask him about everyone he's ever slept with.

I creep closer to him, pressing my entire body to his side as he rearranges us so that I'm nestled in his arm. *You're mine,* I think, wondering if he can read my mind. How else would he have known that for all my bluster, I needed a moment to breathe? That I was scared of all we stood to lose? That I wanted to know him first?

"I think I'm going to get going now," I whisper after a while. It's better to go before they want you to.

He turns to me, expression unreadable. "Let me get you a car."

My heart sings. It's such a small gesture, but I'm grateful for the offer. I shake my head. Hopefully he'll see my refusal as I intend it. That I don't take up too much space. That I'm agreeable, low-maintenance, chill. I decide not to leave anything on his nightstand. It wouldn't work on a Patrick.

I hope this ensures that he'll want to see me again.

"I love the subway," I tell him in a small, light voice. "I'm easy."

chapter 26

Patrick walks me to the train. We're huddled under his umbrella, and he's tilting it to favor my side, his shoulder getting soaked in the process.

When we get to the subway, he pulls me under the marquee of the Mediterranean restaurant on the corner. He closes the umbrella and hands it to me.

I shake my head, like a child, leaving the umbrella to hang between us.

"I'm older than you," he says, urging it forward. "You're taking it."

It's a nice one, a real one, not even the five-dollar kind you buy off the street.

"Thank you." I smile at him.

He pulls his hood up and smiles back.

We stand there, cheesing.

He grimaces right as I feel it, the rude flick of cold water spraying us both as we're almost decapitated by an advancing golf umbrella to our left.

I wipe my face as Patrick ushers me close with a hand to my hip.

We resume grinning, this time for being so oblivious. I nod at the subway stairs behind me.

"Wait," he says, taking my hand. "When do you leave for Texas?" His warm thumb brushes the length of mine.

"Friday."

"Let's hang out before you go."

"Really?" The hopeful lilt in my voice is mortifying.

"Yeah, really." He chuckles.

"Okay."

"Okay."

He leans in and kisses me.

"I'm glad you called," he says, mouth inches from mine. I hug him hard. "You can keep the umbrella," he says in my ear. "But I want my fucking sweats."

I hug him tighter, my *New Yorker* tote stuffed with clothes mashing between us. I want to tell him I love him, but instead I say, "We'll see," and clatter down the stairs. I wave before disappearing around the corner.

I imagine Patrick talking to his friends. The dude group chat. Wondering if he'll say we hooked up anyway. That I took him in my mouth. Or that I led him on. Calling me a prick tease. Immature. I close my eyes. Things seemed fine, but you can never know what anyone else is ever thinking. Or what they'll say about you.

I dig for my MetroCard, hitching my bag onto my hip so I can feel through the different shapes for the right one. My fingers catch loose change and various hard crumbs native to the bottoms of purses before curling around the metal carabiner of June's keys. I fish them out along with my wallet.

Instead of going to Brooklyn, I take the F uptown. On the train, seated across from me, is an older white guy with wire-frame glasses and an orange beanie pulled up high on his forehead. He has his notebook out. He's doing line drawings of different passengers. Sketching quickly as if trying to capture everyone in New York. I want to take the seat next to him and flip through his book to look for Cruella.

The New Yorkiest New Yorkers aren't exactly like *Pokémon Go*, but they also sort of are.

I wonder if Patrick has any favorite New Yorkers. I'll bet he does. He loves details. I replay the last twelve hours in my head, plucking out different aspects of his apartment. The movie poster. His heavy art books. That goddamned avocado egg timer. The way his kitchen towel felt in my hands as he washed and I dried. I don't know what this feeling is, this crawling, spreading sensation that feels at once joyful and like shame. Why didn't I know before this that Patrick was perfect for me? I can't believe he has that flower hair catcher thing in his tub. I picture us in London. In Paris. At Léon in front of Jeremy, who I can pretend not to recognize as I walk by. I hug myself, smiling.

"Jayne!"

I look up, stunned. Suddenly I'm at June's building and I'm still smirking stupidly with my arms wrapped around my middle. June gets off the elevator with her eyes wide. I let the smile drop. I thought I'd have a few seconds to get my bitch-face situated.

"What are you doing here?" She's wearing denim overalls and a raincoat with a hood. Meanwhile, I don't remember the last time I saw her in jeans, let alone dungarees. She's holding a neon-yellow plastic folder. Something about the color reminds me of a crossing guard.

She glances at my oversize sweatsuit. And then down to my clothes from last night, which are swinging in my bag. "Where were you?"

"I'm just gonna grab my stuff," I tell her, sticking my foot in the elevator door before it shuts. "I'll leave the key with the doorman."

"Okay," she says. Her expression's unreadable. "I'll get out of your way."

"Wait, where are you going?"

A beat. "Uptown," she says.

"Doctor's appointment?" I nod at the folder in her hand. She's always bitching about crosstown traffic when she's headed over there. She looks down at it and frowns.

"Nah, I'm just meeting with an old client," she says with a penetrating gaze. "Are you still coming to Texas? At least tell me if I should cancel your ticket."

I let the elevator doors close without answering her.

She didn't blink once.

"Jayne!" I call out.

This time it's my sister who looks up from her phone. Startled.

It takes seventeen minutes from June's apartment to Fifty-Third Street and Madison if you take the F or M train. It's right where the line arcs toward Queens. You pop out at Lexington. Easy peasy.

It's different in a car.

June's Uber spent eleven minutes just crossing over from Park Avenue on Fifty-Second and then flipping back around the block because Fifty-Third's a one-way. I trailed her big mouth right to the medical pavilion. She's been here twice this month.

I'm leaned up against the thick metal column with my arms crossed. She has every reason to feel unsettled and paranoid. I still can't believe she thought she would pull this off without me knowing.

She gets out of the car, stalks straight up to me, and grabs my arm.

"What's the matter, Jayne?" I ask her. Her eyes flit over to the security guard by the revolving door. Then she pulls me toward a flank of plants away from the building. It's still drizzling.

"What are you doing here?" she whispers angrily. "And don't lie to me. I know you're never in this part of town." Her eyes slide down my outfit again. I'm still wearing Patrick's sweatsuit since I'd never made it back to the apartment to change.

The truth is I'm not sure why I'm here beyond getting in a pissing match with my sister. "Me?" I ask innocently. "I have an appointment here. I thought *you* had to meet an old client."

"Just once I'd love it if you didn't make everything about you," she says. Her nostrils flare. I can't believe she'd have the nerve to be angry with me. "And where were you last night anyway?" She glares at my clothes bunched up in my tote and shoots me a knowing look. She rolls her eyes and turns on her heel.

I follow her into the building without answering.

I beat her to the counter. There are two brown-haired white guys in their midthirties at the desk. Their name tags read NICK and ADAM. I flash June's ID, the one I've been using in bars. I smile at her. She flashes mine, the one she obviously picked up off the kitchen counter, where I left it.

Even standing side by side with identification displayed at the same time, we're given sticky name tags with each other's name and nobody notices.

Not that Nick and Adam don't have the exact same face to me.

They take our pictures with a tiny round camera and hand us our sticky name tags. "All right, this one's for . . . Is it Jay-eye Heyoon? Jee . . ."

"June's fine," I tell him, grabbing for it. Our IDs read Ji-young Jayne Baek. And Ji-hyun June Baek, respectively. It's actually not that hard.

In the blown-out security photograph, I'm two little dark eyes in an expanse of white.

I hand June hers. He's only managed to capture the top part of her head. My sister doesn't even get eyes; she's a hairline with a middle part.

We take the elevator, and I follow June into the labyrinthine corridors. It's eerily quiet for how many people there are.

We're silent on our walk. The linoleum floor is glossed to a high sheen. In the too-bright lounge in the waiting area, there's a thin, drawn man with dyed black hair drinking a coconut Bai staring into middle distance. He's propped with a striped cushion on the midcentury sofa and struck with a general air of incredulousness.

June pulls me toward a cluster of chairs as far away from him as possible. "Seriously, why are you here?"

"Why wouldn't I be?"

"Jayne."

"June," I correct her. "My name is June. You can call me Ji-hyun if it makes you feel better."

We watch back-to-back *Property Brothers* episodes without talking. Every single ad is for prescription drugs.

A woman in maroon scrubs calls my name. We both look up and follow her behind the door into a hallway.

We're led to another room, where a tiny woman with hair parted down the middle gets up from behind a desk to greet us. "Hi, Jayne, come in."

"This is June, my sister," says June.

"Her older sister," I tell the doctor, smiling. "I'm sorry I couldn't be here sooner. I had work." I know I'm overexplaining, but part of me is having trouble believing we're doing this.

The doctor's hand is cold when she shakes mine. "Dr. Ramirez."

Dr. Ramirez has huge eyes, made larger by glasses, with a serious face and a tiny mouth. She looks like a friendly mouse. Her nude pantyhose wrinkle slightly at the knees and her severe foamy loafers give her the appearance of someone older, but I'd peg her in her midthirties. She has great eyebrows, full lips, and a reedy voice.

"So, Jayne, how was your week?" Dr. Ramirez takes a seat, gesturing to the leather-backed chairs across from her.

June sits. I sit beside her, reminding myself not to slouch.

"Fine, I guess."

"Did you get a chance to speak to Steph?"

June shrugs insolently. I almost kick her shoes.

"Who's Steph?" I pipe up.

June throws me a sharp look. "She wants me to talk to a counselor."

Dr. Ramirez leans back in her chair. I can't tell if she has eyebags or if she has one of those faces that come with eyebags. Silence settles around us.

"She thinks I need to talk about my feelings before having my uterus removed."

"It's a big decision," says Dr. Ramirez, clasping her hands on her desk. "Of course it's all up to you, but fertility preservation is an option if you wanted to explore it."

My gaze trawls the beige walls around us. June seems to shrink in the seat next to me. I find myself staring at the innocuous Ansel Adams mountain print to Dr. Ramirez's right. This office feels so set designed. None of this feels real. As if the walls will fall away to reveal stage lights and a live studio audience. Dr. Ramirez cannot possibly be a real doctor.

I hadn't given enough thought to this. I presumed I'd come here, terrorize June about her idiot scam, scare her a little with the threat of her stupid baby sister spoiling everything, but this is horrible. I'm struck with self-disgust that I didn't consider the terminal illness part of this whole equation. There's got to be something wrong with me. June was right. I can't actually handle any of this.

Dr. Ramirez turns to me. "Are there any questions you'd like to ask me? Or Jayne . . ." She smiles warmly. It's a jolt to hear her refer to June as me. "It's a lot of information to process at once," she finishes.

I'm dumbfounded by how resigned June seems, how passive. I pull out my phone and hit the voice memo record button. My heart is pounding as I type Jayne as the file name. "I didn't bring a notebook and I want to make sure I remember . . ."

I set it on her desk, with the screen up. Dr. Ramirez smiles. "If it's all right with Jayne."

June shifts beside me. "It's fine."

"Dr. Ramirez, what's going to happen?" My voice is shaking. I have to sit on my hands to stop pulling on my bottom lip.

"The recommended treatment for uterine cancer is surgery. We've recommended a total hysterectomy and bilateral salpingo-oophorectomy."

"Salpingo's a weird word, isn't it?" It's the first thing June's said unprompted since we arrived. "Sounds like a Filipino dessert."

Dr. Ramirez removes her glasses and cleans them with the sleeve of her white coat. Without them her features suddenly recede. She puts them back on and becomes our doctor again. "Totally," I tell her. I don't know what else to say. "With ube or durian or something."

"Totally," echoes June.

I swallow hard.

"What's a bilateral salpingo-oophorectomy?"

"It means they're taking my ovaries," interjects June. "And my uterus. If you didn't know what a hysterectomy was."

"Okay . . ." My knee's shaking so bad, I uncross my legs. The surgery plays like a gory movie in my mind. I imagine the wetness of my sister's organs sliding over each other for a brief second before my focus swings in a wide arc, out of the windows, hurtling away from this room and into outer space.

The black mirror of my phone screen flashes. I'm shocked that it's been recording for seventeen minutes. I understand what June was talking about. How you can comprehend all the words but that the sentences themselves are inconceivable.

"Jayne," says Dr. Ramirez, and I look up sharply, glancing away when I remember who Jayne is in this room. "It's laparoscopic, so it's minimally invasive." Her small hands steady a laminated diagram. Pink. Peach. Red. It occurs to me that the female reproductive system looks like the flux capacitor from *Back to the Future.* There's no way this drawing has anything to do with either of us. I breathe and count what I see.

One: my sister watching the doctor intently.

Two: my sister's chest rising and falling.

Three: my sister in her overalls with her size-six sneaker jogging in place.

It is the foot of a child. *For sale: baby shoes, never worn.*

Dr. Ramirez slices an area on the diagram with her capped pen. "Detaching the uterus . . ."

I'm pulling my lip so hard my eyes water. There's a gummy buildup on the corners of my mouth that I scrape with my thumbnail. It's harrowing. June will be giving birth to her own womb.

Poor June. Poor, poor June.

I wish there were adults present. A mom and dad other than ours.

My older sister is too young for this, but I see the wisdom in her decision not to tell. The only thing that would make this worse is for her to translate to our parents and watch the terror unfold on their faces.

"Wait," I interrupt. June looks up at me dazed, as if she'd forgotten I was there. "Are you saying that the only treatment is to take everything out? Isn't that . . . I don't know, a little drastic? How bad is it? Do you have to do it now?"

"Uterine cancer in your early twenties is rare. There are options to preserve fertility with hormones, which is what we talked about, but that's a deferment of surgery, not an alternative. Eventually Jayne will need the hysterectomy and oophorectomy." Dr. Ramirez keeps referring to her patient by name. It's jarring each time. Maybe it's a med school thing. Maybe it's a bedside manner thing, but it lends a surreal, automated quality to our talk. As if it's prerecorded.

The thought flits into my mind that my sister is just another appointment among ten or fifteen Dr. Ramirez sees in a day.

"But with specialized care with her multidisciplinary team, Jayne could absolutely deliver a healthy baby before surgery."

June laughs, a dry mirthless snort. "Thank you, but I'm not about to get knocked up in the immediate future," says my sister. "I wouldn't even know what to put on my dating profile to requisition sperm like that."

"Jayne," says Dr. Ramirez, this time looking right at me. My blood runs cold. It's as if she knows. Then she turns to her patient.

"Thank you," says June. I know this tone. Her mind's made up. "But you said so yourself. I'm the one making the decisions. It took me forever and a mountain of literal faxes to even get a referral to see you. I'll pass on risking my life for the next few years on the off chance I'll get knocked up." June shakes her head. "I've thought about it. Do the surgery. Just take everything." June's open palm brushes against her middle as if to scoop it out.

"Also." June sighs. "Dr. Ramirez, I'm not trying to be difficult, but don't you think egg freezing is kind of a scam? The actual percentage of live births is, like, maybe eight percent. For thirty grand of drugs and drama?"

"It's about knowing that you have the choice if you want it," says Dr. Ramirez.

"They throw your eggs out like on *Storage Wars* if you accidentally miss a bill."

To her credit, Dr. Ramirez remains completely composed. She nods. "I see."

June flips her neon folder open. It's full of paperwork. Her narrow handwriting is scrawled all over the various bills. "I just want to set a date."

"We can do that."

"Terrific." June riffles through some papers. "And another thing, don't you think it's, I don't know, distasteful to demand the surgery deductible before you'll cut me open?"

Dr. Ramirez places both hands on her desk. She's instantly mouselike again. I imagine her tiny feet dangling in her chair behind her desk.

"You'll have to speak with your insurance carrier and . . ."

"Well." June flips through the reams of printouts until she pulls out what she's looking for. Meanwhile I was convinced my sister wasn't doing anything all day but watching garbage TV. The morass of logistics spread out in her lap is exactly June's wheelhouse. Turns out being sick is a full-time job. "They told me to take it up with you. It's based on hospital policy. I just talked to them"—June confirms it with her notes—"yesterday."

"I'll get a number for you."

"Thank you," says June, putting her folder away. "So, I just have one more question."

"Ask whatever you'd like."

"How much is this going to hurt?"

The question stops my heart.

Dr. Ramirez studies my sister carefully before continuing. "Patients have reported discomfort in the abdomen and shoulder—"

"Hold it right there." June closes her eyes. "Why is it 'discomfort in the abdomen'? It's pain. Do me a favor and just call it pain if it's pain?" Her voice cracks on the final "pain." She opens her eyes.

"Women have reported pain."

June exhales.

"We're basically creating an air pocket in you so that we have room to move around. You're going to feel the effects of that in your abdomen and shoulder. It feels like a soreness in your muscles. You're not used to having air caught in different regions of your body, and that's how it may register. I can't tell you how uncomfor—how much pain you'll experience." She pauses for a moment and takes a deep breath. "You know, we're trained not to use the word 'pain,' but I can see how discrediting that can be."

"It scares the shit out of me," says June. "It makes me feel like you're going to downplay everything because of some malpractice lawsuit and I'm going to be in fucking agony."

"I get that," says Dr. Ramirez, nodding slowly. "So, I'll call it pain."

"It'd make me feel better if you called it fucking agony," says June petulantly.

"Okay," she says. "Patients have reported fucking agony, but honestly"—Dr. Ramirez's shoulders drop—"if you experience what you would characterize as fucking agony, please tell me immediately. You shouldn't be in actual fucking agony, all right?" A tiny hint of a Bronx accent peers out from her doctorial veneer.

That's the moment when I realize that Dr. Ramirez is chill.

"But think about counseling?" Her brown eyes soften. "At least give Steph a call so that if you need her, she's right there. This is a lot."

"I like her," June says as we walk out, tucking her folder under her jacket so it doesn't get wet. "You can tell she kills at poker or something."

"Yeah, she seems cool," I tell her. "She probably drinks whiskey."

"Whiskey neat," she says. "She definitely also cusses like a sailor."

"Definitely."

I don't know what else to say. I root around my brain to see if I can summon any anger at June. I can't.

"Do you still need to grab your stuff?" she asks me when her car arrives. I nod, and she lets me in.

chapter 27

I pull my suitcase out from behind the love seat and fling it open. I can't believe I'm packing again.

June kicks off her shoes, unhooks her overall straps, and leaves the pants in a puddle on the living room floor. She sits heavily on her couch with her eyes closed.

I grab my laundry from her dryer and sit on the floor with my legs crossed, dumping it out in front of me. The last twenty-four hours have felt like a year. I can barely keep my eyes open. I do socks first because they're easiest.

"I got fired," she says. Eyes still closed. "I didn't get laid off. I found out in an office-wide email an hour before they told me."

I stop folding.

She balls her hands and cracks her thumbs under her forefingers the way she always does.

At my eye level, there's a book on her coffee table. It's not an encyclopedia. It's a small hardback. The spine reads *When Breath*

Becomes Air. The title is familiar to me.

"They called security while I packed up my desk."

I imagine her being frog-marched out of the building.

June leans over and picks up the book from the table. There's a 30-percent-off sticker on the front, and the back shows a black-and-white author photo of a doctor in hospital scrubs. She starts tapping the hardback against her bare knee.

"They said I displayed a lack of understanding of the company culture," she says, and then sneers. "Code for: my boss hated me."

I hold my tongue. There's no shortage of people getting laid off all over the world, but of course June's firing is about a personal grudge.

"Believe me," she says, bitterly. "It wasn't about my performance history, that's for damned sure. He was just mad that I wouldn't suck his dick. Shit was fucking high school all over again."

I don't have the energy for this.

June's voice shakes. "People hate me for no reason," she says, doing that nodding thing again, as if she's convincing herself.

Tap, tap, tap. She keeps knocking the book harder and harder on her kneecap. I remember it now, how the man who wrote it died. He was a cancer doctor who died of cancer. I want to grab it from her and fling it across the room. It's maddening that she'd rather read about it than talk to anyone.

I make myself take a moment before I respond. "That sounds tough," I tell her evenly. I've been hearing some version of this refrain my entire life. June's always right. It doesn't matter what it is—daylight savings, parking restrictions, the neighbor's newspaper—everyone else is a chump and she's right. It's as if she can't concede the statistical improbability of being correct 100 percent of the time. I peel my T-shirt off her towel, the static electricity crackling. I remind myself to get dryer sheets before remembering that it's not my problem anymore.

"Are you fucking kidding me?" she balks, voice strangled, agog. She flops her hands against her naked thighs.

"What?"

"*That sounds tough?* The fuck am I supposed to do with that? I confide in you about the greatest humiliation of my life and it sounds tough? Are you even listening to me?"

"Fuck, June. God." I hurl a sock ball at the large window, where it *thunks* feebly.

She sits up, openmouthed, head swiveling to the window, then back at me as if I'd tossed a brick through it.

I roll my eyes. "What do you want? It's always the same fucking story with you. What did you do? You definitely *did* something."

"Just be on my side!" she yells, face purpling. "Just once."

"No. You're delusional!" I uncross my legs, ready to pounce if this escalates. "You did something! Just like you did something to me." It feels good to say it out loud.

"Oh my God, what do you want?" she says, throwing back her head. She looks like her stupid avatar.

"Fuck you, June." The gall makes me want to knock that smug expression off her face.

"Two grand." Her gaze locks onto mine. "Just let me pay you. Two thousand dollars or however much the fuck it takes you to stop crying when I have way bigger things to worry about. Empathy? Ever heard of it? If you could just think of someone else for one fucking second, you'd see that this has nothing to do with you. I don't have a job, asshole. And I have cancer. For once there's something you can do for somebody else and you're bitching and whining about it. Nothing's changed. You don't have to lift a finger, no one has to know, and you're still being a little bitch."

I get to my feet, the rage swelling my chest. If we were younger,

I'd be going after her hair, her clothes. I'd smash her head on the cof-fee table. There's no way she's turning this around on me.

She stares up at me from the couch.

"No," I snap, balling my hands, searching for something hard to launch at her. My eyes land on the cancer book, but I can't take the irony. "I won't shut up. You don't get to tell me to shut up. This is about you, not me. About how you're fucked up."

"You wouldn't even be in New York if it weren't for me," she rages. "Who the fuck are you to tell me what's not okay? Just look at your life. You have no home—"

June pushes herself up from her low couch, rising in her granny panties. She almost falters, and the whole thing would be funny if she didn't have murder in her eyes.

"You have no home," she shouts, sticking out her thumb, count-ing my faults. "School is bullshit because you're too chickenshit to commit to a real major." Her index finger snaps out, her hand a gun in my face. "And you have zero focus because every ounce of energy is spent alternately obsessing about your stupid body or chasing after some boy." That's three. "Where the hell do you get off coming to my doctor's appointment with your smug stupid face and your dumb bag in some Tinder dipshit's clothes . . . ?"

"*Your* doctor's appointment?" I counter, looming over her. It's times like these that I love outsizing my older sister. "I went because you need help, you delusional bitch. You practically black out when you're there. You said so yourself and now I know why. You just sit there pouting and rolling your eyes like you've been called to the prin-cipal's office. That woman is trying to help you. I am trying to help you." My throat strains from the effort.

"You?" she taunts. "You're more help to me when you stay out of my fucking way. Christ, Jayne. Look at you."

Her voice catches and she stuns me by bursting into tears. "Fuck," she says, arms finally falling to her sides. "How are you going to help me?" At this she covers her eyes with her palms, shoulders heaving in heart-wrenching sobs. "I have literal fucking cancer but we both know . . . we both know that you're sicker than me."

I'm dazed. Blood is hammering in my ears. She's always been conniving and ruthless—no one fights dirtier than June—but I'm thunderstruck that she'd turn this around to humiliate me. I wonder how far she'll take it. Whether she'll speak the words we both know she can't take back.

"You're fucking insane," I seethe. I shake my head pityingly. I back away, almost tripping over my suitcase.

"Mom and Dad might be fucking blind, but I know," she says in a low voice, gaze unflinching.

I hold my breath, willing her to shut up and spare me.

June sniffs hard and composes herself, wiping her cheeks roughly.

"Look," she croaks. "Your part's done. You can forgive me or not—I don't give a shit—but I did it this way to protect you. All of you. My way is the only way it was going to be okay."

"Yeah, well, what if you die?"

She blanches. "Wow, thanks a lot."

"Seriously, what if you die?"

"I'm not going to die," says June, catching her breath. "Besides, if I die, lucky you. I'm leaving you everything."

I don't even realize I'm crying until I taste salt on my lips.

"I'm not going to die," she says again. Quieter this time.

"June." I say it slowly. "If you die, then Jayne Ji-young Baek is dead. I'll be dead at the hospital. They'll file a death certificate in *my name*. I'll be dead at school. New York City, New York State, the United States of America—they'll all think I'm dead. Your will won't matter. You're the one who'll be alive in name, June. It'll be me and Mom's dead baby who will be gone. I'll be fucking trapped in some nameless purgatory. I'll be some in-between ghost."

June's eyes widen. The color drains from her face. She really is so smart at a lot of things and dumb at others.

"Fuck," she says.

"If you die, I die." I spell it out for her.

"If I die, you die," follows June.

She sits back down on the couch.

I take my place on the floor. All the piles of clothes blur in front of me. I fold a pair of her white underpants as small as they will go.

"You'd better not fucking die, June, I swear to God."

For once my sister doesn't have a response.

chapter 28

When I meet June at the Delta terminal three days later, I'm no longer angry. In fact, I'm no longer much of anything.

I hadn't realized the extent to which I'd grown accustomed to my sister's apartment until I went back to mine. This time it wasn't just a dead roach that greeted me when I opened the door. It was a dead roach and the startling movement of a red baby roach in my peripheral vision. Until that moment, I hadn't known roaches scaled walls. I watched as it hesitated at the perpendicular obstruction of the ceiling. But then it pushed ahead, hanging upside down, before clinging stubbornly for dear life, unable to move forward.

I'm nowhere near as determined.

I almost capitulate and apologize so I can return to June's before remembering that I'm the one who's mad.

That first night was death by a trillion cuts. I'd left June's in the midafternoon when she fell asleep for a nap so we wouldn't have to say goodbye.

Back at my apartment, the heat came on. Finally. Except I'd forgotten that the warmth I'd prayed so fervently for has no thermostat. Unlike at June's, where there was a central command system operated by smartphone, which glowed blue with exactly your desired temperature, I had baseboards that encircled me in a ring of fire, and they were outside of my control. The exposed pipe in the living room that stands stupidly close to the only available outlet fills with steam, hissing angrily and scalding the tops of my knuckles whenever I have to unplug anything.

I didn't sleep at all. I was tormented by a persistent, arrhythmic clicking in the radiator that was so loud, I found myself listening for it but managing to be startled awake by it each time.

By the morning, when my moldy shower curtain clasped my leg with cold, slimy insistence just as shampoo slid into my eyes, I cried. I sobbed ramrod straight, unable to lean against the tile or collapse to the floor in a proper cinematic meltdown because every surface seemed so filthy.

Jeremy's comings and goings only added to the psychological turmoil. The second day, I didn't leave school until late into the evening, completing all my homework in the library. I never knew when he'd be home, and I'd slowly open the door, searching for evidence of him. I scoured the room. He'd rearrange small things for maximum unraveling. A single mug that I'd left in the sink appeared on the counter. His vintage Lakers sweatshirt migrated from couch to chair.

In my sleep-deprived fever dream, I caught myself believing it to be the handiwork of a particularly lethargic poltergeist. But the lingering smell gave him away, Le Labo Santal 33. It was olfactory retribution for my ylang-ylang shower spray. It worked every time. I felt instantly, violently ill when I'd smell it. My head would whip around in a paranoid frenzy whenever I caught it on other people at school or on the street.

When I told Mari at the store that I needed her to cover me because I was going home for the weekend, she asked if everything was all right. I burst into tears. She ushered me into the back and let me cry all over her shiny, lemony-smelling hair as she hugged me. I wanted so bad to tell her that my sister had cancer that I could taste the words in my mouth. I could imagine her understanding it all and knowing exactly what to say. Instead she just held me and gave me an Ativan.

When I retired that night, the apartment was filled with an acrid, warning smell. The charger cube for my phone had melted from the radiator pipe, so I cried again. By the time Patrick canceled our dinner after seeming what I felt to be aloof in his texts for the previous three days, notably from the hours of midnight to 3:00 a.m., which to be clear, was my most vulnerable shift, I was unsurprised. I could barely remember a life that hadn't been a blistering hellscape.

When he texted his apologies—he'd had a deadline—I was lost to Terrace House reruns tented under a humid sheet with every square inch of my head and body covered as protection from falling infant roaches.

He'd called twice later that night, but I let it go to voicemail.

I listened to his messages over and over, waiting for the pipes to clang, checking his Instagram stories to verify his whereabouts, but of course he was too sneaky to post anything.

He said he wanted to see me for lunch before my flight, but I preferred to remain deeply offended yet demonstrably chill on text.

"It's work!" I'd told him zestily. "It happens!"

He should have known how sad I was from the exclamation points.

By the morning I was due at the airport, there was no water. I tried the bathroom first as the pipes groaned, yielding nothing. The kitchen faucet emitted a rust-colored trickle. It was just as well. I felt strangely clean. It was clear that my soul had left my body.

"You look nice," I tell June when I see her at the gate.

"Thanks," says June. It feels like it's been a month since I've seen her. It's oddly reassuring that in her black suit and tall, spiky heels, she's back to the June costume I'm most familiar with, the version of her I know least well. She may as well be a memoji. I'm still in sweats.

"I need to grab something to eat," she says, nodding to the ambiguously European restaurant. Watching her heels clack, I marvel at her hard-shell suitcase, which glides alongside her. In airport taxonomies, we don't at all look as though we belong together. I wonder if she ever feels as bewildered by me.

"When'd you get here?"

I arrived three hours ago, trying to figure out who the fuck David Buxbaum—the man I've been writing rent checks to—might be. I hadn't realized that flushing the toilet to see if it worked was the one flush I'd have. I brushed my teeth at the airport but June doesn't need to know that. "I just got here," I lie.

She nods her approval. "A half hour before is plenty," she says. "Especially if you have CLEAR." My sister is such a specific breed of asshole. As if I can afford CLEAR.

We sit at the bar on leather-backed stools and look at our phones. The number I have for the broker rang and rang—ominously—without ever going to voicemail. The text I sent remains green.

She orders a glass of white wine and a pressed sandwich. I order a water. She asks for our check with the food. I somehow feel as though I'm on a terrible first date. With my sister.

It's too bright in here. Too loud. Everyone around me seems unhappy in distinct ways.

In the little seating pods to the right of us, clustered around a café, are stooped heads with noise-canceling headphones, scrolling through iPads and phones, hiding behind sunglasses, sitting under hats while flipping through magazines, and sprinkling chips, candy, trail mix, and beef jerky into their mouths. Down the bar there are huge, sweaty glasses of beer, wine, cocktails, french fries, calamari rings, and a thick slice of chocolate cake.

Airport departure halls are like enormous day care centers where every adult baby has a credit card.

Even still, I would kill for a pound of Reese's Pieces right now.

"How do you feel about seeing Mom and Dad?" June asks.

"Fine." I shrug.

Strangely, I'd thought about this trip only as far as seeing June at the airport. My brain may as well be an animal in a carrier. I can sense that I'm going somewhere and that it's most likely going to be unpleasant, but there's nothing I can do about it. I don't even know what to imagine. I've never gone home before. I was only ever there already.

"Fine?" She flips open the black pleather check folder and scribbles the credit card receipt haphazardly.

I gaze at the receipt. Her signature's a mess. It's a cross between a tilted Z and an N.

"*That* is not your signature." I snort.

"Sure is," she says.

I pull out a black spiral notebook from my bag, open it up to a blank page, click my favorite black metal Caran d'Ache, and scrawl a swooping cursive J. I add a Y with a jagged series of barely distinguishable loops that bookends in an elegant K. I do it over. I love signing my name. It's aesthetically pleasing and precise. It signals good taste. It makes me feel well-bred.

"Do you even know how to sign my name?" You'd think someone who'd stolen someone's identity would do a little homework.

"We've got face recognition and chip cards. Nobody gives a shit about signatures." She takes the pen from me. "This," she says, "is my real signature."

She scribbles what could be a *J* and a series of hillocks that could be anything. She does it again. And again. Each one is different. She side-eyes me. "You can be vain about anything, can't you?"

"I read that if you turn the paper upside down, it's easier to copy." I flip my notebook. "Upside down you can focus on the shape and not what the word's supposed to say."

"You idiot." June snorts. She sips the last of her wine. "First of all, it's not like I'm going to be at the hospital, like, uh, hold on, Doc. I have to turn this page upside down. Besides, I'm the one who taught you that. The upside-down paper thing."

A memory scissors through. "Treat it like a drawing," June's saying. It's the two of us at the dining room table, and I'm copying Mom's signature from her checkbook duplicates. I'm signing June's marine biology field trip to Galveston. Mom and Dad were at work, and I'm getting scared reading the small print. The school claimed no liability in cases of accidental drowning, allergic reactions, or any other issues arising from any activities whatsoever. "It's only, like, three hours away," says June. "But we're supposed to be back at eight, so if I'm not back by . . ." She shrugs, without meeting my eyes. "Maybe call Ms. Hoover at school. Or the cops." I'd thought it was weird that she'd asked for my help until I realized what she was really doing. She was telling me where she'd be because she wanted someone to know. Someone to worry about her if she needed them to.

"You wanted me to know," I tell her.

June looks up from her sandwich. She's plucking out sprigs of arugula. Arugula, raw onions, beets, all June's enemies. "Know what?" She takes a bite; it smells garlicky.

"You wanted me to find out," I tell her. "You need my help. You just didn't know how to ask for it."

"What are you talking about?" she says, chewing wetly. Sometimes eating with June makes me want to gag. It's always so anatomical.

I finish my water and shake the ice cubes at the bottom of the glass. Then I pinch the stray arugula off her plate between my thumb and forefinger and put them in my mouth.

"Fucking disgusting," says June to me, shaking her head. "Chew away from me. I can smell it."

I chew right up in her ear. "If you didn't want me to find out that you're snaking my identity, you wouldn't have told me you were sick in the first place."

I know my sister. She could have just as easily signed the permission slip herself. We were constantly filling out our own permission slips and tardiness notices. June wanted to tell me where she'd be that day without having to tell me.

"You don't think you'd *notice* if I had cancer?" She pushes me away from her, eyes flicking skyward.

"You *could have* hidden it from me." Before the confrontation, before she invited me over, she absolutely could have pulled it off. "Instead you came to me. And then you let me move in. You *handed* me your mail."

"You're insane."

"You need me."

She snorts.

"You need me emotionally," I tut, with a sympathetic little frown. "It's okay that you need me. You don't have to admit it. Your subconscious spoke for you. I heard you loud and clear."

"Bullshit." She stabs the air. "If I didn't save your ass by letting you stay at my house, you wouldn't have found out any of this."

"I don't believe you, June," I singsong. "You wanted help from your little baby sister."

"Shut up, Jayne," she says, and grabs her purse and suitcase. I watch as she storms off and joins the service desk line at the gate.

"Call me June," I tell her. "It's okay. This is a safe space."

I've never beaten her at an argument. I'm high with the thrill of it. I eat the rest of her sandwich innards. They're delicious. Like victory.

When the upgrade announcements come on, she boards with first class without looking back at me.

It's fine. I board eighteen classes after my sister, and when I see her, she doesn't look up from her magazine. I mush the side of her face with my palm as I'm walking by in the aisle. "You're welcome," I tell her.

chapter 29

When June and I arrive, we know the drill. She's waited for me at the gate even though we're not officially speaking. "Dad." June phones him as soon as I disembark. "We're here."

It's funny. No matter how successful June becomes or however many ride sharing apps spring up, Mom and Dad will forever insist on picking her up from the airport. It's my first time coming home from college, and the irony doesn't escape me.

Today is the day I became an adult because I had to get picked up by my parents.

The trick is, we have to exit from the second floor in departures. That way they don't have to spend money on parking. That's the deal. The great hack.

We step out into the muggy night. The air's bloated and cloudy with mist and the sky is navy and huge. I breathe deep. Even with the blond woman smoking a skinny cigar next to us by the no smoking sign, the air is incredible. It's rich and earthy, almost as if it had to travel great distances to arrive at my nose. It smells as if the sun's still out. I take off my puffy coat and wad it into my bag.

I search the ramp for their car.

The quiet is deafening. As though the sky is filling my ears with huge nothingness and swirling into my brain. A half-terminal away, Dad's rectangular Volvo headlights glow larger. I know it's him because he also has his fog lights on. The shotgun-side door opens and shuts in shadow, as Mom's tiny silhouette hops out while the car still rolls.

"Jesus." We both say it. At the same time.

This is everything you need to know about our mother. That she'd exit a moving vehicle because she believes she's faster on foot.

"Is this it?" she says as a greeting. She's so much smaller than I'd remembered. And she's dressed in a pink polo with a popped collar and black slacks. It's not only the glasses that have changed, but her hair is different, pulled back in a black scrunchie. I feel unnerved by the changes. As if my nostalgia's been fueled by the wrong information.

My sister bear hugs her and gets in the car. "What do you mean 'Is this it?' The bags or the state of your daughters?" she retorts in Korean. June's Korean is flawless. There's something in the age differ-ence when we moved to America that allows her to joke freely with them. Mom and Dad chuckle.

I don't know that I've spoken Korean since I left for college.

"Hey, Dad," I call out in English to the front seat.

Dad's wearing transition lenses, so his eyes are hidden when he waves back in the rearview and smiles. "Hello, Jayne," he responds in English. Then he turns up the stereo. A dulcet, piano-backed baritone fills the car. The lyrics are about some woman crying in a window. I don't know exactly when, but a few years ago, Dad started humming or crooning all the time. We didn't grow up with music in the house, but by senior year they'd started listening to Korean songs that some-one from church put on a thumb drive for them. Old hits from their childhood or random French tunes, like warbly Édith Piaf. Mom gets hammy for "La Vie en Rose" with her phonetically learned lyrics.

Our mother wordlessly passes back bottles of lukewarm water and a pump-top Purell.

The familiar action pushes up against the pressure already thick and uncomfortable in the back of my throat. The thousands of times Mom has turned to us. Me in the seat behind her, June behind Dad. I've missed her so much, I want to crush her in my arms.

I lean back into my seat, the roiling unease building as we climb the highway seemingly to shoot off into heaven. Some people get nervous when they lose their bearings, when they're out to sea and can't spy land anymore. That's how the Texas sky has always felt to me. As if the world is falling away all around me.

It's not just the sky. It's the negative space of the quiet, too. I will never be found here. It seems as though there are no other cars on the road. If the world ended, we'd be the last to know. We wouldn't even know we were lost.

The familiar pyramid bank building with its stacked, setback ter-races glides into view on my right. The mirrored Spectrum building that looks straight out of *Tron* slips by after that. It's distressing that the architecture of a town where I've spent most of my life barely comprises a skyline. A pair of churches that seem to claim no specific faith other than worshipping at the altar of bigness loom ahead.

At home, my true home, in New York, I overhear people com-plaining all the time about the city, how it's busy, that the din of traffic makes it impossible to hear their own thoughts. This is pre-cisely why Texas scares me. The silence makes my thoughts too noisy to bear.

I search the horizon. *I am only visiting,* my brain tells my body. I push my Brooklyn apartment out of my mind. My stomach growls. I attempt to locate myself.

One: highway.

Two: Taco Cabana.

"I'm gonna kill a bean and cheese," whispers June as the neon sign sails by.

Three: the back of Mom's perm.

Four: Dad singing.

Five: June looking out the navy-blue window.

This is why I'm here. My sister needs our family. And I am a decoy.

"Get over," says Mom, patting Dad's forearm and pointing to the left. "This man has no designs on changing lanes. He's left his blinker on like a lunatic."

My mom is the worst back-seat driver. Her road rage becomes truly homicidal when it's secondhand road rage.

"He forgot he switched it on," says Dad good-naturedly.

"Impossible. He'd hear it." She taps my father's forearm repeatedly. "Okay, now. Get over."

Dad gets over.

"If this psychopath can pass the driver's test, you'd think Jayne could pull it together," says June.

That does the trick. I can sense the tension building in Mom's knotted shoulders.

The three of us may as well count it down under our breaths: three, two, one . . .

"Jayne, I bet you could get your license on this trip if you tried," says Mom.

There it is.

I'd kick my sister if it hadn't gotten Mom off Dad's back while he's driving.

"Dad's car is for dummies," says Mom. "It beeps whenever another car's nearby, and there's a rearview camera for parking. It practically drives itself. You could do it. It's so easy. Ji-young, you absolutely cannot let this develop into a phobia." She says "phobia" in English.

"Fifteen-year-olds can drive, Jayne," says June.

I search for an ally, but my father's eyes are impassive in the rearview.

With my screen brightness set low, I check to make sure there are available cars near us on Lyft. I download Uber again just in case. If I need to make a getaway, I can. I go to Patrick's page and deep-like a post instead of responding to his latest text. I like the way it looks on my phone. That the last text from him was asking whether or not I'd arrived safely. This way I can respond whenever. Plus, I want him to stay worried about me.

I'm bucked by the Volvo's wheels bumping over the tracks as the gate to our neighborhood opens, and a tightness rushes my chest. The sense memory is almost violent.

When we first arrived from Korea, eighteen hours after we'd left, it had been evening then, too. That first night, in our rental car, a stupidly big SUV, on our way to our new house, we were tired and uneasy. June and I watched silently while our parents fell into child-like helplessness at the car rental place, gesturing, pointing at pictures, broken English clattering conspicuously around them, grinning while muttering gravely to each other in Korean.

I looked out the window as we drove.

I'd never known true night before this; it was so dense and black. The quiet was unsettling, and as we turned off the deserted highway onto gentle pitch-black hills, Dad halted at a stop sign for a long time.

I'd thought he'd grasped the full weight of his mistake, but instead he whispered with wonder in his voice, "Do you see that?" He pointed through the windshield and flickered his high beams, and we saw them out there. Their outlines.

"Are those deer?" Mom asked.

We waited for them to pass. "It's a whole family," June breathed excitedly. I felt as though the car was running out of air. I couldn't believe we were expected to make a life here. Out in the wilderness. With literal fucking deer.

The quiet screamed in my head.

When we turned onto our street, our tiny brick house stared back at us with white-shuttered eyes. It looked like a home in a picture book. We thought it was hilarious that it had a real pitched roof, the kind of house we'd only seen in cartoons. It wasn't until daylight that we realized that our brick house wasn't brick at all. It was brick veneer. Gift wrapping studded with brick tread that was only a half-inch deep. And our home sweet home was a replica of every third in the sprawling anonymous subdivision erected hastily to accommodate the air force base nearby.

"You haven't had dinner, have you?" Mom asks, struggling with our luggage. She grabs the suitcases, one in each hand. We know better than to offer help.

"I'm starving," says June.

"I knew you would be." Mom climbs the short flight of stairs into the house, sets her shoes aside, and presses the button for the garage door to shut.

I follow them in. The garage opens directly into the kitchen, with a pass-through to the living room and the dining room on the left. I'm unprepared for the smells. I'm viscerally transported by the scent of Mom's floral perfume overlain with the nuttiness of rice and a metallic whiff of oily fish. I feel my fingernails dig into my palms.

The house is a museum, the bright-white overhead lighting only adding to the ghostly quality. Each stick of furniture is exactly where it's always been. Chair legs eating into their assigned grooves in the cream-colored carpet, black leather couch settled in the middle, the reclining massage chair in the corner. The enormous lacquered coffee table is covered with a lace tablecloth and a pane of glass sandwiched on top. It's still there, seemingly petrified. A setting indifferent to its inhabitants, one that will outlive us all.

My eye lands on the kitchen counter, on a rectangular vase that's filled with easily a hundred pens. I'd bet money that a third have dried out. The vase sits in a shallow wooden tray that also corrals several bottles of vitamins and supplements and a green-lidded square Tupperware container filled with condiment packets. I flip over a blister tub of Smucker's jelly with a peel-back lid. My parents don't eat jelly. It expired four years ago. There's also a stack of *Reader's Digest*s that have been there since I can remember. I'm tempted to believe they were there when we moved in.

I've always associated this kind of light hoarding with being Korean. My parents' scrupulous scraping and saving was mirrored by every other church family whose homes we visited. Their love of containers. Takeout napkins stacked and socked into holders. Kikkoman soy sauce packets were gold since Kari-Out was watered down. Both were diligently stored. Golf balls were gathered from the green, rinsed and collected. Ingenious contraptions involving clothespins and wire hangers were strung up to dry herbs, vegetables, and flowers.

So many rosaries draped throughout.

"Let's see," Mom says, inspecting us as she slips into house shoes. "Are you thinner or fatter?"

She reaches over and lifts my sweatshirt to peer at my midsection. I instinctively suck in my gut and shrink back.

"We're exactly the same, Mom." June rolls her eyes and washes her hands in the kitchen sink.

"You should have seen the way your mother started cooking when she heard you were coming, Ji-young," says Dad, clapping me on the shoulder. "It's all your favorites. You'd think you were getting married."

"Nonsense," says Mom sharply, swatting my father and putting on a green apron. "I've been cooking as I normally do. You're acting as if I starve you. The way I labor over your breakfast, lunch, and dinner. You eat wonderful meals every day of your life."

"It's true," he says, winking over her shoulder at me. "We're all very lucky."

"Did you at least make some of my favorites too?" asks June. Mom ignores her.

It's stifling in here. And loud. Dad's switched on the TV, a flat Samsung LED the size of a full mattress that's set to stream Korean television from dubiously legal sites. A US golf tournament in Arizona has traveled all the way to Seoul to be commentated by Korean sportscasters to find my parents in Texas. The origin of the setup is a mystery to me. They can't restart their router or personalize settings on their phones. June keeps their Apple IDs on a Post-it on her fridge in New York.

I watch June and Dad, framed by the pass-through. It's as if I'm watching a television show of people watching a television show.

June looks good, I decide. Passably healthy in her trim suit. My hand travels to my stomach, gauging the way it fills my cupped palm.

I tip my suitcase over and unzip it, pulling out a light, cotton house dress. I slip into the downstairs bathroom, closing the door behind me. The light here, too, is unforgiving. I lift the hoodie over my head, turning sideways and tiptoeing to see as much of me in my tank top in the mirror. I pee, engage my core, then look at myself again. I turn to the other side to check the thickness of that arm. I'm grateful that my roomy navy smock has sleeves. I don't show Mom my arms. I don't remember the last time she saw my naked body.

And then I do.

Of course I do. Five years ago. My face burns at the memory of the pale-purple silk, crinkly and delicate in my hands. I was swaying side to side. I was too old to be trying on her hanbok. The dress was voluminous, like crinoline, and princessy, with trillions of gathers in the Empire-waisted pinafore. The skirt tied in the back with thin silk strings, and the jeogori—the long-sleeved bolero jacket of the formal gown—tied in front with a full, wide sash. I felt so pretty.

The door opened. I hadn't heard them come home, hadn't thought to lock it, and I saw the circle of her pale face in the mirror like a moon hung above my own round face. I have no idea how long she stood there, but I'll never forget her eyes. They landed on my hands, which held the top closed because it was drawn too tight across my widening back and wouldn't fasten over my boobs.

My hands drop. Mouth hung open. The moment seemed to smear around us, unending. I was horrified that she'd caught me doing something as silly as dress-up, so obviously pretending to be her and so obviously failing, but part of me wanted to show her. Even lit with shame, I'd held hope. In that beat when no one spoke, I allowed myself to think that my mother might say I looked lovely. That her eyes would soften when she realized how badly I wanted the dress. That I wanted anything of hers.

That's when she slapped me. Straight across the face with no hesitation as hard as she could.

I dropped to the floor, tasting metal from the force of the fall, still looking at the scene through the glass. I held my cheek, pedaling my sock-clad feet, digging my heels into the carpet so I could get away from her. The layers of skirt crumpled beneath me, dress straps biting into my shoulders. It had to be a misunderstanding. My instinct was to tell her it was me. I heard myself whimpering. Pleading. Imploring her to see. I thought she'd be filled with gut-wrenching regret when she realized what she'd done, when she'd see who I was.

Instead she pointed at me, eyes gleaming, dark as holes.

"You girls don't get to have everything," she'd screamed before collapsing onto her knees, hiding her face as she bawled. I had never before seen my mother cry. "Take it off," she pleaded into her hands, and I did. Hurriedly. Ears ringing.

My fingers were numb and alien as they fumbled with the front sash. I was trying to go fast, desperate not to tear the fabric, reaching behind me to undo the tricky knot in the back. I threw the jacket on her bed, unslung the straps of the skirt. I grabbed my sweatpants and held them against my body, hiding as much as I could. I kept my face turned away.

I left Mom in a heap. Afraid to look at her, desperate not to confront the disgust in her eyes a second time. I was sick with remorse. I was so glad June wasn't home to see my total humiliation. I closed Mom's bedroom door in the dark hall just in time to hear Dad close the door to his office and lock it.

Two weeks later, Mom left.

I knew it was my fault, and I didn't tell June.

When I emerge from the bathroom, sweatshirt pressed against me, Mom's right there. I startle. I freeze as she reaches over to finger the hem of my dress. "Is this cheap or expensive?" she asks. The truth is that it's both. It's from an extortionate Japanese designer. I stood in line for seventy-five minutes to buy it at a sample sale. "Cheap," I tell her, letting out the breath I'd been holding. I know better than to get into a conversation about how I've gotten ripped off.

"Good," she says. "I was going to say it looks cheap." Mom ducks her head and *licks* the fabric. "See," she says. "The way it discolors when you sweat. It's not at all practical." She then scrunches it into a fist to watch it wrinkle. "And it's so hard to maintain. Is it dry-clean only?"

I have no idea. "No."

"Because even if it is, I'd bet I could put it in the cold cycle and it would be just as good." I make a mental note to never change out of it. I can't give her a chance to test her theory. If it shrinks or discolors, it'll be my fault. Once she disintegrated a bias-cut silk sundress with straps strung of semiprecious stones and she accused me of wearing clothes that were capricious, unserious. Most of Mom's theories are like witch trials.

I follow her small shoulders and perm back into the kitchen, wondering how it would feel to be touched by my mother without bracing for criticism.

"Set the table," she instructs in Korean.

"Thanks, Jayne. I love it," says Dad, in English. I whip around. He's holding what appears to be a red, cellophane-covered ceramic golf bag. I'm guessing it's a mug.

"There are chocolate golf balls and matching tees in the bottom," says June. I take it it's from both of us. "Sorry we missed Father's Day," she continues. We don't do Father's Day. May fifth is Children's Day in Korea, so we usually do something special for all of us, since Cinco de Mayo is huge in Texas. I widen my eyes at June. It's insane to me that they don't see right through her sentimentality.

"Jayne, please," says Mom, regarding me with impatience. I have no clue how I've managed to disappoint her in the last ten seconds. "The table?" she reminds me with a sigh in her voice.

I snap the silverware drawer open. I'm confused by the lack of matching chopsticks. I search around the sink, greeted by the row of inside-out Ziploc freezer bags, handwashed and tented. Their logos have been rubbed off from reuse.

"Dishwasher," says Dad. I reach in, remembering June's detergent pods and half-full loads. She's too busy talking to look at me. I grab utensils, making sure the chopsticks have mates.

Mom posts up in front of the refrigerator, pulling out an infinite number of shallow dishes, setting them on the table behind her as if there's an assembly line of factory workers inside the appliance handing them out.

"I'm glad you're home," she says abruptly. When she swallows hard, I look away.

I precisely remember the day Mom left. There's that Maya Angelou quote how people will forget what you said, people will forget what you did, but people will never forget how you made them feel. For a few hours, I felt my mother's love for me in a deep and profound way, and then she was gone.

That whole morning had been dreamlike. It was the first time I skipped school, so the day's events stuck out even before I knew it for the day it would become. I couldn't believe how easy it was to cut class. I felt stupid that it had never occurred to me to do before. I wonder if that's how Mom felt when she got to where she was headed. Whether she realized how arbitrary it was to stay in one place when she could just as easily be in another.

She didn't seem surprised when I walked back into the house

three hours after getting on the bus. A girl I'd newly become friends with by our mutual appreciation of thrifted Doc Martens was leaving with her boyfriend, and I'd impulsively asked for a ride. I rode in the back of the truck with my eyes closed.

I came through the front door and was entranced by the aroma of cooked food. The dining table was set, not the kitchen table or the squat, lacquered foldout we sometimes used on the floor, and it was laden with delicious treats. It was as if I were happening upon a cottage in the woods in a fairy tale. I wondered who she was expecting.

I could sense someone in the house, but the TV wasn't on. I walked upstairs. My mother turned to face me. She looked beautiful in the late-morning light. She was dressed in a white bra and a simple gray skirt, as if she were going to work in an office. I was astonished. It was Mom, but I'd caught her in another life. A secret one. As though she played a mother in my movie, but here I was, watching her in another film entirely.

It had been so long since I'd seen her out of the wrinkle-resistant polyester slacks she bought at Costco. Her hair was pulled back in a silver clip. She even seemed to move differently.

There was an open suitcase on the bed. It was small, bright green. It usually sat on the floor of her closet. The part of the closet I wasn't allowed in. I knew better than to ask where she was going. She wouldn't tell me, and I longed to earn her affections for not asking.

She held up a jewel-toned silk square to the light. "Do you remember when you'd use this scarf to make a little boddari?" Even her voice seemed different. Happier somehow. Breathier. "You were always so keen to leave."

I'd been steering clear of her when it was just the two of us, her rage for the hanbok incident fresh in my memory, the heat still stinging my cheek, but I sensed an invitation. The acknowledgment of a special occasion. A parallel universe. I walked through the portal and sat on her bed, careful not to rumple the clothes laid out there, flattened as if intended for a paper doll.

I was hungry for her to tell me anything. Mom was unsentimental. Heartachingly disinterested in us. Rarely nostalgic. Halmoni was kind when she came. Slipping us crisp banknotes and patting our cheeks as I pleaded with my eyes, questions leaping at my throat. I couldn't understand why everything was a secret. Why everything I knew about my mom was ill gotten. I spied on her at the organ at church one time as she played a full classical song without making a single mistake, stepping on the pedals at all the right parts. She'd never once played for us before. And I'd seen old-fashioned black silk stockings with a garter belt rolled up carefully in her underwear drawer, hidden away and speaking to a version of her that I'd never know and would never become.

"What is it?" she asked me in Korean.

Mom slipped on a silky ivory blouse. I imagined it felt cool on her bare arms. She was backlit, and even with her C-section scar that I knew was underneath her skirt, I thought she was the most beautiful woman in the world. She's always been the perfect size. So dainty. The small bones that protruded from her skin were breathtaking. She had nimble hands and tiny feet, with eyes that were the biggest of all of ours even without surgery.

"I almost fainted," I told her. Quickly adding, "They sent me to the nurse, and she sent me home." I didn't tell her that I'd deliberately not eaten since dinner *the day before* yesterday. That it was an unspoken pact between me and my new friends. Toward the end of freshman year, one of us had gotten *thinthinthin*. Only I knew her secret. How she ate everything and then un-ate it. Hit reset. We'd never talked about it, but I heard her. And I know she wanted me to ask, so I didn't. Instead, I'd watch the door in the bathrooms at school, at diners, turning on the tap as a warning when someone else would come in. I ignored the repeated flushing, the sour smell of her hair and her breath. I loved studying her, both of us pretending I wasn't. Secrets are like wishes. Everyone knows they don't work if you tell. But if you really want them to gain power, you can't acknowledge that they even exist.

When Mom left, my secret kept me safe.

"You don't feel warm," she said, absently cupping my cheek.

I closed my eyes when she touched me, enjoying the whiff of jasmine and white flowers. I leaned into her cool hand. When I was young, I couldn't fall asleep unless I was rubbing her earlobe. I still remember how I worried the tender flesh between my thumb and forefinger, the nubbin of ear piercing scar lulling me. June did the same thing, tugging the back of Mom's neck, but she'd been bumped from our mother's lap when I was born.

She pulled away and turned to the window. I watched the delicate beads of her spine. I loved observing my mother, as unknowable as she was. The way she held her pinkie aloft while arranging things into a silk pouch, which she laid in her suitcase. I watched myself in the mirror, straightening my posture to appear leaner when I heard the expensive *click* of the jewelry box.

I tried to guess what she'd select for her blouse, running through the tangle of costume jewelry in my mind, the cold strands of faux pearls, the gold Nefertiti pendant, mysterious amber statement pieces, and the jade bangles stacked on the right. I remember guessing it would be earrings. I was startled when she sat down next to me and pressed a thin gold band with two small rubies into my hand.

I left my fingers splayed as it bore a hole into my palm.

"Pretty, right?"

I nodded. She leaned in. I held my breath as she took my hand in both of hers and folded my fingers in. "It's yours," she said.

I slipped it on my ring finger, my wedding finger. My hand could've been someone else's, it was suddenly so beautiful. My fingers had always been my best quality. They are my mother's exactly. The ring fit flawlessly. I aspired to one day have the rest of me be as pretty as my hand in this moment.

"Are you hungry?" she asked, smiling conspiratorially.

I nodded again.

We headed into the kitchen. I inspected the table this time. Myriad small dishes, jewel-like, glinting under the gloss of Saran wrap. She lifted the steaming glass lids of the largest saucepan. Kimchi-jjigae with fatback. June's favorite. A black earthenware cauldron of steamed egg. My favorite. There was even mapo tofu for Dad.

She pulled out a chair and served me generously. Not the half servings I'd been getting from her and from all the church ladies who had been forbidden to overfeed me. My weight was a joint concern.

It felt like a fable. The kind where you eat what's forbidden, where you desecrate offerings to the gods and you wake up squealing, wordless, transformed into an animal, punished for your greed. In Korean folklore, women were mercurial, constantly turning into bears, cranes, or nine-tailed foxes. Sometimes as punishment, sometimes as reward.

I kept eating. Past the point of discomfort. My mother talked about her mistakes and how it would be a sin to expect forgiveness from her girls. I remember thinking that the Korean word for "punishment" was the same as "bee." I already knew she was leaving, and I ate slower so that she'd stay longer. Part of me ate hoping she'd take me with her. Only me. I ate with the ring held tight in my fist as she extracted the smallest bones of the fish, the tricky feathery ones below the fins, and fed me the meat. And when she told me to go lie down, I did because I was tired. And sick. I could barely lie on my back, I was so uncomfortably, painfully full. I'm not sure I heard the garage door opening, but when I came back downstairs, she was gone.

I still held the ring when I woke up.

I felt as though I'd failed a test. That I'd sold her out for a piece of jewelry. I needed to fix all of these acidic, roiling feelings that arose in me. I needed to undo my mistakes. Be forgiven for my sins. I was desperate to get rid of the salty, unctuous, sick, thick bribe inside me. I pulled the cord.

There was this dream I used to have during those months after Mom vanished. That I was standing up to take Communion in an enormous, Gothic church. It was cold and bright, and I had to climb hundreds of steep stairs into the light. I was always too scared to look down, and when I reached the top, I offered up my hands, one exposed palm over the other, to receive the dried-out wafer of sacrament. And that's when I'd feel the searing heat of a sting on the outstretched flesh of my palm and watch the bee disembowel itself.

While Mom was gone, I tried rubbing my own ear and was shocked by how loud and insistent it was, how unpleasant. It never occurred to me that she might not be experiencing the exact soothing, quieting sensation I was. I hadn't known I was a nuisance.

I never told June or Dad that I'd seen her go. It became so clear what she'd meant when she'd screamed "You girls don't get to have everything," gesturing wildly to the dress I'd defiled. June stayed up for her night after night, but I knew she wasn't coming back. And each time Dad called when he thought we were asleep, I lost a little more respect for him. I had seen the look on her face. She'd given me her ring, and I'd betrayed her by taking it. I'd given her permission to leave when my sister or father would have demanded she stay.

When June left, my secret exploded.

chapter 30

Mom turns to me with an expectant face. I sense she's been talking to me.

The harsh lighting casts heavy shadows at her cheeks, filling the grooves by her lips, her neck. She rarely wears makeup, just a chalky film of SPF one zillion sunscreen, and her hair is heathered in between light brown and gray.

I shake my head. "I couldn't hear you," I tell her in Korean.

"Doesn't matter," she says, seemingly annoyed as she busies herself with saucepans. Chopsticks in hand, she sets down trivets on the table and plants saucepans atop them.

For a brief moment I wonder why we're eating in the kitchen and not at the dining table. Why the only time the dining table has ever been set was the day she left.

"Wow," June says, coming up from behind me. "What a feast." She dangles a small robin's-egg-blue Tiffany's shopping bag by its white handles. "This is from both of us," she says, nodding at me. Mom looks to June, then to me, and wipes her hands on her apron before taking it.

"Oh, it looks expensive," Dad says, smiling.

Mom cuts him a sharp look. "I'll look at it later," she says, visibly embarrassed. "Dinner first."

"Just open it," says Dad. For an unsteady second, I'm convinced it's a ring.

Mom takes off her apron and slings it on the back of a chair. She hands the bag to Dad as she tugs her scrunchie off and gathers the loose strands into a tighter ponytail. She wipes her hands on her thighs again and reaches for it. My heart aches when I recognize her actions for what they are. My mother felt the need to change, to be presentable, before she could receive such a fancy gift. If she weren't so self-conscious about her self-consciousness, I know she would have excused herself to put on lipstick.

She carefully removes a flat, square box from the bag. She stares at it for a moment, almost suspiciously. "Thank you," she says, to the box, unable to look at either of us. When she tugs at the ivory satin ribbon gingerly, it's as if she half expects it to detonate. Set atop a rectangle of cottony fluff is a delicate chain with a tiny diamond-studded cross. Mom lifts it and holds it to the light. It's beautiful.

"Thank you," she says again. In the same breath, she adds, "You shouldn't have spent so much money."

"Do you love it?" asks June, grabbing Mom's shoulders from behind, jostling her until she smiles. "It's an early birthday present."

Mom's birthday isn't for a month.

"I love it."

Mom hands it to Dad for him to fasten, turning and carefully lifting her ponytail.

"It's not like anything else you have," says June, crowding them, casting a shadow so Dad can't see.

Dad ushers Mom into the light. "The little clasp is so small," he says, frowning and craning his neck away to help his farsightedness. My parents seem so old and June seems so needy, I can't look at any of them.

"It's platinum," says June.

Finally, Mom touches the cross where it falls on her chest. "I can tell it's platinum by the weight," she says, smiling at all of us. "A woman my age shouldn't have to wear silver."

She says it so silkily that we all laugh. June loudest.

"Now, that's enough," she says, hurriedly unwrapping all the dishes covered in plastic. The moment is over. "Everyone sit. I timed it all perfectly."

I take my usual seat at the square kitchen table. "You should stop losing weight," she says, setting down yet another earthenware pot of stew. "It makes you look older."

"I am older."

"Don't be ridiculous. Drink this." She holds a mug under my nose as if its contents stop time. It's murky and smells somewhere between nuts and feet. "Chaga mushrooms," she says. "For your skin." She reaches out and pats my cheek, not with affection, but as some kind of diagnostic probe. "You look . . . puffy. Your unlucky ear is sticking out more than usual." Only one of my earlobes is attached. I forget which is the unlucky one.

I touch the liquid to my lips without drinking. It's the game we've always played. Later I'll tip it down the sink and feel bad when she tells me how much it cost and how far it's traveled. Mom's love language is to scrutinize and criticize all the physical attributes that you're most sensitive about. I glance at my sister, willing my clair-voyant mother to detect June's cancer from the size of her pores or the sheen of her hair.

"I thought the food was getting cold," I remind her.

Halfway through dinner, Mom leaves the table and emerges from the garage with a store-bought pie in a black plastic tray with a domed lid. "Happy family!" she announces, as if collective birthdays are a thing that's commemorated by eating pie. "They had blueberry, but it wasn't as beautiful. And at least it isn't pumpkin. What a disgusting pie."

"You just don't like nutmeg," says Dad.

"I got the last one," she says, presenting it with as much pride as if she'd made it. "Kim Theresa says that all H-E-B's get their pies from the same place as some expensive restaurants."

"Happy family!" says June, smiling at me.

"Happy family to you," I sing, and June actually laughs.

My sister snores softly on my bed above me. I'm lying on the mat on the floor since June pulled rank because her room is filled with restaurant supplies. I stare at Patrick's text and send him a thumbs-up that I've arrived safely. I then send him the cowboy smiley because I'm feeling chatty.

The woolly stuffiness of the room presses up against my skin. I get up quietly, monitoring June for movement, open my desk drawer, and remove the flat-head screwdriver. I check her again, then step out and quietly close the door behind me.

The thermostat in the hall is set to 84 degrees.

I switch on the bathroom light, blinking furiously in the mirror. This is the mirror in which my face looks most disgusting. I'm almost sure it's not all in my head. I once googled that unflattering mirrors are an empirical scientific phenomenon. They bulge under their own weight, making you appear shorter and wider. And this one, my childhood one, the one I studied most intently during my formative years, distorts all the time.

I've stared in this mirror until I can't see myself. My face loses meaning. My eyes have been wet and ringed red, lips slick with spittle, cheeks swollen and purple. There have been so many nightmares in this place, but I'm grateful not to ever think about most of them. How I'd sit in the bathtub crying silently. Doing everything silently. It was the only room where the door locked. My bedroom door gave way if you shook the handle and shoved.

I stand on the lip of the tub, steadying myself with a palm to the ceiling, unscrewing the metal air vent with my other hand. The cover swings down, held in place by a screw. I reach inside. My fingers brush against a familiar shape. I clutch the bundle of small hardback notebooks and an old packet of cigarettes. I sit on the bath mat with my legs crossed and flip the blue box open and bring them to my nose. The filters smell exactly as they should. Like raisins. And something else. Something acrid. I tap the box upside down against my palm, and a half-smoked joint slides out.

Tucked between the notebooks, there's a stack of folded-up yearbook pages that I'd ripped out of the copy in the library. We all pillaged the school copies. Yearbooks were a fortune at $75 a pop, and most of us couldn't afford them.

I unfold the first page. It's been handled so much, the creases are worn white. It's one of my few pictures of him. Him being a dirty-blond boy with hair in his eyes. Him being Holland Hint, the destroyer of hearts, the decimator of self-esteem, the great love of my life, poised in a rare display of academic engagement. He's wearing safety goggles and a lab coat. Gangly, head hanging.

In the background, you can make me out staring as if willing him to turn around. It's the only picture of us together. Listed next to my name in the appendix of our yearbook are the three pages where I'm featured, and this is one of them. I was mortified. I never asked if he noticed. By the time it came out, we'd returned to not knowing each other.

I slide off the string from around the bundled notebooks. I grab the ribbon bookmark tail sticking out of the bottom of one and flip it open.

"Why is June such a fucking spaz?" I'd written in red pen.

My greatest fear in high school was that I would be like her, like my older sister. June and I were never in middle school together but even still I felt stupid for not anticipating who she'd be in high school.

I knew she was a hard-boiled dork at home. And it was the consistency that scandalized me. In the hallway, at her locker, she made no effort to stifle her braying laugh. She'd roll out of bed and throw on worn leggings and a sweatshirt without any thought. She was indifferent to makeup trends, the right jeans, vanity backpacks that hung just so. The only people who dressed as carelessly at school were the super-popular boys who were gods in their hoodies. But they could get away with it. June couldn't.

It was still dark out when we waited for the school bus that first morning. There was another kid at our stop, and the three of us stood in silence. The bus was quiet when we got on, everyone still half-asleep. There was something adult about how subdued it seemed. I was convinced they could hear my galloping heart. I followed my sister into the aisle. When she beckoned me to sit with her a few seats from the front, I was shocked. When she asked if I knew where to go for first period, I could feel their eyes on us. She was so loud. It was as awkward as if she had burst into song. I heard whispers and giggling. I wanted to shush her when she asked if I had money with me. The rules were so clear, yet I could see June had no idea.

I saw how she walked by herself into school, past the clusters of kids catching up after summer.

I hadn't known that other sixteen-year-olds vaped surreptitiously into their lockers all wearing white Air Force 1s and white sweatshirts.

I hadn't known that they spent all vacation at their food service jobs or at summer school while June was mostly at home taking online classes.

There was so much I didn't know.

Juniors were glamorous in a way June wasn't. They were cultured. They knew when to smile and how to smile so they still looked mean. They knew where to buy lipstick that looked like gloss but was somehow matte. And their earrings bore evil eyes of various sizes. Every single junior girl other than my sister wore shirts that stopped exactly half an inch above their pants. Without exception. And they knew all the dances but laughed goofily through the choreo as if they didn't.

I was ready to learn it all.

And I learned to see June the way they did.

I learned to sit in another seat near the front of the bus.

I learned to leave campus for lunch because pretending not to see her in the cafeteria seemed cruel.

She had friends, I told myself. They were just friends no one else wanted.

The journal entry's from freshman year. "She needs to grow up! This is not okay." I flip a few more pages.

"She needs to wash her hair at least 3x a week."

"Tell June not to talk so much."

"Tell her not to laugh when no one else finds it funny."

"Make her stop selling candy."

Ours was a football school, and twice a year, our star cheerleaders sold candy for fundraising. June had taken to selling rival, cheaper, better candy at exactly the same time. She also regularly sold Hot Cheetos because we didn't have them in the vending machines. It was bad enough that my parents worked in restaurants. I lived in constant fear that kids would talk to me about my sister the Cheetos girl. I didn't have anywhere to hide. There were only six Asian kids in a school of two thousand.

I open the orange notebook, the one from senior year. June was long away at Columbia by then. Here the rules apply only to me. I'd gotten into bullet journaling by then, and beside each handwritten date is another number. My weight. Most days feature a string of numbers, the entries crossed out and rewritten over and over. My weight after peeing. Before and after the gym. Before and after drinking water, eating two inches of a six-inch subway sandwich, a bag of Baked Lay's, not eating at all. I remember how it felt, pushing the surface of the digital scale with my toe, stepping on with my eyes closed, praying for a miracle.

I climb onto the edge of the tub and screw the vent back into place.

I stow the diaries in my bag. As well as the cigarettes.

I'm awake now and I need something. A diversion. I pad downstairs, phone in hand. Avoiding the creaky parts of the steps.

The family pie's sitting on the table. They'd all had a slice, but I hadn't. I pop open the lid, muscles clenched so as not to make a sound. I lick my finger to catch a crumb and dissolve it in my mouth. Then I break off a piece of crust. It melts on my palate. The doughy butteriness floods my senses. I open the dishwasher, again tensing to dampen the noise, and reach for a fork, but since there are none, I grab a pair of chopsticks. I poke into the pie, in a dotted line, perforating a small slice for extraction, and eat it standing in four bites. I brush the crumbs off my house dress, close the lid, and toss the chopsticks into the sink.

Guided by my phone flashlight, I walk over to the enormous lacquered armoire next to the looming black television and open its doors. A silk butterfly charm dangles off the rounded knobs. Inside are our photo albums. There's one for each of us. All our photos used to be kept in paper envelopes from the drugstore until I organized them in color-coordinated albums. I grab my favorite. The red one. The one assigned to June. As I open it, a page falls to the floor, separated from its glued binding. She was always the cutest kid. Sweet, expressive eyes, always in the middle of something. There are three photos to a page, and in the center one she's about four, cross-legged on the floor, looking up at her porcelain clown doll, the one that she broke, propped up on a chair. I slot the page back in and put it away.

The fridge rumbles. I look back into the kitchen. That slice of pie was way too small. I'm aching for a proper slice now that I've broken the seal. I get up. This time I get a butter knife and cut a good-size wedge. It's a calorie bomb, but I want it. I deserve it. I came home and I'm owed. I slide it onto a paper towel and then, using my hands, I mash all the stray crumbs together to make one giant crumb and eat it. They're mine.

I hear myself sigh.

Body humming with sugar and fat, I help myself to a glass of water and peer at the pie box again. Dread creeps along the ridge of my shoulders. There's only a third left.

I google "twenty-four-hour H-E-Bs." There's one an eighteen-minute Uber ride away.

A plan forms. I need to finish this pie and buy a fresh one. I must eat three slices out of the new one to cover my tracks.

"Hi, Jayne Baek."

I whip around. It's Dad. With his own iPhone flashlight shining into my face.

"Oh." Even in the swampy heat of the house, he's wearing a cardigan. I brush crumbs off my T-shirt. He shines his phone at the open armoire. "Why are you up?" I ask him, clearing my throat. I'm struck by how small he looks in the dark. How angry and foreboding he seemed when we were young. I watch as he opens a low kitchen cabinet to pull out a large mason jar. In it is a pale-brown sludge.

"I have to feed the mother," he says, shining the light under his face as if he's telling a ghost story around a campfire. For a moment it's as if Mom's power lies in this jar of muck under the sink.

He pours liquid from another jar into the murky vessel and returns it to its hiding place. "It's my SCOBY. For kombucha."

Another large glass jar comes out, this time from the fridge. This one with a wide mouth. "Sourdough starter for bread," he says, spinning off the lid. "I have to keep my family alive."

He smells it and then holds it up to my nose.

It's inviting. Warm, not quite bready but beery.

"It's gluten-free," he says.

"You've always been into this stuff since way before anyone else," I tell him. I remember all his failed businesses. How the magnets and crystals and jade face rollers were so prescient for him to sell. How it had all been too early. How Texas had been all wrong. My father was the first person I knew who'd tried to import sheet masks from Korea. This was before every Korean product purveyor practically minted money. Before the Danny Songs of the world were on the covers of *Vanity Fair*. Before random non-Koreans at work would ask me which K-dramas I watched and then instruct me on the ones I *should be* watching.

"How are you?"

"Good," I tell him, nodding to make it convincing. "Fine."

He smiles gently. "It's been so long since you've been back," he says. "I think I saw more of my parents when I served in the military."

"I know," I tell him. "I'm sorry."

"Nothing to be sorry for," he says. "How are you and June getting along?"

"Okay, I guess." He chuckles, stirring the fluffy, shaggy dough and then lifting some of it out with a wooden spoon and putting it into a Ziploc bag.

"Where's he going?"

"I have to separate this little guy for the good of the rest of the family." He places it into the freezer. "Thank you," he says to it, and then shuts the drawer. "We can't keep feeding everyone, so he goes into suspended animation."

"Tough break."

He pours some flour into the rest of the jar. "It's a pretty heroic role, if you think about it." He mixes with the handle end of his wooden spoon.

"It's good that you and June are together in New York," he continues. "Life's too hard over there to do it by yourself."

He adds water to his mix.

"Even if being together feels just as hard sometimes," he says. "Family's like that." He stirs for a while and then screws the lid back on. "But they're the ones who will help when no one else will."

He stoops down to return his jar to the lower cupboard, closing it softly. The other back into the fridge. "It's when you really don't want to ask for help that you might need it the most."

He pats my shoulder.

I remember when Mom was gone. How sad he was. And how mellowed he seemed after.

"Put everything back exactly as you found it," he says, swinging his light to the open armoire.

"I will."

"Because she'll know." He shakes his light in my face, chuckling.

"Yeah, I know."

"Good night, my daughter."

"Good night, my dad."

chapter 31

"You get in line," she says to me the next morning, shoving the
shopping cart toward the register. Mom's a genius when it comes to
tricking us into manual labor. June wanted Mom to take her to the
Korean store to get snacks, and I'm a sucker, so I tagged along. There
are about four people ahead of us in line. I used to hate this as a kid.
Having to awkwardly let people go ahead when my mother invariably
vanished at the crucial moment. "You, see if you can find some gluti-
nous rice flour." She directs June down another aisle. "The good kind.
If they have the Vietnamese variety, even better. It has an elephant on
it. Also, grab a fish sauce, the one with the three crabs on the label,
not the one with the fish."

I'm pretty sure June doesn't know what she's looking for.

"I'll be back," Mom tells us both.

June saunters over with the right fish sauce but the wrong rice
flour. "This is my fault," she acknowledges.

"Yeah, it is."

We've already been to the bank. I had to run in and deposit a blue leather envelope of cash while June and Mom got to wait in the car with the AC running. I am the youngest, which means I draw short straw until death.

"Let's have lunch at the restaurant," Mom says as she oversees us loading the car in the parking lot. "You, take this," she says to June, rolling the cart over. "Jayne did the bank."

June meets my eyes before trundling away. There's no telling what we'll have to do at the restaurant.

Seoul Garden is Korean in name only. Truthfully, the cuisine is more Pan-Asian to cover all the bases, with a sushi bar right in the center and Korean barbecue, as well as Chinese noodle dishes trooping out of the kitchen at all times. Logistically, it's a clusterfuck splitting tickets between the kitchen cooks, the raw bar chefs, and the actual bar staff serving drinks.

The parking lot's jammed. Mom bypasses the customer lot, driving through the narrow alley to the additional parking in the rear. She stomps the brakes at the blind corner as another car barrels toward us. As she does, Mom instinctively sticks her arm out, crossing June's chest. "Sorry," she says softly, and pats my sister's hair. I watch June watch our mother with such tenderness that my heart cracks open.

We pull into the active driveway of the back door.

We follow Mom, who carries her purse tucked into the crook of her arm, trailing her like ducklings past the dishwasher, the walk-ins, the slip mats squishy under our feet. It's been forever since I've cut this course with her. "You remember my daughters," she says as we pass the heat of the kitchen. June and I bow slightly. Wave. Say hi. Mom instructs various people to unload the supplies from the car.

Our usual table, the one where we did all that homework, is laden with a gilded red melamine boat heavy with raw fish.

"Is that for us?" asks June.

There are bowls of miso soup and rice and iced tea for the four of us.

"I called Rodrigo to have it ready," she says. Rodrigo's their sushi man. There's June's Unagi Enchilada roll, which resembles a wet burrito more than it does a purist's idea of sushi. And the Izzy roll, my favorite. The whole thing's deep-fried. There's also gyoza, kimchi pancakes, and jewels of nigiri sushi dotted throughout. This is why I can't ever bear to pay for sushi in New York.

Mom turns to us and peels off a few twenties from a brick of new bills. I wish she'd hold it up to her face like a phone so I can take a picture.

"You didn't bring tip money, did you?" she chides, shaking her head. "Waiters don't like credit card tips. How many times do I have to tell you that?"

No matter how stern she sounds, I know she's pleased that she timed the meal perfectly.

"Ji-young," she says. "Get your father." Dad's office is back behind the kitchen. When I pull out my phone to text him, Mom kisses her teeth. "If I wanted him texted, I would have done it," she says. "Have some respect."

I get up, and June smiles at me, sugaring her tea.

"Hurry up," says Mom. "The sushi's going to get cold." It's an old joke. Now they're both cheesing at me.

Both of them are firstborns. And firstborns can suck it.

chapter 32

I wake up from a two-hour nap to catch June, in a bra and suit pants, threading her arm into a white blouse. I was pretending to do homework on my laptop, sprawled out on my belly, when I passed out, and I'm struck now by how beautiful my sister looks with her face in repose. I pretend to be asleep so she stays this way. Her shoulders sag, lending a weariness that makes her seem older. She's less decisive, less a bully to her surroundings. Without the bluster, she's a different person. She reminds me so much of Mom, the way she lets herself show sensitivity only when she thinks no one is watching. June takes a deep breath, and when she lets it out shakily, I can't bear it. Her frailty scares me.

"God, seriously? You're wearing a fucking suit to church?" I sit up. I have a headache from sleeping so long. "You're such a suck-up."

"I want to look nice," she says pleasantly, not rising to the bait. "It'll make Mom happy."

Her garment bag hangs from the hook behind the door. "Jesus, how many suits did you bring?"

There's something about the somber black bag for church that seems funereal. I tug my lip, hard, but when June eyes me, I sit on my hand, which only sets my leg jiggling.

"I wanted options."

Meanwhile, I haven't brought a single nice thing to wear. I'm still wearing the same dress Mom licked.

"Pearls though, really?" I roll over to check my phone. Patrick's left a voicemail. It's almost three minutes long. The tightness at my temples twists.

June shrugs. "It's what I have," she says, tilting her head and attaching the earring back.

She tucks in her blouse.

"Great." I sigh. "I'm going to look like a bum compared to you."

I stare at the notification again. A voicemail has to be bad news. Or maybe he butt-dialed.

"First of all," says June, "you are a bum. Second of all, borrow something."

She unzips her bag and pulls out a sleek black suit. "This one's long as shit," she says. "I brought heels if you want."

"It won't fit," I tell her automatically.

"Yeah, it will," she says. "Mom's going to pop such a holy boner if both her daughters look like little politicians at church."

I finger the fabric. It's a high-end British label that I'm surprised she knows about. It has a peak lapel and gorgeous drape. I slip it over my arms.

"Oh, that works," she says, and tosses the trousers at my face. I try on the pants in the bathroom. When I return, I look at both of us in the mirror, dressed in black, with demure makeup.

"Hi, I'm June." I wave into the mirror stiffly. "I like Domino's Pizza and finance dipshits. The *A Star Is Born* soundtrack is the most important thing that's ever happened to me despite never having seen the movie. Or even being aware that there're four of them."

June hip checks me. "And I'm Jayne," she parrots back. "I'm partial to oat milk, bands that no one cares about, white boys who hate me, trust-fund poverty, and I still think tattoos are subversive even though literally every-fucking-body has one."

She smiles. "And tote bags for boring magazines."

I laugh. To be honest, I'm a little touched that she knows so much about me.

I take a deep breath in the lot as June parks. She drove us in Dad's car since our parents had choir practice beforehand.

"Don't get worked up," she says, applying lipstick in the rearview. I pull out my compact and powder my forehead.

"Easy for you. You love this shit."

June blots her lips and checks her teeth. "Nobody loves this shit."

"Then why do you do it?"

June rolls her eyes and caps her lipstick.

"Because being in a family is about doing shit you don't want to for the benefit of other people," she says. "Mom and Dad sacrificed everything for us, and they want the stupidest, basic shit in return."

"What? Like lying to them about still having a job?"

June side-eyes me. "Do you listen to the words other people say to you, or is just a high-pitched droning?" She tosses her lipstick in her purse. "Mom and Dad want to know that we're safe. They want proof that they did a good job. Why the fuck would I tell them I got fired? Mom calling me three thousand times a day and losing sleep won't get me a new job. I'm protecting her. And whatever. I'm already talking to headhunters. I'll have a new job as soon as all this shit is under control. People don't really want to know how you're doing. They want to wait until you're done telling them so they can tell you how they're doing."

June shrugs. "Mom's the same way. I don't think it bothers me as much as it used to."

My sister smiles at me with deranged brightness. "People like capable, positive people. It has nothing to do with reality." June flashes her teeth even wider. "See? Boom. Different person."

She pops open the door. "Just make us look good, okay? For me." June gets out before I can answer.

Mom's church is called, aptly, Church of the Korean Martyrs. Dead serious. At least that's how it's referred to once a week on Saturday nights. The Korean Catholic community in the greater San Antonio area leases the church at 6:00 p.m. every Saturday from a Catholic high school. A different, richer Catholic church gets the prime time slot of Sunday mornings. After mass, we eat in the gym. I snap a picture of the plastic banner that we sling on top of the regular Sacred Heart sign. I want to send it to Patrick even though I still haven't listened to his three-minute sermon on my phone.

"You think one day we'll get to have church on an actual Sunday?" asks June as she opens the door.

"But then we wouldn't be martyrs," I tell her.

"Yeah, right," she says, nudging me. "As if these fools only martyr on weekends."

It's our bit. We'd said some variation of this every Saturday. I stopped coming when Mom left. I couldn't stand the hypocrisy of pretending we were still a family. To her credit, Mom didn't make me. I took it as an acknowledgment of her guilt.

A sour man in the back glares at us for talking. I smile serenely without teeth, then pretend to dip my finger in the holy water to dab the sign of the cross on my forehead and over my heart. I don't care how blessed it is, this shit could cure smallpox *and* still have pink eye floating around in it.

"Jesus," mutters June, taking it all in. She leads us to our usual spot, the row immediately after the pews reserved for the choir. Right behind the organ. It's all so much smaller than I remember. The wood-paneled, maroon-carpeted box looks like the waiting room of an old folks' home. My eyes search the room, landing on the brown-ish water stain that resembles Italy's boot on the back wall. I used to zone out on that stain, staring until it melted and I could feel myself melting along with it.

June gets up to say a few hellos. Hugging choir members spiffily done up in their freshly steamed purple robes, bowing deep as she greets each one. I hang back. Even fortified by my sister's suit, I can't stomach it. There's Kim Theresa. Im Theresa. Park Helena. The other Kim Theresa, the one that lives out by Fort Sam Houston. I watch June shrewdly navigate the flock. She has a mind like a steel trap for differentiating Theresas.

"You look fantastic, Jayne," one of them calls out to me from two pews over, wriggling her fingers in greeting. She has a dewy, open face and frizzy bangs. "You'd never know how fat you used to be," she stage-whispers. "You're a stick. A stick! And you must be at least a hundred and seventy centimeters tall. You could model."

Park Helena, who I've always liked, waves. She doesn't do the Korean compliment roundhouse, where the nicety detonates into an insult a half second later. These mom proxies remind me of those fishes that bloom around you and eat the dead skin cells on your feet. Patrick's Mom was never among the nudgier women. She didn't sing or play golf. In fact, I can't remember talking to either of his parents beyond a perfunctory hello.

June punches my leg in solidarity when she sits next to me. The familiar chirp of KakaoTalk rings through the hubbub. The organist plays the first few notes of the opening hymn.

Mom enters to take her place, followed by Dad. As choir leader, she wears a gold-and-white sash on her robe. The priest is the only other member of the congregation with a sash. His features a slightly thicker gold border, which probably hasn't escaped Mom's notice.

Mom turns around to thrust a worn pleather-bound hymnal into June's hand. We hear another KakaoTalk chirp. There's another. And another. People check their phones self-consciously. It's always old people who fail to keep their phones on silent while upbraiding us for our attention spans.

The first hymn begins.

I stare at the water stain and wonder what games Patrick played in his head while he was trapped in here with me.

As if sensing that I'm not contemplating spiritual redemption, Mom spins around and conducts directly at me and June. We can actually feel the whoosh of air from Mom's enrobed arms flapping. June's better at fake-singing than I am. She gives great, big spirit face. Boisterous on the first syllable, then letting the phrasing peter out. I barely move my lips. June elbows me again, harder. Her eyes light up as she pops her chin on the chorus. She's so close to cracking up.

Our mother smiles and mouths with the exaggeration of a stage mom. She frowns, then smiles brightly, pointing at her mouth, instructing me to smile.

The song ends just as I find the right verse.

I can't bring myself to take Communion even as my face burns when I have to get up to let people pass.

Afterward, we make our way over to the gym. June and I walk behind Mom. The sky is purple.

Before we burst through the double doors of the gym, Mom turns around and loops my hair around my ear. I wait for the barb. How the pants are a little tight across my thighs or that I need to brush my hair, but it doesn't come. Instead she smiles and squeezes my arm affectionately.

I pocket this moment for myself. This memory alone makes the trip just about worth it.

chapter 33

We hear another Kakao chirp.

The gym already smells like the dankest Korean food, all garlic and fermented fish guts. Mom rushes ahead into the kitchen behind the row of folding tables arranged with large aluminum trays and Sternos burning beneath them.

I watch as she slings a navy apron around her neck and pulls on disposable plastic gloves. She flips her hair coquettishly to show off her necklace. The ladies admire it while Mom tilts her head this way and that, making them laugh. Then they return to serving ban-chan, scooping the fiery red vegetables and marinated meat with their hands, keeping the portions modest so everyone will be fed. Everything smells incredible.

Park Helena comes in behind us. We both bow deeply. "It's so good to see you girls," she says to us, eyes crinkling in a warm smile.

"You too." I realize I mean it. It's good to be back. Following June's advice, I'm smiling compulsorily, trying not to internalize anything, and it's working. It's like an instant lobotomy.

"Especially you, Jayne." Helena squeezes my elbow. "You should come home more often. Your mother's been relentless all week. She raided my freezer for my homemade dumplings, radish kimchi from Oh Theresa. She's been bending our ears and showing off for days how both of her girls are coming in from New York. She's so proud of you two. It's just a shame she never gets to see you."

"I'm here all the time," interjects June.

Helena laughs. "And we're all so lucky for it. You always did take such good care of your little sister." She pats June on the shoulder. "How's work? Your parents couldn't be prouder."

"It's fantastic," says June. "Challenging yet rewarding. A wonderful growth opportunity."

They talk about her son at Wharton, about all his scholarships. My eyes glaze.

"You girls should eat," says Helena, before crossing the room to talk to the priest, who's seated at a long card table with the rest of the men.

"I think if Mom ever said she was proud to my face my head would explode," I tell June while we watch a flock of women descend on the priest to offer food. "Like, there would be blood pouring out of my ear and shards of skull and hair everywhere."

June rolls her eyes. "It's Mom. What do you expect?"

I look over at Mom again, heaping piles of food onto her plate. Suddenly, I can't bear to see her.

"I'm not hungry," I whisper before turning on my heel and walking back into the evening air.

The pea gravel that lines the parking lot crunches under my borrowed heels.

I watch a junky white hatchback pull up to the gas station across the street, taillights glowing red. Two girls hop out, wearing short skirts and tights and oversize, candy-colored hoodies. They both have scrunchies in their hair. I used to fantasize every Saturday about how my friends would come get me at church. Central to this fantasy was that it would be in front of everyone and that all the church kids would see how cool I actually was. How totally I didn't need them. How they'd been wrong to ignore me and leave me out of their games.

I sit on an aluminum bench and pull out the cigarettes. It's dark, but the seat's warm from the sun earlier in the day. The smoke feels heavy in my lungs. The sprinklers have been turned on for the football field behind the school, the mist forming an arc where the lights hit.

I listen to Patrick's voicemail.

He's at work. Having lunch. He describes a chicken katsu sandwich in glorious, mundane detail. *They cut the crusts off, which is a nice touch.* He's wondering what I'm doing, where exactly I'm standing. He asks if I've been to the restaurant. Whether or not June's with me. If everything's okay and says that he'd neglected to ask if I was going home for any particular reason. He says he's thinking about me and that he's still sorry that he had to cancel dinner. He asks if I've had barbecue. How the air smells.

I see the appeal of voicemails for the first time in my life.

There's a prickly sensation inside my body when I think about him. It's the nettlesome conflict between the him I know and the other him he becomes when I'm away. He's flattened on Instagram. Bloodless and scarily intimidating for it, a stranger.

Patrick feels like my only tie to New York, and right now my link to him feels tenuous and imagined.

I recall him carefully pulling the hair out of my mouth. His steady, dark eyes. The rise of his shoulders above me. Warm and breathtakingly present. It's my favorite moment of the ones I've experienced so far. The sweetness of it startles me no matter how many times I play the tape in my head.

I stub the cigarette out on the bottom of my shoe. My heart hammers as I dial his number.

He picks up on the third ring.

"Hey," I say into the dark.

"Whoa, hi."

"I'm at church."

"How is it?"

"So unchanged that it's distressing."

He laughs. "I was convinced for a second that you were pocket dialing me."

"Yeah, phone calls aren't really my scene. This whole real-time communication business."

I hear him chuckling down the line. It tugs at my chest.

"This is my first time back since I moved."

"How's it feel?"

"It's a lot," I tell him. "I have this paranoia that New York won't let me in after this. That it's like Shangri-La or El Dorado or some other magical place that will punish me for leaving."

"Like all the hard work you've put in will get washed away?"

"Yeah." I smile into the phone. "Like the score card goes back to zero."

"I get that," he says.

"But you have a real life in New York. It's your home."

"Yours, too," he reminds me.

The two girls in the gas station across the street return to their car. They look tiny and insect-like climbing back into it. The green-hoodied girl pulls her friend out of shotgun by her backpack. She stumbles, and they laugh their heads off.

It seems strange to me that I've been their age.

"What are you doing this weekend?"

"Working. And then I have some people in town." He sighs. "When are you back?" he asks.

"Tomorrow."

"Thank God."

"Seriously."

He laughs. "Can y'all drive around and do something fun tonight?" I warm at him y'all'ing for my benefit. "Free tea refills, remember? Brisket?"

"True."

"Plus, Texas gives great sky."

I look up. It's still there. All oceanic and silencing.

"You'll see New York again. I promise."

"I know."

"Besides," he says. "You still have our sweats."

I grin helplessly.

We say good night, and I relight my cigarette and take a drag. I send Patrick the picture of the church. He likes it immediately.

"Seriously?" June sits heavily beside me. "I literally have cancer," she says, gesturing at the smoke.

I take a long pull. It tastes gross, but I don't want to put it out for her benefit. I make a big show of exhaling the smoke away from her.

I feel her cold fingertips on the back of my hand. She takes the cigarette from me and, shockingly, takes a drag.

"What the fuck?"

"Glarg," she says exhaling, and then spits at her feet. "Disgusting." Still, she hangs on to it and inhales again.

I take it from her and toss it.

I want to talk about Patrick but know better. I don't feel like hating her for telling me what I already know. That he's too good for me.

I wonder how much of the phone call she heard.

"When's the last time you were here?" Her breath smells faintly of garlic.

"You know when."

"Yeah."

We sit companionably in the dark. "You want to dip?" June dangles the car keys.

I glance back at the gym.

"They're going to take forever," she reminds me. "All the cleanup and the bullshitting." She gets up. "Come on, I'll take you to Dairy Queen."

I don't know why she's being so nice to me, but the thought of cruising around with my sister after all this time makes my heart surge giddily. "Yeah, okay." I shrug. I pop a breath mint into my mouth and spray myself with perfume. I offer some to June.

"You're such a pussy," she says, shaking her head. I spray her anyway since I'm scared enough of Mom for the both of us. If she smells smoke, we're toast.

I draw my hands to my face, sniff, and then spray them, too. "Wait," she says, splaying her fingers. "Do mine."

chapter 34

"Did you know that Jimmy Buffett owns Dairy Queen?" I'd read about it in class. "He basically brought them back from the brink of bankruptcy because he likes them so much."

June pulls us onto the brightly lit lot. "I went to business school too, dummy," she mutters.

The thing is—and June knows this—I love Heath Bar Blizzards more than life itself. Not that the Peanut Buster Parfait isn't pretty incredible too. I ignore the caloric math because what I want is a bucket of frozen deliciousness with shrapnel chunks that get stuck in my molars.

"Did you know you can get a Banana Split Blizzard?" I crane my neck until I can see the big plastic menu. "I didn't know that was a thing until I read it online. Ooooh, should I get Butterfinger?"

I snap a photo for Patrick. There are still four or five cars ahead of us. I'm so excited I can't take it.

"Jesus, get both," she says. "Literally nobody gives a shit."

June leans out the window when it's finally our turn. "I'll have a pineapple sundae," she calls out. I stare at my sister as if she's a stranger.

"Ew, *that's* your DQ order?" It's the most milquetoast thing I can imagine. Of all the desserts in the world.

"It's what I'm in the mood for," she says, shrugging. "This isn't, like, fucking Christmas for me. I get drive-thru every time I'm on the road."

I order a Heath Bar Blizzard.

"Why'd you quit driver's ed?" she asks as she inches the car closer to the window.

"Dunno." I recall the red-faced instructor with the buzz cut. He worked as a waiter at Pappadeaux and told me he'd give me free drinks. He was at least twenty-five and deeply creepy.

I stopped going. I had other things on my mind. Mom was gone.

"What's the point?" I tell her. "You could drive eight hours west *from* Texas and still be *inside* Texas."

"Because knowing that you can leave makes it more tolerable," she says. "It helped me. I just drove around under this stupidly big sky with nowhere to go but at least feeling like I had some say in it."

When June first got her license, she did seem so much happier. After homework, she'd text me and we'd go to DQ for frozen desserts, Sonic for cherry limeades, and Long John Silver's with a side of Whataburger chicken fingers with cream gravy and Texas toast if we were feeling decadent.

June's always been easier to talk to in a car. "Thanks for this trip," I tell her quietly.

"It's not so bad, right?"

"Yeah. I didn't even hate church."

"See?"

"Yeah." I stare at the chess piece-sized Virgin Mary effigy affixed to mom's dashboard. I remember how, when I unpacked my things at school, there was an identical one in the bottom of my suitcase. I threw her in a sock drawer and haven't seen her since.

"Did anyone at church ever ask about me?" I can't tell if I'm disturbed or relieved how little has changed in the last four years.

June laughs. "You mean, did the church ladies light a vigil candle for your scorching soul every week? Or did the priest dedicate his homily to Jayne returning to the flock?" She turns to me. "Is that what you're asking?"

"What I'm asking is why you're such a dick."

June laughs. She pulls up a little farther, then sets the car in park again.

"Did they ever ask you where Mom went?"

She shrugs. "Nah. I'm not even sure they asked Dad. You know how it is, church-folk are all up in your business until that shit *actually* gets dark. Then, they just think you're contagious."

I do know. It's not just church, though; that's everywhere.

"Do you think we'll ever know where she went?"

"We could ask her," says June.

At this, we both crack up.

"You really didn't think she was coming back, did you?"

I think about her packed suitcase. The eerily placid look on Mom's face. "No, I really didn't," I tell her honestly.

chapter 35

The last time I told June Mom wasn't coming back, she'd smashed an alarm clock on my head.

"You fucking whore!" She'd wrapped her fist deep into my hair and pulled with everything she had.

"Get off me, psycho!" I twisted, eyes filling with rage tears. She managed to hook me behind the ear where my scalp's most tender. I raced down the stairs, turning around on the carpeted landing to taunt her.

I'd called her a dumb bitch. Disgusting. A loser. I screamed for her to get a life. I crashed into the living room, grabbing my things, blindly shoving keys, wallet, lip gloss into my bag.

I checked my shallow pocket for the hard contour of mom's ring. I'd tried to tell June that first night. That this was our new life and still she wouldn't listen. It was so pathetic the way she kept pretending that things were ever going to be the same. Her naiveté sickened me. She was supposed to be my older sister. She was supposed to be so fucking smart.

"Do your goddamned homework!" she commanded, getting right up in my face. "What if she comes back and your grades are even worse?"

I laughed bitterly, drawing myself up tall. "You're so naive." I wanted to tell her everything. That our precious mother didn't love us enough to stay and that she'd given me a ring because I'd caught her. I hated that only I knew of this lopsided bribe and how cruel it was. June loved Mom more than anyone, but Mom didn't care. She hadn't left her anything. That's how much she thought of her firstborn daughter.

"Honestly, I feel sorry for you." I shoved her off me, glaring. She looked peaked then, small, as if all that piss and vinegar and moral outrage had been drained from her. She was still wearing her ridiculous Hogwarts sweatshirt from school that was stained at the sleeve. It was humiliating enough that she was a social liability on campus, that she telegraphed her obsessions with magic and fantasy for everyone to see. The fact that she couldn't at least be a realist at home when the truth was excruciating enough to accept was unforgivable.

"She's not coming back!" I screamed for a second time.

June shoved me and I landed so hard on my ass, I bit the inside of my cheek. I hated her so much, I vibrated with it.

"You are such a fucking traitor," she shrieked, blocking the door. "You have zero loyalty. You're so selfish, you make me sick. You don't deserve to be in this family."

"Family?" I screeched into the empty house. "Do you see a family anywhere?" Dad was at work, again, desperate to avoid us, leaving us to fend for ourselves with no explanation.

June needed to wake up. "She's gone. She doesn't give a shit about us. You could be fucking valedictorian and clean the house spotless and go to church every day and pray your ass off and it still won't make her come home. She's gone. She doesn't care." Mom didn't have to say it for me to know. Her voicemail was full. We'd filled it up. And her silence broke my heart.

It had been a month, and I'd moved on. As far as I was concerned, Mom leaving was the best thing that could have happened to me. If she could forget about us, I could sure as shit forget about her first. I'd smoked pot for the first time. I'd stayed out on a school night, drank gin, and puked so hard I'd thought I'd lost hearing.

I summoned all the hauteur in my entire fifteen-year-old body to push past her. I added a snotty head tilt. "I'm going out. It's not my fault you have no friends. Fucking loser."

June lunged for me. I kicked her off and swung the door open. As I ran down the drive, sandals slapping at my feet, wind lifting my hair, I felt high. I slipped Mom's ring onto my finger without looking back.

The car jerks forward.

"Maybe Mom was sick," says June. Her face is haloed in a red glow from the brake lights in front. "She looked insane when she came back."

Mom returned three months later. It was early in the morning. She was drawn and pale and immediately went to take a nap.

"God, Dad was sad."

"Yeah, that's why I couldn't let him go to church by himself."

In the car ahead of us, the driver reaches for four full bags and two holsters of desserts.

"Who gets food at DQ?" June muses.

We both shake our heads in disgust and drive up.

"Oh, hey," says June to the cashier. I hear acid in her tone and duck my head low to see what she saw. I recoil quickly, face burning as I feel June's eyes flick over to me. I recognize him right away when he wouldn't know me at all.

It's Holland Hint's little brother Willy.

With a constellation of acne on his cheeks, he's lengthened out in the last few years, seemingly as tall as Holland but less filled out from what I could see.

Two years younger than Holland, he wouldn't know either of us, but I realize I'm holding my breath.

A horrible fear gnaws at my guts that his brother works here too, even though the last time I stalked him, he'd enlisted in the air force. I turn to see if I can spot a beat-up blue Nissan truck in the parking lot. All those memories. Driving around with the radio on, rarely talking, him making me duck whenever he thought we saw someone we knew.

I hear Willy give her the total. June primly unbuttons her wallet clasp and hands him a twenty.

I pull out my compact. I'm oily. And my lips are flaky.

He hands over her change and tells us to drive up to the next window.

June throws the car in drive. I jerk forward when she slams the brakes.

"That's the brother, isn't it?" says June, jaw set.

I don't respond. If anything, I'm surprised that she remembers. I check the rearview, making sure he's not within earshot, making sure June doesn't see me checking.

She shakes her head, studying me. "Fuck if these assholes don't look exactly the same."

I sense her seething gather steam.

"Why didn't you say hi?" she hisses.

"June, stop."

She grabs my compact from me and snaps it shut.

"Do you honestly think he's about to go call his brother and tell him how you looked?"

I stare at the powder puff in my hand. I wasn't aware I'd gotten it out.

"June."

"He doesn't know you," she says, dumping her change in the center console. "And even if his brother were here, he'd pretend he doesn't know you either. Just like high school."

The anger comes off her in waves.

"Look." I shrug. "I barely even remember high school."

"You're so full of shit," she says. Even in the dark, I can see there are twin splotches of red high on her cheeks.

I sigh and look out the window.

"Let me guess," she says. "You don't want your ice cream."

She's right about that. "I'm not hungry anymore."

"Fine," she snaps. June guns the engine, spinning the wheel wildly to the right, and I'm convinced she's going to clip the tail lights of the sedan in front, when she throws the car in reverse at the last second.

"June!" I scream. My hand shoots up to the ceiling as my feet grind the floor.

"Shut up!" she says. Horns blare.

I turn my head, catching the surprised eyes of a Mexican family behind us. June curses while inching out so we can leave. "Thank you!" We both wave in our rearview, but just as our car lurches forward, we almost pitch into the van coming into the parking lot at a wide angle from the road.

June slams the brakes again. And just like Mom, she sticks out her arm to brace me, but she ends up hitting me hard in a clothesline, elbowing me right in the sternum.

"Ow. Fuck." I rub my chest, glaring at her accusingly.

The van flips us the bird.

"Jesus Christ, June, will you just pull over? Just park for a second."

"Fine." June silently slides into a spot.

There's a maroon van parked next to us. On the back windshield there's a sign written in white shoe polish. NEED A KIDNEY. BLOOD TYPE A OR O. And a phone number.

"Why are you so *weak*?" She's staring straight ahead and I'm braced for the insult, but the last word slices clean through my defenses. She inhales sharply, eyes clenched closed. She exhales shakily. "Look, I know you can't help it. But you're just so fucking . . ." June smacks the bottom of her steering wheel with the heel of her hand.

When I popped open the door of Holland's blue truck, Mom's rubies on my finger, my sister's voice ringing in my ears, I thought I was going to be his girlfriend. That's how it felt. I was finally the lead. I was the love interest. I was the one they were singing about in every single pop song.

"Hey," he said, expression unreadable. I'd expected a smile. I'd hoped for a hug, but he seemed put out. As if I was an imposition. It's true that I'd been the one to surreptitiously approach him while my friends were in the back of Planet K, the head shop where he worked, but he'd asked me to hang out. When I'd hoisted myself up to the cab of the truck, I was startled by the empty plastic bottles of soda on the floor, the stink of tobacco, the grid of duct tape on the navy pleather seat, and the gristle of coiled spring trying to elbow its way out and dig into my ass. I tried to keep the distaste off my face. I didn't want to be accused of being high maintenance. It knew it to be the worst possible insult that could be hurled at a girl.

"I thought I'd take you to the Chateau," he said, without facing me. I'd never been to the Chateau before. We rode in silence, which I chose to think was romantic. We passed railroad tracks, turning into a subdivision that seemingly didn't end. He was silent and brooding, but I knew we'd talk eventually. He'd reward me for my own quiet and let me in. I couldn't wait for him to tell me I was easy to talk to. For him to tell me things his girlfriend wouldn't understand.

We drove into a cul-de-sac where no porch lights were left on as a courtesy. I discovered what few sophomores were privy to. That the Chateau all the seniors talked about at school, the spot for all the wildest parties, was nothing more than a half-built model home in a nothing-neighborhood in a zombie part of town.

The door was ajar, with a hole where a doorknob would be. Holland walked in first, without holding the door for me, and I felt foolish for my crushing disappointment. The floors were littered with beer cans and broken glass, and it smelled powerfully of pee. There was a filthy mattress on the floor and a few plastic chairs around it, a jet-black streak of char coloring the far wall. A gold glimmer caught my eye, and I realized it was a condom wrapper. In fact, there were multiple bits of foil confettied all around the mattress.

I'd thought it would be a mansion, but who knew where I'd heard that. I'd stupidly wondered if there was a pool, whether we'd dip our toes and laugh, but there wasn't even electricity in the sad, abandoned house. The glass had been busted out of the window frames. There were no appliances in the kitchen, a toilet had been dragged into what would have been a dining room.

I could feel my fingernails digging into my palms like teeth as revulsion rolled thickly through my body.

We drank Fireball, which left our mouths spicy and warm. Still without talking, he kissed me, pushing up against me on the splintery wall of that dank shell of a house. His hooded eyes were open but unseeing, and I left my body there, preferring to witness this as a bystander. I knew this was going to have to be a secret—at least for a while—but I was confident that everyone would recognize the change in me. They'd see it in my movements. That this intense, pulsing charge of rage at my mother could be alchemized into power. He was a good kisser. Slow and deliberate, melting into my edges, which were already fuzzy from the cinnamon liquor. For that moment, I didn't mind that we stood in a squatter's den. That there was so much broken glass on the floor. We were both floating.

I led him back to his truck by his hand. It was surprisingly warm and soft. He had a rough, woven blanket in the bed. All I could think while his hands groped my breasts was that I hoped he wouldn't go for my pants. I'd heard that you could contract tetanus in your cervix if you got fingered by a guy with dirty fingernails. I tried to check his nails, but it was dark, and when he switched from sucking on my neck to kissing my mouth again, I moaned in that way that every girl knows how even if they don't want to.

It was surreal when he took my hand and guided it to his fly. I was shocked by how suddenly I was touching Holland Hint's penis. And by how hot his penis felt. It was not unlike petting an unseeing animal wholly separate from him. Like caressing the spine of a small hairless cat. When the spurt of feverish ooze landed on my hand, it glistened as it cooled. I couldn't tell if I was sick from giddiness or loathing. I knew that this part I wouldn't tell anybody about. I checked my own nails. They were clean.

I also saw that my ring was missing.

"My ring." I sat up, heart hammering. It was everything she'd left me, and I'd lost it down some stoner's pants.

"What's that?"

"My ring," I heard myself say, hysteria edging. "We have to find it." Holland, who was prone to doziness in the sober light of day, was practically comatose. He didn't stir. Didn't help me look for it. Didn't jump up and down to see if it fell out of his pants. Didn't so much as pull his phone out to help me search his car filled with garbage.

The next morning, he passed right by me as if nothing had happened. And still, two weeks later, I'd silently lost my virginity in that room. I'd watched my own condom wrapper falling to the floor. I was grateful that we'd done it standing up. Even if it hurt. Even as he crashed into me at angles that felt brutal and wrong. I was careful not to touch anything. A week after that Holland Hint never spoke to me again.

It's how I learned that nothing ever met expectations.

Every time I saw him kissing his willowy, glossy girlfriend in the hallways, pulling her narrow frame toward him as he draped his arm across her shoulders, I felt a deep, digging pain through my midline.

They both had the same straw-colored hair. From the back they looked like siblings.

I thought no one knew. But a few days later, the rumors began. My friends became distant and more boys came calling.

June kills the engine.

"Every time someone hurts you, you find a way to hurt yourself ten times worse."

It doesn't sound untrue even if it feels wounding coming from my sister.

"Whatever, it doesn't matter." I hear the tears fall dully onto my lap. Onto her borrowed clothes.

She's right, though. The completeness of Holland Hint's disregard gave me purpose, direction. It became a brittle carapace of protection. Beneath the veneer I was the thinnest I'd ever been. I didn't need Holland Hint. I didn't need Mom, I didn't even need June. By the time my older sister left for college I was ready. Mom, Holland, my friends, they all served as great practice.

"Can we go?"

She sighs. I keep staring at the white streaks of shoe polish on the van next to us. I hope someone gives them a kidney. Even if I don't know why anyone would.

chapter 36

I sneak up to Mom's bedroom. She and Dad are watching TV downstairs, June's in the shower. When I was little, I'd take off all my clothes—underwear and everything—and get into Mom's bed pretending I was her. An adult. A beautiful woman. A desirable woman.

Little kids are such creeps.

I slide the mirrored panels of her closet aside. The scent of mothballs overpowers Mom's perfume. I breathe deep. I love the feeling of the fabric on my face. I dig in the back, beyond her everyday boring work stuff, for the white garment bag. It's all still there. Unworn. Waiting. I unzip it, pulling the hanger through the hole in the top of the nylon bag, freeing just the blazer's shoulders. Her suit is tiny. With the prim, shiny, outdated buttons so close together that it gives the impression of doll's clothes. I hold my cheek against it, the crepe whorls scratchy against my skin.

I return it and search for my favorite. Mom's hanbok. It's still as delicate as I remember, but as I pull it closer, I see them: pinholes of light. A series of holes. A greedy moth's meal clustered under the armscye of the jeogori. An ache branches along my chest at the stolen potential of all these beautiful clothes. Saved with such earnestness only to be ruined.

When the water stops, I return the clothes and slide the closet door back.

I'm watching June as she watches Mom watch TV. This is it. I'm on pins and needles wondering if she'll tell them everything. The cancer, the surgery, that she won't be able to give them grandkids.

"See, this is not representative of contemporary Korean entertainment," June says to me instead. I glance up at the screen. It's some show where contestants come out singing, while wearing huge, strange masks or cartoon mascot heads.

Our parents are on the couch while we're lying on the floor at their feet. June's using the wooden block that Dad keeps trying to convince us promotes circulation as a pillow and my arm's going numb from supporting my head while lying on my side.

"They remade it here," says Mom, unblinking. June shoots me a look. We're always surprised when Mom actually listens. "Masked singer," she says in English, without tearing her eyes from the screen. She does this sometimes. Defies the version of her in our minds. Like senior year when I discovered she had strong opinions of the Spurs starting lineup.

A cat face sings "Memory" with its head hitched at an unnerving angle, as if its neck is broken. It's made only more creepy by the rich male voice and the slim-cut red suit on the body below.

The camera cuts to a close-up of a young woman in the audience swooning.

"*This* is why you never got into K-dramas," June says to me. "You've been watching boomer TV. Your Korean would be so much better if you got into it. It's passive learning." She turns her pillow longway, as if there's a more comfortable angle on a literal block of wood on your skull.

"Um, excuse me, you only ever watch *Gilmore Girls*," I retort.

"First of all, it's because my Korean compared to yours is incredible. Second of all . . ." She sits up for this part. "Two words: Lane Kim." Satisfaction lands on her face like a gavel thwack. "And don't you talk about Lorelai and Rory like that. Pull it together. And Sookie. Also, Jess."

"Lane's Mom is sus, though."

"That Mom had a lot of disappointments in her life," she says, lying back down. "You can tell she's seen shit. Show some respect."

Dad changes the channel again. Now it's a supercut of sons returning home from the military and bursting into tears as their mothers alternately leap and collapse into their arms. The classical piano music swells without release.

That gets us both right in our feelings.

I think about the YouTube video of Danny Song's return to the states after he did his two years. I wept openly. That one hit different since he was Korean American. Still, I hear my sister clear her throat discreetly as Mom switches the channel over to the CCTV that monitors the restaurant.

"How many times do I have to ask Cherry not to wear white sneakers?" Mom *tsk*s to the screen at the unsuspecting waitress, who can't hear her.

She scans the grid of images and enlarges selectively.

The aerial view of the front of the restaurant by the hostess stand is full of people waiting. Dad straightens up, alert. Mom quickly clicks through to the main floor of the restaurant. Then the view of the booths to the side.

"It's building," says Mom.

Dad's already on his feet and pulling on his puffer vest.

Quick as a flash Mom starts brushing her teeth, kicking off her house shoes, and returning to the TV as if anything's changed in the last fifteen seconds.

Honestly, you'd think they were firefighters.

June's sat up to watch them.

They're ready in less than two minutes. "Don't wait up," says Mom, not even looking back at us. Dad's already in the car because I can hear the garage door opening.

I don't believe them. I look over at my sister to see if she's disappointed that they've abandoned us on our last night.

She takes the remote and shuts off the TV.

The silence bears down on my shoulders.

Other families would have a special activity planned. They'd watch a movie together with a big bowl of popcorn. They'd talk to each other. "Why are they like this?"

"Like what?" She gets up on the leather couch, lies down, and stretches out extravagantly.

"They just *left*."

June yawns. Irritation charges through my spine. She only doesn't care because I care.

I get up and sit right on her legs. "Aren't you mad?" She squirms beneath me. "They could have done this any other night," I continue. "Like, any night that we're not here."

Instead of shoving me off, June pats my back. "People aren't abandoning you just because they go."

"Whatever."

I stomp upstairs, washing my face to go to bed. The room's stifling. It feels as though the carpeting's heating up the memory foam of the fold-out mattress. I can't tell if it's hotter down here or cooler since heat rises. I'm fuming. Livid at June's patronizing tone, pissed that our parents are so insensitive that they can't tell when something is so obviously amiss.

There's a glow-in-the-dark plastic Virgin Mary, a holdover from the eighties, about the size of a G.I. Joe action figure, presiding over us from the bureau. A dim, judgy night-light.

"Hey." June pushes the door open.

I ignore her.

"You literally went to bed a second ago," she says.

I still don't open my eyes.

"Jayne."

"Jesus, what?" I kick the covers off.

"I'm sorry, are you busy?" I can hear the amusement in her voice.

Finally, I sit up. "What do you want?"

June stands in the doorway, backed by the hall light, and I can't see her face. She turns and walks away.

"June?"

I hear the stairs creak. It reminds me of when she used to run ahead, hide, and jump out to scare me as revenge for following her around the house. And how, later, when she was in high school and I was in eighth grade, she'd call me in the middle of the day and bark, "What?" making me think I'd called her. It takes every ounce of restraint not to see where she went.

"It's so fucking hot," she says when she returns. She's brought the old electric fan out from the garage. A Sanyo with blue fins that we used to put our faces right up against. We loved the way it garbled our voices and blew our hair around.

She sits down on the floor with her back up against the bed and switches it on.

Finally, some air circulation. The breeze is fluttery on my skin.

"We should open the window too, though, right?" I ask her.

She rolls her eyes, huffs, gets back up, and mangles the venetian blinds with a plasticky clatter. I get up to help. The vacuum-sealed window lifts after a moment. The house alarm beeps twice in rapid succession. My brows rocket up to my hairline.

"They don't set it anymore," she says and shakes her head. "God, you were so fucking bad at sneaking out. How hard was it to remember that the alarm code is Mom's birthday?"

She sits back down next to me. I feel her warmth settling along my side even though we're not touching.

"Should we open the door?" I ask her.

"You're so dumb," she says, laughing, extending her leg out to hook it open with her foot. "There." This is the best part of having a sister. Since we were raised by the same lunatic, under the same conditions, June knows exactly what I'm thinking.

"It's not a thing, you know," she says. "Fan death."

"Fan death" is a pervasive Korean superstition that if you fall asleep with a fan running without opening a window or door for ventilation, you'll suffocate. It makes no sense logically or scientifically, but there's no convincing Mom. Or me, evidently.

"I just don't want to hear about it in the morning," I reason.

"Sometimes I think most of what Mom told us is stuff she made up." June's voice is becoming raspy. She's pressed her cheek against the knee of her tented legs. Once her foot twitches or she coughs dryly, she's about to fall asleep.

"Fan death is a myth," she says. "Just like lying down after a meal won't turn you into a cow."

"I love how that only applied to kids. Meanwhile Mom and Dad always passed the fuck out after lunch on their days off." I smile at the memory.

"Writing someone's name in red would definitely kill them, though," says June. "That's just science. And possibly the story line to a *Grudge* sequel." She leans and knocks her shoulder to mine. I smile. The first time we watched that movie, I slept in June's bed for a week.

We sit in silence for a moment.

"It's so weird." I stretch my legs out in front of me. "I didn't ever believe her, but I didn't *not* believe her. I don't think to question anything she's ever told me."

"Yeah, I get that." June stretches her legs out next to mine. "I always thought that if I just did everything the way she told me to, or the way she'd do it, that she'd love me more."

I stare at June's doll feet.

"I always figured Mom didn't like me anyway so what was the point?"

"She loves you," says June gruffly. "She's just the worst at letting you know. I don't think you can change people by acting a certain way. Just like how being skinny or smart doesn't make them treat you differently."

"I just want Mom to like me." I reach behind my sister and pull on the white bed skirt, releasing it from where it's hitched up on the box spring like a girl with her dress tucked into her panties. I don't mention the part where I wish my sister liked me, too.

June pats my leg with uncharacteristic affection.

"She likes you," she says and then laughs. "She told Helena Park, so it must be true."

chapter 37

Mom drives us to the airport the next morning. I expect her to say something profound, something worthwhile, but all she can talk about is how she's packed us lunches of kimbap.

"Did you remember everything? I put your clean underwear and laundry on your suitcases."

"Yeah," says June, who's sitting in front. Dad's at the restaurant for payroll.

"When will I see you girls again? Christmas?"

I look in the mirror, daring June to sign us up.

"We'll see," she says. "Depending on your behavior."

Mom scowls, and they both laugh. I watch the backs of their heads. I try to catch June's attention in the mirror, but she only has eyes for Mom. It breaks my heart that she thinks she's doing Mom a favor by not telling. I can tell she wants to.

"Thanks for the food," says June, instead of all the other things lingering in her expression.

"Yeah, Mom, thanks."

Mom turns and pats my leg. I love that she's put on lipstick for the short drive. "Don't wait so long to come back," she says to me.

I pop my door open.

Mom gets out and grabs our bags. Then she does something she's never done before. She gathers both of us into her arms. "Ah, my daughters," she says. "When will we be together like this again?"

She reaches for our hands. Her palms are papery and rough. "You're both going to get married off and probably move away even farther," she says. "Serves me right for leaving my own mother behind. They say that daughters are never yours to begin with." She squeezes our hands tightly, pursing her lips. I wonder if she'll cry. "And I guess they're right. Ji-hyun I knew would go away from the moment she was born. But you . . ." She palms my cheek. "You I thought I'd get to keep, my smallest blood clot."

I feel June watching us.

"Bye, Mom," I tell her, stepping away. June hugs her as I check my boarding pass for the hundredth time.

"Be nice to each other," she says. "You're all you've got."

It's not until we're past security that I burst into tears.

"I'm gonna get us some magazines," says June, turning away but squeezing my arm before she goes.

The moment wheels hit tarmac I text Patrick. I'm home.

He sends prayer hands as I grin stupidly into the aisle.

"Are you staying with me?" interrogates June when I get off the plane.

"Uh . . ." I'd been planning to ask. I have no idea if I even have running water at my place. "Is that okay with you?"

"Yes. God, shut up," she says, yanking my forearm. "Just hurry. I fucked up and already called the Uber. It's coming in four minutes."

As we're sprinting through the arrivals hall, I think of how much June and Mom have in common. Manufactured urgency is their absolute favorite emotion. I get it. Control feels good no matter how small the triumph. If anything, it's amazing that Mom doesn't move to New York. She'd love the energy if she gave it a chance. In New York you always feel late regardless of the circumstance.

Back in her apartment, we slump on the couch with our jackets on. Bags dumped at the door.

"Holy shit," she says. We were silent the entire ride home.

"I know."

"So tired." My sister keels over and closes her eyes.

It feels so good to be back but I know in a matter of minutes, she'll be asleep and we need to figure out food.

My phone buzzes in my hand. It's Patrick. When am I seeing you? and then I want to hear everything.

I smile, remembering our phone call. There's so much I want to say.

Cringing, I take the risk. Tomorrow?

Instead of tossing my phone across the room from douchechills, I leave it facedown on the coffee table and groan like an old woman.

"I'm so hungry," June says.

"Same." I get up to check the fridge. The turkey chili I made for her last week is still in there. The lidless saucepan has a ladle stuck in it. I pull it out and scrape it into the trash.

"At least I put it in the fridge," she calls out.

"We're going to have to get groceries," I tell her.

June groans.

"I can go." I wipe my hands on her crusty-ass kitchen towel. "Do you need anything?" I ask her, reaching for my coat.

"Fuck." June groans again. "I'll come with you."

Trader Joe's is a madhouse. I grab a basket so we can move quickly, but June upgrades for a double-decker cart. I watch the back of her head as she aggressively rips through the crowd. Everything is a contest with her. I wrest her cart away before she can drive us into the tangle of abandoned shopping carts that's been left in the middle of the frozen foods. If June steers, there's no way we're not catching a fistfight.

"Why do people do this?" she asks no one in particular, waving her hand at the carts. "It's so inconsiderate." We've been back in New York for a few hours and already the luxurious spaciousness of Texas is a distant memory. The store is a pit. The kind that requires four flag bearers to negotiate the enormous winding serpent of impatient New Yorkers from devolving into melees over riced cauliflower and smoked trout. Normally I'd rather spend the day at the literal post office than shop at any Trader Joe's, but I need my provisions. My prewashed salads, my zucchini noodles, my tamari rice cakes.

June disappears and reemerges with a paper shot glass of sample coffee. I drink it. I'm touched that she added almond milk. I toss the paper cup into the wooden barrel and miss. I furtively look around when I pick it up. I grab a carton of egg whites, salsa, beef jerky, and a sleeve of tricolor bell peppers. I swap the salsa out for hot sauce. The jar's too heavy.

June throws a stack of frozen meals into our cart. "This is garbage," I remark, picking up the frosty tray of enchiladas.

"It's not garbage; it's vegan," she says, adding one more plastic-enrobed brick while holding my gaze. "I make it when I'm tired."

I grab four more sheepishly and add them to the cart. I feel guilty all the time when I forget she's sick. As if the cancer will discover my negligence and multiply faster out of pique.

June disappears down the bread aisle, so I eye-fuck a pouch of salt-and-pepper pistachios, wondering how many servings it would be if I inhaled the whole thing. That's when I hear my sister yelling for me, Jayne and then *Ji-young*. Mom used to do this, scream our Korean names in public. I'm mortified. I text her back. JFC what? But she doesn't answer. I wind the cart to the next aisle, and there she is, smiling and waving me over. Talking to someone.

Patrick.

I rear back so violently that I crash into a woman behind me, who exclaims, "Ow-wah," as if it's a two-syllable word. I flip around and apologize, lurching forward. As I do, I buck the cart into a South Asian girl in white leggings standing with Patrick. "Ow-wah," she exclaims, rubbing her ankle. Her perfect sable eyebrows are in a full-tilt snit.

He's wearing a beanie and a thick, plaid work shirt. He looks sensational.

I, on the other hand, am wearing his sweats.

I grin, chastened, but something in the way his companion turns to him, indicating her injury, looking up with childlike concern, makes the smile die on my lips.

"Sorry," I mumble uncertainly at her.

Patrick's eyes yield nothing. As cold and resolute as a slammed door.

"Look who it is!" June's double-fisting paper cups of samples but still managing to make game-show hands.

I lose the staring match and blink down at his cart.

"Hey," I relent.

I must have overshot my casual tone because uncertainty flickers across June's face. "You know who this is, right?"

I nod and force myself to smile. "Sure. Hey, Patrick." My tone is pointedly treacly, nearing hostility.

"Yeah, hey. Jayne." Patrick waves a little.

I try to read his tone from the way he says my name. I decide that he seems annoyed.

"Holy shit," says June, turning to Patrick but not before shooting me a look. "I must have conjured you." She elbows him sportingly on his arm. "We were *just* in Texas and we went to church and I totally said to myself, I wonder what Patrick's up to, and now here you are. Fuck."

She looks at me again, like, *Can you believe this?*

"I'm June," says my sister to the girl beside him.

It unfolds in slow motion. Patrick's palm lifts off the red cart handle, ascends, and then lands on the girl's shoulder. Her glossy tresses shimmer from the contact. I'm clutching the pistachios so hard, my hand cramps.

"This is . . . ," begins Patrick falteringly, staring right at me. His eyebrows frown.

"Aliyah," says his beautiful friend as she touches her heart meaningfully.

"Sorry, Aliyah, I'm the worst, but I have to . . ." June pulls out her phone and throws it in selfie mode. "I have to send this to my mom. She'll flip. Patrick, we literally just got back today. Jayne, get closer."

My heart lurches nauseatingly in my chest. I back into them with my hair dusty from dry shampoo, smelling of airplane exhaust.

When my sister goes from portrait to landscape so she can fully include Aliyah, I almost ram our cart into her. "June," I say through clenched teeth.

"Thanks," June mumbles, scrolling through the photos. I make a desperate effort to catch Patrick's eyes, but he's transfixed by the pounds and pounds of trail mix, snack bags of nuts, dried fruit, candy, and boxes of granola bars in his cart.

"Camping?" I smile weakly. I'm desperate to pull out my phone, to check if he read my last text.

"In a sense," says Patrick.

Aliyah smiles up at him, the adoration apparent. "Not exactly," she says, in what I can hear now is a British accent. Fun. I brace myself for when she tells me she went to Oxford, too. Like every other scarily gorgeous woman in New York. "It's a little more mission-based. I'm in the Peace Corps, so I'm stocking up before I head back."

Cool. A genius humanitarian. Even still, the mention of the Peace Corps dislodges something in my memory. "Your sister's in the Peace Corps too, right?"

"Oh, you know Kiki?" Aliyah brightens with the intensity of several poreless suns. "That's how we met," says Aliyah. "Kirsten and I have been friends for a dog's age."

"Oh my God, your accent is delightful," says June, who never says things like "delightful."

A kind of snort-laugh escapes my throat. "Oh, totally," I enthuse. "Delightful." I want to throw a slab of mission figs directly into Patrick's face.

"Anyway, we should . . ." Aliyah nods toward the massive lines.

"Yeah," Patrick and I say in unison.

"What's your number?" asks June, already tapping his name into her phone. "I'll message you these." He leans in close to my sister and carefully recites it. His eyes flicker up to mine so quickly I may have imagined it.

"Good to see y'all," he says, smiling benignly and turning around. Aliyah waves.

"That was nice," says June, handing me a cup of something gray and wet. "It's pulled pork; it's pretty good." She crushes the pork mash into her mouth without a fork as if it's a Push Pop. I shake my head. She eats the other one.

"You know it wouldn't kill you just to eat it," she says. "It's literally a speck of food."

I push the cart down the aisle realizing with disorienting numbness that I'm devastated. I feel ridiculous.

"I've always liked Patrick," says June, oblivious. "But *she* seems like a nightmare. Like, who owns white leggings? That's like people who own white couches. Does she dress like that in the Peace Corps? How is she doing her laundry?"

I toss macadamia nuts and chocolate-covered almonds into the cart. And mini peanut butter cups.

June looks at the sweets and back at me.

"What's happening?"

My eyes blur with tears. "Why are you constantly making me do things I don't want to?"

June does a double take. "What the fuck are you talking about?"

I grab her forearm to move our cart aside so the masochistic woman with a stroller *and* a cart can get by.

"I didn't want the fucking pulled pork. And I didn't want to pose for fucking pictures in the middle of a store."

"Okay," says June, eyes wide.

"Can we just go?"

"Are you serious?"

I nod. Mute. Tears are fully streaming down my face to comingle with my leaking nose. I check my Trader Joe's tote for a napkin, a Kleenex, anything, but there's only a bobby pin and a dusty dime.

"Yeah, okay, fuck it," she says, and ditches our cart, steering me out by the elbow.

We trudge side by side for a block while I blindly search my pockets. My hand closes on the folded sheaf, pulling it out halfway before realizing what it is. I blow my nose on a mile-long CVS receipt.

A spitefully attractive dark-haired couple crosses the street in front of us. They have a baby. The man's sipping from a reusable coffee cup. He's wearing a lean black suit, with a BabyBjörn strapped to his chest. She has a blunt haircut under a blue beanie. And wearing an oversize camel coat, yellow clogs, she's clutching wildflowers wrapped in butcher paper. "Why do men always go for that type?" asks June, just as I was thinking that *she* definitely carries tissues in her purse. "The ones that look like they come with the picture frame?"

"Because men are trash," I say as we speed up to overtake them.

"I just don't get Patrick's girlfriend," says June.

"You think that's his girlfriend?"

"Amal fucking Clooney back there?" June snorts. "Of course that's his girlfriend. Staying together while she's in the Peace Corps? That's a sunk-cost move. That's at least two years deep. Plus, you don't go to Trader Joe's unless you're in it. It's grocery IKEA. Everybody knows that. You have to be prepared to fight. That's long relationship territory. Like, we're talking picking people up from the airport. That's not even healthy. That's codependent. You shouldn't ever go to Trader Joe's with anyone you plan on having regular sex with. That's what the Whole Foods hot bar is for."

I close my eyes. Watching her talk, cheeks puffed up, the way she orates with that smugness, as if she knows everything about everything. She makes me crazy.

"I know you and that idiot roommate-boyfriend weren't going to Trader Joe's together, am I right?"

I glare at her. The closest Trader Joe's to our apartment was on Court Street. It was a proximity issue, not an intimacy issue.

"Well, did you?"

I glare at her.

"See," she says triumphantly. "This is why I'm such a beast at my job. I know fucking everything about the human condition."

"Oh, yeah?" I shoot back. "Is that why you were fired?"

The barb pings off her without a mark. "Let's get Thai food," she says.

chapter 38

I wait until she's asleep to put on makeup. I watch my lips curl over my teeth as the lipstick glides on. The muscle memory of it is quieting. The placid, faraway place that made the rest of high school bearable. Hours of YouTube makeup tutorials prepared me for the rest of my life. I learned exactly how to appear indestructible. Impenetrable. Paint as armor.

I'm strangely calm. I'd let my guard down with Patrick, and that was my fault. I should have remembered: Everyone is disappointing.

June says that however badly people treat me, I treat myself worse. She doesn't get that there's a certain logic to it. When I had my wisdom teeth pulled last year, I couldn't stop rooting in the metallic socket, dislodging the blood clot with my tongue, exposing all the nerves. The pain had been so stunning and clear. It was both precise and expansive. I like that I could control when that zip of agony coursed through my head. It made everything and everyone else so quiet.

My hands sweep the brush across my skin. I'm looking at myself looking at myself into infinity. I could be anyone. I love how all girls' mouths look the same in the mirror. The more we put on our faces—highlighter, bronzer, brows, cat's eye, contoured, carved, concealed, and accentuated—the more we resemble one another.

I need a certain type of night. It doesn't matter where. The kind that doesn't affect you beyond the indescribable relief, the scratching of the itch, the bloodletting because you don't have to remember any of it. None of it counts. I have no use for consequences.

I loot the tequila from June's kitchen cupboard and help myself. It's golden in my throat. I text the easiest person to see, to talk to. The worst idea. It's as if I'm watching me from a distance.

He calls, and I'm thrilled by the immediacy of it. The thrust of intrusion. "What are you doing right now?" he bellows when I pick up. It's loud where he is and he's drunk. He always calls when he's drunk. "Meet us," he says before I can answer. The restaurant is noisy behind him.

I could walk there, I tell myself. It will give me plenty of time to change my mind. But in the next moment, I've arrived at the neon sign. It's a tractor beam. *Bright Lights, Big City.* This Tribeca corner is mythic. It's on the opening credits of the best seasons of *Saturday Night Live.* It feels like Christmas in my heart. It's perfect.

I glide through the door, unzipping my men's nylon flight jacket so that it slides off one shoulder. I'm wearing what amounts to lingerie. My earrings are big enough to ward off predators. The interior is a movie. I catch the eye of several people as I walk in, feeling their gazes graze me. I'm grateful for the ambience. It's easier to be practically naked in dim conditions. The amber glow given off by the globe pendant lamps casts the chatty, upturned faces in a warm, appealing light. Total Toulouse-Lautrec territory.

A thin, smartly dressed woman with a blunt bob greets me at the hostess stand. Her face is a pearl, set against the strong shoulders of her vintage red dress. The lights from the construction outside pulse against the drawn venetian blinds, casting angled shadows across her face and the room. She reminds me of a replicant, but I feel more like the cyborg as I tell her I'm looking for friends, scanning the bar area before I spot him.

He's sitting, clear across the room, tucked behind a beam at a leather-covered banquette in a corner. I wouldn't have seen him had it not been for the mirrors hanging high on the wall. I'm horrified that he's seated in such a snug spot. I can't tell who with. Whoever it is, the shoulders are draped in a dark blazer topped by a leonine head of fair hair. Other than kids dining with their parents, I'm the youngest by a decade.

There are people on dates bustling behind me as the trim, attractive waitstaff in black and white negotiate their way through with hot plates and limitless patience. I'm desperate to leave, and had the hostess not been quite so coolly beautiful, I might have hidden my face, ducked, and hustled out with a mumbled apology. But instead I smile breezily, matching her sangfroid with my own, and make my way over.

I can at least say hi.

The older gentleman with Jeremy turns with his napkin pressed against his face, a flash of irritation disappearing so quickly that I must have imagined it. I reach down for my coat zipper and do it up a bit. There are full dinner plates in front of them, and I'm horrified that I'm interrupting a meal, hanging over them in this awful way. I helplessly gather my jacket around me, so I don't disturb the couple next to them, who are now watching me as well.

"You can slide in with Jeremy," says the man, calling someone over.

"Let's get that coat checked." He eyes my enormous bomber. I do as I'm told, reluctantly baring my arms.

I'm basically naked, gritting my teeth so as not to shiver. I feel eyes on me and then realize it has nothing to do with my scant clothes and everything to do with this incredibly famous actor who even my parents would recognize.

"Hey, you," says Jeremy, pressing his warm cheek to my cold one. I don't know where to put my hands, pressed up against him like this, and when he slings his arm over the back of the banquette and around my neck, I don't protest. Sandalwood cologne wafts over me and fills the sides of my mouth in warning saliva.

The actor watches us, never breaking eye contact or even blinking. He smiles, seeming on the verge of speech, but a calculation is taking place. I am being appraised. His eyes are a watery cerulean but beady. Set against puckered lips and florid, chubby cheeks, with his glinting cuff links and enormous watch, it dawns on me that I'm talking to a royal class of piglet.

Anybody really can be made to look like anyone.

"Have you eaten?" he asks, gesturing to his plate, and when I nod, he nods as well. "I didn't know we'd be having company. I'd have insisted on another table."

"I'm sorry," I falter. "I thought I was meeting y'all for drinks." I glance at Jeremy, who refuses my eye. I get it. Every man for himself. This is an entirely new stratosphere of ambition for him. An establishment that outpaces all the cool downtown art kids.

The actor saws into his fish. "Well, then, let's get you a drink." He chews and raises his brows at Jeremy, who springs into action and orders.

I'm gratified at seeing Jeremy like this. So utterly dominated.

"Thank you." I direct it to him, not Jeremy. "I wouldn't have dreamed of interrupting your dinner."

He glances at me just once. He's done discussing it.

I clear my throat.

"You know, this place used to be crawling with celebrities back in the eighties," he tells me. I have to lean in to hear him. I hold the neckline of my dress against my clavicle with my cold palm. "Marty, Bobby, Keith Haring, Grace Jones. John Belushi used to march straight into the kitchen, into the walk-ins, and make whatever he wanted. Tribeca was obviously different back then. So much cocaine."

Jeremy laughs at the cocaine reference. A quick snort that makes the actor stop chewing and shoot a questioning look. As if to ask what's the matter with him.

I'm surprised that Jeremy isn't bothering to show him up. I wonder who this man is to him.

At no point does the man introduce himself or ask my name.

"I gather you're from the South," he says. I'm astounded.

"Texas," I report dutifully.

He nods as if there's a correct answer. "You said y'all earlier. What do you do for"—he conducts the air briefly with his knife and fork as if looking for a word—"work?" he finishes.

"I'm in school." Our drinks arrive in low glasses. "For fashion."

"But surely you can see that by how fashionably she's attired," says Jeremy. My face burns. I uncross my legs. Under the table, I finger the hem of my short dress. The actor smiles politely.

He raises his glass, so I raise mine and take a big sip. I could take it down in four healthy gulps and run out.

"How do you like your old-fashioned?" he asks with a crooked smile teasing at his lips. It's famous, this particular smile of his. It crinkles his eyes, as if he's finding humor in something just outside of your perception.

The cocktail burns a course down my throat and ends in a treacly cherry flavor. I nod appreciatively, licking my lips, turning my face away from him as I do.

"You know they invented the cosmo here?"

I take another sip. He tilts his chin up encouragingly while I drink, as if helping me along, and when I dab my mouth with a napkin, I'm rewarded with another curving of his lips. It's the patronizing smile particular to super-celebrities doing Japanese instant-coffee commercials. The low-rent kind that come in cans.

I can't help but stare at the hairs on his wrist, which curl over the metal strap of his huge, incredibly expensive timepiece.

"I don't understand fashion, which I'm sure you can guess." The actor's eyes twinkle. It's as if Jeremy isn't at the table. "I've been wearing the same Brioni suits for the past thirty years. Maybe the occasional Loro Piana sweater. My daughter's in school for the very same thing. She says I dress like a senator she'd never vote for."

"At least it's not Brooks Brothers." I smile down at my hands.

"What's your name?" he finally asks. I glance up. It's as if there's a floodlight pouring out of his eyes and into mine. I'm filled with warmth.

"Jayne."

"With a y," interjects Jeremy, and I hear the insult in it.

"Like Jayne Mansfield," says the actor, ignoring him. "It's a beautiful name."

The actor gets me another drink, and I thank him, unaware that I'd finished the first. My gratitude knows no bounds. I can't believe this important man, a man everyone in the restaurant leaves alone out of reverence, is paying such close attention to me. I'm jealous of his daughter.

"You seem like a resourceful young woman, Jayne," he begins. "I have a question for you. My oldest, the one in design school, says unpaid internships are unethical. I can't keep up with all of this"—he shakes his head—"PC business or this new sensitivity. I get it: Don't take your Johnson out and start whacking off in front of the ladies— pardon the vulgarity—but why wouldn't she take a position with a dear friend who can help her out? It's who you know, not what you know, don't you think?"

I'm grateful to be asked. "It's about leveling the playing field," I tell him carefully. "If the position is unpaid, it means that only people who can afford to work for free can qualify for it. It's unethical because . . ."

I feel Jeremy tense beside me.

The actor wipes his mouth, sets the napkin on his plate. It seems to signal something, but I'm unsure of what.

"Believe me," he says, smiling indulgently, crinkling his eyes, but not with any sense of levity. In fact, the sudden hardness in his look stops me short. "This isn't an internship anyone else would qualify for," he insists. "With or without money. If she can afford to work for free, why shouldn't she? I can see it being unethical if she took a paying job from someone who really needs the ten bucks an hour or whatever it is."

I empty a good half of my second drink.

"Oh, of course," I reason. "That makes sense. I can see both sides, is what I'm saying. I think your daughter has honorable intentions, that testify to, um, how well she was brought up, which is amazing. But if we're being realistic, I agree with you on a logical basis."

I can't tell if I'm hallucinating, but I feel as though his shoulders ease a little.

"Creative fields are different," says Jeremy.

"Exactly," says the actor. "Real business is indifferent to business hours. You don't tell Lorne Michaels or Mick Jagger that you clocked out because it's five."

"Amen," says Jeremy with his palms raised.

"I worry about how delicate everyone's becoming. I'm all for women's lib. Civil rights. All of it. But everyone's being ridiculous. Triggered this, triggered that. Some of these men are monsters, don't get me wrong. Especially the ones going after underage girls. That's despicable. They should be locked up. But most of the conversation seems patronizing. As the father of daughters, I know that it's women who are the real ballbusters." He chuckles as if imagining his girls kicking some creep in the stones. "No man would have to be told no twice is what I'm saying."

Suddenly he pushes his chair away from the table. I wonder if it's something I said. I hope to God Jeremy takes care of the check.

"Restroom," he announces.

When he's gone, Jeremy forks up several fries and the rest of his steak and shoves it into his mouth, then takes a sip of his drink. "I knew you'd cave," he says, body language easing. "Fucking drama queen." He wipes his mouth. "Where've you been anyway?"

I'm barely listening as I watch the room hum with novel energy as the actor walks by. As soon as his back is turned, heads duck low, people excitedly mouthing his name to each other. It's as if gold coins are trailing in his wake. I can imagine them telling the story of the sighting to their friends. I wonder if I'll feature in it at all. Some Asian girl, they might say. Not his wife, they'll say, cheapening me. Far in the corner, there's a phone out, set low and at an angle. I know they're taking a creep shot of him, and suddenly I feel protective.

"I'll be back," I tell Jeremy, vaguely aware that he's talking to me about the apartment. I cross the restaurant quickly, and when I get downstairs, I see him. He's posing with a group of three women stooped in a sorority squat for a selfie. When they're done, one whispers close in his ear, red nails clutching the shoulder of his jacket. On his feet, he appears older. And rounder. He smiles his crinkly smile at the woman, and when they step out of the way so I can get to the bathroom, the actor doesn't even glance at me. A flash of anger detonates in my chest.

The bathroom is a beautiful one. A hammered-tin ceiling painted white. More mirrors. Checkerboard tile on the walls. Iconic bathroom selfie lighting. I pee, feeling a little sad. Glad for my own story. I tell myself that I won't go back home with Jeremy, wondering if I mean it.

I sigh, dreading the rest of the night, but when I leave the bathroom, he's there. Waiting for me. I'm pleased to be chosen.

"You're so nice to give those girls a selfie," I tell him, wanting one of my own.

"When they stop asking is when you have to start worrying," he says, smiling.

I gaze at the stairs, elated that we'll be reentering the restaurant together, but instead of offering me his arm, he looks around furtively and steps closer to me. He holds my attention, and before I know it, his wet bottom lip is touching mine. Tentatively. I don't know what to do, but I'm frightened, reluctant to appear rude and disrupt the story for both of us. As I'm kissing him back, as his old-man tongue—a creepy, surprisingly athletic protuberance—blankets mine, I wonder if he'll still walk me upstairs.

"You know, my priest is Vietnamese," he says, pulling away and grazing his lips to my temple. "On the Upper East Side. Tremendous sermons."

I smile back and touch my lip. I realize that I'd thought he'd brought up his daughter as a signal. To indicate that he was safe. A family man. A silly dad.

He encircles my other wrist with his hand and gazes down at it.

"I have an apartment in the city." He pulls my hand and brushes the back of it against the warmth of his crotch.

I'm grateful that there is a staircase, Jeremy, and an entire restaurant standing between me and this imposing man's car.

"I have school in the morning," I tell him. He releases my wrist as I whip around and bolt. "Sorry." I rush upstairs, marching on shaky legs, straight to the hostess area to demand my coat.

Come on, come on, come on. I'm scared to look, but the temptation is overpowering. I glance over my shoulder to catch Jeremy half rising, toothy smile frozen on his face, greeting the actor, who's returned to the table. I can't see the actor's expression, the turn of his mouth or his words, but Jeremy laughs at whatever he's said, and it stings. I know Jeremy's a snake, but I didn't think he'd serve me up in this way. When they return with my jacket, I throw them my last ten bucks, grab it, and run into the street.

Patrick calls. I let it go to voicemail.

chapter 39

"Sex," proclaims June when I come home from school a few days later. "Sex," she repeats, when she realizes any curiosity on my part is not forthcoming. She's eating Stoneground crackers out of the box at the kitchen counter and spraying crumbs everywhere.

I've been too scared to go back to my apartment since the night with the actor. Jeremy's texted twice complaining about the lack of hot water. I hadn't expected him to check in on me, but the full extent of his selfishness is breathtaking.

The thought of sex turns my stomach.

"What about it?"

"I'm having it." Sure enough, she shows me the highlighted word in her bullet journal. "I'm making a checklist to accomplish before November nineteenth."

I pull out my phone and check my calendar. "What's November nineteenth?"

"My surgery date." She flips her datebook and shows that to me too.

The violence of communicating with my sister is outrageous.

"But that's, like, next week."

"Week after next," she says. "Tuesday. Seven thirty a.m. I got the first surgery of the day."

"June." I almost reach out to swat the cracker out of her hand. "Well, can I come?"

"If you want."

"When did you make the appointment?"

"In Texas."

"But I was with you the whole time."

"Can we get back to talking about me?"

I shake my head, completely flabbergasted. "How are we not talking about you?"

"You're talking about my organs," she corrects. "I'm trying to tell you about things I want to accomplish."

"Like sex."

"Exactly."

"How is that not talking about your organs?"

"Fuck you," she says, laughing. "Wait." June tilts her head quizzically. "Is a vagina an organ?"

"What?" Again, I never know if she's messing with me. "Of course it's an organ."

"Is it? No, it's not. Lungs are organs. Your heart, liver, those are organs. They have, like, a wrapping."

"Just because you name other organs doesn't make a vagina not an organ." I can't believe this conversation. "A penis is an organ."

"Right. It has a wrapping," she says, pulling out her phone. I know she's checking, so I google as fast as I can.

"The vagina is a tubelike muscular . . . ," I recite off my screen.

". . . but elastic *organ* about four to five inches long . . . ," she chimes in, and starts speed-reading to beat me.

"November nineteenth?" I set an appointment for 7:30 but then delete it. I hate the idea of JUNE SURGERY sharing space with my work schedule and homework assignments. And there's no way I'd forget.

"So I have to get D'd before then."

"Yuck, June, God."

I haven't had sex in months and I'm fucking relieved. Jeremy had one unvarying move. This numbing pneumatic thrusting that made me feel as though I was being drilled for oil. He also had the mortifying habit of talking dirty. It wasn't that it was crudely kinky or filthy. It was a generic recitation, an almost dry-running commentary of what he was doing.

Now I'm going to put my . . . And then I'm going to . . .

"When's the last time you . . . ," she begins. "Actually, don't answer that." My sister shudders slightly. "Gross."

June pulls down a cookbook from her shelf. "I was thinking of having a party. Invite people over." She flips to a picture of kicky hors d'oeuvres featuring edible flowers. "See," she goes, pointing, "I could do this."

The recipe involves anchovies. I take it from her and shut it. "June, nobody gets laid at a dinner party. Just get on Tinder and be clear about your intentions. That you want to touch organs. Who are you inviting?"

"Work people I can hate-fuck."

I try not to envision my sister's naked body squirming rhythmically under some finance douche and fail.

"And some friends," she adds, clearing her throat. She reads something in my face and her expression shifts. "They're probably not as *cool* as your friends, but they're good people."

"Okay," I say carefully. And then, to add levity, "Can finance people be good people?"

"Fuck you," she snaps. "They're *nice* to me." She watches me closely. I can't tell if she's defending herself from an insult that I have no intention of lobbing or if she's taunting me. "It's not going to be a big party or anything, but it'll be fun. Or not fun, but chill." She rolls her eyes and begins to furiously type into her phone. "You're coming, right?"

Her eyes widen at my half-beat of hesitation.

"Yeah," I manage. "Of course."

"Well, don't do me any fucking favors," she says hotly, and storms off into the bathroom leaving me to stare after her with my mouth open.

chapter 40

I check the awning of the brick and wood restaurant in Nolita before entering. It's a perfectly respectable, bustling trattoria, and I'm told to walk all the way to the back and downstairs. The "secret bar" where June's having her get-together is located in the basement beyond the coat check. For once I made the right decision and wore sneakers so that I can beat an Irish goodbye. I'm not in the mood for some Vyvanse-snorting, *Atlas Shrugged* obsessive finessing me over sixteen-dollar cocktails.

I come straight from school, wearing the least flattering clothes I own. Classic man repellant. Wide-leg black pants, Vans, and a black sweater with holes at the elbows. The space is cavernous, cold. A cellar wine bar aglow in red lamplight, dark carpets, and rows of dusty bottles behind the long wood bar. I was expecting flocks of suits, but the crowd is diverse. Erratic jazz plays, and the gathered clusters talk in low tones. The ambience isn't dominated by any particular energy. I'm surprised June knows about this place. It seems the kind of place Jeremy would hide from his friends.

Booths line the back wall, which is dotted with framed pictures.
I see June standing among the crowd spilling out from the corner
table. She's wearing a low-cut dress, champagne flute in hand. Her
heels must be at least six inches tall. When she teeters toward me, my
insides wobble. I imagine her tumbling, cracking her head wide on a
table. She grasps my forearm unsteadily.

"Hey, you made it," she says. Her blowout highlights her cheekbones, the layers cascading in soft waves around her face.

"Um." I'm speechless from the full majesty of her dress. It's literal
red satin, wrapped around her waist, and her décolletage is hoisted
up in full commitment to the fluttery flamenco hem. The cut flatters
her enormously. "Nice dress," I tell her, instead of what I want to say,
which is: "Tits much?"

"Thanks." Her eyelashes are so long, she's serving uncanny valley.
Compared to how she's looked in the past month, it's almost as if
she's wearing a prosthetic face.

Someone over her shoulder cracks a joke I don't catch, and she
turns around. I look past her to regard her friends. It's an odd mix
of pale-blue button-ups under sleeveless fleece vests, one guy in a
comically slender suit, and a woman with super-short hair in jeans
and a windbreaker. My initial assessment is that they don't look rich.
Or even particularly smart. "No, seriously," insists a sandy-haired guy
with enormous teeth. "Look it up—it's called compersion. It's experiencing joy at someone else's joy even when you have nothing to gain
from it. It's the opposite of jealousy and the highest form of empathy."

"I don't think you're in any danger of becoming an empath," says
my sister, cutting him off and pulling me into the fray. "Guys . . ."

The guys turn to me.

"This is my little sister, Jayne."

"Hey." I smile weakly.

"This is Malick." June gestures to everyone in order. "Wooj, Lyla, Elliot, Chen, Golds, Adam . . ." I make no effort to retain any of their names as I keep my hand raised in hello.

They chuckle and murmur, some of them waving encouragingly.

"So, this is Selina's sister," says one of the middle ones, toasting me with a beer. "Respect."

"Didn't Selina actually have a sister?" the bearded one asks, as if I have any idea what they're talking about. "Wasn't she like a nun? Maggie or something?"

"Silence, nerds," says June, raising a hand.

"Selina?" I ask her.

"Ignore them," she says. "I put a card down." She leans in to tuck a strand of hair behind my ear. "Tell Serge what you want." She points to the bartender behind me. "Did you eat?"

I shake my head.

"I'm getting food sent over even though I know digesting isn't sexy." She huddles closer. She smells of dark, lacquered wood and smoke, a perfume I don't recognize. "I don't want anyone barfing before we get to it," she says.

"Who are these people?" I ask her.

"Work dorks, mostly," she says. "I went to college with Lyla. She's a socialist." June shrugs. "I thought I'd mix it up."

She squeezes my arm. "Thank you for dressing hideously so that I can sparkle. It's so considerate."

"Do you need anything?" I gesture toward the bar.

June knocks back the rest of her drink. "Actually, I'll come with you." She burps a little and grabs my forearm for support as I lead.

"I want to get pregnant," she tells me once we're out of earshot.

"Tonight?"

"While I can."

An odd squeak escapes my throat. "What—and those guys back there are your donors?" I glance at the table.

"Essentially."

"June."

"I'm serious," she says, clutching my forearm with her talons. "Just to know what it feels like at least for a second."

"If you were pregnant for a few days, it's just a few cells. It's like you ate a corn nut. It's barely a shadow."

"I haven't ever even taken the fucking morning-after pill."

"It's no picnic," I retort, and she looks at me for a beat.

"Gross," she says, and then laughs.

I sit sidesaddle on a stool watching her lean onto the gleaming wood bar, boobs hoisted, foot hitched on the brass railing underneath.

"Why?"

"May as well take the ol' equipment around the block."

"Well, do you want to have a baby?" I ask her.

"Not with any of these dipshits," she quips.

Her smile dies when she sees my expression.

"Don't you think if you want to be pregnant for a second, it might be worth thinking about? Dr. Ramirez said you could talk to a fertility specialist. You could still freeze . . . *something*."

She ignores me to hail the bartender. "I'll have two Bombay martinis, extra dry, filthy. With two olives each, up." June points her thumb when she says "up."

For a second I'm distracted that she knows how to do that. To order a martini in that way.

"You're going to have kids, right?" She turns to me.

"I . . ." I think about my period. How long it's been gone. How I'm terrified that I've broken something in there from all the abuses I've heaped on my body in the last few years. "I don't know," I tell her.

Our frosty martini glasses arrive. She leans over to slurp the top of hers before picking it up, and I copy her. It's briny, slippery, and cold.

June takes her cardboard coaster upright and absentmindedly saws the edge of the bar with it. "I did talk to them. The fertility people. I even talked to Steph, and I'm not a good candidate for ovarian preservation. I asked. I can physically do it all—go on hormones, put it off as long as possible, try to have a baby—but nobody advises it. The thing is, I don't want to find an angle on this one. I always try to game things, and it's never worked. The reality is, I don't want to risk it . . ."

She raises her glass to me. "I got to get knocked the fuck up right now."

"Okay." I raise mine. "To you conceiving however briefly at your secret hysterectomy sex party."

We clink glasses.

"And to the science fiction horror show of me giving birth to my own fucking uterus and ovaries."

"Jesus, June."

She keeps her glass held aloft, so I touch it with mine.

We drink.

"Life is fucking weird," she says.

"It is."

"Do you think it gets worse?"

"Probably?"

She laughs and toasts me again, which makes me laugh. My sister hugs my shoulders and squeezes. I wrap my arms around her middle. In her stripper heels, she's taller than me for once.

"Fuck, Jayne," she says after a while, blinking rapidly, eyelashes fan-dancing. "I hate this." She exhales slowly. I hand her a cocktail napkin, which she touches to the corners of her eyes. Her finger-nails are shellacked in an oystery color. "But at least semen is an anti-depressant, I think. It's also basically all protein, right?"

"Totally." I have no idea if this is true.

"Promise me you'll have kids." June blots her nostrils and inspects the contents of her napkin.

"June."

"You'd be a good mom," she says. A lump forms in my throat. "Everyone fucks everyone up, but you're so fucked up already, you'll be understanding about stuff like that."

"Thanks, I guess."

"You're a good teammate." She clears her throat.

I think about the two of us. Our tiny cult.

"And you're sure you don't want to talk to Mom about any of this?"

June shakes her head and extracts the olive at the bottom of her glass. "They have enough going on." My sister places the furry olive pit on her napkin.

I think of Dad's lump of dough, parceled off and tossed into deep-freeze time-out so that the rest of the family can thrive. I won-der if that's what June's been doing all along in plain sight. Hiding her vulnerabilities so as not to be a burden.

When her second drink arrives, she takes another healthy slug.

"Wish me luck," she says, heading back toward her friends. "Gotta get my organ basted."

chapter 41

Patrick walks in as I'm giving June a thumbs-up. Heat prickles my scalp. When we lock eyes, he smiles. I take a sip of my drink to know where to look and what to do with my hands and face.

My heart hiccups against my diaphragm.

"Hi," I say once Patrick's too close to ignore. The effort in my smile makes my left ear pop. All of this is intolerable. My chest is a too-small shoe for the blood-filled foot of my heart. I feel like I'm going to pass out.

"Hey," he says, smile faltering slightly.

I take a step toward him and offer my cheek as I squeeze his shoulder. "Guess I can't get rid of you, huh?"

He slides his beanie off, and his hair is messier than usual. Plus, he's got a good bit of scruff going on. His cheek is cold from outside, and he's as rumpled as I've ever seen him.

He leans in, flashing his teeth with uncertainty. "Actually, wait, I didn't hear you. What did you say?"

I'm close enough to feel the heat of his neck on my lips. "It doesn't matter," I mumble, pulling back. "I said, um, whatever." I flap my hands near my face unbecomingly. "Sorry."

"Is it June's birthday?" he asks.

"What?"

"June . . . ? She made it sound like it was her birthday."

I shrug. "It's just a regular get-together."

"You want to sit down?" he asks.

The things I do for my sister.

My thoughts go scribbly with pent-up bitterness as I pick a small round table and pull out a seat.

I've had three cups of coffee today and little else. I couldn't possibly hate myself faster.

He unzips his leather jacket as he sits and sets it on the back of his chair. The image of the two of us in matching sweatpants feels both so long ago and so far in the future that I'm racked with a sense of vertigo.

He runs his hands through his hair again. He looks tired.

The past few weeks come hurtling into memory, a deranged carousel of indignities that frankly have so little to do with him. The cockroaches at home. June's rage at Dairy Queen. My inaccessible, unknowable parents. Rae's thin thigh. Calling Jeremy after everything that happened. The actor's mouth on mine. The hot scrape of old-man tongue.

I'm lit bright with shame when the kaleidoscope of images refracts all the way back to me groping Patrick in that disgusting bathroom, so slobbering, needy, and frightened.

Of course he has a girlfriend. And she doesn't even have social media. I checked. It's just one more way she's better than me.

I pull my phone out as if to peruse important emails. My arms may as well belong to somebody else.

Patrick clears his throat. "So, I brought her a present." He shows me a tastefully matte shopping bag.

That he went out of his way to buy something for my sister fills me with small, hard, mean thoughts.

"How touching. She'll love it," I hear myself saying woodenly. "You should go say hi." I point to the back corner, where June's meaningfully grabbing the shoulder of a baby-faced brown-haired guy that she's towering over. She's making huge hand gestures. They must have changed the Spotify playlist because indeterminate U2 blusters all around us.

"Yeah, okay," he says, pushing his chair out and glancing back to the bar. "I'll get us drinks first?"

"Sure. A Bombay martini. Up. With two olives. Um . . ." I try to remember the rest of the order. "Yeah, that's what I want."

"So, no vodka soda."

I shake my head, disgusted with the part of me that shimmies giddily that he remembered my drink from last time.

I watch him walk away. His shoulders rise as he leans against the bar. He hitches his foot on the bar railing, and the way his sweatshirt rides up a little in the back, the way the break of his jeans falls on his pristinely clean sneakers, just the way everything seems so effortlessly boy and attractive and unperturbed finally ignites some sense of unfairness. He's so fucking okay. Just so fucking aboveboard and respectable with his stupid thoughtful gifts and his insouciantly mussed hair.

When he returns, I'm braced by the overwhelming urge to hit him. Hard. Right on the arm. Just to see if my discomfort lessens. I'm incensed that his leather jacket doesn't make him appear as though he's wearing a costume, which is how I feel when most men wear leather jackets. I'm insulted that when he sets my drink down in front of me, he smiles easily and that the silence is somehow comfortable when he does.

Remember when you said that New York was waiting? I want to ask him. *That you wouldn't forget about me? Was that literally, figuratively, or bullshittingly?* I want to sustain this anger and indignation in a stalwart display of feminist outrage, anything that even remotely hints to a sense of pride, but it's flagging already.

When he leaves to greet June, she lights up and pulls him in for a hug. I can see by the slack of her torso that she's wasted. She introduces him in what may as well be a silent film, her gestures are so comically exaggerated. She hugs him again when he hands her the bag, holding the embrace a beat longer than necessary and whispering something in his ear. The sudden, piercing thought arrives that she's invited him as an option. My sister is absolutely conniving for sex with Patrick. I can't tell if I'm repulsed or impressed by how undeterred she is by his girlfriend.

My mouth is rank from the olive particles carpeting my tongue.

I stare at the black square of cocktail napkin under the foot of my glass. There isn't even a ring. Fucker didn't even spill a drop on his way over. That's what we're dealing with. As I lift it, it dribbles onto my lap.

I'm heated when he comes back around. Worked up into a full lather.

"Well, it's definitely not her birthday." He pulls his chair out and sits down.

"I told you it wasn't."

He looks over his shoulder "Man, I don't know what the fuck that energy was."

I follow his gaze and laugh. I can't help it. It is a deeply weird vibe. June's standing with her back to us, one hand placed on the shoulder of two different dudes. It's as if they're posing for a family portrait in which she's the dad. I'm astounded by the adult she's become. It both makes total sense and none at all.

"What'd you get her?"

"Macarons," he says. "Nice ones."

Jesus, what a suck-up. "That's such a gift you'd give an aunt," I tell him. "Were they sold out of boxes of fruit or what?"

"I have no idea," he says stiffly. "It's been a long week."

I check the time. It's just after ten. A perfectly respectable hour to leave, but of course now I don't want to.

"So did your friend Aliyah make it back okay?" I take a phantom sip of a martini from the glass that is now clearly empty. "She seems nice." I don't know why I'm opening this portion of the conversation with the unveiled contempt of a sociopath from a reality dating show.

"Yeah," he says, observing me with the appropriate level of caution.

"She's so pretty," I insist. Honestly, I can't stop myself.

"She had some things to deal with in town."

"Nothing bad, I hope." I say this to seem classy even if bad things happening to Patrick's girlfriend isn't entirely without appeal.

"It went okay," he says. He removes a pack of mints from his pocket and eats one.

"May I?" He shoots me a quick look as you would someone who says "may I."

He holds the tiny metal tin toward me. My hand extracts one with the precision of a metal claw game at the amusement park. I accidentally take four and quickly shove them into my mouth as if he won't notice.

He snaps the box shut, and I'm struck by how much I want to reach out and grab his hand. Hold it to my face like a freak.

"I mean, like, *so* pretty." I have no idea who's piloting the control center of my brain at this point.

He takes a deep breath. "I wanted to tell you about her."

I smile brightly. "Well, now you don't have to," I demur. "We're fine, Patrick. Honestly, you don't owe me an explanation. We don't owe each other anything." I am the very picture of detachment. A person with options. I may not have the job he has or the apartment or the significant other or the art, but one day I might.

"I'm getting another drink," he says.

I watch him leave and realize that the bar's suddenly heaving with activity. I check the time. It's leapt to midnight somehow.

Patrick returns with his beer and takes a long swallow. I notice that I've torn the cocktail napkin into little strips. Trying to get from end to end without ripping the strand.

"I called a car." June stumbles over to us. "This is Kazmi," she says, placing her entire open hand on the chest of the guy whose arm is around her waist. "First name, Salim."

"Hey." He up-nods and stumbles back a half step, laughing as he recovers.

"Analyst," she adds. Her eyes are closed as she says this, but then they snap open to follow brightly with "Aries," as if to justify her choice.

Salim's Adam's apple juts out at a true ninety-degree angle, and he's tall and scrawny—a collision of corners—but the rest of his face is all circles. He has huge dark eyes—Disney eyes—a bulbous nose, and bee-stung lips.

"What's up?" he says. They're both spectacularly wasted.

"I think I should go back with them," I tell Patrick, gathering my things. "So she doesn't get murdered." I can't deduce if she knows Salim or she's picked him from the bar.

"I guess I'll head out too," he says, slipping on his jacket.

We trudge upstairs, and I'm overcome by the urge to shake him. We've held hands before. He's cooked for me. I slept in his bed. *Pops!* I want to scream at him.

Patrick waits with us until the car comes. I catch snippets of June's conversation.

Patrick. Church. Can you believe it?

A black car pulls up. Gleaming and morose. June gets in the far door. Salim in front.

"Hey," Patrick says into my ear as I open my side. I stall, wondering what sage parting words he'll leave me with. Instead he asks, "Where are you gonna be while, they're, you know . . . ?" He nods to the lovely couple we've poured into a car. "Like, is this a one-bedroom?"

"Fuck," I whisper more to myself than to him.

"You getting in, buddy?" my sister's sperm donor calls out from the front seat. "It's a party," he continues.

"Party, party," June mutters with her eyes closed. She's leaned up against the window. Little exhales fogging up the glass by her mouth.

"Scoot over," he says. I roll my eyes, nod, and scoot over. He gets in and shuts the door.

chapter 42

Smooth classical music washes over us in the dark. I can already tell by June's stillness that she's asleep.

"What are you doing?" I whisper to Patrick. This is the closest we've been since that night. His thigh is pressed up against mine, and I'm holding myself as still as I can. Not even leaning into his side as the car turns sharply.

June's snoring softly. He smiles at her, then back at me, and even in my irritation I smile. The bastard's breath smells like mint. "We can take a walk when we get there," he whispers. "Or get a cup of coffee." He leans in closer to me. "Do you really want to be third-wheeling it on this little *scrimmage?*" He looks out the window for a moment. "Look, I can get out and go home once we drop them off," he says. "Entirely up to you."

He holds my gaze for a long time. "I just . . . I know I owe you an explanation," he says. "If you'll let me."

My resistance gives. "Fine."

"You go on up," I tell June when we arrive at her building. Her eyes dart to Patrick, then to me, and back to him. She shrugs, and the two of them shamble through her lobby.

It smells bright and clear outside. As if it's about to snow. We're posted up on the street in front of the glass-enclosed white entryway. I cross my arms to conserve heat and tuck my head as low as I can. Anyone reading our backlit body language across from us would take this for a breakup.

"I'm going to sound like an asshole however I say this," he begins, hands shoved in his jeans pockets. I peer at him over my jacket collar. "Aliyah and I broke up."

Maybe it's the cold, but I don't feel immediate relief. I search for a tremor of glee. I locate an ugly speck of smugness, but mostly I wonder who broke up with who.

"You got a Tinder alert," I say accusingly. "In the bathroom. That first night we met at the bar."

This has troubled me more than anything else. The fucked-up truth is that if he'd cheated on his girlfriend with me, I could have forgiven him. Hell, I'm damaged enough that I might have been flattered. But I wanted to believe better of him. The Patrick I knew— rather, the Patrick I *thought* I knew—is a much better person than I am. Better than some dude trawling dating sites for Strange.

"Right . . ." He sighs. "But it's . . ."

"Oh God." I throw my hands up. "Please don't say it's complicated." I feel so stupid.

"We're not actually together," he says. The "actually" zips up my spine, settling into an exquisite twinge at the base of my skull. I find myself smiling.

I imagine Jeremy putting it exactly that way when he was hooking up with other people. "We're roommates," he'd whisper to yet another aspiring performance artist. "We were together, but now we're not together-together."

I am the common denominator. Patrick is an improvement over Jeremy, who is leagues beyond Holland, and for all three I am utterly disposable.

"I don't know if it's complicated," he says. "More that . . ."

He's shifting his weight from foot to foot. I realize how impractical his leather jacket is and I'm relieved to experience aversion. Vain men are weak, I reason. I congratulate myself for dodging a bullet. Fuck this man and the rest like him.

"Why does it bother you that I was on Tinder?"

I roll my eyes at the past tense.

"Look," he begins. "You're the one who hit me up in the middle of the night to meet you at the skeeviest bar in all of New York, including Staten Island. I'm like, holy shit, it's Jayne. Maybe she's new in town. Maybe she's just out and about. I know nothing. I meet you. We get shitfaced; it's fun. Then you pull me into a bathroom even though there's a huge line of people waiting to go before us."

I'm embarrassed to hear myself characterized like this.

"Then you puke, not on the sidewalk but in the literal street, almost getting decapitated by a moving vehicle, and then, just as I'm wondering what exactly I've gotten myself into, you announce that you've got nowhere else to go. Honestly, Jayne, if you were literally any other woman in this city, that would've been it. Actually, no, none of this would've happened in the first place. I would have tapped out a solid seven moves before that. But you're you. I know your family. I've met your mom. I foster a healthy fear of your sister. I wasn't going to leave you falling-down wasted in the gutter. So I loan you my clothes. You use my shower. I cook for you. I act like a fucking gentleman and give you the bed. We hang out the day after. I thought it was chill."

He sighs. I can see his breath. His eyes are hard, then soft.

"Jayne," he says. "I would have told you about Aliyah at any point had we seen each other again. I should have told you that first night. I knew it was fucked up. But it's why we didn't hook up. Why I stopped. But I also didn't want to seem presumptuous and call you, like, *I have a girlfriend.* I was dating a lot of people, and I don't know anything about your situation."

"You were dating a lot of people?" My voice is anemic and pitiable.

I stare at him, face completely numb.

I glance up at the gleaming building, trying to see which unit is hers.

"They're not done," he says, reading my mind. He breathes into his fists and scowls.

"Here," he says, nodding across the street. It's a delivery entrance with a glorious recess and nice thick walls to block the wind. There are even stairs on a stoop.

Without hesitation we run-waddle and sit side by side, huddling close. "We had an open relationship because she wanted one," he says. "It wasn't working. So we broke up."

I'm doubled over with my hands shoved in my pockets, and my breath warms my knees. "I'm sorry."

"No, you're not."

"No, I'm not."

"We were together for two years," he says. "Living together for six months. She didn't tell me she applied to the Peace Corps. Meanwhile, I thought we only had to navigate grad school."

It takes me everything not to ask where she applied.

"Instead she told me she was going to Peru for two years."

"Jesus."

"She slept with some rando a few months ago, but we talked

about it like adults. We said we'd try an open relationship, and that's when I met you."

I tilt my head to look at him. He's hunched over too, with his head turned toward me, temple to knees. It's strangely intimate. Like we're in a blanket fort.

"But then why break up?"

He sighs as he grinds the sockets of his eyes into his kneecaps. "Because I'm not built for this. I tried it. I did all that Tinder shit. Raya. Bumble. Whatever the fuck, Hinge. I thought maybe it was a good idea. I've had a girlfriend from the time I was fifteen. It's like in high school, Asian dudes were one thing, but a decade later it's like suddenly we're all hot. It was ridiculous. I felt like such a trope, like one of those tech bros who gets all cut up and gets Lasik and acts like a totally different person. At first it was a laugh. I liked meeting all these people that I'd otherwise never know. Especially in New York. But having sex with strangers is fucking weird. I think I hate it."

Recognition knocks at my heart.

"I felt so fucking emo." His shoulders shake a little as he chuckles. "Like, I was getting offended that no one seemed to want to be friends with me."

I can't stop a tiny, sympathetic whine from escaping. I clear my throat. Fuck, he's cute.

"It all started to blend together. The drinking, partying, random hook-ups. The shit freaked me out. When you're fucked up, you're not always as careful as you need to be. I started to get tested for STDs, like, every other day because I'm a total fucking hypochondriac and the anxiety was making me nuts."

"Are you okay now?" Reluctant compassion wells squishily in my chest.

He nods. "When I saw you in the bar, man, it made me happy. I wanted someone to talk to, to just spend time with. You seemed a little messy, but the last thing I expected was that we'd hook up. Look, I've met girls like you. Shit, I've been curved by girls like you. And honestly, and I don't know if this is fucked up, but you ask me to meet you at a hipster dive bar, high-key looking like the type of Asian fashion chick who drinks bubble tea but only dates white photographers who speak conversational Japanese, so I had zero expectations."

I sit up. "What the fuck?"

He shakes his head. "I don't know, Jayne. But, that's the vibe. Like, how many Asian guys have you dated?"

Malcolm Ito.

"I haven't even . . ." I'm embarrassed to continue, but I hate that he's turned it around like this. "I haven't even had a real boyfriend."

"But you've hooked up with guys?"

"Yeah."

"And?"

"Well . . ." I scoff. I glance across the street. I stare at the pavement, disappearing into myself. I wonder if he's going to ask if I'm obsessed with white-people things.

"Shit," he says after a while. He rubs his palms on his denim-clad legs, sighs, and then turns to me. "I'm sorry."

"For what?" I wonder if I go sufficiently dead inside whether I'll feel the cold.

"I sound psychotic," he says.

I can't bring myself to meet his gaze. "What do you want, Patrick?" Jesus, men are exhausting. "You're the one with a girlfriend."

"I know."

"And you're cross-examining me about *my* choices."

"I'm just trying to figure you out," he says. "And it's going very poorly. God, I sound like some asshole ajusshi."

"Yeah, you're not coming off great right now."

"Fuck."

Finally, I turn to him. "I wish you'd have just told me about her."

"Same," he says. "Hard same. But again . . ." He smiles ruefully. "Deadass I couldn't tell if you'd care. Your whole thing about being fun and effervescent convinced me, until you *effervesced* all over the place and shit got dark so fast."

I laugh despite myself. He's not wrong. I finally see how wounded he appears. How bloodshot his eyes are. It's clear to me now how much he looks like someone going through a breakup.

"Man." I let out a sigh. "You're kind of a fuckboy."

He grins. "Fair."

We sit for a while. I nudge his shoulder with mine. "Yeah, well." I sigh, my breath misting the air in front of me. "I started hooking up with this grifter who moved into my apartment, and he fucked a whole bunch of other people right in my bedroom while I slept on the couch. So . . ."

I feel him shift beside me. "Jesus. Guess you'd know a fuckboy when you see one," he says.

"I'm like a truffle pig for fuckboys."

He throws his head back and laughs. "You know what?" he says, getting to his feet, shaking his hair, and blowing air out through pursed lips. I look up at him.

He crouches in front of me and whispers close to my face, "I like you a lot, but it's freezing."

"This is dumb, right?"

"Want to come over?"

I nod, teeth chattering.

chapter 43

When our car arrives, Patrick wraps his arm around me in the back seat. I'm exhausted. I wonder if it's hyperthermia setting in. He reaches for my hand as we climb his stairs.

"I feel like, from a medical standpoint," he says, opening the door, "we need to swaddle ourselves in as many blankets as possible."

He hands me the fuzzy slippers I wore last time. I nod in gratitude. I'm so cold that the pressure from my skull defrosting is a vice grip around my sinuses.

"But I think I need a shower." He takes his jacket off and hangs it up. "I just washed my sheets."

"Yeah, me too," I croak, reluctantly removing my coat. "It's like people who wear their shoes indoors. Or sit on beds in jeans. Gross."

Patrick yawns, leaning against his kitchen counter.

I nod, helplessly yawning back.

"You go first." He washes his hands and fills up his teakettle.

I realize I'm crowding him, huddling close for warmth. "No, you go ahead."

He looks down at me. "Do you want to agree that we'll shower together with no expectations or anatomical inspections because we're just both so fucking cold?"

"Yes," I tell him. "I'm also going to need more sweats."

"Yeah, I figured," he says, shaking his head. "And don't think I didn't notice when your ass wore them to Trader fucking Joe's." I poke him hard in the shoulder, embarrassed. He chuckles and grabs my hand and leads me to the bathroom.

We turn away from each other chastely as we undress. I'm so cold, I clutch my naked body, and when the hot water sprays over us, it stings, needling into my numb flesh, my back, my ass, my legs. I let out a ragged breath as he does the same. It's almost as if I can feel my personhood rising into my body as I defrost. I close my eyes. This moment feels like the culmination of so much running around. So much flailing and confusion.

His arms encircle me, and I know my eye makeup is smearing down my face, but the warmth of his arms and the steam crowd out my thoughts. I trace the tattoos on his biceps. A palm with an evil eye. A large red stamped dojang seal on his shoulder with his Korean name: Jang Min Suk. There are smaller ones: A turtle. A cat. Blossoms blooming on his forearms. A stylized dokkaebi monster mask with horns and his tongue sticking out. We stand under the hot water for a long time. He washes his hair, and when he reaches out of the shower to grab a sample-size bottle of conditioner from his medicine cabinet, I know it belongs to her or any number of *hers*, but I try not to let it hurt my heart. I wash my hair, luxuriating in it, lathering up, and when he steps out first, I'm happy to have the roomy tub all to myself.

I press my palm against the tile. I push my toe up against the blue rubber mesh flower in his drain to drag my long black hairs out. I feel like crying. If I lived here, I would be so happy. It's not even that I want to move in with Patrick. It's that his house feels like a home in a way I've never experienced in New York. The pictures on the walls, the impractical number of books, the stupid avocado egg timer. It's festooned with personal effects. Nobody's leaving anytime soon. It feels like a place where people want to stay.

Patrick hands me a white towel as he's brushing his teeth. I squeeze the rope of my hair, wringing it out, and wrap the towel around me, under my armpits. I toss the hair ball I've collected from the drain and dry my hands to grab a few squares of toilet paper and wipe my eyes. It feels rough, but I don't want to soil his towels with eye makeup. Patrick watches me.

He hands me my toothbrush from before. The same one with his dentist's name on the handle.

"Jayne," he says, after a beat. "No one's used it."

I grin as we brush our teeth side by side. In our reflection, I think how unfair it is that men get to look the same all the time. That they don't have to experience the rude shock of their appearance unadorned and without makeup. His mirrored face with its toothbrush dangling from his mouth buckles and swings toward me as he pops open the medicine cabinet to hand me facial moisturizer.

"I have body stuff, too, if you need," he says. There's a green-topped bottle of drugstore lotion on the glass shelf above the sink.

I moisturize my face, then pump some lotion into my cupped hands. With his own towel slung low around his waist, he watches me.

"Do you mind?"

He laughs and lets himself out. I lotion my arms, my legs, smearing it into my thighs, and for once I don't stare at my face and inspect my body. I wrap the towel around myself again and go into the living room. He's in the kitchen, drinking water, and it looks so good, I walk over. He hands the tall frosted glass to me, and it's delicious. He refills it, and I drink that, too, and when he kisses me, our mouths are cool and slick.

I press my steam-poached body up against his as the lip of the towel under my armpits bites into me. He draws me toward him by the waist and the towel loosens, and it's fine because I want there to be less between us. I want to feel his chest on mine and I don't care if our chests suction cup together and make a noise, because what I want is to plunge my entire chest inside his and feel the warmth there. My senses skitter. I clutch the towel to me before it falls away entirely.

"Is this okay?" he asks, expression stormy. He grabs the glass of water left on the counter and takes another sip.

I nod. He waits. "Yes," I tell him. I lead him into his room. It's dark in there, which is better. I take my towel off, fold it into thirds, and lay it on the pillowcase to protect the pillow from my wet hair. Then I lift the covers and get in. He does the same on his side, flinging his towel on the chair by the window. He lies there, offering me his arm, and I snuggle against him.

"This can go however you want," he says. His eyes are shiny in the dark.

His gaze is almost unbearable. I crane my neck, close my eyes, and kiss him.

He kisses me back, deeply. I break away. His lips are swollen, his hair is mussed. Again he asks, "Is this okay?"

"Yes."

We're both on our sides facing each other. I watch as his hand travels up to his cowlick to pat it down, and something forceful cork-screws inside of me. I want to eat him. He studies me openly, with-out any self-consciousness. I'm struck by the solemnity of him. His silence. The scrutiny's intimidating, but it feels good too. He kisses me, and this time I roll on top of him, hair tumbling onto his face and tenting around us.

I smile. "Hi."

"Hey."

I kiss him. Deep. I kiss him with everything. I kiss him, and I'm struck by this insistent pouring feeling.

It's a rubbery vertiginous swooping, and when he flips me to be on top of me, our full bodies pressed up against each other, I feel relief. I trace his face with my fingertips. His cheekbones are so close to the surface. He turns his head and kisses my hand. It's been so long since I've been touched like this. I don't know that I've ever been touched like this before at all.

He leans over to get a condom, and he checks in again and I say good again, and as I watch him, I realize I've always looked away for this part, as if not to be complicit, so later, when the regret comes, I can blame everyone but myself. But this time I watch. He smiles self-consciously. Shyly somehow, and it endears him to me all over again.

He hangs above me and covers my mouth with his, my neck, a shoulder, and at some point I'm no longer looking out of my eyes, wondering how I must appear, whether I smell okay, if I taste good, if I'm fatter or thinner with my clothes off or on, or how I rank against the billions of other images of women that exist in the world.

My heart actually aches, it's so full.

When he presses into me, I don't feel invaded.

I didn't know about this. This other sensation.

A feeling of recognition. Of me claiming him.

It's how he fits perfectly inside of me. It's in the way his mouth tastes. The way his tongue feels. How he smells. I've always understood the transaction of it. That I give something up, that I endure the physical discomfort of intrusion for something in return. For him to like me. To think I'm special. Special enough that he'll want to stick around. But this is more mysterious. The inquisition somehow mutual. I have no idea how this goes.

My breath sounds ragged to my ears as he reaches down to touch me, pulling his hips back before rocking into me. I choke a little on my own spit, I'm so surprised by my reaction to him. His hair's in his face. I close my eyes, and when I feel his hot, wet mouth on my breasts, I feel as though I'm falling.

I sigh when it's over. I don't pretend that I came, but I feel almost as though I could have. That I almost had to stop myself from doing it. It's as close as I've ever come to finishing with someone else, and as I grab his hands and cinch them tighter around my shoulders, he collapses behind me.

"Hey," I squeak. I'm breathing out of my mouth as smoothly as I can, so he doesn't hear the hitch in my throat. The wet in my nose. I'm mortified. My eyes smart.

"Jayne," he says, propping himself up to look at me.

"Yeah?" I angle my face away. To hide the tears leaking out of my eyes.

"Hey," he says.

I swallow, my tears puddling on the towel I've left on the pillow. "Jayne."

I turn around to face him. "I don't know why I'm crying," I say helplessly, laughing, feeling like an idiot.

"Okay," he says, awash with concern. "What do you need?"

"Can you just hug me but maybe not look at me?"

He gathers me in his arms from behind and presses his chest right up against my back.

I exhale. "My reaction bears no reflection on performance," I reassure him, patting his hand, and I can tell he's smiling even if I can't see it.

"I'm sorry," I tell him, sniffing like a child. "What a mess."

The tears take a moment to dry up, but eventually I collect myself. "Can I stay here tonight?"

"Of course," he says. "Are you okay?"

"Yeah."

"I know I haven't been completely honest with you," he says. "But I'm super done with dating randos. I like you. So, um, please stay the night. You're the one who keeps trying to run out of here. You don't have to feel like you're overstaying your welcome with me."

I start weeping all over again, the tears sliding sideways.

"You want a glass of water?" he asks.

"Okay." I sniff.

He grabs a pair of gray sweats.

When he comes back in, concerned look on his face, hair messy, I sit up with the sheets pulled up around me.

I take long, thirsty gulps. "Thanks." I hand back the glass feeling like a child.

He sets it on the bedside table.

"Fuck," I tell him. "I'm exhausting."

He laughs.

Between the vomiting and the sobbing and the yelling, I wonder what's wrong with Patrick that he seems to like me.

"You know what though?" He sits on the edge of the bed.

"Hmm?"

"Remember the part where you used toilet paper to take off your makeup, so you didn't smear it into my towels?"

I turn my head up to him.

He grins. "That was hot."

chapter 44

It's just getting light when I skip down Patrick's stairs and out his door. The air is bracing and crisp. I hug myself, having wheedled another sweatshirt from Patrick, and while the sounds of garbage trucks used to sour my mood after big nights out, this morning I'm glad to be sober and awake at this early hour.

I hop on the subway, surprised that it's as full as it is. It's strangely tranquil, populated mostly by people rousted from bed by jobs that require uniforms. The collective reluctance and resignation remind me of our school bus in high school. I want to see my sister. I'm excited to see her, curious about her evening, ready to laugh at her stories.

I up-nod the security guard in the lobby, halfway tempted to ask if he'd seen June's sperm donor depart.

I turn the corner on her floor, wondering if I'll tell her my story about Patrick, less about the sex and so much more about how I like him, when my smile fades at the sliver of light at her door.

It's open.

I push it slightly with my fingertips, listen, and then push it all the way.

"June?" I say quietly. Too quietly for anyone to hear. My heart hammers. It was a mistake to go with Patrick. I had no business leaving her with some Wall Street pervert ax murderer. I recall his name. Salim. Salim *what*? I can't conjure the rest of it. Fuck.

Fuckfuckfuck.

I sense the atmosphere for any movement. My shoulders coil inward. I inch forward slowly, not taking my shoes or jacket off in case I have to leg it to safety.

"June?" I try again. This time louder.

I turn on the kitchen light. An awful foreboding washes over me. *My sister's dead.*

If she died while I was having sex with Patrick, I'll never forgive myself.

"Hello?"

I see the spots first. Dark droplets. Four inky bread crumbs foretelling her passage, splotched on the ivory hall rug from her bedroom door, leading to the bathroom. I soundlessly make my way over. I feel as though I can hear the walls breathe.

"June?" I push the bathroom door open, knocking quietly just once as I enter.

"Fuck!" she screeches, eyes wide and then indignant, arms wrapping around her boobs. "What the fuck?" She splashes the water with her palms when she sees who it is. "You scared the shit out of me!"

It's a horror movie. I'm astonished by the blood blooming around her in the water. For a heart-juddering, all-consuming moment, I'm convinced she's been stabbed.

"Is he here?" I turn my head toward the bedroom.

"Is who here? What the fuck?" she shrieks.

I'd read somewhere that there are only nine pints of blood in a human body. I try not to stare, but I need to know if I'm looking at enough blood to overflow one of those plastic-handled milk jugs. There's so much of it ribboning around her in the water. The coppery tang, the sediment, I can almost taste it.

"It's just me," she says, and then sighs. "He left. We were going at it until we both realized I was perioding all over the place. It was gnarly. You should have seen him—his dick looked like Carrie, and I thought he was gonna pass out."

"You scared me!" I tell her. "You left the door open."

"He probably did. You should have seen him break out."

"Jesus."

I push open the door to the bedroom and check out the crime scene. June's mattress looks like an abattoir.

"Never trust anything that bleeds for seven days and doesn't die," she says ruefully. "I thought I might be having cramps. But I've also been in such consistent pain, it's hard to tell."

I watch my sister let the old water out and refill the tub. As the water runs clean, I see her naked body for the first time in years. She's sitting with her knees tented. From above I can see that her abdomen is swollen, but her limbs are thinner. Spindly. "I can't wait for all this shit to be over," she says.

"Is this a cancer thing?" I inch into the bathroom from the hallway.

"No," she says. "My period. It's gotten so much worse. It comes every three to four months and arrives like some plague."

There was always an Old Testament quality to June's periods growing up. Mom's was the same way. Mom never gave us the Talk as it related to sex, presuming that someone at school had it handled. But she did pull us both aside when our periods came to remind us that a woman's body was a burden and that nice underpants were a waste of money.

"Jesus, it's fucking metal." There's a silty ring of scarlet around the tub. "You look like you've been making kimchi in here."

She chuckles and then groans. "Stop," she says. "I feel horrible. I can't even tell you how many blood transfusions I've had this year."

I had no idea it had become this bad.

She lifts her hand out of the water and stares at her fingers. "I think I'm still drunk."

I tiptoe through the blood droplets and sit next to the tub on the bathmat.

"I refuse to buy adult diapers." She closes her eyes dopily. "It's like a miracle if I don't soak through a super-plus tampon and a pad in between subway stops."

"Yeah, but"—I gather my legs in my arms—"when's the last time you took the subway?"

"Fuck you," says June, smiling through gritted teeth. "God, you should have seen me at work. Trapped on the toilet in between meetings. I went to the bathroom so much, this analyst had the nerve to intervention me. She thought I was a cokehead, which, let me tell you, everyone would have been way more okay with."

June runs more hot water, and when her hand rests on the lip of the tub, the dewdrops from her fingertips are pink. My sister's insides are outside of her, and a flutter of panic takes hold of my heart.

She closes her eyes, grimacing.

I can't tell if the dampness of her face is sweat, condensation, or tears. She looks a bit like Mom then. I didn't think either of us looked like her, but I see it now. I shouldn't have left her alone.

"Wait," she slurs, leering at me. "Did you and Patrick *bone*?"

"June." I roll my eyes, but I can tell I'm smiling.

"Oh my God." She splashes her hand excitedly. "Does his girl-friend know?"

"They broke up."

"Suuuuuure," she says, shaking her head before exhaling noisily. I'm touched that she'd ask about it when she's clearly in pain.

"Want me to wash your hair?"

My sister doesn't say anything. I hold my breath, embarrassed suddenly to have asked.

"Yeah, okay," she says, finally opening her eyes.

We clear out the dark water and fill it again. I detach the shower nozzle, testing the temperature as she leans, tilting her head back. Her black hair tendrils out. My sister wipes the water away from her eyes with the heels of her palms. I grab the good shampoo. The Frédéric Fekkai travel bottle that I brought over. I lather her head with the tips of my fingers, with enough pressure that it feels good but carefully so I don't get soap in her eyes. When her face crumples and she starts crying noiselessly, I keep going without another word.

My sister and I have been tormented by our bodies in different ways. A few weeks before the end of June's last year of high school—one random Thursday—she leaked all through her leggings. Most of the semester was over. Senioritis had settled in for the upperclassmen; finals were a week out—the days were protracted and dull. It was almost as if people were waiting for something to happen. And this was particularly inviting.

A disparate number of factions—the popular kids, her advanced-placement adversaries, the kids who owed her money for snacks, even Holland and the burnouts—joined forces against my sister. For someone playing such a minor role at school, she incited so much collective cruelty. She'd been sitting in some genius IB course, and when she stood up, it was a *Saw* movie on her ass.

Kids from class cornered me, wanting to know if I'd heard. The friends whose demeanors had cooled after the Holland Hint debacle flooded my phone. All day people had been throwing tampons at my sister and sticking maxi pads on her locker. They'd printed out Japanese flags and taped them on her back, on her bag, even on Mom's car, that she'd borrowed. They told me gleefully, telegraphing what until then I hadn't known was common knowledge, that they'd witnessed my shame about my sister and presumed us enemies.

It's true that since my first week, I'd memorized her schedule, bobbing and weaving to avoid her flight patterns, but other than rolling my eyes and writing in my journal, I never told anyone.

Stomach in knots, I hid in the library at lunch. My cheeks burned as I made my way to fifth period, shuffling, eyes downcast, until a huddle of senior girls I barely knew but certainly knew *of* beckoned me over in the hall. "I just had to tell you," said the most beautiful one as I held my breath, "that you're nothing like her." She smiled at me, as if she'd provided clean drinking water to countless future generations of my third-world family. And honestly, that's how I'd felt. It was as if my tattered reputation, my indiscretions were pardoned in that moment.

I chose not to defend her. Craven gratitude suffusing my body with loose-limbed relief as I loped away. She'd brought it on herself, I reasoned. I didn't choose to be related with June, besides which she'd thrown me away. I was furious at her for getting accepted to school in New York and clearly planning to leave.

All day, I'd steered clear of the bathroom, afraid of what I'd overhear, but between fourth and fifth period I couldn't hold it any longer. I'd run into the ladies' room, when moments later June came in after me. I saw her through the crack of the stall, face pale with blotches the color of live coals high on her cheeks, and held my breath. I gathered my feet up so she wouldn't recognize my shoes and watched as she looked at herself in the mirror for a while. Her eyes seemed hollow, unseeing; she seemed genuinely bewildered.

She got in the stall next to mine. The one I was always careful to avoid. The one that called me names on the left-side partition. I prayed that she hadn't seen me, that she couldn't sense me, and barring that, I hoped she would not speak. I told myself that it was for her benefit, to save her the humiliation, but so much more of it was that I wanted no part of her anguish. She cried so hard, the dragging, chest-racking sobs seeming to rise from some elemental, rooted pain. I sat there, eyes glued shut, feeling as though my body were trembling along with the bathroom stall doors, tears streaming down my cheeks.

Mom was gone. It was just the two of us. And still I'd forsaken her.

I rinse her hair out. Apply conditioner, working through the knots carefully.

"At least this part will be over after the surgery," she says. "The bleeding."

"Yeah."

"And then I can move on to the next part," she says, wiping her eyes with the backs of her hand. "The menopause, the fatigue, the shitting, and the vomiting."

I hand her a towel for her face. "If I had to, I would probably wipe your ass."

She laughs. "I've wiped your ass so many times. That's all I did for two years."

"I'll give you two weeks."

June flicks me with water. "I'm taking two months, whether or not I need it. I'll get a bell."

I strip June's bed, remake it, give her a fat white prescription pill of ibuprofen, and tuck her in. I clean the bathroom, scrub the grout, throw the towels and bath mat in the machine. I spend an unknowable amount of time on my knees, crouched low, blotting at the blood in the hallway rug with a Tide stain stick and paper towels, crying so hard I feel wrung out.

She's going to die.

I grind the paper towel into the carpet.

Get it out get it out get it out.

I can't fight the roaring in my ears.

The familiar galloping in my chest.

chapter 45

I call Gina Lombardi's office. They fit me in for an emergency session. I walk in meandering circles, to kill time. She'll fix this, I tell myself as my fingernails bite small red smiles into my palms. The familiar whir of the noise machines in her waiting alcove is so soothing that I run my fingertips over the textured eggshell wallpaper, lulling myself into a trance.

I don't know what I was thinking, canceling my last appointment. I force myself not to hug her when she opens the door.

"How have you been?" she asks, taking her place in the cream velvet club chair closest to the window. In a starched white blouse, open at the neck, and pleated woolen slacks, this is a woman who will tell me what to do. Her honeyed hair has been trimmed, no longer brushing her clasped hands when she leans toward me.

"I'm fine," I tell her. It's true enough. Enclosed as I am in her dome of good feeling, her force field of hardy mental health and cognitive clarity. "Did you know . . . ," I begin, trawling my memory for anything interesting, "that Germans have a word for when you're longing for a place you've never even been?" I'd written it down in my notes from June's encyclopedia when I snooped in her apartment that first time. It's inconceivable how long ago that was. We were different people then.

"Fernweh," she says. "The Germans have words for a lot of things. Are you experiencing that right now?"

I shake my head. "I had it when I lived in Texas. For here, for New York. I would picture the buildings and try to hear the sounds and focus until I felt like I could teleport myself here."

"Do you feel more grounded now that you *are* here?"

I consider lying to her, but the vision of June's swollen body in the scarlet bathtub stops me. I know how to be good. How not to test a God I don't trust.

I shake my head. "It's not at all what I thought it would be. Nothing is. No matter how much I love it, it doesn't love me back. If I weren't so broken, it would fit. I feel like I don't have a home." My voice breaks. Hearing myself say it strikes me as so sad, so pathetic, so lonesome that I burst into tears.

"I'm just wrong," I tell her raggedly. "I have, like, fernweh for myself. Or something."

I feel the weight of Gina's gaze even as I avert her eyes.

"Fernweh is rooted in pain, or sickness and sadness," says Gina. "It's directly translated as 'far pain' or 'far sickness' as opposed to 'heimweh' or 'homesickness.' But it's also longing for the unknown, since the familiar is stifling or challenging. The foreign can seem fantastic, exalted, since its possibilities are infinite. We have no data or experience around it. But once we arrive and the faraway is known and becomes familiar, then what? You've got all that energy and longing and possibility that no longer has anywhere to go. It's got nowhere to be invested, nowhere to live. Have you ever considered that it isn't a place that will improve your life? That there is no such thing as a geographic cure?"

"Jesus." I cry harder, thinking about my sorry, extortionately expensive apartment and my perverse relationship with Jeremy. "Then what is it all for?"

She stands, her slacks are wrinkled, and her belt is Hermes, and I hate that I notice it even before registering the box of Kleenex held out in front of me. I take it in both hands, fighting the urge to crush it. "So, this is it? Nothing will help me?"

"Is that what you're hearing?"

I roll my eyes. Why can't anyone ever give me a straight answer? A flicker of irritation juts my chin and I find myself staring combatively. I despise her suddenly. Her imperious, ice-queen exterior goading me with its impenetrability.

I pluck two Kleenex and blow my nose noisily at her.

"I feel like I'm out of control." I state it plainly as possible. Make the cry for help explicit.

"On a scale of one to ten—with ten being extremely hopeless and out of control—where are you?"

I continue to stare. I can't locate any of myself to make the assessment.

"Jayne," she says evenly, writing something in her yellow notepad, which I always take as an indication that I've done something wrong. "Can you name five things that you can see around you, four things you can touch, three that you can hear, two you can smell. . . ."

I didn't remember there being more parts to this, the smelling portion and the rest of it, but of course I'm remembering now.

"I'm sick," I tell the blond woman in front of me whose life I know nothing about.

I stare at my palms and flip them over. They're strangely mottled and hideous.

Gina waits.

For some reason I'm reminded of June holding the cancer book and tapping it against her leg. The one with the doctor, *Where Breath Becomes Air*.

I wonder if I'll ever escape the cinematic irony of that exact moment once she's dead.

"What if I told you I had cancer?"

She stills.

"Do you have cancer?" It's uttered in such a placid tone that I half expect her to yawn.

"It would explain the depression."

"It would." She holds my gaze.

I know it's spoiled and reckless, but for a moment I'm jealous of June's cancer. There's such powerful recognition in the diagnosis. Everybody respects cancer. Being sick with cancer would explain my sadness, my sickness, my anxiety, and the horrible suspicion that everyone in the world was born with a user's manual or a guide to personal happiness but me.

If I had cancer, Gina Lombardi would help me.

I have fernweh for cancer. I'm disgusting.

"Jayne," she says patiently. "We're just about out of time."

Of course we are. I rise out of my chair as if guided by strings. "Fine."

"Would you like to meet this time next week, or go back to our usual day?"

"Whatever."

Gina retreats to the chair behind her desk and clicks on her mouse. She picks up her silver wire-framed glasses and puts them on, her mouth easing open slightly in concentration. She glances at me and clears her throat.

"I'm sorry, Jayne."

Something in her tone makes me sit back down.

She comes around from her desk and joins me. "I should have informed you before, but this marks our eighth session. If you want to keep meeting, you'd be responsible for a seventy-five-dollar copay."

"Are you serious?" There's no way I can afford seventy-five dollars. The worn leather back of Gina Lombardi's very nice flat lifts off the heel of her crossed leg. I feel nothing but disgust at her four-hundred-dollar highlights.

"It's the policy for your health insurance. I could refer you to some colleagues who operate on a sliding scale, but . . ."

"I make myself throw up," I tell her. "Just so you know. I can't stop doing it. And I haven't had my period in a year."

"I'm sorry," she says. The corner of her mouth sinks slightly, but she's otherwise completely composed. She swivels around to pull something out of the bottom shelf of her bookcase. "There are resources that can help you." A xeroxed pamphlet is waved at my knee. I take it wordlessly despite the air bubble of laughter at my throat. I can't believe this woman thinks a leaflet will save me.

"I don't have cancer," I tell her, arms crossed. It vaguely registers somewhere in the hinterlands of my perception that I'm crying again. "Or the other thing."

"Jayne," she says, eyes shining with infinite patience. "Please look into it." She nods at the folded paper in my hand. "It's where I refer all of my patients who struggle with disordered eating. They'll help you. New York is just a place. It's the people who will become a home for you."

I force myself back toward June's, stopping off at the deli on Broadway, the nice one, the one I like. I just need gum. I need coffee. I need TUMS for the coffee, and possibly more of those delicious chocolate-covered banana chunks. I could get some for my sister, too. She should probably also have something with iron. What has iron? I fling open the door, and my eyes immediately land on it. On me.

It's my picture by the cash register. There are three other people featured along with me—the WALL OF SHAME, as it says in black Sharpie. The others have their grainy black-and-white faces turned away from the security cameras, but mine is tilted at an angle, looking straight into the lens. The wanted posters are for various petty thefts. The balding guy in glasses above me has a yen for RX protein bars. The teenager to the left is a little more lowbrow, Cheetos and Arizona iced tea. The other woman, to the upper left of me, has a genuine need—she's taken cans of sausages, sacks of dried beans, nutritious, filling, dense. And there I am: CHOCO-BANANAS, it reads under my startled, ghostly mugshot.

The shame is so immense—instant and physical—the wind's knocked out of me. I hide behind my hair, looking only at my shoes, as I elbow a woman, pulling the door open with such force that something in my shoulder clicks strangely in its socket. I can't even mutter *I'm sorry*. I'm too desperate, too frantic, too repulsed. I sprint to the subway, body incandescent with humiliation, nauseated and frantic to burn off some of this horrible energy. The embarrassment scorches down to some essential wound inside me.

I blindly pull out my card. I can't believe I've ruined this neighborhood too. Everything I touch turns to shit.

I'm shaking on the train.

The roar.

The gallop.

I take a deep breath, searching the skyline as the train goes aboveground. The murky trench and soaring residential buildings of the Gowanus Canal. The Statue of Liberty the size of a grain of rice behind the dingy glass of the subway window. I peer down, searching for my piles of smashed building, but I see that it's all but been tidied away. I'm filled with an awful regret. Why can't things just stay where I want them?

My joints are coiled with a hectic friction, and my body tingles in anticipation as I walk to my block. As I pass dollar stores, the Laundromat, and the man who sits out there on a plastic chair in a coat, with a cat. My mugshot rises up in my mind, and it recalls the blown-out security photo of June's forehead at the cancer center. Various sense memories slice through my thoughts. Water warming my fingers as June tilts her head back, crying, as I rinsed her hair. Mom's robe-clad arms flapping at us in church. Dad not meeting my gaze in the rearview, the rumble of highway beneath my seat. Jeremy laughing when the actor returned to the table. The abstract look on Ivy's face when we're both bleary-eyed and blissed out while randoms grope us through thin dresses. A flash of us giggling as we pull each other into a bathroom. Taking turns. Sharing sugar-free breath mints or Listerine strips. Spraying perfume on each other before we had to leave our bubble of privacy. Patrick can never know this side of me. His wholesomeness, the sanctity of his apartment, I can't taint any of it, him, with me.

Another image surfaces: my ex-roommates, Megan in front, Hillary at my doorframe, unwilling to step into the squalor of my bedroom. It's not usually as bad as this, I want to tell them, but they don't care. Tones rising. Faces luminous with rage. I'm struggling to focus on their features, the contortions of their mouths; I know they're mad, but I'm so tired. Tired enough not to get up, so tired that I don't bother to upright myself and hide the empty bottle of wine that I'd stolen and the remnants of Hill's demolished birthday cake on my bed.

I was smiling then, too. Partly out of discomfort at having been caught but mostly with a curiosity for how far they'd take it. Initially, I'd been judicious about helping myself to their cabinet. Then I became more haphazard in what I'd replace. It started with passive aggressive texts. A single house meeting where I apologized profusely and privately rolled my eyes. The thick, ropey vein on Megan's neck throbs with the higher registers as she shrieks. I'm impressed by her convictions. It takes courage to display such vitriol. I go silent. Remote. I back away from the scene in my mind.

It was Hill that finally pulled her back, blinking slowly, allowing for unalloyed disdain to slide off her nose and down at me. She told me I had a week to gather my things.

"Yeah, okay," my sour mouth mumbled, heart reanimating as panic shot scratchy spidery impulses all over my skin.

This can't be all there is. I'm finally here.

I envision June again. In the bath. The spatter of dark on white tile.

My sister died.

My sister died.

My sister died.

The supermarket doors slide open and I take a deep breath. The bright, glossy packages in the aisles call my name. My legs threaten to give, I'm so grateful. Relief is so close. I need donuts. I need the exact vanilla-glazed yeast donut that they had at the diner with Patrick. When it was raining, when we were matching, when it was safe. I also require an apple pie. A whole one. A happy family pie but my own. And real Parmesan. The kind that looks like a pink Himalayan salt lamp, the kind I'd never had before. I make a beeline for the refrigerated section of the grocery store. I don't need a cheese grater; there are going to be teeth marks in mine.

I'm scandalized and impressed by how expensive real Parmigiano-Reggiano is. Nine bucks a hunk. It lands heavily in my basket. The anticipation in my salivary glands make my temples ache, and by the time I'm at the cookies and cakes, I'm drunk with options. I could get Entenmann's. I peer into the windowed box, but their donuts are the wrong texture. The dry cakiness, the way you can pack them in your guts like a drug mule swallowing condoms isn't what I want. I need the greasy, fluffy, bready ones. I need the exact one I had with Patrick or it won't work.

Patrick.

The thought of what he'd think of me skitters across my mind. It dawns on me that I left his apartment just this morning.

I send him a heart emoji, and when he sends me one back, it feels like a blessing.

In the bakery section by the bread, I spot a six-pack of donuts. According to the plastic dome, they were packaged four days ago. The top one has kissed the inside of the box, leaving a smeared ring of glaze. It looks obscene. They're the exact ones I want. There are half pies packaged in semicircles, but I get a whole one. Apple. It'll go well with my cheese.

I select a sleeve of macarons. Not very nice ones. Not at all the kind you'd get for an aunt.

I grab a coconut water for health. A tub of mac and cheese from the hot bar, because why the fuck not.

I rove the walls of snacks. The metal basket handles pressing urgently at my forearms. I grab a box of Nilla Wafers and Wheat Thins because Triscuits by the box are too scratchy and pointy and because I want a snack I would never normally buy. One that feels as though it belongs to someone else. I also pick up an entire barrel of non-GMO cheese balls.

I pay for it all on my own debit card. Rent is due in three days and I haven't checked my balance in weeks.

I hurtle myself to the apartment. Flying so I can't change my mind. I shove my arm into the plastic bag twisting round and round my wrist and scratch the top of my right hand, trying to pry open the clamshell of donuts. I retrieve one and cram its cloying stickiness into my mouth. Press it in as I gnaw. Heaven. I lock eyes with a girl in a cheetah-print jacket talking on her phone. She has the decency to look away.

I lick my lips and grab another. Gorging. The streets are packed with commuters. Flocks of moms. Some are even jogging. Jerks. That's what I both love and hate about Brooklyn. It's so densely populated, I'm camouflaged. They barely see me. And if they did, they don't care. By the time I'm back in my lobby, I realize my mistake. Six donuts is not enough. I should have gotten twelve.

I race up the stairs, pulling myself up with the banister handle, calves complaining at the fourth-floor walk-up.

Galloping.

Thundering.

I'm so, so close.

Cumbersome fingers fumble with my keys. Part of me wishes Jeremy were home when I crash through the door. I would vaporize him if he tried to obstruct my course in anyway.

I kick off my shoes. I lock the door even though I'm alone. I peel off my coat and my sweatshirt, dump them into the tub, tie my hair up, and sit on the floor in my bra. It's dirty and it's exactly what I deserve. I gather my companions around me as I eat and eat as fast as I can, before the rest of me notices and tries to stop.

Adrenaline is shunted straight into my heart.

Gratitude floods my nervous system as the sugar takes hold. I eat so fast that it doesn't count. I eat as a velveteen curtain of serenity descends over me, the mechanics of my jaw hypnotizing me the way competitive marathon runners hit a rhythm. I swallow and swallow until my stomach is distended and my head aches from repeatedly grinding away at the mouth-fucking. I stack Wheat Thins three high and bite into them. I put the flattened part of the Nilla Wafers together and make little spaceships and destroy them and do it ten more times. Twenty.

Sweat gathers at the small of my back and seeps into the waistband of my jeans. At some point I'd undone the top button and unzippered them but at no point do I personally witness this occurring.

The macarons look like those cupcakes that are actually soap, but they're pretty. Colorful and like jewels. I hold the glassine box to my nose and smell nothing. The pads of my fingers are impossibly sensitive, trembling, and I'm gripped by a singular purpose. I eat them in order. Begin too bright, tart, or even too dark and robust and you'll deaden your taste buds for everything else. Green is pistachio, and pistachio is perfect. The sensation of my teeth piercing the delicately crispy outer layer, easing into the ganache, the viscid chewiness, makes me close my eyes—it's too narcotic, too pleasurable, and still I can't even tell if it tastes good. Orange. Brown. Lilac. I'm bludgeoned by sugar. I can't discern perfume from texture.

I'm thrilled at the devastation. Destroying beautiful things so carelessly and so fast.

The mac and cheese is a paste. It's gloriously gluey, sticking my mouth together, cementing all the sharper foods, lending a contrast. Some cushioning. I crash-land a Nilla spaceship into the tub and scoop it into my mouth. I eat a fifth donut. And then just the top of the last one. I dig into the glaze with my thumbnail and rip it off and scrape it into my mouth.

It's almost time.

I run my tongue on the roof of my mouth. It tastes metallic. It's pulpy and stinging, cut up from all that's going in.

The cheese balls are a mistake. They dissolve too quickly, so they don't provide that choking feeling as they're going down. But they taste great after vanilla glaze. The whole ritual feels as though I'm being run over by the slowest-moving train. I can't get off. I vaguely want to, but it's overruled. Because truly this is the only thing I can count on. This has never left me no matter where I am.

I polish off the last macaron, and there is no enjoyment. Finishing is drudgery and it's still all in my teeth. I'm still chewing when I crawl out on my knees. This view I hate. Looking at the toilet bowl from this angle. Directly into it. As if at an altar. I retch into my hand, another kind of sacrament. I do this so the telltale splash doesn't give me away. Even when I'm alone. I've always been a little proud of this. How quietly I can hit reset. I keep going, putting my mouth where people shit and abasing myself the way I always do, trying to exorcise the hate and anger and never managing to get it all out.

The Korean word for punishment is "bee."

When I flush again, the swirl is still a sour, hazy rose-orange.

Blood.

Body.

I sit in the tub, on top of my clothes, knees gathered to my chest. The faint whine of tinnitus tethers me to reality, alerting me to my movements. It feels like the high-pitched hiss of air escaping my head. It's only then do I notice how cold the room is. That the heat is out.

I hoist myself up and I look in the mirror. Eyes watery, panting, cheeks purpling, bright-red lips wet. Flecked with slick clumps of undigested food.

I am ruptured.

I'm crying. And watching myself cry only amplifies my sadness. I'm filled with devastating pity for every single mirror version of me, all those times before, the youngest ones making me saddest of all. Watching myself have compassion for me in the absence of anyone else makes me cry harder.

I wash my hands with soap. Thoroughly, front and back. I dry them. I bring my fingers up to my nose. They still smell of ruin and spoil. I rub toothpaste all over them, hating myself, hating the way it feels. Hating that I have to watch myself do it. Unable to tear my eyes from this horrible shadow version of me that gets its way every time.

My phone rumbles on hard tile. It's still in the plastic bag where I'd chucked it. I reach over and drag the bag toward me by the handle.

It's Jeremy. He wants to know if I'm in the apartment. I listen for sounds. A jangled key, creaking floorboards in the hall, but it's quiet.

Three dots. He's thinking.

When the dispatch comes, a burble hints at the back of my throat. I'm confused at the list until I realize it's a series of his records that he'd like me to look for.

He asks if I can meet with him today to deliver them. He reminds me that there's still no hot water. As if this would inure me to his request.

In the mirror my face cracks open into a smile of genuine amusement. My eyes are blood-shot but my lips stretch wide with glee and then I'm laughing.

It feels good.

Deleting the text feels even better, and when I go to my contacts and delete him entirely, I feel a floating sensation in my arms.

I pull my rumpled sweatshirt out from the tub and throw it on.

Surveying our collective possessions, the threadbare couch, the stained mattress, stray clothes and books and the milk crate of records, I feel peaceful. Finally, nothing is missing.

I don't know if I'll be able to stop hurting myself in this way, but I don't want to keep doing it for Jeremy's sake or anyone like him ever again.

I fish my coat out from the tub by a sleeve as the folded-up pamphlet from Gina hits the floor. I clutch the sink, steadying myself as I pick it up, seeing stars as blood rushes into my body and out of my head.

I unfold it and read.

The air is redolent with the smell of flowers. I've emptied both spray bottles of Ylang Ylang shower cleaner. The mattress is suffused with it. Couch, too. I lift sofa cushions and crop dust the springs. I darken all of Jeremy's clothes with layered mists of the fragrance that makes him gag.

I hitch the box of records on my hip with my coat slung over it and a bag of books at my shoulder.

I lock the door and slide my key under. My regards to David Buxbaum. Regards to the management company that I couldn't find online to fix the heat or the water, no matter how many monthly TexStar bank checks I dutifully sent to a P.O. box in Canastota, New York.

I carry the box of Jeremy's precious vinyl out to the curb. An offering to the New York City sanitation system should they have an interest.

I'm at June's door. Again. With nowhere else to go. She's on the couch watching TV in her pink bathrobe. My sister has a white Korean sheet mask on her face, head tilted awkwardly toward me so as not to drip. She looks like a Japanese Noh theater actor with pancake makeup. "Is it possible that I'm still drunk from last night?" she asks. *Gilmore Girls* plays in the background.

I check the time. Absurdly it's just 8:30 in the evening, of a day that seems to have so many days nested into it. I dump my bag and shoes.

"I have to talk to you," I begin.

She sits up as I take my place on the love seat.

"Wait," she says, and tosses a foil package from the coffee table onto my lap. "If this is serious, you have to wear one too. I have another ten minutes."

I pick up the envelope. It features a tasteful macro shot of flora with dew droplets on it. I flip the pink packet over to read the back.

"Wait, this one has actual stem cells in it?" I ask her, picturing microscopic bits of fetus. "Is that legal?"

"Apparently snail serum is passé," she says, shrugging. "This is the hot new shit."

"Can I just have five minutes and then I'll put it on?" I've been practicing my speech the whole way over.

Her masked face nixes it.

I tear the package to extract the slimy white parcel and unfold it. Gingerly so I don't drip on the couch or on my clothes. I carefully peel the mask off its plastic backing and position it onto my face, matching it up to my hairline. It's cold and unpleasantly wet. I dock the holes over my eyes, nose, and mouth, pulling errant strands of hair out from under it.

"You got to wipe the remaining serum onto your neck and hands," she instructs. "This shit is like twenty bucks a pop. Everyone's using it post-op. It promotes healing."

"Wait," I tell her, reaching for another pink packet. "Open your robe for a second."

Once I get the mask unfolded, I slap it onto her belly.

"Holy!" exclaims June with a laugh in her throat. "It's fucking cold."

"Can't hurt." Maybe it will absorb deep inside her. The face on June's torso looks up at me as her slimy pancake face looks down.

"So, what were you going to tell me?" June tightens the fuzzy belt of her robe.

"I need a place to stay."

"Yeah, dingus, I know," she says. "You've been literally living with me for almost a month."

"Yeah, but . . ."

June picks at the edge of her mask and peels it off. Her face is slick, her baby hairs clinging to her forehead.

I reach for mine, but she sucks her teeth in reproach. "You have at least another fifteen."

I peel it off anyway and hold it in my hands. Warmed by my face, the wetness makes it feel vaguely alive. "I'll put it back on," I tell her. "I just need to actually see you."

"Okay."

"I have to move out of my apartment."

"Also, to file under, 'criminally obvious.'"

"June!"

"I'm sorry," she says, eyes wide with impatience. "I'm waiting for the part I don't know."

"Well," I barrel on. "It's filled with roaches, there's sometimes no water at all for days, and the heat's going to kill me if the cold doesn't. You asked me a long time ago if I was on the lease." I shoot a sidelong glance at her neck roll. "Anyway, I'm not. It's an illegal sublet and I've tried to make it work, but I failed. I can't do it. I'm a huge fuckup and I left for good and I need to stay with you for a while."

"Okay," she says evenly. "How long would you need?"

"Two months."

"Is that a real number or is it the longest you figured you could get away with asking for?"

Fuck, she knows me so well. "The second one."

"You can stay here as long as you want," she says. "But you have to do something for me."

She reaches under her robe, plucks the face mask off her tummy, and flings it onto the coffee table.

"You need to quit doing the shit you're doing," she says quietly, crossing her arms.

The inky horrible feeling drops over me again.

"What are you talking . . ."

"Stop," she says, raising her hand. "You can't lie to me if you're going to live here. I know when you leave. When you go back to your apartment and what you do. And if you can't do it there, you're going to do it here. So we have to talk about it."

"June," I plead. The morning's shame rises up in me like bile. I close my eyes.

I sense June approaching as the cushion next to me dips. When she reaches for my hand, I look down at it. Her palm is warm, smaller than mine, and covers my knuckles like a shell.

"I've seen them," she says softly. My sister's eyes shine with a tenderness I can't bear. "The bags of stuff. In high school, I kept finding so many of them in your room at home. Food wrappers, boxes, all those wadded-up pieces of toilet paper. The Ziploc bags . . ."

"Stop."

"I've seen it, Jayjay."

"June, please."

"I've seen the bags of vomit under your bed."

I recall the warmth of the plastic pouches, heavy in my palms. I'd never meant to leave them there. Bags are my last option. They were only for when she was in the bathroom or if I'm having a really rough go and I can't get out of bed. I must disgust her.

I wipe my knuckle against my face, crying numbly.

"I was so scared." June covers her face with her hands and bursts into ragged sobs.

Her crying makes me cry harder.

"You scared me so much. Worse than Mom. Worse than anything. I almost didn't come here," she says throatily. "If anything had happened to you while they were at work and I was here . . ."

I hadn't known. And the shame of it throttles me.

I hated June for going to New York. At the time, I couldn't believe that she would. She knocked on my door as she was leaving. I was catatonic when the garage door closed, this time with my sister on the other side. I cried so long and hard, my shoulders cramped from heaving.

"I thought maybe if I brought you here, if I kept you close by, you'd be okay." She searches my eyes. "But I know you're still doing it."

My sister grips my arm. "Jayne," she says. "It's your hands. You can't stop smelling them. That's your tell. That's how I know when you do it. We can get whatever help you need. We'll get you the best. You just have to get better."

chapter 46

I look up the address. I'm early, but I'm in the right spot.

According to the pamphlet, there are meetings all over the city, but this one, the only one at this time, is in a claptrap playhouse in the West Village. I walk from June's. I pass the bakery where I met Ivy, the basketball courts, and a slice spot across from a church. The Thanksgiving decorations are up. It's perverse how Americans need their cartoon turkeys to seem thrilled at the prospect of being eaten. You'd think they'd slap googly eyes and cartoon smiles on smallpox blankets to go with them. On the corner where I hang a left, there's a Chihuahua tied to a bike rack, an upturned U. He's wearing a tiny lilac cowboy hat.

The location is sandwiched between two comedy clubs and features a narrow corridor, black sticky floors, and a rickety, uneven staircase with silver skid guards trimmed on the lip of each step. I want to leave but don't.

On the second-floor landing, I pass a closed door, behind which someone's singing a lusty rendition of "Be Our Guest," that song from *Beauty and the Beast*. I have no expectations and I'm not a joiner, but the invitation to snoop in New York buildings I don't know about is irresistible. There's a bathroom on the third floor. There are two stalls and it's just me. I'm never in the West Village, but I catch myself thinking that in a pinch, it's not a bad bathroom to add to the collection. Even when I hope not to ever need them again.

Three thoughts persistently bang around in my head. That they'll laugh me out of the room for not being fat or thin enough. That the lack of any cost of admission means it's a cult. And that I'm not sick enough to be with sick people and that being with sick people might wind up being contagious. A truly diseased part of my brain wonders if I'll be able to pick up any weight-loss pointers.

The room is bleak when I poke my head into the indicated door. I check the time—we're only four minutes from starting and there are only two people in there. An older Black woman with bright-green eyes and her raincoat zipped over her lumpy purse and an Asian woman in workout clothes who seems like the type of Asian who folds all her underwear the same way.

They're chatting amiably while setting up chairs, so I grab one off the pile and do the same.

Voices echo in the hallway, and three women enter. They have expensive blowouts and wear designer rubber boots and enormous engagement rings. They're fancy, these women. I've never been to the Hamptons, but I'm willing to bet they have.

They're followed by two men who smell like cigarette smoke. One has a neck tattoo, and the other, a silver-haired man of about eighty, wears his hair in a small ponytail. Bright hellos and hugs abound. In three minutes the room is filled with the most random assortment of humans.

All told, we're a smiling group of about thirty straight from central casting, varying ages, races, and sizes. A heavyset man with a yarmulke on his head unravels an iPhone charger and plugs it into the wall. More hugs are dispensed, but they seem to have gotten the memo not to touch me. I position myself in the back for a swift exit and so I can study everyone from the rear. A figure sits next to me. She's greyhound slender, a teen. In worn Stan Smiths, with a pierced nose and a thigh gap you could lob a softball through, she smiles at me with this beatific light and I feel as though I've been lied to.

No one looks like they're in enough pain.

No one looks like how I feel.

No one looks like they do the things I do.

We gather in a circle holding hands, and the intimacy coupled with the praying in unison instantly freaks me out. At the mention of God, a door in my head shuts with a definitive *no*. These people—these weirdos—all take deep cleansing breaths. And as we sit down, I pull out my phone and mentally set a timer. After fifteen minutes, I'll leave.

We take seats. There's a row of six chairs in front facing the rest of us. It's not unlike the configuration at church. The Hamptons lady sitting dead center reads a placard from a binder. There will be a speaker, she announces. I'm hoping for one of the fancy women, perhaps the one in a Moncler jacket and mink lashes, but it's the dude with the beatnik ponytail seated next to her. I have no idea what this old white man can possibly tell me.

He smiles ruefully. He announces that he's given up. He chuckles nervously and asks his higher power to speak through him, and I wonder if he'll fall to the ground in a rapturous fit and ululate in tongues. The preemptive secondhand embarrassment radiates from my chest down to my arms and legs. I can't look at any of them, but I listen.

"Hi. My name's Cyrus, and I'm a gratefully recovering anorexic and bulimic," the speaker begins.

"Hi, Cyrus," they call back cheerfully.

I'm boggled that what I've seen of meetings in movies is real.

"I'm also an overeater, exercise bulimic, sugar addict, and laxative abuser." I can't believe this man who's old enough to live through wars and probably protested against Vietnam would admit this to a roomful of people.

I didn't know bulimics even came in male. Especially grandpas.

As he talks, my desire to leave dissipates. It's like overhearing an argument or watching a fire. Witnessing a rando who could have come off the B52 bus enumerate all of his shameful pathologies is deeply fascinating. It seems so out of place in polite society. He may as well be naked.

Cyrus recounts how he'd always been a fat kid. He calls it husky, which makes a few of the attendees laugh. I brace myself, searching his face for indignation, waiting for ridicule, but Cyrus seems to light up at the amusement. He talks about how his parents were perfectly nice people. Suburban. His father was a doctor, his mother a fundraiser, and neither of them was particularly around. He confesses how difficult it is to find a reason for it, but he was always filled with a deep loneliness. He leans forward, and his knee starts to jog.

He says that from a young age he'd always felt as though he were observing all the people around him as if through glass. That everyone always seemed to know how to have friends and joke around and that he didn't. That they all seemed to know what to do with boyfriends and girlfriends and that it all looked so easy.

When he gets to the part about an accomplished older brother who'd been a Rhodes Scholar, a genius and an athlete who excelled at everything, sweat prickles my scalp. When he says that his anxiety was so awful that he couldn't even learn how to drive, I can't catch my breath.

This man may as well be talking about me.

His parents divorced when he was a sophomore, the same age I was when my mom left. He says that liquor helped. He calls himself a double winner and says that he's part of the "beverage program" and that he's an alcoholic. But then drinking turned to drugs, which quickly became destructive, so he turned to food. His freshman year of college, he'd ballooned to almost three hundred pounds.

That's when he took matters into his own hands. He'd vomited, chewed and spat food, tried every commercial diet possible. From eating only pepper-infused water, Weight Watchers, Paleo, meal-replacement cookies, eating for his blood type, Whole30, Atkins.

A memory bobs up from the time I tried Atkins in high school. I'd lost eight pounds but had eaten so much cheese and bacon, peeing every ten minutes until I realized I hadn't taken a crap in almost three days, eventually passing a gruesomely painful bowel movement the consistency of a diamond after straining on the toilet for so long my legs went numb and I saw stars.

He'd had his ears stapled, his jaw wired. He'd even lost the deposit on gastric bypass surgery because at the very last minute he found these rooms instead.

He said he'd never forget how it felt to finally name these feelings. To learn that there are others like him. He recalls a checklist from his early days. And as he goes down it, reciting offhand the signals, I realize with a sickening clarity that we really are the same.

Have I eaten spoiled food? Yes.

Burned food? Yes.

Frozen food? Yes.

Stolen food?

More times than I can count.

It's as if there's a key turning in my heart. I picture myself groggily, helplessly eating my roommate's brownies from the trash in the middle of the night. Chewing around the dish soap I'd squeezed onto them to thwart myself.

The stories around the room are astounding. I experience the repeated diagnosis of a feeling I had no words to articulate before. Secrets I didn't even know I was hiding. They talk about how desperately they believed that if they only lost enough weight that they'd feel at home in their bodies.

That if they were skinny they'd finally be treated the way they deserved.

But it's not the high drama or the gross-out stories of abused GI tracts that break my heart.

It's the psychosis of knowing that your eyes are broken. That we all know what it's like to look at yourself in the mirror one minute and then see something completely different the next.

Most of us have left our bodies in times of crisis. We've been stuck in scribbly, maddening thoughts of what to eat for lunch, paralyzed that a wrong choice will turn us down the road to a binge that ends with aching bellies and sour mouths.

A binge is defined as that freight-train feeling I know too well. That rush. The helplessness. The hostage situation. The compulsion to eat everything to blot out the feelings of anything else. The peace of feeling as though you're choking because putting things in your mouth and then taking them out is the only thing in an unmanageable world that feel you can control.

Shit.

ShitShitShitShit.

I am them.

They are me.

I've canceled plans to eat or not eat. I've "called in fat" to work. I've gone to the gym instead of confronting someone. Eaten or gotten shitfaced instead of standing up for myself. I've been stunned and injured when I've lost the weight and not been given the respect or recognition I knew I deserved. I've starved myself skinny and been absolutely fucking miserable.

A notebook lands in my lap. There they all are. Everyone's names and phone numbers, just like they said. There are no last names, but this blackmail collateral is breathtaking to me. It's unbelievable, this trust fall. I can't bring myself to add my name, but I'm moved by the gesture. It's the stupidest, most touching gift I've ever known.

There's so much laughter. Not mean-spirited, contemptuous mirth, but joyful, knowing laughter. Every invitation to an impending social event that necessitated the losing of ten, five, three, forty pounds in two days inspires the snapping of fingers. Chuckling at fights picked at the table so we wouldn't have to eat pasta. Or so that we could eat the pasta and then storm off to buy secret ice cream on the way home.

There's talk of cake. Leftover birthday cake. One of the mothers had gotten up to eat a sliver. Then another. And another, until the whole thing was gone. She'd had to put a rush order in at the specialty bakery with a slew of lies to have another one made. Another frosted intergalactic spaceship that she'd had to eat down to the same spot to make things right. I think of how prepared I was to go to H-E-B in the middle of the night for pie. And how the pie I'd eaten after hadn't changed the perception of my childhood home.

I have never felt so known. So fucking spied on. It's the limited-edition ginger ice cream. The loaves of bread, the peanut butter. Ramyun. Coq au vin. Ketchup.

There are stories of hope. How things have changed. Hollow teeth salvaged. Missing periods retrieved. Bridges burned and mended. Families left and returned to.

Then a woman with a tidy brown bob and wire-framed glasses, wearing a preppy fisherman's sweater, cries about her father who died a week ago. After eight years of freedom, she'd started throwing up and hasn't been able to stop. Tears slide down her cheeks, and she calmly removes her glasses to wipe her eyes. Last night she'd slept for an hour on the bathroom floor next to her toilet. When her three minutes are up, I'm enraged that she's not given more time. But she smiles and thanks the room and says she knows it will get better because it has so many times before.

There are only ten more minutes of the meeting left, but I'm desperate to leave. I need air. I grab my things to duck out, refusing to look over my shoulder.

In the narrow, airless hallway, I see her come out of the bathroom. Cruella. A vision in lilac with her dog in her arms. Up close she's somehow younger than I thought even though I'd never assigned her an age. She was nothing more than a cartoon. A caricature of the unwell. She's wearing a lilac sweatsuit with a matching fringed cowboy vest to match her dog's hat. The ink slick of her hair is drawn into a bun so tight, it slants her eyes.

"I thought that was you," she says. As when Jeremy first talked to me, it's like a painting peeled itself off the canvas to address me.

Her voice is a revelation. It's far lower and more mellifluous than I could have ever conceived. Cruella has NPR voice.

I'm so stunned that I don't know what to say.

"Ingrid," she says, placing her hand on her chest. "We don't really know each other, but we also do. I see you all the time near my apartment. You must go to fashion school. I can tell because your eyeliner's always perfect."

"Thanks." I'm overcome that I'm not anonymous to her. That she likes my eyeliner. That she's collected me in some way too. "I love your clothes. The monochrome always pops in a crowd."

She smiles warmly.

Her dog sneezes. "Christ Almighty, Duffy, bless you." She hugs him close to her chest.

So, it's Ingrid and Duffy. I remember now, how I'd seen the dog with the lilac cowboy hat outside. How she and her dog have always foretold good things.

"His allergies are insufferable today. Cranky old man." She shakes her head. "So, are you one of ours?"

"Um." I nod slowly. "I guess I am."

"Uch." She pats my hand. "The beginning's the worst," she says. "But keep coming back. I was a gutter, gutter bulimic. Worst of the worst. I'm still crazier than a treeful of cockatiels, but I'll tell you what—you're only as sick as your secrets. The second you talk about it, *ffffffft*." She blows a raspberry and waggles her fingers into the air. "It all starts to get a little better. Humans need to share their darkest parts. Unburdening makes you closer to everyone. There's that thing that all addicts have, that you're a piece of shit in the center of the universe. That everybody's obsessed with the ways you fall short. But the truth is, we all have the same, boring problems. Sometimes the best thing you can do is talk about it. It makes no sense, but glory if it doesn't work like a charm.

"Oh," she says, plucking a pen from the knot at the nape of her neck and pulling a note card from a pocket. "What's your number, dear? I'll call you. I don't text, I'm old school, but I'll call you since you're new."

I'm equal parts suspicious and flattered. I consider faking her out but don't. I'm so curious about what she'll say. She writes her number and tears off a corner of the card and hands it to me. With a sky-piercing "I" and a decadent swooping "G," her penmanship is exquisite.

"Good luck, dear." She slides the pen back into her hair. "Keep coming back. This is the only place that will help you. Don't go floating off to Tahiti and think it's a cure. It doesn't work—I can tell you from experience. Florida doesn't work, either." She laughs at this. "Anyway, we'll always be here."

Her surprisingly warm hand pats mine again before she opens the door and lets herself back in.

As I walk toward June's, I realize I'm hungry. When I cross Union Square, there's a small protest, for universal healthcare. I think about the person with the van. Wonder whether they got their kidney. I pass by work. All the winking trinkets in the display window that I only know now don't make for a home.

I have wasted my entire life focusing on the wrong things and the wrong people. I don't know how it came to be that I believed changing everything about me would change the way people treated me.

I thought a polished appearance and stellar behavior would be the passport to belonging. And when I inevitably failed at perfection, I could at least willfully do everything in my power to be kicked out before anyone left me.

I duck into a narrow sandwich shop. It's been a fixture since 1929 and features a lunch counter where I've always wanted to eat. There are black-and-white framed pictures all over the walls and a nice man who wants to know what I'm having. Until I establish a usual, I order a matzo ball soup.

I text Ivy and tell her I'm thinking about her. I ask her how she's doing. I realize how superstitiously I believed that if I just got away from her, I'd stop. That maybe we both would. I tried to blame her for everything when all she did was remind me of the ugliest parts of me.

When my food arrives, it's beautiful. Golden and steaming. The soft mound of matzo a gift. I take a picture and send it to Patrick.

I eat my New York meal in a New York restaurant all by myself.

When I'm done, I say a small prayer to be willing to keep the soup I've eaten. I pray that I'll get healthy. That my mangled body will be restored. I speak the words in my mind with sincerity and hope. I don't know if it works, but if it doesn't, I know where I'll go. I know who to call.

chapter 47

When I get back to June's, there's a twentysomething curly blond dude with a tool belt getting ready to leave.

"Hi," I tell him, surprised, shooting a questioning look at my sister. There's a bookcase right in the middle of her living room.

"TaskRabbit," says June, and thanks him.

We watch as he laces up his boots. I have so many questions and thoughts. He takes what feels like eleven minutes to put on his shoes.

"Thank you," we say in unison. June widens her eyes at me. Seriously, sometimes it's like white people pretend they haven't had to take their shoes off in years.

"Ta-da!" she says brightly once he's gone, walking me over to the white shelving grid. "Okay, so from here . . ."—she taps the far side of the shelf and walks around to the back of the couch—"to here . . ."—she glances at me to make sure I'm paying attention—"is your room."

I'm speechless.

She points at the TV on the wall. "Obviously, the Samsung's not yours, but you can use it occasionally. And we can get a pull-out couch if that makes more sense. I don't care what the fuck you put on the shelves."

I think of all the versions of home I've mood-boarded over the years, and this is somehow my favorite.

"Thank you." I hear my voice thickening.

She waves this off, and when she sits on the love seat to avoid sitting on my "bed," the heavy droplet threatening to spill over my left eye quavers. I brush it away quickly and sniff hard. "I take it the view is mine, too?"

"Just as far as the edge of the couch."

I sit beside her and she turns to me. "So, how was it?"

"A whole lot of God talk."

"Yikes. What flavor of God?"

"More of a Build-A-Bear, Choose Your Own Adventure kind of God."

"Is it a cult?"

"Yeah, but there's no leader. It's like an independent-study cult where your homemade God helps you learn about your feelings."

"So, it's a small cult."

I think about my talk with Patrick. About cults and families and the secrets and stories that bind strangers together.

"Yeah."

"And you feel better?"

I consider Ingrid. "Yeah, I do."

"Good." She sighs heavily and gets up. "Gotta change my tampon."

She winces when she returns, doubled over slightly. "I wish every muscle in my body would give it a fucking rest."

That's when I remember. I go into June's hallway closet for my suitcase. I grab my crushed pack of cigarettes and slide out the half-smoked, vintage joint.

"Yo, you want to get high?"

"With you?" She sits back on the sofa.

"Sure," I falter. "Or you could just have it. For your period or whatever."

"Spark that shit." June points over at the stove.

I light it carefully, making sure the dried-out paper doesn't completely catch, and hand it to her first. "I don't know how old this shit is," I warn, walking back into the kitchen to grab a plate.

"There's an ashtray in my sock drawer." I don't all the way believe her until my hand lands on a hard corner. Sure enough, there is. And, shockingly, it's a Supreme ashtray.

I hand it to her.

"Old weed, new weed. I wouldn't know the difference. I was always too scared to try. Like, I'm paranoid enough as it is."

She holds the joint tentatively to her lips. She takes a baby puff and holds her breath. She exhales carefully, eyeing the smoke as if to check that it's working. "You know, I didn't mean to say, 'With you?' earlier. Like, as if I didn't want to smoke with you. I was more surprised that you'd want to smoke with me."

"Can I ask you something?" The weed is pleasingly scratchy in my throat.

June nods as I hand it back. "Sure."

"Why didn't you want to hang out with me when I moved here?"

"Um." June plants the joint in the ashtray with such force that embers fly. "Excuse me, I called you twice when you came. I had to buy you a bed just to get you to talk to me."

"But you never want to hang out. You called out of obligation and I'm grateful for the bed, but it's like, that's such an older sister duty move. That's basically to look good to Mom."

June reels back, an incredulous look on her face. "Oh my God. Lastborns are the worst. That is not why anything! Oh!" She stabs the sky triumphantly. "You hid from me."

"What? When?" Fuck, I already know what's she's going to say.

"Union Square subway, by the 4/5/6. Maybe a year ago." She shoulders into me and laughs. "You're so fucking stupid."

I try to keep a straight face but can't. The weed keeps dissolving all the edges of my feelings.

"You, like, leapt." She jerks up dramatically with little bunny hands in front of her. "Behind a trash can or something. I saw you. I was late to a meeting and so annoyed, but I should have stopped just to embarrass you in front of all the cool New York commuters."

"It was a harp. I hid behind a guy with a harp."

"That shit hurt my feelings," she says, still smiling but less so.

I can't believe she saw me.

"I'm sorry," I tell her and mean it. "I'm sorry for all of it. I'm sorry that you couldn't rely on me when mom was gone. I'm sorry I was such an asshole to you in school. I'm sorry that I didn't help you when everyone was being a dick about your period."

She shrugs. "You had your own shit." June clears her throat. "Siri, play the Romeo and Juliet soundtrack," she calls out. The Des'ree song comes on. It's perfect. I recall the fish tank scene in the movie. Baby-faced Leo in his chain mail and Claire with her half-pony and raver-girl angel wings gazing longingly at each other, separated by glass. It's so weird to me that June's never seen this movie and how I have no idea what she pictures when this song comes on.

"It's amazing that either of us made it out of there when I think about it." June picks up the joint and relights it at the stove. "We both suffered," she croaks, walking back. June hands it over, eyes narrowed.

"I was such a nerd. And you . . ." A plume of smoke obscures her face. "Were such a chink slut."

I laugh—truly laugh—when she says that, and she cracks up so hard she starts coughing.

"You know, I bought one of those Japanese paint markers and covered it over before I left." She holds her fist in the air and mimes a box. "Made a big-ass square and blacked it out."

There's a knot of pressure at my sternum. "Really?"

"You didn't see it?"

I shake my head. "I never went back into that stall."

"Wait," she turns to me suddenly. "So, you did fuck Patrick?"

"What?"

"Sorry, it's just where my brain went when we were talking about what a gigantic slut you are."

"Oh my God."

"Did you tell him about everything? About what's going on with me?"

"God, no." I shake my head solemnly. "I would never."

"Okay." Her face relaxes. "It would just be weird if he knew and Mom and Dad didn't."

"Of course. It's not my story to tell."

"It is, though, I guess." She yawns. "Partially."

"I didn't say anything," I assure her.

"Okay, so what does his body look like? Can you count his ribs from the front, or is he, like, stealth jacked?"

"I'm not fucking telling you."

She beams. "But you like him?"

"I like him."

"Fantastic. Now get me a glass of water."

I roll my eyes and get up.

"Don't drink from it first," she calls out.

I hand it to her.

"Thank you," she says, and drinks thirstily and sets it down next to the ashtray. "You want to know why I really got fired?"

"Yeah."

"This." She holds the white ashtray up. "I stole this from my boss." She shakes her head, smiling at the memory. "He was such a sexist, racist asshole. I knew layoffs were coming and it wasn't a secret that he hated me." June shrugs. "So, I took it. He searched everywhere. He was so fucking pissed. He knew I had it but couldn't prove it. And you know what? It was fucking worth it."

I stare at the ceramic prize. June is the strangest person I know and quickly becoming my favorite.

"It's why they call me Selina," she says proudly. "As in, Selina Kyle. Catwoman. Nobody could figure out how I did it. I'm a fucking legend."

chapter 48

The day of the surgery, I get up before her. It's the middle of the night, but I eat a quick breakfast of rice with hot water poured over the top and pickles. That's what Cruella told me to do, make an action plan to eat and follow it. June can't eat, and I don't want to be hungry and distracted if I need to pay attention while she's under. She can't worry about me.

We take a car over to the hospital in silence.

"How are you feeling?" I ask her. She's watching the predawn city through the window.

"I'm fucking sad," she says.

I squeeze her hand. She squeezes back.

We check in at a desk that's called the concierge, and it doesn't feel like a hotel no matter how state-of-the-art fancy the cancer building is. The overhead lighting is a buzzkill. And you'll never get rid of that smell. That sanitized, deloused smell. We're told that we'll be going to the pre-surgical center for examination and that I'm not allowed to be in the surgery, which makes sense, and frankly, I'm a little relieved.

We're reminded that the surgery would take only three hours, but that my sister can stay the night if she wants. As long as she's out ten minutes before her twenty-four hours is up, we won't be charged thousands more.

Every time I glance over at her, I'm struck with the thought that I might never see her again. That we're arriving together, but that she might not leave. I have her overnight bag by my side, along with her ugly fuzzy pajamas from Mom. We've been shown pictures of the room she'll stay in. It's decorated to look like a decent-to-nice motel for business travelers with this ash-colored fake-wood paneling covering a wall, but I still can't imagine her there. June doesn't make sense in hospitals.

We're led to a changing area. It looks, unnervingly, like any old dressing room in a strip mall store. She's told to remove any jewelry.

"Will you stay?" she asks me in a small voice. I nod. "Of course."

She's given two paper gowns and a box for her possessions. She hands me her phone. I put it in my pocket. This is the wrongest part by far. My sister sleeps with her phone under her pillow. That she won't have it with her is so unnatural and scary.

I open up my phone, and when I see her face icon hovering over mine in the exact location of the hospital, the squeezing in my chest gets tighter.

We don't talk as I wait for her to change.

"These are pretty cool," she says, wriggling her feet in socks with little rubber grips. "They're probably like two hundred bucks a pop." She grins, but when we're told she has to have an IV put in, we both stop smiling.

We're taken to a waiting area in what seems like a warren of different waiting areas. There's a stretcher in there, but she's told she can wait in the recliner for the moment.

I concentrate so as not to look down at my own name on her tag. I'm trying so hard to be chill, which means I'm smiling often and unnaturally. They keep calling her Jayne.

I can't bring myself to look at the stretcher. I hate it so much.

Her vitals are taken. Blood drawn. She's being hammy, in that June way. Cracking jokes and being affable, putting everyone at ease, and I almost want to strangle her. To demand that she pay attention to what's going on. To understand what a big deal this is. That it's November 19. That it's finally happening.

A super-short, smooth-skinned Black woman with wide-set eyes and distractingly good brows comes to see us, immediately followed by an equally diminutive Asian woman with freckles. They're both wearing thick-framed tortoiseshell glasses, and I wonder if there's a story behind the matching eyewear.

"Jayne," says the first woman to my sister. "How are you feeling?"

June exhales and says, "Okay."

The doctor extends her hand to me. Her palm is cold but soft. "I'm Dr. Ellington, Jayne's surgical oncologist. Your sister tells me that I'll be coming to speak to you afterward."

"Yes," I croak, and then clear my throat. "Yes," I repeat. I'm already feeling like a disappointment. That she was expecting a real adult, a more convincing advocate for a person undergoing surgery.

"It's good to meet you," she says warmly, turning to the woman beside her. "This is Sandy Chee, our nurse liaison, who'll be updating you throughout the surgery."

"Hi, June," says Sandy to me. "I can also answer any questions as you have them. And I'll let you know when you can see your sister in the post-anesthesia care unit. Oh, and please don't bring flowers until she's set up in her recovery room."

June pipes up. "Sandy?"

"Yes?"

"Did you get the glasses first, or did Dr. Ellington?"

Dr. Ellington laughs abruptly, then clears her throat.

Sandy smirks and taps the right side of the frames. "It was a joint decision," she says. "I got them first, but then Suze tried them on, and they looked better on her." She rolls her eyes and then laughs.

"They were on sale," pleads Dr. Ellington.

"They were on sale," agrees Sandy.

"They're really good glasses," says June, nodding.

"We'll come get you shortly," says Dr. Ellington.

As soon as they leave, I'm terrified that I'll start crying hysterically. I pull my lip. Rolling the meat between thumb and forefinger.

My phone rings. I check the screen.

"Tell Patrick I say hi," says June cloyingly. And then, "What does his dick look like?"

"June, stop." I grab my phone and walk out into the hallway.

With Patrick I've been as honest as I can be. I already told him that I'd be out of pocket for a few days. That I'm dealing with a family thing but that I'll see him on the other side. He didn't press, and my heart was so grateful, it hurt.

I need to show up for her. I need to get used to the strangeness of helping June for once and not the other way around. This phone call is the best way I know how.

Once I'm back, June sighs extravagantly. "I think the last half hour is the longest I've been without my phone," she says. "You were gone, what, five minutes? Without a phone it was like an eternity."

I check the time. They'll be taking her in shortly.

"June," I tell her.

"Don't you mean Jayne?"

"I did something."

I know from the tone in her voice and the crumpling in her face when she says "Umma?" as the door opens that I did the right thing.

"Oh, Ji-hyun, Mom's here," she says in Korean. "Don't worry." She rushes in, kissing June's temple.

As soon as I'd gotten home from school yesterday, I'd called her. She'd left last night, made two connecting flights to arrive in the early morning after a thirteen-hour flight that would have normally been three, just to be here. Even when she called me from downstairs, asking what room we were in, I couldn't believe it.

Our mom's here.

Mom's tears fall freely as she cups June's cheeks. "Everything's going to be fine."

There are no more jokes. No snappy chatter. My sister begins to sob. "We're here," says Mom. "Don't cry, Ji-hyun, or you'll make your sister cry."

I've *been* crying. I've been openly weeping from the moment June said "Umma." Mom smooths the worry lines on my sister's forehead with her hands. "Shhhh . . . Stop crying, stop crying. Honestly, you'll get wrinkles."

June laugh-sobs. Even if Mom's deigned to descend upon us in filthy, freezing, godless New York, she's still Mom.

There's a knock on the door as a nurse comes in. She's young with bright, round eyes and shiny dark hair. "Good morning, Ms. Baek. I'm Celia," she says, and slots June's arms into the blood pressure cuff.

"Aw, y'all make me miss my sisters," she says in a distinctly Brooklyn accent. "I have two sisters. One in the city, the other in Westchester. I love them so much I want to kill them all the time. Who's older?"

I look over at June sharply. "I am," I tell her.

Celia takes a quick look at Mom. "You don't look nearly old enough to be their mother. You look like sister number three."

Mom smiles charitably.

"And what's your name?"

I feel my mother's eyes on me. "June."

The air's sucked out of the room. I can't even look at my sister.

"Jayne and June. I love that," says Celia, taking June's temperature and then shooting the plastic thermometer cover into the trash. "All right, Ms. Jayne, I'm going to need you to get on the stretcher, so hop on up." She slides down the sides so my sister can get in.

Celia fixes it so that June can sit up. The look is complete. With the gown, the IV stand, the hospital bracelet, and now this.

When Celia leaves. I brace myself for Mom's questions. All I've told her is that June's having surgery.

"I worry so much about you girls," she says, blinking through tears. "Moving so far from home, struggling to make a life. But I'm so proud of you both." Her voice breaks. "You're both grown now and you'll make your own decisions. I might not approve of all of them, but I'm so proud of the way you're taking care of each other right now."

Mom starts crying openly and takes June's hand. "Ji-hyun, you've always been so good at taking care of everyone. I wonder if that's why you're sick. If my failings are what did this to you."

"Mom, you didn't fail us," chokes June. "It's no one's fault. Cancer's just a motherfucking son-of-a-whore," she says in Korean. Even in this emotional moment, I'm impressed by my sister's fluency.

Mom pinches June for cussing and laughs in between a sob. "Why are you like this?" she asks.

That's when they come in. To take her away.

"Jayjay?" The adrenaline jolts me to my feet. I grab my sister's hand. They're doing it; they're wheeling her. Pure terror is written on her face, as I'm sure it is mine.

"Juju," she says, eyes locking on me.

"I love you," I tell her. I've never said it to my sister before. Ever.

"Fuck, same," she says urgently, reaching for my forearms. "I love you. I love you, Mom."

"I love you," says Mom in Korean, holding my hand when June can't anymore. I watch her lie back, and then that's it. She's concealed behind people. We walk with her stretcher as far as we're allowed, and then the doors shut.

There's a burning sensation in my chest. We're both standing in the hallway, staring like statues.

When the door swings open again, we startle. Sandy Chee emerges and smiles. "Hi," she says, looking at my mom expectantly.

"This is my mom." I fall into the role of my parent's spokesperson easily.

Mom nods several times and smiles with far more warmth than she would in Korean. "Hi," she says, and takes a half step back. Mom lives in constant fear of being hugged.

"I'm sure June can tell you more." Sandy gestures at me. "But Jayne is in very good hands. It's a relatively straightforward procedure, and I'll give you updates as I have them."

She leads us to yet another waiting area, this one identical to the one before, with tasteful furniture and a television, but more private. "I'll meet you back here as soon as I know more."

Mom takes a seat positioned optimally for the TV and pulls out a Kleenex, but instead of wiping her eyes, she wipes down the coffee table in front of her.

I sit next to her as she pulls out a lunchbox and sets it down.

"I brought kimbap," she says. "I made it with no kimchi so it won't smell."

"Okay."

Neither of us touches it. Finally, Mom turns to me. "Are you going to tell me why you were calling her Jayne?"

"She had to be me," I tell her in stilted Korean. "So, when I come here, I have to be her. Her insurance was messed up." I don't know if the words for car insurance and health insurance are the same, but she gets it.

Mom sighs and pulls out a tiny Purell from her bag and offers it to me. "One of the boys at church had to do that for his brother. ACL surgery. You know Cho Theresa? The one with the super-pretty face and the unfortunate husband? I think the rehab was thirty thousand dollars. This country is ridiculous. Of course you helped her. What choice did you have?"

She takes a quavering breath. Her cheeks collapse as she starts crying again. "I'm so glad you have each other. It lets me know that however much your father and I make mistakes, you'll ultimately be okay." Mom puts her arm around me. "I kept having this dream," she says, handing me a warm bottle of Poland Spring from her purse. I scooch low into my seat, settling in. "I was eating from this huge platter of fruit, the juiciest, ripest fruit, but it was all gritty like soil and I could only taste metal. My teeth were crumbling out of my mouth." She shudders. "I sensed something was going on even before you called me."

She pinches my leg. "You should have called me sooner."

I can't believe Mom's here. I've lost all sense of place. It's almost as if we're in a hospital in a parallel universe. Not in New York. Not in Texas. Not in America at all.

"Your father knew something was wrong," she says. "When you

girls came home. I told him to stop being so cynical, but he said it was suspicious that you were together. That you were speaking to each other at all." She turns to me, searching for answers. I say nothing. I can't tell what she actually wants to hear. "I don't know what happened between you two, but you have to know that you owe it to your sister to help. She loves you more than anything in the world. You were her baby. She was hysterical when we thought we'd lost you. When you kept playing in that stupid flower bed. She threw Flora—do you remember Flora? The porcelain clown doll? She wouldn't let anyone touch it, she adored it so much."

I think of the photograph at home. The one that fell out of June's album of her as a child, looking up prayerfully at the doll. June sitting on the floor, the toy presiding over her from the chair.

"She tossed it out of the window to show you what would happen. I didn't know what she was doing, but she took you to see it, and you finally understood. You stopped playing out there. It was her most precious possession, and she sacrificed it for you."

I realize I do know that. That it's always been true. That there's nothing June wouldn't do for me.

Mom grabs my hand again in her small one. Her palms are rough. Her knuckles thickened by work. Her wedding ring is a plain gold band, lacking in any adornment.

"Mom," I ask her, drawing up a breath for courage. "Did you wish that I was a boy? When I was born?"

"Yes." She says it so quickly that a small laugh erupts from my mouth.

"Thanks a lot."

She looks at me impatiently. "Who wouldn't have wanted a boy? Everyone wants one of each. We were hoping for a boy with Ji-soo, too."

My heart stops. I've never heard Mom's dead baby's name.

"Your other sister," she says. Again, in a tone that's shockingly unvarnished. "I would have been happy with three girls, too. That would have been wonderful, to gather all of you in my arms like a bouquet. My sweet daughters with your enormous heads." She leans back in her chair. "You girls weren't easy on the way out, let me tell you."

"Mom?"

"Hmmm?"

"Where did you go?" I barrel on before I lose courage. I want to be able to tell June when she wakes up. "When you were gone for so long?"

She sighs. "Your father said you would ask," she says. "I wonder when I'm going to start believing him."

I stay silent. Hoping this time she'll say what I need her to.

"I went to Korea," she says. "I had to go home."

"Why didn't you bring us with you?"

She shakes her head. "That wasn't your home. I can't explain it. I needed to be in Korea. Your grandmother was furious, crying, hitting me every day, telling me I was a disgrace, but I just stayed at my childhood home and cried. And slept. I went to Ji-soo's grave every day. That's the only thing I did."

I picture a small grave. A child's grave.

"I missed you girls every day. I hope you believe me. I was haunted by thoughts of you. But Ji-soo needed me too. My body didn't want to be in America. This life we chose, it was so hard. Your father and I had worked sixteen-hour days for over ten years. I thought I'd made a mistake. That I'd made a mistake to choose this life and that I'd brought you girls into it, which was unforgivable. But one morning, when I went to talk to her, it was pouring rain and then it cleared up.

I was on my knees, clearing off the clumps of grass that were sticking to her, telling her about everything we'd seen, what our house was like, what the two of you were doing, and I felt a sense of calm wash over me. The horrible feeling, the weight that was pressing down the moment we landed in Texas, the way it would bear down on my chest until I couldn't breathe, was lifted. I knew it was time to come back. To my real home. With you two and your father."

She looks at me.

"I'm sorry I don't have better words to describe it," she says. "When you have children, you'll understand."

I picture my mother, in the suit she'd left in, in her blouse, on her knees. The way the dirt and small stones bit into them, ruining her pantyhose. I imagine her talking to her dead baby on a green hill.

I don't know if I'll ever understand what my mother felt. Whether it was grief for herself or her dead daughter that kept her away. I know what it's like to want to leave. How it feels when the home you have is a mirage, an illusion. But I know that wherever I am, if June's around, I'll be okay. Even if she hates me a little. Because even when she hates me, she loves me the most.

"You know, the trick to taking care of your sister is letting her think she's taking care of you." She scoops my hand in hers. "I suspect you can ask your father the best way to do that since he does it so well with me." This makes me laugh.

"Your unni needs you. You're the only one who can get close enough to help. Be good to her. Especially when you two have to do this again."

I give her a questioning look. "When it's your turn to have children, you'll have to be June, because after this surgery 'Jayne' won't be able to. At least not according to your medical records. You'll have to switch places and help each other again."

My heart stops. I realize she's right.

The thought of doing all of this over makes my soul leave my body. I can't imagine how tiring it's going to be. But I also love the idea of June's name looking after both of us. Maybe my kid's name will carry her Ji. Or maybe it will be inspired by a poison or a war general.

"Umma?"

"Hmm?"

I scooch low in my seat so I can put my big head on her bony shoulder. "What does Ji-soo mean?"

I feel her heartbeat in her small chest. "I never told you?" She pulls my hand closer so she can trace the characters on my palm with her finger.

I shake my head, eyes closed. "Tell me."

resources

If you experience shame, obsession, and perfectionism around food and body weight, you are not alone. Please reach out to the support systems below.

The **National Eating Disorders Association** (NEDA) is the largest nonprofit organization dedicated to supporting individuals and families affected by eating disorders.

Call or text: (800) 931-2237

For crisis situations, text "NEDA" to 741741 to be connected with a trained volunteer at Crisis Text Line.

www.nationaleatingdisorders.org

Overeaters Anonymous (OA) is a community of people who support each other in order to recover from compulsive eating and food behaviors. There are no dues or fees to join.

Call: (505) 891-2664

www.oa.org

acknowledgments

Lol. This book.

Remember when I said the second one was hard? Well. Just . . . Wow.

I am grateful to so many people for their love and patience. Edward Orloff, my agent. You are decent and kind and I love the way you do business. Thank you, Susan Hobson at McCormick, for all the beautiful international editions.

Thank you to my family at Simon & Schuster. Kendra Levin, I didn't know that editors like you existed. Thank you for your wisdom. And for extracting me from the hellscape of my own making when I decided I wanted this book to be done before it was ready. Dainese Santos, thank you for understanding my heart and reading with such sensitivity and care. I feel so stinkin' affluent that I got to have a pair of Asian eyes on this trust-fall of a manuscript.

Justin Chanda, I'm grateful for your unwavering support. Chrissy Noh, Lisa Moraleda, Anna Jarzab, Anne Zafian, Lauren Hoffman . . . you guys! Here we are again. How even? I miss y'all! Remember offices? Plus, hi, Mackenzie at S&S Canada. Hearts.

To gg, a genius. And Lizzy Bromley, a legend.

Thanks to my people: Phil Chang, Asa Akira, Minya Oh,

Eric Chang, Leilani Zahn, Kenzo, Eric Hu, Steven Yeun, Yoonjin Ha, Trish Hook, Naomi Zeichner, Rose Garcia, Kerin Rose, Sara Vilkomerson, Jess Gentile, Soo-young Kim, Keith Abrams, Gabriella Ainslie, Maeve Higgins, Melanie Campbell, Imelda Walavalkar, Brooke Nipar, Stephen Porto, Usha Khanna, Ginny Hwang, Emily Pai, and Kyoko Fukuda.

Suze Webb, thanks as always for the astute read. Karen Good Marable for the voice notes and the sentiments. Mark Lotto, thank you for bearing witness to every single multiverse version of *Yolk* and straight up telling me which ones were trash. Jami Attenberg for the perspective and reminders to be gentle. Aminatou Sow, Dr. Betty Nyein, Emily Eagan, and Dr. Jennifer Mueller at Memorial Sloan Kettering for your time and guidance around reproductive health.

Thanks to Zareen Jaffery for all the hand-holding and the love.

Thanks to Jenna Wortham for hanging out with me in outer space.

Thanks to Jenny Han for being a Virgo and for world-class discernment and courage.

To Jermaine Johnson, Priya Verma, Jason Richman, and Mary Pender. We are the most beautifullest together. I am so lucky.

To my therapist Ryan and the fellowship of now two different flavors of 12-step group. You guys stay saving my life and my sanity. Thank you for teaching me that feelings are not facts and that the universe is a benevolent conspiracy hellbent on showing me magic if I simply get out of the way.

For my family. Especially Ollie since he's new. Especially—*especially*—to the mom one. I love you to the moon, Peaches. I'm so glad you're still here even though you don't read a lick of English.

And, of course, Samuel Reinhard. My favorite human being on this bum deal of a planet. I love you so much, it's stupid.